BLOOD AND BETRAYAL

BLOOD AND BETRAYAL

LEGACY OF THE DRAGON: BOOK ONE

S. H. BLODGETT

Version 1.0

Cover by Selkkie Designs

Developmental and Copy/Line Editing by EJL Editing

Light Line Editing and Proofreading by Elizabeth Merck

Artwork by StarGazerCreations

AUTHOR'S NOTE

(READER BEWARE!)

This book contains a word or two that may be difficult to pronounce. There are a lot of elements to the magic system as well. At the back of the book, you'll find a guide that may be helpful with both as you read along!

Dedication

First and foremost, none of this would have been possible without my husband, Ian Blodgett. I'm incredibly blessed to have such a supportive life partner. I love you to the moon and back!

To my Dad, thank you for reigniting your love for reading and diving into my work with such enthusiasm. Your feedback during the final edits truly made this book better, and I'm deeply grateful for your support throughout this journey.

To my Mom, my greatest cheerleader, thank you for sharing the news about my book and believing in me every step of the way.

To Gramme, who nurtured my passion for reading, thank you for all those visits to the local Books and Bagels shop! I cherish every book you gifted me and hold those memories close to my heart.

To my family, who shaped me into the person I am today, I will always be grateful. Your unwavering support has made this journey possible.

Thank you all from the bottom of my heart! Here's to publishing book number two!

CHAPTER ONE

CAENRYA

Rancorous cheering sounded behind Caenrya as she descended from the arena's battlefield. Her feet moved on their own accord as she repressed the wave of disgust and hatred she harbored for the patrons of the underground fighting ring. Revealing even a hint of weakness in her bearing would lead to repercussions for her sister, should her actions reflect poorly on their daimyo. Only a nod from her masked handler reassured her they'd survive another day as she passed through the tunnel. Her bruised fist loosened a hair by the time she was guided into the holding cell.

A metal grate clunked to the floor behind Caenrya. Her black leathers rested against the chilled stone of the room as she was left waiting—always waiting—at the daimyo's beck and call. The daimyo was a calculating man of vast power and wealth, a lord in his own right within a lawless land where no true ruler maintained structure.

Caenrya's final match concluded the evening, and the other fighters lined the endless hallway around her. Only one fighter rebelled in their holding chamber when he refused to obey his handler's order to stay silent. One Caenrya knew to be new. No seasoned fighter would dare the whip, and the sound of the lash almost made her flinch.

Don't react, she recited, suppressing the wave of fear and forcing that indifferent mask to remain locked in place.

Caenrya's handler stood like a statue beside her cell, waiting for their daimyo to collect them after his gambling business concluded.

Once more, the hall fell silent to footsteps. A thundering of them reverberated through the ceiling. She knew then it would only be a matter of minutes before her daimyo collected his winnings for the evening's bets. It was only natural there was much for him to gain. After all, Caenrya was the most profitable fighter in his collection. Having never lost a match in the underground fighting rings, her victories were assured, just as her cooperation was with her younger sister held hostage back at Shikei—the nightmarish bunker where she, and the daimyo's other fighters, were imprisoned. Their sole purpose in life was to earn money for a lord who'd kill them when they proved useless.

It was only a matter of time before she, too, wasn't a financial asset.

One by one, the fighters were claimed by their owners, a handful traded to a new lord or lady through clandestine deals shaken upon over a glass of sake. More than a few jewel-clad people gawked at her in appreciation. Some with outright jealousy that they didn't own her. Caenrya ignored them all and pushed her exhausted frame from the wall when a man's obscenely elaborate silk kimono shone in the minimal lighting of her cell. Without glancing at his face, she knew his up-swept eyes spoke of permanent superiority as he hailed his handler to unlock the steel grate between them and Caenrya.

They were eyes she learned the hard way never to meet.

Without a word, Caenrya fell in behind her daimyo, an intimidating man of extraordinary wealth with a penchant for seeking priceless treasures. His armored guard of four divided themselves to escort their charges through the underground exit. Their emergence garnered reverent whispers as they passed through the exit into the forested mountain range beyond. The daimyo signaled for her to fall in step, and her stomach curled inward as she listened.

"Upon the commencement of the following week, you are to embark on another contract at the behest of the contested lands." The daimyo's deep voice lacked the emotional depth any normal person had.

It was a voice that never ceased to chill her to the bone.

Caenrya distracted herself by wondering which faction she'd be aligning with this go-around within their disputed land. Who was next on her list to assassinate. Her daimyo's loyalties lay with whoever produced the most coin.

The daimyo's silken hair swayed across his lower back as they passed the dense line of pines, the pathway worn by the influx of visitors the arena received every other full moon. "I need not remind you of our arrangement."

Nodding in response, Caenrya wouldn't speak without explicit permission.

The daimyo signaled their departure with a flick of two fingers. They collectively pooled their taiji—a mystical inner energy that ran through their veins—and bounded toward the river weaving throughout the valley. Caenrya once used to relish the harmony of energy that allowed all beings to interact with the earth's natural taiji. Balancing hers against the ground gave her a spring-like mechanic, allowing her to bound vast distances with speed rivaling that of a mountain cat. It made journeys much more tolerable.

Now, though, Caenrya felt indifferent to it as they flew beside the rippling water and only visualized it as another tool of survival.

One day. Caenrya dreamed of a day when she and Verina could escape their soul-crushing lives. Perhaps Caenrya could find a way out, taking

Verina with her, and return to the home they were stolen from. Only the faintest of impressions remained in her mind from their life before their capture, but Caenrya adamantly believed it was a better life than they could find here. Every day was spent fighting to survive. Possibly a foolish hope, but it was everything to her.

Even if it meant damning her soul in the meantime.

A clear sky twinkled overhead. Two full moons graced the center of it all with a pearlescent hue. The scuffle of nocturnal animals caught her ears, and the slight scattering of dirt with each leap filled the air as the distance passed in the blink of an eye. Each of the four ronin—the hired guards of the daimyo—kept on high alert. Their eyes searched at a constant pace, and their heads swiveled toward any movement in their perimeter. Weapons of varying types littered their crimson lacquer-dipped plates. Silk cord tied them into a fine mesh of the highest caliber.

Everything about the masked ronin put Caenrya on edge. Especially knowing they'd turn on her the instant she attempted anything deviating from her orders.

Hours passed on their trek back to Shikei before the air tangibly changed. Her shoulders tensed, and her skin tingled at the feeling of being watched. The towering trees around them seemed to lean over her. The ronin leading them slowed, and their group condensed around the daimyo as they stilled beside a copse of pines. One held out a palm, warning them to be quiet and still.

Every internal alarm was blaring with abandon, raising goosebumps along her arms. Her fatigued limbs groaned at the thought of an impending battle. Her reserves were close to being depleted after the countless matches Caenrya had to endure, and it brought a grim edge to her mouth at the thought of an ambush. Truly, it was—

A kunai shot from across the banks of the river. Only a flash of moonlight caught her attention before her body reacted instinctively to the airborne double-sided knife. Caenrya threw herself forward, taking the sharp blade to her shoulder to protect the daimyo. Pain lanced from the deep-rooted injury, and her teeth gritted as the ronin leaped into action.

The lead pulled the furious daimyo into the safety of the overflowing foliage, and the others engaged with emerging black-clad figures. In mere seconds, the sound of clashing metal overtook her surroundings.

Having no weapons put Caenrya at a distinct disadvantage. Her near-empty stores of taiji downright guaranteed anything but a fair fight.

However, it didn't prevent her from joining the fray.

Mid-air, Caenrya felt the shift in her blood as her right hand created the *zen* hand seal—a unique hand movement that activated the taiji in her body. At the same time, she recited an incantation in her mind.

Her taiji's nature shifted, and her body thrummed with a power unique to her bloodline. Pale blue taiji formed a crackling blade around each hand. Her shoulder sung with pain as she blocked the barrage of katana-borne blows one assailant greeted her with. The slightly curved blade sliced through the air, sizzling when it met the resistance of Caenrya's taiji blade.

It took but seconds to determine these opponents were vastly different from those she triumphed over in the ring, even those she felled in war zones.

It was the lack of shock that widened her enemies' eyes at her ability, the grace in which her current ones flowed in unison between attacks within their tag-teamed pairs. And the fact that she was steadily losing ground and being corralled toward where her daimyo had been pushed into hiding.

Her breaths became ragged gasps as she parried between well-timed blows, her footing almost catching on a protruding root.

These enemies were faster. More precise and brutal than nearly any she'd encountered before. Sparks flew as she blocked a nasty blow racing for her healthy shoulder. A grunt escaped her from the angry flare of agony radiating from it.

Minutes passed. Caenrya knew she wouldn't last through the duration of the skirmish. Two of her daimyo's ronin had already fallen, only one remaining at her back to repel the onslaught of four attackers.

Out of the corner of her eye, she caught the flash of flame summoned, a fiery tornado erupting from an enemy's taiji attack around the last of the ronin. His shrieks cut off within seconds. Seconds where she was forced to navigate herself toward the river amid dodging several blows to avoid being caught in the flame.

Caenrya's feet balanced on top of the flowing water, and her movements were purely defensive as they circled her. It wasn't long before a katana cut into her leg, and her taiji faltered.

A distant part of her hoped the death would be fast. That the enormity of her duty would at last be over. She was a shell of a being while working for the daimyo. Only the rare moments she could visit Verina ever brought any semblance of genuine emotion back to her otherwise darkened heart.

But now... Now she'd be ashamed to admit she willingly released her hold on the taiji flowing through her limbs. Ashamed to confess she wanted nothing more than the end of the horrific life she led. She didn't deserve it anyway. Not when a dreadful part of her wished to be rid of the burden of her sister, knowing Caenrya could have fought her way out and escaped ages ago.

When a powerful blow connected with the back of her skull—her vision blacking out—Caenrya's body slackened. A ghost of a smile graced her lips.

She knew then a split second of true contention, an emotion found not in piles of gold coin or a lover's returned smile. Rather, it was within the knowledge her time spent suffering was at its bitter end, her burdens shedding like a snake's skin.

Though it was dampened by a lingering memory of her sister. In that moment, all those years ago, Verina's pleading face made her promise everything was going to be okay.

Deep down, Caenrya knew it never would be, but she would die trying to make it so.

***

Drifting in complete darkness proved to be rather soothing. Such silence made her feel at ease. Caenrya couldn't remember the last time she could let her guard down in such a way. To do so was death, but now that she had fallen to it, it was...

Lonely.

Until a strange presence wormed its way to the edge of her consciousness. It prodded at her steel-clad mind. Caenrya's curiosity allowed her defenses to crumble at the effort the foreign presence put forth. It was then she heard a voice—one unmistakably alive.

"I'm in," a man said. His words echoed in the recesses of her mind. "I'm searching now."

A flash of memory crossed Caenrya's void, a time she'd repressed violently and refused to recall. She knew then she had survived. Not even death would rescue her from the daimyo.

Of *course*.

But a piece of her was relieved. There was still that last thread she clung to, one that whispered she could still save her sister.

Now, though, it was threatened by the man using his taiji to invade her subconscious.

Growling in rage, Caenrya grabbed that vine-like probe with ferocity. Her fist drew it close as she whispered, "I'll enjoy ripping your mind to shreds."

The man's fear leaked through, and his voice was urgent as he shouted at someone to wake the captive. Her. The thought made her grimly laugh at the irony. The invader's consciousness squirmed as her mind struck back, his own mind easily falling apart at her efforts.

From her years of training, Caenrya knew the mind and soul were fragile things. When a person used their taiji to attack with their intangible spirit, they were in their weakest state. Only if a person was assured they were more powerful than their foe could they engage in such an attack.

She was being underestimated.

And. It. Pissed. Her. Off.

A rush of adrenaline laced through her body, and her lungs gasped for air while her eyes snapped open.

Details flooded her sight, from a dreary concrete bunker to an entire company of panicked adults circling the room in a hurry. A balding man was slumped at her left, his glazed eyes unseeing as they faced her pinned form. Liquid rushed through a tube into her arm, metal wound around her leaden limbs. Blaring white lights shone, making the finer details of the white-coated forms and the weapon-clad ronin blurred.

Blinking, Caenrya spotted a bizarre insignia on their person. Some had it over their hearts; others wore it on their shoulders. Six people total.

These weren't ronin. Ronin didn't affiliate themselves with any organization. They were worse.

Shinobi.

By the appearance of their insignia, these warriors belonged to a clan, a crucial and disturbing distinction. As her eyes grew accustomed to the lighting, she picked out the black uniforms identical to those who had ambushed her. She saw emblems of jagged wings over their right shoulders.

Only one figure remained calm at the end of Caenrya's cot, and his stance said more than the set of his face would have. Unflinching with a confidence that spoke volumes. Formal silk attire with royal hues of blue and silver, a cape draping over his left shoulder with the emblem of a jagged wing clasping it to his uniform. The same emblem as on the others. With another blink, Caenrya made out the stern set of his expression, warring on a face that appeared naturally kind.

She ignored the flurry of a white-garbed medical shinobi analyzing the slumped man beside her. "You're wasting your time. My obligations are to another, and no number of honeyed promises or veiled threats will persuade me to fight for you."

For a clan.

There were five sections of divided land on their continent, four of them belonging to individual clans. The section she lived in was the only rogue territory where everyone fought each other to rule. Clans had an established hierarchy, but that didn't make them any better for it.

They certainly never helped the innocent in her territory.

A second passed. Her brows furrowed when the man's steel-gray eyes analyzed her without reaction. His bronze hair was mostly tied in a wrapped topknot up high, a gold wing pinned through the middle. The lower half of his hair fell straight to his shoulders, a neatly trimmed beard wrapping around his jawline. A regal countenance.

A white-garbed woman shook her head, brunette curls bouncing around her heart-shaped jawline. Her voice was urgent as she reported to her lord, "Shogun Arundel, Shinobi Aaric's taiji is too far distressed for me to neutralize. The girl's Kū nature is superior to mine."

Kū nature, one of the five elements of taiji: the mind. Caenrya's strongest affinity.

A pacing black-clad shinobi behind her appeared as if he might launch at Caenrya at a moment's notice. His tanned jaw was locked as he faced the shogun.

A flicker of confusion crossed Caenrya's eyes. Why was she in the presence of a shogun? *This man is the leader of the clan*, she thought grimly. With that morsel of information, the dynamic shifted.

The shogun marked her lapse, folding his arms across his chest as his eyes assessed her.

Tucking away that information, her mind reevaluated the situation.

Caenrya hadn't ever crossed a clan leader's path, hadn't thought them involved with the illicit dealings of the war-torn territory they intruded. In fact, none of the people in the room blended with her perception of the average criminal.

What was their goal in ambushing them? Caenrya had misjudged them. At first, she thought her ambushers wanted her as their fighter in the rings. But there was more to it. Were the clans now vying for the contested land along with all the other warlords? That would make sense since they had targeted her daimyo, who was one of the many figures of power there.

"You're not a member of the Kriv Clan." A statement, not a question, asked by the shogun.

Caenrya blinked, her brow pinching. Kriv Clan? She knew little of their land's history, but that name had never been whispered to her ears. She greedily clutched to her chest every bit she could glean of the unknown world and would have remembered the clan's name.

Knowledge garnered power, after all.

And right now, she was powerless.

Understanding lit the shogun's eyes. "We refer to the contested lands by the clan that used to rule it. The Kriv. There are enough members from the Kriv Clan remaining among the warring lords, thus it remains titled as such."

An incredulous laugh escaped her before Caenrya could suppress the noise. There wasn't an ounce of humor in it. "I have no clan. I don't belong to any Kriv Clan lord. I thought *you* knew who you were slaughtering before you ambushed us," she accused with more than a hint of venom in her tone. Caenrya despised losing to *them*. It hadn't been a fair fight. Now what would become of her?

"She's obviously lying," snapped the pacing shinobi, his hand reaching for a tanto blade slung across his black trousers. His ebony eyes blazed with raw anger, and his unbound hair waved about his broad shoulders with each step.

The length of the blade was a third of a katana's, something Caenrya subconsciously noted as her mind devised ways to combat it.

"Rainer." A black-clad shinobi slapped Rainer's hand, her thin mouth a fine line. "If she dies, Aaric has no hope of regaining his mind." The man who tried to probe Caenrya's mind. "Do you wish to make his daughter, Owena, an orphan?" Her auburn head tilted at him with a grim look.

Closing her eyes, Caenrya attempted to focus her taiji.

"It'll do no good," the shogun said, his calm voice drawing closer. "The surrounding graphite-imbued metal prevents the use of taiji."

Her eyes snapped open. Caenrya glared at his squared face in response, her mind circling a method to escape. It appeared she wouldn't be able to rely on her power. "How about this? Release me, and I'll release your friend here. I don't particularly have any fondness for the ronin your people have killed. There won't be any hard feelings on my end."

The shogun gripped a bar on the side of her cot with calloused hands. "Are you a hired ronin?"

Drawing a deep breath, Caenrya tuned out the deadly stares she accumulated around the room. "No," she finally said, a hint of acrimony stretching the word.

"We acquired intelligence that a ring of black-market trading was occurring in the vicinity of your capture. A prominent figurehead of the Kriv Clan was said to be present. If you can trade any further information, then we could discuss an amicable arrangement." The lines deepened on the shogun's forehead.

They moved Aaric carefully into a chair, and the white-garbed medical shinobi monitored his condition closely.

"I've never known anyone from the clan. I've never known much. Even if I had crossed paths with one, I would never have been told," Caenrya responded coldly. Her fists clenched under the metal biting into her skin. "The only thing I do know is that you managed to kill everyone who might have provided such details and captured the single one who is completely *useless*."

Rainer snapped, lunging forward several steps before the two others reined in his arms. Cursing at them, he snarled beside her, "You're lying!"

"Quiet, Rainer," the shogun shot at the man. "She was not responsible for the loss of Serillia. Your team confirmed that your wife passed at the hands of another. We won't get answers without first listening."

They were going to kill her.

An impossible hollowness brought her eyes to the ceiling. Try as she might, there was no reasoning with them when their verdict had already been made. All she could do was disassociate from her body to withstand any torture they tried.

She only hoped Verina would live. Caenrya's throat grew thick.

There was something to be said about devoting her entire life to achieve one tiny dream and for all of it to amount to *nothing*.

"Sit her up," the shogun ordered, motioning to the medical shinobi to adjust the frame.

The brunette medical shinobi avoided eye contact with Caenrya as she elevated the back of her cot, the latter steadying herself for whatever may be in store. Caenrya tensed as the shogun gestured once more, the indication sending a jolt of irrationality through her despite her best attempt not to react.

There was one thing she could never forgive in her years of servitude. The permanent reminder was etched into a story of shame on her back, something she never allowed anyone to see.

Jerking away from the woman, Caenrya bared her teeth in a violent promise. "If you touch my back, I swear I'll enjoy fragmenting your mind." A cornered frenzy lit her eyes.

Everyone quieted, the shogun's expression mellowing as he waved the woman away from Caenrya. "You're a slave then," he determined, knowing full well that each had a brand burned into their backs.

Caenrya only lifted her chin in response. Humiliation and resentment tightened her face.

"Why defend the lord you were escorting if freedom is this close? Why not expose his identity and divulge the information you've gleaned?"

Heartbeats thudded loudly in her ears. Caenrya met his heavy gaze, regaining her composure. "For every day I work in his service—do his bidding—I gain a day where my younger sister lives."

"What if I promised my aid in retrieving her?" That gold wing pin shone as his head inclined, catching the lighting.

Her body froze at the thought. Such a dangerous one.

Damn the shogun and her precarious situation. Damn her shrunken heart for skipping a beat at the thought, at the possibility, as faint and hopeless as it might be.

But the sliver of light must have shown in her distrusting eyes, for the shogun's fingers danced on the bed rail beside her. "In exchange for any details you can offer about your knowledge and experience thus far, however insignificant you might distinguish them to be, I can offer the Duša Clan's full efforts in this exertion."

Duša Clan. She'd never heard of the clan's name before. The shinobi who ambushed her were Duša then.

Caenrya's throat worked for a moment, Rainer's protests barely recognizable over the roaring in her ears. Shaking her head, she cautiously asked, "Why go to such lengths? You must stand to gain something."

"My clan has many enemies, both within our territory and in the surrounding lands. If I can mitigate the threat from any of them, the effort would pay dividends." His tone grew a hair darker, and his spine straightened. "We've lost many good shinobi in ongoing feuds, and if we continue on such a warpath, we'll be left defenseless against the other vultures awaiting our failure. With the Kriv Clan resting on a majority of my clan's border, their civil war is spreading through the edges of my land." Those imposing eyes weighed on hers. "I ask that you join our ranks."

The other shinobi protested along with Rainer. Caenrya's heart sank. She'd be trading one lord for another. But hadn't she already settled on the path she was inevitably fated to tread?

Holding a palm up, the shogun silenced his shinobi. Directing his next words at them, he said, "She already proved to overpower our strongest shinobi in the Kū nature, and she's capable of holding her own against a number of our jōnin-ranked shinobi. Such a bloodline gift would prove substantially advantageous." His thick brows lowered dangerously. "Would the other clans hesitate?"

Licking her lips, the auburn-haired female shinobi sighed. "No, Shogun Arundel."

The others ranged from reluctant to outright spiteful.

Caenrya debated her options, though common sense dictated she could only give one plausible answer.

Throughout her indentured years in the daimyo's care—if she could call it such a thing—whispers of the elusive clans reached the ears of every slave. Some stories were terrifying, detailing the ways many would hunt their own kind for deviating from a single rule or for forsaking their ancestors. Though Caenrya had a gut feeling there was some truth to those rumors, it was said their blood ran thick. Family above all else. A homeland that valued trivial things such as honor and loyalty.

She always resented them for never bothering to show that *honor* and *loyalty* to the victims in her discarded territory. But if there was the slightest chance Caenrya could enter their fold and bring her sister with her... wasn't it worth betting on those forbidden tales she gleaned from other slaves?

After all, she sold her soul once to spare Verina from a life fighting in the rings. Caenrya's life. Why not once more?

"I'll agree to your terms."

Caenrya started from the beginning, her eyes low to the floor. "My younger sister and I were kidnapped at such a young age I can barely remember anything. I don't know where from, but I do know we were sold upon arriving at a bidding event to the daimyo I've worked for." Caenrya fought the urge to touch her pointed ears. She circumvented many truths to prevent history from repeating itself. If these people knew everything...

Caenrya shivered.

"We were too young for fights, but our capacity was measured in various ways. I fought to be the best to leverage my worth. Eventually, I succeed at being the daimyo's prized possession." Her fists tightened. "His highest-earning fighter. In exchange for my efforts, he kept Verina, my sister, out of the fighting pits and separated her from the others." Everyone fended for themselves at Shikei, but she made sure Verina was given better treatment. "As for the daimyo, I learned about his routines. About some of those he made deals with. What he gained from it all."

Her eyes flicked up, catching how everyone was enraptured by her tale. Shogun Arundel nodded for her to proceed.

Caenrya recounted every memory to the tiniest detail, selecting to skip over a few minor things they need not know. But she kept her word, explicating many aspects of her daimyo—her *previous* daimyo—and the constant fighting she underwent at the arenas. She didn't know the daimyo's true identity. Only his face. One she described with a detail only the finest of artists could hope to capture. There were several other faces she'd memorized after frequent appearances at many of the fights she participated in. Some she carried out hits for. Their contracts took her deep into the warring lands, where men fought tooth and nail to climb higher than the rest up that mountain of prestige and power.

No one suspected death to be served by an unremarkable girl, and it was always her target's undoing. It made her daimyo very, very rich.

The shogun's face darkened when Caenrya recounted a number of her contracts. She was careful to leave out anything too damning, skipping over those she thought would raise far too many questions or may have been against one of their clan.

There wasn't much beyond speculation and the general location of her latest arena, as the daimyo had been excruciatingly careful to knock her out whenever they neared Shikei or any other remarkable location. However, from how these people drank up her words, she knew they gleaned something significant.

By the time she wrapped up her story, her shoulder healed by the brunette woman and cuffs unlocked, Caenrya had released her hold on Aaric's mind. They ushered his limp form to the infirmary for monitoring as he came to, leaving only her, the shogun, and Rainer in the room.

For a beat, Caenrya thought they'd double-cross her, laughing all the while at her gullible belief in them. She waited for it too, for a kunai to be sheathed in her heart and her existence to end.

But when the shogun extended a hand to help her ragged form rise from the cot, Caenrya speculated if she traded the devil she knew for the devil she didn't.

Chapter Two

HALDEN

Halden soared from one of the many sloped rooftops of Riverside Square, his lithe body bounding across the vast land the Citadel claimed. Sunlight shone brilliantly above him. Merchants, artisans, and common folk lined the winding streets below on both sides of the clear, rushing water. During those insignificant moments, he felt alive, almost as if the possibilities were endless. In one direction, he could take make for the training grounds stationed within the mountainside. In another, he'd be only minutes away from the Shinobi Academy—a school he was glad to be long since finished with.

But there was one place he was summoned to: the Duša Clan Temple.

While studying a new technical balance of yin and yang to perfect a water-based taiji attack, a messenger eagle squawked from his bedroom window. If it weren't for the shogun's seal on the letter, Halden would have placed it aside and forgotten it until the afternoon had passed.

When his father asked for his presence, it would be unseemly to ignore for long.

An unintentional frown crossed his mouth as Halden landed on the third-floor balcony of his father's office. The presence of the place was enough to dampen his cheerful countenance. Despite the breathtaking view of the valley hosting the Citadel behind him, his mood was soured when he reached for the door's dull brass handle.

He ignored the flutter of a sparrow's spirit as it flickered into existence above him, the slight transparency and shimmer noticeable even during daylight. The weight of being summoned overrode his respect for the spirits and the overlap between their worlds, but only momentarily.

When the door opened wide, he was greeted with his father's disapproving stare behind his cypress desk. It was petty of Halden to enter from the balcony to the shogun's workspace, but the slight still managed to bring a sliver of smugness every time.

A curly blonde mane tilted in his direction. Under it, a pair of earthy, exasperated eyes he'd developed a healthy fear of stared back from his commander's face. "You sure took liberties with your time getting here," Eirea said.

Treading across an elaborate woven carpet of elegant design, Halden performed a necessary bow to his shogun before standing at attention beside his commander. His father's face remained indecipherable, half of it hidden behind clasped hands. Examining the Duša Clan leader's paper-scattered desk, Halden said, "I was in the middle of a task. I'm here now."

A look of reproach pulled at Eirea's prim face, her arms crossing over the standard black uniform shinobi were gifted upon graduation. Fitted, thigh-length robes. Slits on the side went up to a black belt tied around their middle. The flexible fabric tucked into leather bracers on their forearms, similar to their loose-fitting pants, slipping into shin-high boots.

"Our team has been assigned a new member, and she'll arrive here shortly." Eirea glanced at him expectantly, their gazes at an almost even height.

Shock buzzed through his spine at that, Halden's face portraying his confusion as he faced his father. "Did something happen to Ryu?"

"Sahkara isn't being transferred," his father answered, wrinkled eyes flicking toward Eirea. "I've already debriefed Cadigan as you were... indisposed."

Halden refused to balk.

"Team Cadigan is to receive an additional member at the commencement of this meeting. A refugee of the warring lands who has claimed asylum within our clan. I have only called the two of you in to discuss this matter before the other relevant members arrive," he explained.

Such a grave air emanated from the shogun, one that grew more common as the frequent skirmishes progressed. Halden shook off his childish grudge against his father for the moment, knowing when the shadows edged Ilias Arundel's expression, trouble was nearing the horizon. Needless to say, the small tidbit about the clan taking in a *refugee* would have had the same effect. Adopting any person from another clan was traditionally forbidden, and if this news reached foreign ears—*when* it did—the next summit between all clans could mark the beginning of a new war.

One they wouldn't survive.

"Why risk everything on one refugee? To integrate her into our shinobi way of all things..." Halden couldn't find the words to end that trailing thought.

"You'll have to trust that this is the best course of action, Halden. There is much you remain unaware of," the shogun said.

Halden's nose flared at the constant reminder.

"Though today, a part of that must change." His father's bulky frame rose from its cushioned chair. He held every ounce of Halden's attention as he distractedly tapped the deserted region on the wall-hung map. "You and Commander Cadigan are to undergo a jōnin-leveled assignment that must remain between us."

Skin pinched between Halden's brows. His team had never received a mission above that of mid-ranking chūnin, much less one only half of the team was aware of. When they were students in the academy, they were at the rank of genin. After years of study, training, and field exercises, they would graduate to chūnin. The next tier a shinobi could advance to was jōnin. Each rank came with its own missions the shogun could assign, though it was rare to be given a mission above one's rank.

Usually, it was a good sign someone was being eyed as a possible candidate for promotion.

He despised admitting it, but Halden felt a thrill at the prospect of such a tasking. However, more than a small corner of his mind wondered at the reason Ilias justified giving it to *him*. Was it truly a sign of Ilias recognizing his potential? Or was it an olive branch to grow closer?

Eirea remained statuesque beside him, already informed of the situation. Her pristine posture made the casualness in which Halden hooked his thumbs into his pockets outright disrespectful.

Good.

"You are to aid Commander Cadigan in three imperative areas. The first is that you are to monitor Caenrya, a jōnin-capable girl, and report any intelligence you glean from every interaction she makes. She's withholding secrets, and of what nature I have only vague inclinations." The shogun's eyes gazed out the window beside him. "The second is remaining on guard for potential threats, whether they stem from her or an outside group. I suspect others will be searching for her, and I entrust her safety to your team."

A fleck of light glinted from his father's bronze hair, his eyes peering out of the corner toward Halden. "The last is to gain her trust. For the future of our clan, I require her loyalty. Without it, we will surely fall into a dark era in the foreseeable future." His words were somber, sending a chill down Halden's spine. "The ancestors have spoken to this decree."

Blinking, Halden felt the moment's gravity, a similar sentiment mirrored in Eirea's eyes. It was rare when the dead crossed into their dreams and only to depart wisdom solely on matters of great importance. "What will others know of her? How will you explain her presence?" he carefully asked.

"Should I lie, I'll lose the trust of my people. A stake I cannot risk, and so it'll be a part-truth. Caenrya will be accepted as a refugee from the warring lands. Sahkara has been briefed on everything but the specific tasking I've given you both. As with any mission, this is strictly confidential," Ilias reminded, continuing to describe the girl's background and what to expect upon her arrival.

Throughout it all, Halden couldn't help the flicker of disbelief crossing his sight, nor the incredulous look he gave his commander. He opened his mouth to press the matter when his father took his seat again, a hand held up to command his silence. But a second later, knocking sounded from the hallway. Javan, the shogun's kampaku—assistant—entered with Ryu and a slightly shorter, rail-thin girl in tow.

His plaited hair swayed on the way out, and Javan closed the door behind him.

Refugee. The word tumbled in his mind as he took in her frail-appearing profile.

Braided hair of gold fell to her oversized ivory robe's waistline. Her sharply tilted jawline and pale, low-set cheekbones were haunted by the dark skin under her near-vacant eyes. The only true emotion Halden could discern was distrust, her feet maneuvering her carefully away from another at every given moment. Her back was only to a wall, those eyes observing every movement around her. It was unbelievable that such a person would be capable of much damage, much less worthy of such an assignment.

Then he noticed her ears. Pointed far more than those of any Canecian—any person who lived on their continent of Canecia—or one of five continents Halden knew of, but even then, he'd never heard rumors of any bearing such traits in this age.

Halden fought the reaction threatening to surface, the implication clear as day. *I'll have to give my father credit where it's due.* All clans had bloodlines intertwined with that of the fae. Elves, in particular. Though their human blood diluted their prowess, those with a higher ancestry of Elven blood harbored a sharper point on their ears. Since Elves had been long since extinct, those with mildly sharp ears like Halden's, Eirea's, and Ryu's were held in high esteem.

Either the Caenrya girl hailed from two immensely strong bloodlines within a clan, or she was bastard-born from two ancient houses in different clans to have such a strong connection to their heritage.

Houses have killed for less.

A knowing glint shone from the shogun's eyes before he addressed the girl. "Welcome to your new team. This will be your commander." He held out a hand toward Eirea, who gave Caenrya an appraising face.

"Eirea Cadigan." A quirk of her lips showed, her hand moving to rest on her hips.

Unimpressed, Caenrya frowned at Halden, then Ryu. The latter appeared in a rare mood. His finger tapped on a crossed arm. To her credit, Eirea didn't react when the girl ignored her and turned to the shogun.

"When do we leave to rescue my sister?" Caenrya asked, her soft voice contrasting heavily with her bearing.

Before Ryu said something inappropriate, his father addressed her question. "Two criteria must be met before I'd consider sending Team Cadigan out." He gestured to the map behind him, continuing in a neutral tone, "We must pinpoint the location and scout as much intelligence as we can glean before risking lives. Then your team will be required to prove capable of handling such an assignment."

"I'm more than capable now," Caenrya pressed, placing her palms flat against the shogun's desk as she leaned toward him. "Every minute I spend out of Shikei is another where she's in danger, and—"

The shogun's hand raised, halting her words. Leaning back into his chair, his father calmly rested his hands on his lap, saying, "If you can beat me in a shinobi's duel, then I'll permit you to leave this instance."

At this, Halden's interest was captivated.

His great-great-great-grandfather was a legendary figure during the turbulent times of establishing borders between the clans after the dissolution of the empire, his youth inspiring many to achieve great heights. He passed on all his brilliance to Halden's lineage. The current shogun, his father, managed to keep the Kriv Clan from gaining any purchase within their territory. In the middle of a war, Ilias single-handedly removed the Kriv Clan's shogun with brutal effectiveness, thus stalling their advances for a decade.

Ilias had never lost any fight in his years as the clan's leader.

Besides that tidbit, he was interested in how a girl without state-of-the-art training would compare to one of the land's best shinobi. Ilias had elaborated that she was skilled and blood-gifted and not with a gift hailing from any major house that was accounted for.

"However, should you lose, you'll agree to dedicate yourself to training both on your own and with your team. In all likelihood, it will take several months before we can locate any leads and organize a team to retrieve your sister. This time will be crucial for you to learn and integrate into the clan."

Halden could feel Ryu's distaste cloud the room. Eirea shot Ryu a look that promised he'd be in for it if he acted out. Eight years their senior, the commander was a terror when provoked and took every liberty to reinforce that when they didn't meet her expectations.

Even though he and Ryu were eighteen, she tended to treat them as if they were her own age, which meant their training was often brutally exhausting.

"Fine," Caenrya agreed, dipping her chin.

Turning to his assistant, Ilias said, "Reserve the training grounds for this afternoon through the evening. Ensure that the academy is granted privileges at the Shinobi Stadium for drill relocation. We'll require privacy to not attract undue attention."

With a trained bow, the kampaku took his leave to carry out the orders. A flutter of wings sounded at the window overlooking the patio. An eagle landed on the sill with a scroll tied to its leg. The shogun promptly reacted, unraveling the missive with a tight face. Without a glance in their direction, he said, "I'll meet your team there at five after noon, Cadigan. For now, I have other matters to attend to. See that in the meantime, you show Caenrya to her quarters in the Wisteria Square."

His tone left no room for argument.

With the clear dismissal, the team left. Ryu signaled to Halden to hang back as they took to the streetways, putting a generous distance between them and the women before he ranted.

"Who's to say this crazy bag of bones isn't going to turn on us when she doesn't get her way? Because of her, we aren't going to collect any decent assignments for who knows how long," Ryu grumbled, kicking a stone with his boots. "Besides, why is she even being placed on a shinobi team? It's not like she'll become a member of the clan. She's not blood. She doesn't even have a last name."

Staring at the back of Caenrya's head, Halden couldn't help but experience creeping pity for the girl. While he did empathize with her plight, he also couldn't disagree with Ryu's point. Breathing hard from his nose, he said, "We are at the will and whim of the shogun."

Shoving his hands in his pants pockets, Ryu shook his head angrily. "We were on the cusp of receiving our first jōnin-ranked assignment, Halden. *Jōnin. Ranked.* We are incredibly close to taking our jōnin assessments. I can't even fathom how far we will be set back."

"Ilias wouldn't give us a genin-ranked addition," Halden pacified, giving his teammate a face that read *you're being a slight overdramatic.* "Besides, this could be an opportunity for us to build up leadership experience. We'll need it if we are to command our own units."

Ryu's near-black eyes squinched up at him. "You know something."

Shrugging his shoulders nonchalantly, Halden only said, "Reading between the lines."

Ryu and Halden had bonded over their shared goal of becoming better than the one person in each of their lives who overshadowed them. For Halden, it was his father and the reputation as an Arundel descendant Halden was expected to maintain. For Ryu, it was his elder brother, who was a shinobi prodigy everyone admired. Before they had enrolled at the Shinobi Academy, they were already training together.

Taking on a jōnin-ranked mission would propel them one step closer. If Ryu only knew they had just started one.

A drifting wind spilled the scent of grilled seafood, bringing Temple Square alive with patrons as they passed through. Every counter steamed with freshly cooked meals, and children ran around a central statue of an eagle mid-flight. Behind them, the Duša Clan Temple appeared a replica of the creature, with its towering central hall surrounded by twin L-shaped wing halls on either side. A sharp tower rested in the middle, imitating its head with a grand golden-etched bell in the center.

Ryu stared with longing at each food stall they passed, only distracted by another stall displaying the latest weaponry and other tools fashioned. A handful of artisans bowed in respect as they passed.

Halden acknowledged them with an uncomfortable dip of his head. He'd never adjust to the prestige his father's station gave him and despised it when people attempted to worm into his graces. At least Ryu never had such sentiments. His friend's interests were limited to his own career progression, shinobi tools, and the occasional dalliance with a merchant's daughter who stole his heart long ago.

Straightening his back, Ryu appeared as if a thought struck him—a mischievous one Halden dreaded already. "I bet I can scare her off within a week. It's not like we'll go search for this sister of hers or whatever. She won't ever amount to much, not even close to what she'd need to be to join us on such a mission."

Ahead, Halden saw Caenrya's hands twitch, and his gut clenched at the possibility that she had overheard everything, despite the sizable distance between them. Wisely, Halden shook his head, trailing behind his commander with a conflicted mind.

Halden could see where Ryu was coming from. Clans didn't take in strays. They didn't chase down and rescue anyone outside their own clan. Caenrya appeared far too weak to pose much of a threat. A single shinobi was required to have a decade of training before advancing to the level of genin.

Which only made Halden more curious as to why his father believed she was jōnin-capable.

***

Halden and Ryu reconvened with Caenrya and Eirea at the training grounds, the former appearing as dour as ever. At least she had a fitted shinobi uniform on this time around, though it revealed how thin her starved frame was. The belt they all wore wrapped several times around their middle only accentuated it further. The clan's emblem of a jagged wing rested on her right shoulder. She had dark eyebrows, and her cheeks were shrunken in. Her critical eyes absorbed every detail of the widespread obstacle courses to her left, the wide-open dirt sparring ring in the center, the high-ropes fighting course looping far above their heads, and the blooming cherry blossom trees threaded throughout.

"It's the pride of our academy's architect," Ilias said behind Halden, Ryu nearly jumping out of his skin to his right.

Halden had had years to adjust to his father's stealth. Well, the years Ilias had been around anyway. Caenrya's blue eyes flicked to the shogun, unreadable.

"Would you care for any weapons before we begin?" Ilias asked, his chin lowering in Caenrya's direction.

Caenrya's back straightened. "I don't need such things."

Raising his brows, Halden stared on with growing interest. Eirea frowned slightly next to him. A quiet scoff sounded from Ryu, his straight eyebrows pinned low.

"Well then, shall we?" Ilias confidently strode into the dirt ring, Caenrya following without missing a beat.

It spoke volumes Ilias didn't bother to change into appropriate clothing for a fight.

Ryu snickered, a nudge with his elbow drawing Halden's attention. "Do you think she'll be able to throw a punch?" Reproach lined Halden's face. His reaction wiped the smirk off his friend's. "I'm kidding," he mumbled. "Kinda."

Eirea waltzed over with a fake smile, wringing an arm around Ryu's neck. "She's going to be a part of our team, and I fully expect you to treat her as such. Otherwise," she cheerfully added, lowering her head a couple of inches to be level with Ryu, "you'll be stuck at the academy as a punching bag for recruits during the entirety of this month and next."

Their commander stood alongside Halden at a height two centimeters over six feet tall, and it only helped her become more intimidating when she lorded it over them.

Swallowing, Ryu reluctantly apologized. Halden knew it was not genuine, and by the glint in their commander's eye, she was well aware too. His father squared up against Caenrya, pausing for a moment to pull out a piece of fabric and wrap it around his eyes. A furrow creased Halden's brow, and a shared moment of confusion passed between him and Ryu.

The girl's jaw ticked, obviously off-kilter from the action of the shogun. Halden caught Eirea's smirk, and his father curled his fingers in the signal to start. Ilias made a quick hand seal of *zen* and awaited his opponent's move.

It dawned on Halden then what Ilias had done. A tingle crawled along his spine, and his head leaned forward.

It spoke more than words ever could. Ilias would handicap himself.

Despite her size, Caenrya moved with lightning speed, zipping forward with basic sparring techniques his father easily blocked. It was a dance of sorts. The girl took the lead with an ever-increasing advancement of taijutsu—hand-to-hand combat. Movements even Ryu's eyes widened at.

Too bad Caenrya was sparring with the head of the Arundel house, a branch with the bloodline gift—otherwise called vin—of visualizing the world's taiji with a third inner eye. The ability allowed them to observe the flow of energy within natural materials and people alike, rendering sight unnecessary in combat. The waves of taiji were lights within an otherwise dark world, only requiring a steady flow of one's taiji to visualize within their mind.

It was nearly impossible to outperform an Arundel in taijutsu alone. A fact that brought a snarl to the girl's face when she realized it minutes later. Leaping backward, Caenrya performed the hand seal for *zen*. A semi-transparent aura enveloped her elbows, sharpening into razor edges past her fingertips.

Even from his location, Halden could discern a near-inaudible crackle emanating from the visible taiji. "I've never seen the energy manifest into a physical form," he mused. His interest grew further in his assigned mission and what knowledge his father must have been withholding.

Zen.

It was the only one out of nine seals to require a single hand to shape, and the only seal a select number of houses in each of the five clans could create. It insinuated even more that Caenrya wielded a bloodline ability that wasn't prevalent in any of the established. The circumstances made him wonder about his father's campaigns and where this was going to lead.

"I've been told it chipped away at our shinobi's blades when they sparred with her," Eirea remarked, Ryu's frown creating creases across his face.

The shogun withdrew two kunai in the nick of time, and the twin blades clashed in an array of sparks with Caenrya's taiji blades. Whirling, her long braid whipped around with her form, one blade aiming higher than the other. What would have disemboweled an ordinary foe was deflected with a graceful sweeping motion, the ebb of the match turning as his father fell to the defensive. It put him at a distinct disadvantage to not have a weapon of equal length or strength, the snap of a kunai confirming Eirea's rumor.

The shogun's hands swiftly fell into the *toh* seal. His palms stretched in Caenrya's direction as a wave of water roared.

A ninjutsu technique. One where the user activates their taiji through a mental incantation and hand movement, otherwise called a seal. Each element had a specific hand seal to weave, and Ilias used the one for the water element.

It was inescapable at their proximity, and Caenrya was forced back a dozen feet as the water knocked her down. Her head hit the ground hard. A moment lapsed before the water settled into a pool around her.

Red-hot anger flashed in Caenrya's eyes as she regained her footing. She circled Ilias's still form. Caenrya's foot turned inward, and Ilias's hand wove the hand seal for wind. Both hands gracefully swooped low, and his fingers intertwined at the end of the movement.

A tornado of wind erupted around the shogun, gales ripping from the center strong enough to send Halden back several steps to regain his balance. Beside him, Eirea had braced in place, but Ryu hadn't been as fortunate.

Like Caenrya, Ryu had spun toward the ground. Unlike Caenrya, he didn't have taiji blades that steadied his bearing.

Caenrya's damp hair whipped wildly around her. Both of her blades pierced the ground as the wind threatened to send her airborne. All around them, tree branches and leaves fluttered with abandon.

Halden's eyes watered as the noise muffled Ryu's curse.

Before Halden could blink, Ilias's hands formed the earth seal. The ground shook recklessly all around them. Halden dropped low, the gale and shuddering incapacitating. The world became unhinged, and his vision vibrated with the force. He squinted his eyes toward the scene before him, tightening his jaw to prevent the rows from clacking.

Two more seals in rapid succession. Water and fire.

Twin dragons of each element rose far above the shogun, roaring in the maelstrom of elements.

Far below, Caenrya barely kept her blades dug into the trembling ground. Her eyes were wide as the display unfolded. Her arms struggled to maintain her place, and she grimaced as she forced her head to tilt up at Ilias.

Without moving a step, Ilias swept one hand in her direction.

Dragons whirled down from the sky. Their long bodies writhed around each other as they aimed for Caenrya. At the last second, both elemental beasts collided, sending a sizzling cascade of steam around them. The wind subsided, taking the last of the haze with it, and the earth stilled once more.

His father was merciless, lunging forward as Caenrya regained her footing. He threw the broken kunai at her, which she swiftly dodged. She moved to attack, but it was too late.

A single palm blocked her spinning movement at the shoulder, causing the taiji to sputter throughout the affected arm.

Halden winced.

He knew how it felt to have his father use the other half of the bloodline gift they wielded: the ability to block the chakra points taiji ran through. Much like joints for limbs, taiji circulated through their own channels in the body. Junctions were located at every joint, and Ilias had blocked one in her shoulder. It immobilized the mystical energy in a person's body, rendering any ninjutsu impossible to use past that chakra point.

A quick glimmer of shock shot through Caenrya's eyes. Her other arm rushed to defend against the kunai racing for her abdomen. Switching directions, Ilias deftly tossed his kunai to his other hand in a feint. He took advantage of the confusion and impacted her elbow with his palm.

Before she knew it, Caenrya's second taiji blade dissolved. Ilias's kunai was pointed at her unprotected face.

"Your blocked chakra points will be recovered within the half hour." Ilias stepped back, placing the kunai back within his layered robes. "One creed we shinobi adhere to is the Eternal Forge. It represents the need for continuous improvement in taijutsu and ninjutsu, two of the most crucial elements to better ourselves so we may be a lethal force. You'll need to learn the ninjutsu arts beyond your bloodline gift. With time, you could expand upon what you already wield, but you lack a foundation that will force your teammates to come to your aid in any real battle. They'll be the ones to sacrifice their lives first because once your enemy determines the extent of your abilities, they'll quickly outmaneuver you," he said. His words were harsh, but his face was patient and understanding as the fabric around it was removed.

Ryu puffed out his chest. Halden glanced sideways at him, frowning as he caught Eirea's eyes rolling at Ryu's smugness.

Ilias straightened out his overgarment, a half-sleeve fitted silk robe fastened on his right side. "Shinobi equipment, from a kunai to a katana, are all hard-pressed to fail while taiji is bound to. You must learn to defend yourself with weapons outside other than your taiji blades. Your taijutsu is excellent. With time, you'll determine where your elemental inclinations lay with taiji. Simple words of power, such as my water technique, will unlock a variety of choices when confronted with a challenging enemy. What I displayed here was but the surface of what shinobi may achieve with time and practice."

And innate talent, but Halden didn't say that. Not all shinobi became jōnin. Some weren't capable of the vast requirements. And not all jōnin could wield every element as the shogun had.

What was more terrifying was the reality that Ilias had taken it easy on Caenrya.

Ilias retrieved his broken kunai from the ground. Placing it in a different hidden fold of his robe, he continued, "You'll never be confronted with an impossible situation if you equip yourself properly. Until then, train."

Caenrya's face remained unreadable, and her chest heaved from combat.

Ilias's face grew somber. He released his taiji with the *zai* seal, a necessary step to end the expenditure of taiji on his bloodline gift. "Train so when the time arrives, you can lead us to fell the daimyo who committed the atrocities against your family."

Caenrya's lips pressed into a firm line, and her eyes fell to the ground. Only a subtle dip of her chin indicated her response. When she brushed by all of them without another glance in their direction, Ryu huffed.

"How is *that* jōnin-ranked capable?" he complained, his slightly upturned eyes narrowing at Eirea.

An arched brow rose on Eirea's face. "Because unlike you, Ryu, she can throw a punch."

In response, Ryu closed his mouth, the skin under his lower eyelid bunching further. His meticulously kept black hair had blown in wild directions, and the gelled point in the front was sideswept.

Ilias's face radiated disappointment at Ryu's shortsightedness. The latter's shoulders drooped when he saw it.

"What you aren't aware of is that her taiji excels in the Kū nature, managing to overcome even our strongest in the mind arts. Without this crucial knowledge, nearly any foe would be felled the moment they made eye contact with her," Ilias said, Ryu's whites showing as he stared after Caenrya. "Possibly even myself."

And that was what Halden had discerned when his father used his vin and blindfolded himself. A revelation that had Halden wondering at the extent of Caenrya's true bloodline gift.

Eirea *tsked* in distaste at her charge, leaving them to follow Caenrya. Unable to help himself, Halden rubbed an eyebrow—a stress-induced tick he could never manage to get rid of. It was concerning how easily the girl could turn on them all, make a joke one minute, then obliterate their minds the next. Perhaps he should learn what sets her off and strive to avoid that at all costs.

He preferred to keep his sanity.

CHAPTER THREE

CAENRYA

Caenrya credited that loss to the shogun's bloodline gift. Having a vin like that made Ilias her natural opposite. A perfect counter to her mental prowess. And being able to block her chakra points... Caenrya didn't stand a chance not knowing what she was up against. If she could do it all over again, she'd keep more distance between them and wait for an opening to...

Her teeth ground as Cadigan took the lead.

There had to be a way. Perhaps if she cut the cloth around Ilias's face, she could secure a line of sight to his eyes. From there, Caenrya would have no trouble defeating him.

Tomorrow, she'd see about a rematch. She could do it.

Caenrya followed her new commander to her quarters, refusing to say a word as she was dropped off at the Wisteria Square apartments. Along with her brief tour of the Citadel, she was introduced to her new home before being shepherded to the training grounds. It was beautiful in that particular residential sector, a thought that made her frown grow further. Apparently, the location hosted most of the representatives of every major house in the Duša Clan.

Green petals were scattered across the cobblestone streets, falling from high-rising, twisted ahari trees—trees native to the continent with their thick expanse of branches and minimal green foliage. The slopes of each rooftop ended in a dramatic, upswept arch, meticulously kept gardens lining each building.

Hers—such an unnatural thing to claim—was extraordinary, with dark wood pillars lining the front and a spiral stairwell leading to her second-floor residence overlooking Wisteria Square. Lanterns were alight with a flame of gold, the metalwork elegantly finished with an eagle on top. Spirits of grasshoppers darted about the cedar floorboards, dissipating into the air within seconds.

Inside, Caenrya was given a simple, white-sheeted futon mattress along the right wall and a tatami mat lining the floor. A bamboo-framed alcove inlaid the wall across from the doorway, and a simple desk was built in with a stunning view of the bustling marketplace below. Thin shoji windows could be slid to the side to block the view. Such a luxurious feature that she almost despised it. It amazed her how even a room designed for one held a private bathing area, an entire stone-encrusted shower, a porcelain toilet, and a matching sink within.

Shikei had shared bathrooms. Metal, cold, and clad with an eerie darkness.

They even gifted her what they called a refrigerator, which held various food items inside, and a small electric stove top beside it to heat food. A tall wardrobe held an array of clothing, more than she'd ever owned, of such fine quality she knew it wasn't something a fighter would ever possess in Shikei.

And it was hers. All hers.

The coals burning within her extinguished, leaving behind such a plaguing cold.

When she shut the door behind her, Caenrya didn't bother with the lights. It brought a twisted comfort to remain in the dark, alone and without the added responsibility of maintaining the ever-draining façade she upheld. Her eyes burned, and her body moved out of necessity toward the shower. By the time hot water ran down her, it melded with the tears streaming down her sobbing face. How long she stood there, her chest hurting and steam clouding the tiny bathroom, Caenrya didn't know.

Didn't care.

All that mattered was she was free at last, achieving the dream she and her sister had yearned for.

But Verina wasn't there.

No small amount of guilt tore at Caenrya's heart. The haunting moment where she willingly gave her life instead of continuing to fight for their freedom replayed over and over. She could have given more when ambushed by the Duša shinobi, but it spoke more than words could ever say she was relieved it was over. Her burden was no longer her duty to carry. All of those bloody tournaments she suffered and the abuse she endured were at last gone. Even if it meant her sister would be forced to pick up her mantle.

How Caenrya could have such awful thoughts... it killed her. Ate at her inch by inch as she slid to the ground, water burning into her skin.

She dug her nails into her arms, pain blossoming in each spot. Her mind was tormented over what the daimyo and other children were putting Verina through. There was an entire wing in Shikei for them, different rooms dedicated to the level of skill each wielded. When they arrived all those years ago, Caenrya quickly picked up on the pecking order, getting into frequent brawls and threatening others to establish herself higher in the chain to protect her sister.

Verina was a gentle soul, growing up with wistful eyes whenever Caenrya described the beauty of the outside world. Seeing blood terrified her, even more so when the prospect of learning to fight arose.

Five.

That was the age when any child became fair game to the rest of the fighters. A day she dreaded more than any other. Caenrya had already been incorporated into the chain by then, sitting in the middle of the rankings despite most of the others being older than her. Her taiji blades served her well to compensate for her lack of real skill.

When Verina kicked and screamed as she was drug into the challenge room, Caenrya instinctively knocked out the boy who wanted to raise his status. It was meant as a punishment for defying orders when the daimyo demanded every child challenge Caenrya afterward.

Little did they expect it would awaken a second part of her bloodline gift that fateful day: the ability to mind-walk.

Caenrya knew the other kids feared her by the end of it. Each successive challenge that same day ended with her opponents mumbling incoherent thoughts on the ground or so bloodied the next kid would slip on the floorboards. But she became number One, guaranteeing that her sister would remain untouched.

Caenrya went as far as to strike a bargain with the daimyo, swearing to serve at every tournament and even as one of his guards if need be.

She would have paid any cost to keep Verina safe, and that day, it was her soul.

For the last decade, Caenrya would be allowed one monthly visit to check on Verina, a silent reminder of her sworn duty. Those brief minutes meant the world to her, giving Caenrya the strength to carry herself through the rest of the weeks before the next visit. As time passed, though, she saw the changes before she felt them in herself. It began when Verina was startled whenever she visited—a brief expression of fear before her sister realized who was there. Then, it was in those moments Caenrya would remember to be happy. To smile.

She lost touch with her humanity, all so her sister could keep hers.

Numbness shaded every thought and action of hers for years. It was the only thing she felt after her energy was spent, making living under the daimyo's thumb somewhat tolerable. It crept in now. Her hand found the handle to shut off the pouring heat. A part of her wished those shinobi had ended her miserable excuse for a life instead of bringing her to this place. Another wished she had the courage to give up herself. But after years of giving everything she had for her sister, Caenrya didn't know how.

A whisper in the back of her mind told her to wait another day. Maybe it would bring something worth living for. At least, that's what Caenrya imagined as her body folded into the white cotton sheets of her bed. Her eyes were unable to close to the comfort of sleep. A vacant ache echoed in her stomach, and the familiar pain of hunger was the least she could endure in solidarity with her sister. She owed Verina for leaving her behind, so much so that Caenrya wasn't sure she'd be capable of waiting around.

Should she stay? Should she go?

Back and forth, her thoughts swayed in each direction. Her eyes stared into nothingness, and her fingers absently thrummed on the soft sheets. Something in her gut tugged at her mind to hurry back before it was too late. Before the damage was done and she lost Verina as a punishment for not returning.

A sharp pain tugged at the center of her back, a taiji-imprinted slave mark there to remind her not to stray for too long away from her daimyo. And it would only worsen over time unless...

Hopping from her bed, Caenrya switched back into her close-fitting training garments. Pulling wide her windows, she gathered taiji in her feet as she leaped, gracefully landing amid the dinner crowd gathered below. She hated the way the common folk treated shinobi there, with a near reverence. Her hair billowed about her as she dodged bows, ignored greeting smiles, and made for any direction that would lead to an exit.

Time was a luxury Caenrya didn't have.

Her mind recalled the map spread behind the shogun in his office. From the Citadel, a vast volcano rested north, marked half a foot away on the parchment. The enormous outline had been faint throughout the day as she toured her new surroundings, giving her the impression she could reach it within two days. The slave mark on her body guaranteed it had been a week since she separated from the daimyo. Pain only radiated from it as early as the seven-day mark. The time she'd spent in the Citadel, both conscious and not, was about two days.

Meaning, she had at least a five-day journey to the mountain range where she'd been kidnapped. If two days equated to half a foot of map distance, five was a foot and a quarter away. That gave her a general circle of distance where she had been taken from the daimyo. She determined that journey would lead to what they called the Kriv Clan territory southeast of the Citadel, precisely where a mountain range was depicted on the map.

Caenrya chewed on the inside of her mouth.

Within the coming weeks, the mark would become incapacitating with pain. Her body would not survive once it grew too potent. If she left now, at least she'd stand a chance at seeing her sister again. Caenrya owed her that much.

Besides, she couldn't linger here, living a life of luxury while her sister continued to suffer. Waiting wasn't an option, especially when there was an enormous chance these people would never fulfill their end of the deal in time.

Months. Caenrya didn't *have* months.

She'd be dead in a matter of *weeks*.

It was the daimyo's final assurance Caenrya wouldn't take her own leave during any of her contracts.

What good would she be to Verina here? Caenrya would be better off working for the daimyo, knowing her sister would be safe all along, rather than wasting her days here with the genuine possibility Verina was facing the consequences meant for her. A punishment for Caenrya abandoning them.

The streets were a maze of confusion. The only guide point was the river she walked alongside for direction. A small part of her stomach gnawed with guilt at leaving after all that had been given to her, but the words of her would-be teammates quickly snuffed that out. It was clear that Ryu child detested her. His insults scraped at her last nerve. If he were in Shikei with her, Caenrya wouldn't have tolerated such disrespect.

Besides, she could level him in any real fight. The shogun won only because of his bloodline gift, a situation she'd never cross again. Caenrya had never lost in such a manner, and she'd never do so again. It was humiliating.

People laughed and happily chatted as she passed through them all. Children chased each other along the riverbank with figurines clasped in their soft hands. Hers were bloodied at their age, stained and calloused from a world that couldn't ever compare to the indulgence these kids were graced with. They hadn't a single worry beyond when they'd meet again, whereas hers had been innumerable. Insurmountable. When her next meal would arrive, where her next contract would take her, if she and Verina would survive all of it... Caenrya walked faster, pressing her lips into a fine line.

None of these people understood.

The sun had dipped behind one of the surrounding mountains. The Citadel's outside wall showed on the horizon. Caenrya selected an isolated chunk of the wall tucked between trees, carefully sticking to the shadows. She focused her taiji to her feet and palms. One hand adhered to the stone wall above her head, and the taiji from her body bonded to the natural energy in the wall. Scaling it like a lizard, Caenrya heard the sound of footsteps approaching from her left. She paused halfway up the wall, gluing her body against the stone. Her taiji tingled in her limbs as it adhered to the barrier, and her heartbeat thudded in her ears along with the cadence of footsteps passing over her.

She waited for the duo of shinobi to pass before pulling herself over the top and sneaking across the walkway. With a quick glance at the shinobi's back, she lowered herself on the other side of the wall. The grittiness of the stone bit into her palms as she scaled halfway down. She landed in a roll, shooting to her feet and dodging between the ahari trees as she descended the slope. Wind whistled through her long locks, the landscape whizzing by as she bounded through the sparsely forested hills. The tax on her energy was minimal, Caenrya breathing a slight easier when the distance between her and the overcrowded village grew. Though a part of her dreaded going back, she owed it to Verina.

But... did she owe it to her in this way?

Did Caenrya owe a life of servitude, with her sister benefiting only from meager meals and her own life in stone cellars? Was it worthwhile, even if it ensured her sister was kept from the bloodied arena?

Slowing, Caenrya halted beside a thick trunk and leaned a hand against it. Closing her eyes, she lowered her head with shaking fists. *Think*, she demanded of herself.

As skilled as she was, there wasn't the faintest hope Caenrya could rescue Verina of her own accord. The other fighters wouldn't dare miss the opportunity to repay the years of beatings Caenrya gave them in the rings, much less the air-tight security throughout the massive complex. Even to this day, Caenrya didn't comprehend the floor plans because they ensured whenever she entered or left a blindfold had been in place.

Caenrya had weeks remaining before the slave mark on her back became deadly. With the resources of the Duša Clan, there was an honest chance they'd discover further information on Shikei's location within a reasonable time. For the opportunity of both of their freedom, it could be worthwhile to wait one more week before abandoning them.

There was still a future with Verina leading a normal life, even if Caenrya never would. She could almost visualize Verina sitting at the food stalls in their beautiful market squares, laughing with others her age rather than being fearful of them.

Verina would have a comfortable room in the Wisteria Square, enjoying the spring breeze and the sound of the river flowing close by. She'd have the opportunity to select her path, whether it be an artisan or a shinobi. Painting with vibrant colors or training with a variety of blades. Over time, she'd have a whole room of friends, and her outgoing personality would flourish in such a welcoming environment. She'd be the first to adventure and discover new nooks and crannies in the Citadel, returning each day with a wide grin and stories to share.

That was a life worth living. What Verina had now wasn't.

Caenrya would continue the cycle of misery if she went back to serve the daimyo. There was never a real chance of escaping that place.

The daimyo would never allow his prized fighter to leave, much less the leverage he blackmailed her with.

She'd use the clan for now. While she didn't have months, Caenrya would allow them to divulge their secrets and training to her for as long as she was willing to wait. There was a chance they'd find a lead sooner than the several months Ilias warned of. And if Caenrya had any hope of defeating the daimyo's elite guards, she'd need the time to better her capabilities.

It would be premature to leave.

Turning, Caenrya knew she had been rash. Patience wasn't something she was good at, but if she could wait longer, maybe, just maybe, it would pan out to be the opportunity she'd been waiting for decades to happen. It was difficult to allow that ray of hope to brighten, to believe that the time was *now*.

None of it felt real. It seemed too good to be true.

Above, a squirrel chittered at her, annoyed Caenrya decided to stop at that tree of all in the area.

One foot in front of the other, Caenrya began the trek back to the Citadel.

One week. She'd wait at least a week to give these people time to earn their promise. If it was the one chance she'd been waiting for, it would be the best path for Verina's future.

A second later, a flurry of needles buried themselves in her back.

A gasp of pain escaped Caenrya's mouth, and her body lurched toward the ground. Two black-clad figures jumped from the height of the trees, another two walking toward her from behind. Catching her balance, she gritted her teeth at the array of wounds throbbing across her back. Her attackers circled in front of her.

She didn't recognize any, unsure of whether they were Duša or foreign ronin hired outside of a clan. Did the shogun realize she betrayed his trust? Were they disposing of her?

Two wielded shuko, their claw-like blades protruding a foot from their fists. The others held pockets of undisclosed tools; the thought sent a throb of pain ricocheting from the multiple weapons in her back. Then she noticed her limbs drooping of their own accord and the gentle sway of her unstable body. The attackers edged around her, taking their time closing ranks. One took the lead, drawing a hidden katana from his back and pointing it at her.

Caenrya attempted to form a hand seal at the same time her knees gave, and her body unsteadily propped against the ground. Her eyes blearily focused on the grassy blades below her. The edge of a sword buried itself into the dirt at the top of her vision.

The needles were drugged.

The ronin kneeled beside his sword, taking her chin in one gloved hand to inspect her face. "Confirming, it's One."

One. One out of the thirty-two owned by the daimyo.

Her stomach rolled.

"Excellent. Retrieve her, and we'll make haste to the designated transfer location," another ordered. The sound of a weapon being sheathed echoed in her ears. "Looks like she made it easy for us."

A snicker sounded from another arrival. Her body was numb as she was slung over the shoulder of a man. There, her consciousness faltered, a heavy fog clouding a majority of the words passed between them as they retreated further into the woods.

Her choice ended up being irrelevant. Caenrya was destined to be claimed by the fighting pits once more. Her body wanted to battle against her helplessness, and her thoughts struggled to function against the haze of the drug. This time, Caenrya thrashed against the creeping wave of unconsciousness roiling at the fringe of her mind. Despite her efforts, her breaths became shallower, and her leaden lids darkened her vision.

Chapter Four

CAENRYA

How much time had passed, Caenrya hadn't a clue. She took care to regulate her breathing, preventing any hitch of her lungs or twitch of her fingers from giving away her sluggish alertness. A stark brightness contrasted against the earlier darkness she had left in, indicating at least a half day's passing. The daimyo's men were resting, the chirping of squirrels near where her body was bound against a tree. Bark grazed her neck, and the smell of sap was abundant. By the words she managed to pick up, she discerned they were discussing the matter of her bounty over their midday meal.

Anger flooded through her. She'd have fun ensuring they wouldn't make it back to beg for forgiveness when they returned empty-handed.

Keeping still, Caenrya focused on her toes first, attempting to move them discretely within her boots. It was slow—painfully difficult actually—but she managed a slight shift. Time was all she needed for basic movement, and then she'd plan her escape.

"Quiet," one of the men whispered, his footsteps closing in on her position.

For a dreadful second, Caenrya feared she had given away her waking. The sound of leaves crunching grew closer, and one of the ronin kneeled beside her. It was an immense challenge not to react and launch herself at the man.

Another ordered, "Untie her. We need to move now."

Wind whistled around her as a man positioned himself next to her, unbinding a slim rope around her middle. A muscle flinched in her back, and her heart nearly stopped in her chest at the hesitation the ronin inspected her with. A hand waved by her uptilted face, another shaking her shoulder once that didn't incite a reaction. She could feel his breath on her cheeks. He was close, waiting for the moment she might give any indication for concern.

"What's the hold up over there?" snapped one of the ronin, sounding as if he were hidden in the thick, sparse leaves of ahari treetops.

A moment passed. Then a frustrated, "I'm moving."

"They're here!" another shouted.

An arm looped around her waist, and the ronin beside her rushed to evacuate the area. Popping sounded, and the hiss of a gas being released into the vicinity drowned out the sounds of nature. The roar of fire erupted somewhere in the near distance, shouting ensuing from two nearby voices.

"You two go ahead. We'll stay back and take care of the pursuers," someone bellowed, a confirmation sounding from another.

Caenrya ticked a finger amid the distraction, a sense of relief building when her body became more responsive. *Almost there*, she thought grimly. With more time, she could join the fray. However, whether those pursuers were friend or foe, she hadn't the faintest inkling. It could be she was vastly outnumbered. If that were the case, she'd at least go down fighting.

When a minute passed of them bounding through the woods, Caenrya had thought herself fortunate they'd lost the others. By what she could distinguish, there were only two ronin left. Much more favorable to her odds.

A man started, "Who—"

A sharp whirlwind spun around them, causing the man to slide to a stop before meeting the edge of it. The whistle of a weapon clashed with a blade and the *thunk* of metal into the ground near her. Something large flew by, the sound of an enormous object crashing in front of her. Hair rose on her arms, the sizzle of electricity crackling into the man holding her. He flung back with a cry of pain, and Caenrya's body tumbled into the grass. She rolled twice before hitting something sturdy, and the smell of burning flesh squinched her nose.

Cracking an eye, Caenrya's curiosity got the better of her.

Smoke drifted from an armor-clad shinobi's palm. The royal blues and silvers on lacquer-dipped plates were eerily reminiscent of the Duša shogun's formal attire. Black hair was shorn close to his scalp around his head, the top a longer length and styled in a way that made him appear even more egotistical.

Ryu.

If Caenrya could have wrinkled her nose, she would have.

Ryu drew a pair of kusarigama from their sheaths on his hips, gripping the weights to the sickle's handle as he lunged toward the sprawled man beside her.

The masked ronin grunted as he flipped to his feet, taking one glance at the bloody gash on his leg before pulling out his claw-like shuko. Swinging forward, Ryu knocked back a blow with one of the weights at the end of his chain, meeting a second blow with the sickle held by his other hand. Out of the corner of her eye, Caenrya could make out another blue and silver figure engaging in combat with a swordsman.

His sai were flying about him. The long center prongs of the fork-like weapons deftly parried attacks. His steel-gray eyes saw his opponent's every move as he attempted to disarm the other shinobi. Bronze hair shifted around his head as he ducked low, the strands short and straight.

Halden. He was moving with a fluid grace she hadn't seen before.

Ducking low, he narrowly escaped a blow meant to decapitate him. His eyes tracked the blade as it swept by.

A flicker of something Caenrya couldn't decipher caught in her throat. Perhaps it was annoyance she couldn't secure the win on her own. But a part of her was reluctant to recognize it as relief. As awful as it was to admit, she wanted nothing more to do with Shikei beyond being the one to burn it to ashes, something she wasn't confident of achieving mere moments before.

That relief was short-lived.

An overshot attack by Ryu sent him straight into the path of a three-pronged blade. The steel ripped through the seams of his light armor and tore flesh across his chest with a sickening noise. Gathering her strength, Caenrya's limbs shook as she propped an elbow to push herself upward. Somehow, Ryu managed to keep his footing, his wrists holding the chains of his weapons as his hands wove the sign of *pyo*.

Currents of air twirled around him before racing toward his opponent. A single hand seal, and the other ronin summoned a wall of earth between them before leaping backward, his blades dragging through the grassy floor to stabilize his momentum. Blood dripped from his other weapon, a cruel glint crossing his sights as a laugh burst from his chest.

"You are outmatched, kid."

Caenrya clenched her jaw so tightly it hurt when she managed to rise to her knees. Her eyes were locked on those gashes across Ryu's abdomen. Noticing her, Ryu shook his head and repositioned his weapons.

"Keep out of the way. I've got this," he warned, jolting forward and leaping over the rock wall.

Further back, Halden created a snake of water that stole the katana from the other ronin. He sliced forward, only to meet a fang of ice mid-air. The ice proved too heavy, knocking him backward against a tree trunk. Appearing dazed, Halden was too slow to combat a heavy punch to his jaw.

Impressing her, Halden rolled with the momentum, making the most of his off-kilter balance by throwing a sai toward the recovering shinobi. The sharp blade embedded itself deep into his attacker's shoulder and gave Halden the reprieve he needed to leap back into the fight. He did so with a series of foot techniques that ended in a precise sweep that knocked the ronin down. From there, Halden pulled him into a tight spinal lock.

A blast shook the tree limbs above her. Another battle occurred further down the hillside.

Caenrya took a single step toward Ryu before the ground rose to meet her again. Growling in fury, her hands clawed into the grass as she struggled to rise. The distraction caught Ryu's attention. His head swiveled back too late to deflect the double-wielding attack locked on him.

A new kind of horror sunk into her stomach at the grisly sight. The entire world slowed before her. Three blades sunk deep into his heart, and his ribs crushed under the force of metal. Another three tore across his throat, crimson spilling under those agonized eyes. Caenrya's blood boiled, guilt hitting her hard as his lifeless body collapsed to the ground.

Anger, so much anger, coursed through her. She barely registered her hand creating a seal. Taiji raced from her fingertips, weaving and wrapping toward her shoulders as it cloaked her. The sluggish edge ebbed. Caenrya was able to rise to her knees quicker than last time.

But still far too slow.

Across the small glen, Halden had accumulated a variety of cuts up and down his body. His opponent managed to resecure his katana. He breathed hard, slicing through a variety of taiji-made icy spears thrown his way. Then his eyes caught Ryu's form on the ground, and the slight second ended with a spear impaling his left calf.

Caenrya's body shook with rage, and her taiji warped around her arms into razor-sharp mockeries of blades. The ronin standing over Ryu noticed her. His sharp eyes looked at her arms before his black pupils began to wander upward.

"Don't look into her eyes," his partner shouted, backtracking to avoid a sweep of Halden's single remaining sai.

Too late.

The ronin's face paled, and his pupils dilated when meeting hers. And Caenrya grinned a wicked, merciless thing.

Time froze as she mind-walked, contorting space around them. Her prey's brain struggled to comprehend how they suddenly appeared at the edge of a vast canyon. Twin knives appeared in her hands, and his legs were unable to move. Panicking, the man thrust his arms about before she halted those too, his eyes terrified of the wrathful visage that approached him.

"Please," he whispered, his head shaking violently. "Please, no, no, no!"

Caressing his face with the tip of her blade, Caenrya assured, "I'm going to enjoy this."

His screams echoed as Caenrya withdrew her consciousness from his mind, blinking as reality came into focus once more. Only a second had passed in real time, but the man's empty husk fell to the ground and gave out after his mind had experienced a day's worth of shallow cuts.

Weak.

Caenrya checked on Halden only to see his back against a tree. His last sai was upright in the ground a foot away. Regaining her feet at last, she bolted forward to try to save at least one life since she had failed Ryu.

The katana rose in a deadly arch, the blade gleaming in the midday sun as it swung downward. She knew it was futile. The distance between them was far too great. For once, it had *hurt* to watch another die. Her heart had clenched, a sentiment she was unaccustomed to.

Was this what it was like to have a team? To care for others and watch them die?

Her contracts had always taken her to eliminate some target or another, and not once had she regretted snuffing out a person's existence. Never thought twice of the hundreds of others she broke inside the fighting ring. Now, she'd lose two so-called teammates in one fell swoop, and it didn't sit right. While Ryu had been an upright arse, he'd at least come to lend his hand. No one had ever given her even a free morsel of food.

He'd sacrificed an entire future.

The katana was but inches from Halden's heart when a sickle cut it out of the air. Ryu's body materialized beside Halden, a knowing grin spreading from the latter's face. "Good timing?" Ryu asked, his chest labored.

"Just have to hold off until Cadigan arrives," Halden acknowledged, dipping his chin.

Shaking off her surprise, Caenrya marked the muddy spot where Ryu's body used to be. *A bloodline gift*, she realized. Her body was still wobbly, but she managed to take another step before the hair rose on the back of her neck. Diving forward, Caenrya avoided a lightning bolt coming from their flank by mere inches.

"There's another," she called out, searching the tree limbs for the ronin hiding among them. Already, fatigue nipped at her heels from the use of her ninjutsu. The drug still ate at her reserves.

Halden threw a kunai to where he marked the taiji across the clearing. The sharp end stuck into a tree trunk beside a shifting figure.

He has the same gift as Ilias, she thought. Being able to see everything during a battle was a huge advantage.

"Mine," Caenrya said, pooling her taiji and jumping into the tree. Leaves brushed her face, a bug fluttering by as she landed on a thick branch. Her taiji pooled in her feet, clinging to the tree's energy while she balanced. Combat clashed below, Ryu and Halden teaming against the disarmed ronin there. She heard a twig snap across from her before the person wrapped around the wood.

Lanky, but significantly more built than she, Two stood there. A smirk rested across his blocky bone structure, and his air of superiority peeved her instantly. "Imagine my surprise when the daimyo contracted me to rescue his One."

Snarling, Caenrya jumped forward, meeting his katana with her taiji razors. Her arms shook as they stood across the branch at a stalemate in strength. There wasn't the slightest chance she'd be able to catch his eyes. He had long since learned to avoid hers at all costs after years of their power struggle, a fact that had her mitigating her taiji in the next moment to conserve energy. Sinking low, she balanced on the branch and swept a foot out to catch his. Stepping back, Two clucked his tongue as he whirled his weapon about his wrist.

"Too bad he already took out your punishment on Thirty-Two." Two sighed mockingly. "You should have heard her screams."

Verina.

Freezing, Caenrya suddenly found herself short of breath.

"The daimyo is furious with your betrayal, and without you to take it out on, he's unleashing that ire on the rest of us."

She couldn't help it. The worst possible outcome had happened, and it brought her to her knees. The world swam around her, and a faint ringing sounded in her ears.

Kneeling in front of her, Two continued, "She's still alive. For now. The daimyo has grand plans for her. For you, too, when you return."

The world closed in on her.

Cocking his head, his face twisted. "Though I'd rather that not happen." His foot flung out, kicking her across the abdomen.

Pain spiked across her middle as Caenrya fell twenty feet into a thorny bush. Cuts tore into the side of her face, through the fabric, and across her arm and thigh. Two landed beside her, and the tip of his katana pointed at her sternum.

"I'll be sure to tell her how you had a coward's death, and how you did everything in your power to abandon her to live in a fool's dream." Considering that for a moment, Two shifted his gaze upward. "Though I don't know if she can hear anymore after the damage done to her."

Something primal snapped in Caenrya.

Dark and sinister, taiji crawled from her bones, coating her existence as it writhed around her. Thrusting a hand forward, it cackled through his stomach, the sharp end impaling the trunk of the tree behind him. His scream of agony went unheard by her ears. Closing the distance, Caenrya brought her face within a foot of his.

"I know now why the daimyo sent you here," she purred, enjoying the agony wrenching his expression. "He sent you as an offering." She gave a cold laugh at his flash of understanding. "He believed me to return of my own volition and gave me your life in exchange for my forgiveness."

The daimyo hadn't hesitated to escape that night when they were ambushed. Realizing she'd hold a grudge, he gave Caenrya Two's life. It could have been enough in the twisted game he played with her, only if she decided to return.

He lost that bet.

The boy realized it too. "No." Two coughed, blood bubbling at the corner of his mouth. "H-he couldn't. W-wouldn't." Frantic emotions crossed his face, a new expression tearing at his mouth every second.

"He has," Caenrya cruelly reassured him, pinning the edge of the other taiji blade over his heart. "And it will be in vain."

A chilling cry of pain caught her attention, and Caenrya's head darted in its direction. Another ronin had joined his partner, cutting deep across Ryu's back before Halden could parry the blow. A fatal blow aimed at Halden the moment he turned his back.

She stood at a crossroads.

Caenrya could end one of the most hated lives she ever had to bear, one of the people who tormented her and threatened her sister's life at every turn. He'd gone so far as volunteering to be the one to deliver her lashes whenever she'd act out against the daimyo's wishes, and went even further when he threatened to bully Verina in the weeks Caenrya wasn't permitted to see her.

Or.

Caenrya could bound over and save two strangers' lives. She might lose the opportunity for revenge, and Two might escape to report it to the daimyo. Verina would be devastated, and if what Two said was true, she could receive further punishment on Caenrya's behalf.

There was also a chance, as slight as it was, the daimyo would spare Verina's life instead if it meant Caenrya wouldn't return. He'd want her sister to replace her fighting prowess, even if she hadn't yet shown signs of displaying the bloodline gift. There was a chance Verina possessed it in a dormant state. Her life would be secured, at least well enough until Caenrya could destroy that place. After all, they both had the same parents.

It was settled.

Taiji blades met the ronin's, and Caenrya's eyes connected with the surprised ones of her opponent. Before anyone could register it, she entrapped him in mind ninjutsu. He flailed against it, stronger than any opponent she'd ever faced in the art. Without toying with him, she hastily impaled his physical heart. There was a chance he'd escape if she took too long, and she had to ensure Ryu and Halden's survival first and foremost.

After all, she was apparently a soppy team player.

By the time Caenrya turned to address the last ronin, he was already gone. A swift sweep of the perimeter indicated he had taken his leave with Two.

She cursed.

A fact that didn't sit well with her, but she'd made her bed. The cackle of her taiji withered away, and an immense wave of exhaustion blacked out her vision. At the time, she didn't register the hand steadying her shoulder as she slouched against the tree, nor Halden's hasty check for injuries before helping her to a sitting position.

It was only after her vision cleared that she questioned whether it happened. By the time Halden was packing Ryu's wound, Caenrya knew it was. It didn't sit well with her, but at the moment, lifting a finger was extraneous. Even with her taiji repressing the drug in her veins, it still lingered. It seemed it was only temporarily suppressed when she used her vin.

How unfortunate.

Caenrya's eyes drifted to the wavering leaves far above. The repercussions of her actions played through her mind. Without intending to, her mouth moved of its own accord. "You two shouldn't have come here." Even to her, the words were hollow. "There is still at least one ronin left fighting back there, and if he wins, he'll wipe us out where we sit."

"Cadigan won't lose." Ryu grunted, lifting his arms to allow Halden to bandage the packed gash. His chest rose in ragged heaves by the time it was done, Ryu's eyes somewhat glazed as he laid down.

As he stood, Halden appeared worse for wear, with flecks of blood smeared in his chestnut hair. With a grimace, he collected both of his sai blades. He glanced over at Caenrya. "I would thank you for saving our lives, but you also placed us in this danger."

"You'd give anything for your clan, including your life for an assignment given to you, correct?" Caenrya asked, meeting his heavy stare with one of her own. At his nod, she proceeded. "I'd do the same for my sister. At first, I didn't believe staying with your clan was in her best interests. I decided to return to the Citadel before I got too far, but they discovered me first. I plan to stay with your clan now. Hence, why I wasn't too reluctant to save your lives." She frowned. "You're welcome."

A half-hysterical laugh burst from Ryu before a wince of pain cut it off. "You know," he wheezed, "I take back my doubts about you. You are a piece of work."

Not knowing how to take that, Caenrya ignored him. Facing Halden's pacing form, she quirked a brow. "Why don't you go assist Cadigan if you're concerned?"

"I don't disobey my orders. Shinobi Creed: Oath of Allegiance. All shinobi will maintain unwavering allegiance to their leader and mission regardless of personal desires." His fists clenched, the worry gnawing at him. Seeming to need something to distract himself with, he asked, "Where did you learn your Kū control?"

The dancing around irked her, but she must have had a moment of insanity because she decided to answer the question. "I didn't. My daimyo forbade any... instructor... from teaching me any form of yin and yang balancing to achieve ninjutsu. I only know how to access my bloodline gift from the third reserve. Fortunately, it has a Kū element affinity and allows me to shape my taiji in loops outside of my own body."

Only those with a bloodline gift had a third reserve outside of yin and yang's individual reserves. Caenrya knew nothing of how to balance anything outside of her reserves for taiji usage. She was fortunate her bloodline gift was powerful in the Kū nature. Others varied with different elemental affinities.

"If you were a fighter of his, then wouldn't he equip you with every tool of the trade?" An incredulous note crept into Halden's words, and his feet stilled at last.

Closing her eyes, Caenrya released a deep breath. "'Ronin need not be overburdened with unnecessary tools; rather, each should be capable of selecting one and cultivating it for all purposes,'" she quoted her daimyo, sensing Ryu's interest grow as the conversation continued. "Indeed, he spouted that nonsensical response each time I pleaded my case. It took me years to discover the true reasoning behind his reluctance."

Both men were watching her when Caenrya peeked an eye.

"He knew I'd slaughter them all if I were capable of more," she said.

Silence fell, Ryu's huff audible from where she sat. "It's crazy that you mean that," he muttered.

"We've been given different lives," was all Caenrya said, her attention caught by an incoming figure as she bounded across the field.

Halden's relief was palpable at the commander's return.

Ragged but determined, Cadigan slid to a stop beside them. Her gaze evaluated their condition within a second. "How serious are your wounds, Ryu?"

"Painful enough that I should be getting far more than a chūnin's pay," he grouched, a sharp inhalation taken when he struggled to sit.

Cadigan rolled her eyes and addressed Halden. "Keep on alert. We have to move now. I had four on my tail earlier, but one vanished. They may attempt to reorganize themselves if there are more, and we can't give them the time to do so."

Nodding, Halden performed the hand seal to unlock his taiji-seeing capability again, his eyes scanning and seeing far more than Caenrya's ever could. It made her jealous. Cadigan slung one of her arms across her shoulder, helping Caenrya up despite her protests. A glare from the commander shut her mouth, and she allowed the commander to assist her as they began the trek back to the Citadel. Halden supported Ryu beside them.

"Commander, I'm sensing three signatures to our left and one in front of us," Halden warned, his expression solemn as his eyes asked the unspoken question. *How are we going to survive this?*

A troubled edge shifted her face, her mouth opening as a figure blurred before them. Cadigan shifted, throwing Caenrya behind her as the form materialized. Both of her hands clasped forward around the length of a katana thrusting toward her face. The ronin pushed with all his might.

Blood streamed down the commander's arms as the blade pushed through her grip, impaling her left eye before it came to a sickening stop.

Caenrya froze on the ground behind her, and her mouth parted at the attack that would have otherwise impaled her heart.

Instead, the commander had sacrificed herself.

Chapter Five

HALDEN

Halden had never witnessed such a heart-stopping moment in his life, and all for what? He and Ryu were outclassed. Even the girl proved more capable than them. Someone with far more advanced proficiencies should have been assigned to her. Eirea alone shouldered much of the last fight against *four* of the ronin, and now he and Ryu were useless in the face of this new threat.

"Cadigan!" he shouted, releasing Ryu and moving to interfere.

The ronin dropped his blade, leaning back to dodge the kick Halden swung. His anger got the better of him. The flurry of punches was wild as he threw himself into combat. Sidestepping, he narrowly missed a powerful kick, swooping in to grab his leg. With a practiced roll, he locked the ronin into an airtight hold with his hands incapacitated. Nearly half a minute ticked by before the man passed out. Halden only relaxed his hold when certain. Three more figures emerged from his side, and this time, his haunches relaxed a hair.

Duša shinobi.

With shaking limbs, Eirea dropped the katana, a bleeding hand managing to form the *zen* seal. Metal erupted from the earth, forming chain bindings that would secure the fallen ronin from movement when awoken. Massive swelling already puffed her left eye. Her hands fell limp at her sides. Her face was twisted in an excruciating way as she evaluated her injuries.

Halden's gut clenched. The skin was cut to the bone on both of his commander's hands.

"Owena, provide aid to Cadigan," Daven ordered his subordinate, turning on the somewhat spiky-haired chūnin next to him. "Niko, stay beside the enemy. We don't need any surprises."

Caenrya appeared stricken all the while. Her knees were wobbly as she forced herself upright beside Ryu to move out of the way of the oncoming shinobi team. Halden had never seen the commander of Team Pernelle concerned until his green eyes saw his friend's state. Once, Eirea and Daven Pernelle were on the same team when they were chūnin. They often held joint training with their current teams. The two were thicker than most friends.

Resting on a nearby rock, Eirea filled in the arrivals on their situation while Owena poured her taiji into healing the commander.

Several times, he caught Owena's dark eyes glaring at Caenrya's. Though it wasn't until he perceived Ryu's abnormal silence he noticed his teammate had fallen unconscious.

Halden dropped beside him and palpated a faint pulse in his neck. He clenched his jaw, moving next to check Ryu's wound. Feeling the bandage, Halden swore when his hand came away crimson. "Owena, Ryu needs aid fast."

By now, Eirea's hands were mended, and the bleeding around her eye had stopped. She appeared steady once more, though pain glazed her good eye. She pushed Owena's hands away and said, "Care for Ryu. I'll be fine."

Owena blinked and shook her head. "I don't have enough taiji for both of you. Your eye isn't healed yet, and if the extent of Ryu's injuries is severe, you'll remain blind if not treated immediately." Her black hair shifted back and forth as she glanced between them with uncertainty.

In a firm tone, Eirea said, "See to Ryu. An eye is not worth a life."

With a second's hesitation, Owena made to kneel beside Ryu. Her lips pressed into a firm line as she worked with the *sha* seal, beads of sweat appearing on her forehead. It wasn't until Caenrya spoke that a peeved expression pulled at her face.

"I'm... sorry."

"You almost caused the death of an entire team," Owena bit back, hostility flooding her almond eyes.

Niko took it upon himself to turn his back at the edge of their perimeter. His usual *I-do-not-want-to-be-involved* attitude came out as strong as ever.

"Owena!" Daven sharply cut off her next words with a deep tenor, and his bulky arms crossed as he took a no-nonsense stance.

Raising a hand, Eirea stopped his impending lecture. Halden could discern the amount of respect the jōnin had for her by following her wishes. When Eirea fumbled with her medical pouch, Daven swiftly kneeled to assist her. An edge of worry lined his heavy eyes, his narrow jaw tense.

"Caenrya is part of my team, Owena." Focusing on Caenrya's regretful face, Eirea said, "No apology is necessary. I'd do the same for any of my students. We managed to eliminate most of them and have secured one valuable resource to give us the intelligence required to proceed within our timeline."

Leads for Caenrya's sister.

Lowering her chin, Eirea promised, "This is a win." She eyed her team, each in turn. "All will be fine this go-around."

It was a saying Eirea always repeated at the end of a difficult mission, and when she did, she believed it.

A spring of pity shot through Halden. Caenrya gave everything she had for her sister, going as far as abandoning the security his clan offered to turn herself in. It was selfless, though he had the distinct impression that wasn't how she saw it.

When Caenrya winced, and her back straightened as if something sharp prodded it, Halden's brows bunched. "Were you injured?"

Suspiciously fast, she replied, "No." A hint of pain held that word down.

"Just everyone else was," Owena snidely remarked, her back hunching in fatigue.

Turning on her, Halden's fists clenched. "Knock it off. She saved our lives."

Owena snorted. "Yet she's somehow not hurt?"

Caenrya's head lowered across from him, and her otherwise empty façade returned. A defense mechanism, he realized.

Owena's lips pursed. "She almost killed my dad, and somehow, you guys trust her to *save your lives*?"

Ilias had debriefed him that Caenrya arrived on harsh terms. But who wouldn't have when they thought they were in the den of an enemy?

"Shut up already, Owena," Niko's voice called out, his groan loud enough it caused a squirrel to scatter away. "Your dad is fine. It was a misunderstanding." At the venomous stare he received, he added, "His words, not mine."

Halden left the two to bicker. He sighed through his nose and elected to take a note from Niko's page. Keeping his eyes peeled, he continued to scan for any living taiji signatures in the area, relieved to find they were alone. The tidbit of information about Caenrya was concerning, though. His father had stipulated a situation that hadn't sounded dire when she'd arrived.

Almost ten minutes passed before Owena collapsed from taiji depletion, and Ryu was mostly healed from her efforts.

It was relieving how quiet it grew after that.

Together, both teams aided each other in their return. Taking in the massive stone wall encompassing the Citadel, it astounded Halden how everything changed so quickly. He'd left with Ryu and Eirea the moment a shinobi under his father spotted Caenrya leaving the village. A second team was to follow them. It had been taxing to rely on his vin for such a long duration but a necessary precaution when tailing her and the rogue ronin so they remained hidden. Ryu had been furious the whole duration, a sentiment Halden had started to share.

That was before Caenrya paused and moved to turn back.

By the time he registered a total of nearly nine different taiji markers, they had to regroup and plan a decisive course of action. They waited for a moment when the enemy separated out to give the backup team time to catch up.

Nine was far too great a number to take on with three people. But the further they went, the more likely the enemy was to receive reinforcements. They had no choice but to attack against bad odds.

Eirea took the brunt of the group while Halden threw in the smoke bombs and small explosives to split them further. It had gone well enough at first. While it was painful to admit, they were outmatched, and it didn't take long for them to realize it. Even drugged, that girl had done more damage than Ryu and him combined were able to deliver. They were a simple distraction until she could step in.

And if what she admitted regarding her inability to manage yin and yang to produce normal ninjutsu was true, Caenrya would be a monster when properly trained. How any one person could be gifted with such raw power was beyond him.

When his father gave him this assignment, Halden had to confess it was ludicrous to be classified as jōnin-ranked. But he understood now. She must have belonged to someone incredibly influential to have such disposable ronin chasing after her, and with a skill set like hers, he imagined she made that daimyo quite the fortune.

He did pity her for it all.

However, something about that entire encounter with those ronin didn't quite sit right with him. The way the masked ronin *played* with Halden rather than outright strike with consecutive kill shots made him uneasy. Perhaps they were overconfident in their capabilities and wanted a distraction to ease their boredom, but even that thought was troubling him enough that Halden discarded the line of thought.

He'd revisit it when alone.

Walking back in the middle of the night was not ideal, but Halden guided Caenrya in silence as the remainder of the team broke off to the healing clinic. At a later time, he would be seen, but he wanted to ensure she didn't lose herself. The streets were close to empty. Their only company was the occasional stray cat and their enervation. He felt as if he were in a trance as his mind reeled. He and Ryu had several close calls in the past but not where they were close to death. That shadow had mulled over his thoughts all day.

"Should I leave?"

The question was spoken so softly he nearly missed it. Nothing about her countenance gave away that she'd spoken, nor had any inclination to listen to a word he'd say. "Why?"

Not as much as a twitch as they passed through an empty passage between residential buildings. "They'll not stop coming. It's a liability." A pause. "I'm a liability."

Trying for a joke to lighten the mood, Halden said, "Too late to try, I'm afraid. Ryu is beginning to like you, after all."

She didn't even blink. Could she blink? Halden didn't remember.

"We were caught off guard, is all. Once we all learn to trust each other more, we'll be a team for the books," he said.

"I've never had anyone in my corner. It seems, though, that I've only caused pain here," Caenrya replied, the words almost inaudible. Her posture shrunk inwards as if she were wrapped with her own guilt and sorrows.

A corner of his mouth downturned at that. "How old are you?"

Blinking—so Caenrya *did* blink after all—she thought for a moment. "I think I'm eighteen years old."

The same age as him and Ryu then. "Well, you have plenty of years left with us to cause us even more grief." They turned through the roadway he lived on, though her apartment appeared first.

"I'll try not to."

A crook appeared along the curve of his mouth. "I have a distinct impression that you'll fail miserably at that," Halden mused, resting his aching hands in his pockets. The handle of one sai glinted in the lantern light.

"I don't fail at much." Caenrya sniffed, a shade of personality leaking through that maintained demeanor at last.

Shrugging, Halden put on a disappointed face. "You couldn't beat my father."

Her jaw slackened at that, and her face morphed into vivid annoyance.

A cheeky grin split his face. His assumptions on where to push were correct. "Maybe next time," he said.

Halden noticed her narrowing blue eyes had a thin rim of gold around the pupil. He'd never seen such a stunning blend of shades, all surrounded by thick, dark lashes curving at the tips.

Scoffing, Caenrya pointedly did not stare in any direction where those eyes could see him. Dried blood stained the ends of her long hair, a small splatter across her face and arms. Halden gleaned the impression her state was not unusual for her. Only time would tell what visual he presented at the moment. Some part of him wanted to try to see if he could crack a smile on her face, but a larger part knew what his assignment entailed.

"What's your sister like?" Halden casually asked.

Her shoulders tensed, a vast range of emotions fluttering across her face before smoothing into nothing. Caenrya shut down again. He should have seen that coming, but he had to figure her out first, and this was the only way. Opening his mouth, his word only halfway out, she leaped onto the second-floor open hallway, entering her apartment with a distinguished slamming of the door before locking it.

A loud and clear message.

Pinching the bridge of his nose, Halden sighed for a moment before pivoting back the way they had walked. One of the cuts near his elbow stung with pain at the movement. His eyes connected with one of his father's privately hired shinobi across the way. He shared a quick nod before leaving Caenrya in his hands. Halden hadn't any idea how he would glean any important knowledge from her, but he had to try.

***

The following afternoon, for they were all too exhausted to attempt a meeting early, his father summoned Team Cadigan for a debriefing.

Formally, the shogun was expected to punish Caenrya. It was one of the most severe crimes a shinobi could commit to abandon a posting, but since she wasn't technically a member of their clan or even a contracted ronin, there weren't any legal ramifications. All the same, Halden was impressed by how she withstood the verbal assault without even a grimace.

Both Ryu and Halden were attended to and healed, Eirea now sporting a black headband lowered over her missing eye. Over the course of the meeting, she appeared in her normal spirits. Somewhat happier, if anything. Halden wondered if Daven had anything to do with it.

When they were dismissed, the team was assigned time to recuperate. That was when Caenrya spoke.

"I don't have time to be doing nothing while you interrogate the ronin," she stressed, lines appearing beside her eyes.

An appraising expression crossed Ilias's face before he nodded once. "There's no one better than the elder of House Dagon in the nature of Kū. If you, in particular, happen to request her mentorship, then you may stand a chance of acquiring her services to better your odds of joining the extraction team to retrieve your sister."

Ryu's eyes were bulging from his square-shaped face as he refrained from outright laughing. "You'd have better luck with a tree than that retired pile of hatred." He snickered. At Eirea's glare, he grew defensive, a higher pitch in his words. "Hey, don't bite the messenger. That woman despises her own house, which is the only reason she lives here rather than in her daimyo's territory. She even whacked me once when I stepped within two feet of her while on an errand."

Halden snickered at the thought, earning a swift glare from the elder that could have cut steel.

"Where does she live?" Caenrya cut to the chase.

"Halden, would you show Caenrya to Aya's residence?" Ilias asked, lowering the bamboo blinds when the sun's glare began infiltrating his office.

After a confirming dip of his chin, Halden led Caenrya through the central hall of the Duša Clan Temple and down the blocky stairwell. Lined throughout were portraits of their notable ancestors, each house represented. A part of him was envious Ryu would have a day to relax, a fact he gloated about the entirety of the way to his father's workplace. Though, at each portrait Halden passed, he wondered at whether he'd ever achieve something so grandiose as the honor of being recognized. His house was among the major ones in a clan that cherished bloodlines and separated the weaker gifts from the stronger ones. Ilias had already achieved more than most when the daimyo of each house voted him in as their shogun.

It placed an expectation on his shoulders Halden wasn't sure he could live up to.

He was certain the elder would throw that in his face, too, as they climbed up the steep stairwell to her mountainside home. A simple yet traditional house fixed in the center of a large koi pond with an elegant red and gold bridge leading to the sweeping archway of the entrance. Two suspicious eyes flashed behind an open window, and it slammed shut when Halden spotted her. A handful of seconds passed before he heard a lock snick into place, his hand halfway risen to knock.

"Elder Dagon," Halden started, readying himself for the berating that was about to be unleashed. "We seek your experience on a matter."

Folding her arms, Caenrya stared at the door as if her eyes could see through it.

A cackle sounded from within. "You think I haven't heard that a million times, child? Go away. You have a fancy academy to teach young minds."

"This is a matter that cannot be resolved elsewhere," Halden tried, his hand ticking in annoyance.

"Oh-ho-*hooooo*," the elder cried out, mocking them in a muffled tone. "And my ancient ways are the only method left to help you in your self-centered quest? Nothing I haven't been pleaded with before. Completely." She paused purposefully. "Unique."

Shifting his stance, Halden rethought his approach. "Not exactly."

Another cackle.

"You're the only one, though, that is advanced enough in Kū to train a shinobi gifted with a bloodline version of the mind arts," he explained.

"No one in our clan has a bloodline capable of such," Aya denied with passion, a hint of anger leaking into her words.

Speaking up, Caenrya said, "I do, but I'm not of your clan."

The door cracked at that, a pair of lined near-black eyes examining them. "Why should I bother assisting someone not of our clan?"

"Because I need *help* to rescue my sister," Caenrya answered. Her fists balled at her sides.

"And here I thought it might be something new," Aya drawled, unimpressed by what she saw. "In my prime, I was renowned for my title as the Warrior Goddess of the Dagon house. Earned through blood and sweat, my title was granted when I slayed the demon of Dych Clan. It was an accomplishment no man could ever come close to achieving, for his mind nature was superior to that of any mortal besides mine. You," she wrinkled her bulbous nose, "are not worthy."

Placing a fist over her heart, Caenrya stepped forward. A fierce grit overtook her face, and her chin rose in defiance of the elder's perception.

"I have fought in the darkest pits of this land, been sent to the internal fray of battle to collect the heads of the Seven Warlords of Taft."

Aya lowered her gray brows at that.

"I have survived under the thumb of cruelty to spare my sister from a similar fate. I've endured the greatest pains and will go to any lengths to achieve what must be done for my sworn oath. To also redeem myself for my own lapses." A haunting note crept into Caenrya's words.

"Let me see your ears," the elder demanded, the door inching open farther to reveal a stunning satin robe of cream and burnished gold hanging on a dainty figure. Pulling back the impractically long strands of her hair, Caenrya's sharp ears stood in stark contrast to their less pointed ones. The girl held Aya's look until the elder released a sharp exhalation. "The Dragon of the Warring Lands. What a pathetic sight you are."

Caenrya didn't react to the dig, though the title raised questions for Halden. "What do you mean by that?" he asked, shoulders pulling back when Aya turned to him with a temper.

A scathing twitch of the woman's nose. "Have your head buried so far in texts that you aren't attuned to the world's events? You Arundels are infuriatingly ignorant." When Halden crossed his arms, a finger tapping impatiently, she huffed. "Perhaps you should ask her."

Caenrya spared him a second before her gaze returned to the elder. "I killed some important people."

"Articulate," Halden remarked dryly, the mystery of her background clouding his thoughts. This girl, with the appearance of a ghost wearing a person's skin, somehow had a story worthy enough of being whispered about across the clans.

He itched to know more.

"They say those who survive an encounter with you are traumatized by a lady with the eyes of a dragon in their dreams, often struggling to differentiate between waking reality and the ghost that haunts them in their slumber," Aya hummed. Her manicured nails drummed against the doorframe before her posture straightened. "I'll make you a deal if you'll acquiesce, Caenrya."

A jolt shot through Halden at that. His eyes narrowed on the wrinkled lady. How did she know of the girl's name when it was only shared with a select few? And why would his father withhold such crucial information about Caenrya's past from him? Clearly, it was public knowledge if the elder was aware.

"Name your terms." Caenrya motioned.

"My training is grueling. The number of people I've taken under my wing is less than the number of ears on your head. You'll do everything asked of you, else you forfeit any further instruction. For every lesson I depart, I'll be given an answer to a question of my choosing, and *never* will you lie to me." A glint of cunning unmasked behind the elder's sight, a visual that set Halden on edge.

Shifting his weight, he interrupted, "What business is that of yours?" He had an inkling of the nature of those questions and where Aya would pry. Beside him, Caenrya grew deathly still, waging an internal battle.

"Watch your tongue, Arundel," the elder scolded, the curl of her mouth unmistakable. "I take the ideal of apprenticeship none too lightly, even less so for one outside our clan." Squaring her shoulders, Aya tightened her fingers gripping the door. "There are already whispers of an outsider among our ranks. The new narrative has been set in motion, and there is scant time to determine the direction before the common folk do in our stead. If you wish your father not to be deposed, I encourage you to remove the shroud over your eyes and wise up."

Our stead.

So then. Aya's decision had already been made. The question was, when had it been definite? Nostrils flaring, Halden had the overwhelming urge to confront his father. It was clear a throng of information wasn't provided to him, and it irked Halden that the fact was being thrown in his face.

"I accept your conditions," Caenrya said, her chin lowering a hair.

"We'll begin immediately." Opening the door, Aya permitted Caenrya entrance. As Halden made to follow, a wrinkled hand almost palmed his face. "You are not welcome here," the elder grunted, slamming the door in his face,

A whoosh of air tousled his hair, his fists whitening as he quelled his rising anger. He half raised one, wanting nothing more than to bang it against the embellished wood. Only his ingrained respect for decorum had Halden turning instead toward one source of his frustration.

It stole another nineteen minutes of his day to trek back across the Citadel. The spirits were almost as agitated as he was, with an influx of animals and insects appearing around the sprawling, lacquer-thatched rooftops, dangling between golf-leaf-decorated lanterns, and peaking among the plentiful shrubbery before disappearing back into their spirit world.

It was a bad omen to sense such troubles from those who no longer walked with the living.

The off-kilter air plagued Halden as he breezed by his father's kampaku, Javan, who berated him for intruding without notice when he whipped open Ilias's office door. Words were cut off between his father and a graying man the moment he entered. His father appeared aged by ten years whenever the elder man frequented the Citadel. His uncle, Markus Arundel, held low esteem for Ilias's family. An exasperated huff escaped his uncle.

"Yet another example of your never-ending list of shortcomings, I daresay," Markus Arundel goaded, a flick of his fingers in Halden's direction.

Behind Halden's stiffening back, Javan hissed, "I was trying to warn you away from this course of action for this reason. Your father already has enough on his shoulders."

Bitterness sunk Halden's stomach at the scene, a multitude of aspects hitting him at once. He held no fondness for the daimyo of the Arundel house and detested the resentment with which his uncle treated him and his father. Markus believed the title of shogun was stolen from his grasp. It didn't better his mood that his father hadn't notified him of Markus's arrival from their territory, nor that Halden had proven himself irresponsible for barging in recklessly.

Clearing his throat, he backtracked his anger to neutralize the damage he may have caused. "I carry an imperative update for you, shogun." Halden even managed to bow his spine despite wanting to go in swinging.

"You can say it and crawl back to your hovel," Markus insisted, his attempt to appear disinterested only giving way when a gray eye twitched.

"Daimyo Arundel, we'll have to resume our previous conversation at a later time," Ilias said, the command pressing in the tone of his voice to his elder brother.

The corner of the daimyo's nose pulled, and his chair jerked back. His waist-length gray hair was bound by fabric at the end, jerking from side to side at the abrupt movement. Both of his peaked ears were on full display, as they always were, with his hair tucked behind them. Markus would never stop flaunting their house's stronger lineage to the Elves, even if it had been over two thousand years since any had been alive. His nose always raised whenever he passed a Canecian with rounder ears, namely those in the lesser houses. And the minor houses comprised a much more significant portion of their clan than the major houses.

Everyone had some degree of Elven blood in their lineage, but his uncle didn't see eye to eye with anyone unless their ears were sharp.

"I'll see myself out then, *shogun*." He spit it out with vehemence. "The matter will be resolved today. My house grows weary of your transgressions."

Stepping aside, Halden watched as his uncle slid the door shut with force, Javan's reedy limbs ushering him down the hall. A weary droop crossed his father's face, a flicker of concern appearing in Halden's mind before his anger was remembered. At his father's gesture, Halden took the seat across the desk before speaking.

"I didn't deserve to be left unaware of the crucial elements of my assignment," Halden said, his voice level. "Not only was I blindsided by the Dagon elder today, but now there are rumors I've not been debriefed on circulating the Citadel. Including how Caenrya nearly killed Owena Dagon's father."

Intensity sharpened Ilias's face. "Did Aya take her in?"

Of course. Of course, that was all his father cared about. The *noble* shinobi cared more for his clan than his family. "And sent me away after the fact." Sullenness coated Halden's tongue.

The shogun's face lightened at that, a nod to himself as he became distracted by some inner dialogue. "Then all is well."

The room darkened around him.

"Nothing is well," Halden snapped, bracing his hands on his knees. "I'm not able to observe Caenrya during her training, Cadigan lost an eye, and my entire team almost died in the process of retrieving the foreigner after she attempted to escape!" *And you hardly seemed relieved I made it back.*

Clasping his hands, the shogun arched a brow at him. "I've told you more than any other, with the sole exception of Cadigan. Beyond that, I am not required to divulge anything further should I wish it. You forget yourself," he corrected with stern words.

Leaning back, Halden schooled his face into neutrality. Such pent-up anger threatened his control, but he knew better. Always knew better than to show disrespect. "I apologize, Shogun Arundel." Empty words, but he knew he had overstepped.

A dip of his father's head. "Now, what did Aya reveal in regard to Caenrya? I need any words that carried importance during the exchange."

Back to business, as usual.

"Aya called Caenrya 'The Dragon of the Warring Lands,' to which she explained a tale of how people remember the dragon's eyes in their dreams long after any encounter. Otherwise, all I learned of was Caenrya collecting the heads of the Seven Warlords of Taft," Halden recounted, too disgusted with his father to meet his burning gaze.

"As I suspected," Ilias quietly said, a moment hanging between them. "Have you gleaned anything further?"

Suspected of what? A puff of air forced its way out of his nose. "No."

Standing, Ilias faced the wall-wide map depicted behind his desk with a thoughtful stance. The royal blues of his robe stood in stark contrast to the faded color of the paper spread before him. Halden made to leave before his father's deep voice cut off his tracks. "I was given a prophecy by dream, the previous shogun warning me of events to come."

Warning...

Facing his father's profile, Halden frowned. For the ancestors to depart caution was one thing but to instill a prophecy... "How bad is it?"

Ilias ran a hand over his bearded chin. His eyes searched for a vague answer within the confines of the map. "Precarious enough that I'm unsure how we'll manage to overcome," he murmured, low enough that Halden double-guessed what he heard. "To be frank, I don't think we'll find any viable leads on the girl's daimyo for several months, not when we've been searching for years. After we discover one, it will take several more to act on it. We have at least six months before we can act for her sister. We must use this time wisely to shape the future in our favor. It's our only hope."

Six months. Halden's mouth curved downward. Would Caenrya be willing to stay that long? Could they fend off whoever was after her for that duration? Half a year was nothing to blink at. "What did they say?" Halden took a handful of wary steps toward him.

Sighing, Ilias shook his head. "Once I determine the meaning of that, I may discuss the matter more at length. Until then," his neck swiveled toward him, "we must ensure Caenrya's cooperation."

"She's in it?" Halden recalled how strangely the spirits had behaved on his way there, wondering if that had any part in the prophecy.

Ominousness overtook Ilias's expression. "Caenrya *is* it. She is the linchpin that determines whether our people will survive. Whether we will falter when faced with the greatest threat of our lives."

CHAPTER SIX

HALDEN

Asaki's ramen shop boasted a compact bar-sitting arrangement, where Halden and Ryu watched as the skilled staff hurriedly prepared bowls of noodles. Above Halden's head, vibrant lanterns danced, casting a warm and flickering glow. The air was filled with the tantalizing aroma of savory ramen and broth. Bustling activity echoed throughout the shop as the staff catered to both seated and takeout customers.

Though Halden was a regular at Asaki's Ramen, he couldn't help but feel numb to his surroundings in his agitated state.

"For you, Shinobi Arundel." Asaki smiled, serving his ramen across the countertop.

With a nod and word of gratitude, Halden waited for Ryu to be served seconds later. Halden stabbed his chopsticks violently into his spicy miso bowl, a severe frown pulling at his mouth. "For once, I wish my father would be more forthcoming and honest."

Beside him, Ryu slurped up his own noodles. His head bobbed in agreement as he swallowed. "My parents are being secretive right now about some new mission Ren was given." Ryu's older brother. "Apparently, it's some high-clearance, classified, more-important-than-me tasking that they can't stop flaunting to me."

The clatter of utensils and the sizzle of ingredients filled the air all at once, breaking the conversation for a moment.

"To be frank, I don't think I'd want to know more about the whole Caenrya situation," Ryu said. His face pinched. "She reeks of trouble. Eirea won't tell me anything beyond that she's a refugee running from the—" Ryu cut himself off, looking each way before whispering into Halden's ear, "Kriv Clan." He straightened. "I can't imagine her being allowed to leave them with her bloodline gift. She's a terrifying one at that. I don't want the shogun to tell us more." A shudder shook Ryu's shoulders.

Leaning an arm on the polished counter, Halden rested his chopsticks on his bowl. He didn't have much of an appetite. "I'd like to know more about what we are dealing with. Especially after that ambush."

Ryu's hand lowered his chopsticks before the boiled egg reached his mouth. "That's a fair point. If it weren't for my cloning vin capability, I'd be dead right now."

They were silent for a moment as a customer paid for her food, grabbed the to-go bags, and left with haste into the afternoon crowd. The air hung heavy between them.

"What's going on with Ren?" Halden switched topics.

Eyeing the boiled egg, Ryu said, "He's gone all the time now. He only comes home to sleep, and at odd hours, too. My parents are oh-so proud of his every fart."

Halden smirked.

"Worse off, Ren won't even tell me about any of it. He's always been such a rule stickler with his stellar reputation, but usually he at least gives me the time of day. With our five-year age gap, no one expected us to be close. But... he's more closed off than ever," Ryu said.

"Must be an important mission then." Halden wondered at it. Did it have something to do with intelligence gathering? His uncle was more on edge than usual. Ilias would use his shinobi to gather information on the goings-on of their house.

Within the feudal system each clan had, a shogun reigned supreme. The leader of the clan was elected by the conglomerate of daimyo to protect the clan and guide them until retirement. There were thirteen major houses and sixteen minor houses in the Duša Clan, but only the leaders of the major houses were given the rank of daimyo and control over a number of minor houses. Each minor house was larger than any major house in terms of population, making the role of the daimyo crucial to the system.

Deciding to eat the egg, Ryu chewed before shrugging. "Every mission he's given is important. It sucks, though, because my father couldn't help but rub it in that everyone is doing better than I am. Even Hina. Which I don't like saying because I'm not jealous, but it sucks being compared to my girlfriend."

Ryu had been head over heels for Hina when they enrolled at the Shinobi Academy. Everyone thought the two of them were made for each other. Hina's sweet demeanor calmed Ryu's arrogance. She was, perhaps, more skilled than any other in their class, and two years ago, they made it official.

Wincing, Halden rubbed a hand behind his neck. "Ouch. Yeah, there's no way around that. He's harsh."

Ryu's house was one of the major ones in the clan, and it came with the expectation he'd surpass the most achieved of shinobi. His parents fawned over Hina, and her presence attracted more attention than his own, despite her being from a minor house. Her prowess as a shinobi exceeded that of her birthright, but perhaps more important to them, her ears weren't round. Ryu struggled with not being the more renowned shinobi in that relationship. His parents' blatant jabs, the comparisons to his exceeding brother, and his own self-doubt crippled him. Whereas Ren bent over backward to fall in line, Ryu grew jaded from the constant pressure.

"Yeah. I'm thankful Hina can withstand it all. It's awkward and uncomfortable for her too. Her family has been far more welcoming." A wistful note entered Ryu's voice.

"I think you're pretty lucky to have someone who can put up with your antics on top of it all. I'll never forget the time you pranked our instructor right before we graduated from the academy. I thought Hina would run then and there," Halden joked, trying to ease some lighter topics into their joint troubles.

Snorting, Ryu could only grin as he recalled the day. "I still can't believe how *we* managed to move everything from our classroom to the lawn outside. Don't forget, you helped me. Willingly."

Grinning, Halden still was proud of the fact they got away with it. "Your idea. I wasn't the mastermind behind that. I think it was impressive that we managed to get everything in the same exact setup within a couple of hours."

"When I told Hina it was us, she tried her hardest to get me to confess." Ryu chuckled, polishing off his ramen.

"Wait, that was you two?" A high-pitched voice gasped behind them.

Ryu and Halden turned to see Owena and Niko walking up to the ramen shop. The raven-haired shinobi was dwarfed by Niko's stout frame.

Owena appeared positively delighted. "I was never able to get you to confess, Halden."

Ryu winked at his partner in crime. "We don't break easily."

The two newcomers sat to Halden's right, and Owena ordered tonkotsu ramen and plopped into the seat beside him. A seat further, Niko ordered hakata, silently watching Owena with his brown eyes as she gravitated into the conversation.

"You two were always either fixated on studies or up to no good. There was no in-between," Owena said, sipping on a glass of water as her eyes mischievously glanced at Ryu, then moved to hover on Halden.

Folding his arms, Halden rested on the back of his chair. "I'd say more of the first than second." Looking at Ryu, he amended, "For myself, at least."

Niko's mouth downturned as Owena laughed, resting a tiny hand on Halden's left shoulder.

"True on that. There's a reason why you're the highest-ranked guy in our class." She thanked the owner of the shop when he delivered her ramen.

Ryu lifted a brow at Owena. "How are you and Sven doing?"

Behind her, Niko's face fell further into displeasure. Halden couldn't help but feel bad for the guy. He and Ryu knew Niko had held a crush on Owena for years, even as she dated around.

Her face grew bored. "Fine enough for now." She twirled noodles onto a chopstick. "But, more pressing, how are you two holding up with that girl on your team?" Owena's voice dripped with sympathy. Her head lowered toward Halden, giving him the distinct impression she expected him to say *it's been absolutely awful.* "We were told that people from the Kriv Clan were mad that she claimed asylum here. It's awfully selfish that she'd place you in danger, especially when she doesn't belong here."

"I think it's bringing a new perspective to our team by having someone with experience beyond our borders." Halden knew that wasn't the answer she was digging for, and judging by the flicker of annoyance in her eyes, he judged it correctly.

"Though she is a heck of a killer," Ryu muttered, swiveling in his chair to face them.

Niko's body turned toward them, his eyes growing a tad wider. "What do you mean?"

Owena shot him a look.

"Caenrya single-handedly eliminated two of the ronin that attacked us." Ryu's voice was grim, something rare for him. "Even though she was drugged."

"What I'm hearing is that she's dangerous," Owena said, her face tightening. Both of her brows raised. "She shouldn't be on any of our shinobi teams. She isn't trained or trusted. It's only a matter of time until she turns on us. So far, she nearly got four of our clan killed."

Even Niko appeared slightly concerned.

"That's not what he meant," Halden said, his eyebrows pinching.

Two more customers retrieved to-go meals, and the chatter momentarily overshadowed their conversation. When Halden peaked at Ryu to confirm, he was shocked to find his eyes searching anywhere but near him in a nervous way.

"Was it, Ryu?"

Ryu blew out a long breath. "I'm not sure yet."

"Hey, that's okay," Owena said, her face concerned. "She's a foreigner. There's a reason clans stick to their own. Outsiders can't be trusted. None of us knows her or her true motives. It's best to keep our distance until the shogun can see reason and remove her from our territory."

That was enough.

"My father knows what he's doing," Halden said sharply, rising from his seat. At Owena's large eyes, he turned to Ryu before she could rush to apologize. "I have some business to attend to. I'll see you later, Ryu."

"Halden, I didn't mean any offense," Owena started, moving to stand in front of him before he could leave. Her full lips pouted.

Niko continued to eat his ramen in silence.

Such a conflicting mix of emotions weathered Halden's patience. He nodded in Owena's direction, moving around her and through the square before he said something he might regret.

And it was on the tip of his tongue.

CHAPTER SEVEN

CAENRYA

Caenrya's lips pressed together at the elder's pinched face, her eyes drinking in the lavish expanse of quarters Aya owned for but a moment before tuning it all out. "I don't have the time to learn how to sit still." It was an effort to refrain from scorning the lady and the cashmere cushions she rested on around the indoor pond of koi.

The marble steps winded down into a shallow divot central to a gold-leaf-adorned and statue-clad entry room with several enormous fish swirling beneath lily pads. Mouse-like staff members had taken to the halls when Aya asked her first question: What was the extent of her training?

Caenrya detailed the extensive hand-to-hand combat she was forced to learn, and the threshold testing of her mind by those in the employ of her lord. All the elder said in response was to *sit her rump down* and *empty her mind*.

What nonsense.

"Today, we hone in on one crucial element of the Shinobi Creed: Tempest's Calm. A shinobi must wield the ability to be clear of mind and maintain composure in all circumstances." A hint of impatience crossed Aya's words. Her lightly veined hands rested on either side of her own pillow across from Caenrya, and a sweep of grayed hair rested above Aya's slim brows. "To increase your own adaptability for taiji balancing, you must conquer the act of zazen. It is the cornerstone of shinobi mastery and will set you down the path of Awakening."

Caenrya tracked the elder's hand as it hovered over her gray head.

"Here, you must empty the mind and tune out all but the breaths you take. In particular, notice the depth of your inhalation, the calming energy as the air passes through you when exhaled from here." Gesturing toward her chest, Aya's eye cracked open. "Do it."

"If I meditate, will I be able to move on to the important aspects right after?"

Scowling, Aya said, "It takes the common shinobi years of practice during their time at the academy. Even afterward, they continue their regime, hoping to unlock their Awakening and open another gate of power."

The first tidbit of information sank her shoulders, and her fists balled in frustration over her black trousers. Caenrya hadn't ever been parted from the daimyo for more than a matter of weeks. She could only have a month to live with the slave mark, perhaps less if the distance remained great. Whatever was requested of her, she needed to excel at and perfect quicker than anything she'd managed in the past if there was any hope of being among those who rescued Verina.

"What is the Awakening and gate of power?" Caenrya hadn't heard those terms before, even when she racked her mind back to the scant memories of her previous life.

Something shifted behind those ancient eyes, a darkness clouding what lurked in the background. "There is much you lack," Aya noted, her chest rising high. "We'll begin with a summary of the fundamentals, and you'll study the rest within the texts every shinobi is given at the academy. Before you leave today, take with you a few manuscripts from my library and read."

Clearing her throat, the elder continued, "Every living creature is given a spiritual seed at birth that defines them into the Five Categories of Beings. Depending on the category you're gifted at birth, that seed can be nurtured into determining one's capabilities. Most of us fall firmly into the first category where that seed remains as a seedling, never to bloom into fruition. Those people are found in minor houses and can't use taiji. Those with a category three or higher spiritual seed tend to comprise the major houses since we have more Elven blood in our veins and a greater connection with taiji. For the blessed few with a seed capable of flourishing into the fifth category, we can achieve the greatest shinobi accomplishments with our taiji so long as we endure for perfection."

Eyes focused, Caenrya drank in every word. The tips of her fingers curled.

"The Awakening is a state that all shinobi strive to achieve. To become a jōnin, one requirement is that you must reach this state. It is independent of the seed you were born with and requires intensive zazen to unlock each of the Five Paths in order. Once the Five Paths are unlocked, one may regenerate taiji from nature's stores. It permits your body to reach its full potential, excelling in the categories of strength, speed, and healing. Your primary focus at this time is simply to learn the fundamentals of meditation to begin your journey along the first Path of Self-Realization."

A tiny splash sounded from a koi.

Pinching her brow, Caenrya asked, "Where do the gates fit in?"

"The Art of the Eight Gates is mastered through zazen." Aya's wrinkled face turned toward her. "The more time you spend on self-inquiry to reveal your true identity and unity with the universe, the more your taiji may grow. There are eight phases our taiji may prosper into, and with each gate you unlock, the strength and nature of your taiji will fundamentally increase."

Caenrya's index finger dug into the pad of her thumb as her mind drifted to the previous day. "I've already unlocked one, then. Yesterday, I was able to diffuse a drug that inhibited me while using my vin, and I healed from several wounds within minutes."

The elder took a beat before replying, "Tell me more about what occurred during those moments."

Recalling, she said, "I needed to act. I used the *zai* seal to form my taiji into weapons and grasp the mind of an attacker."

A peculiar expression crossed the elder's stern face. "Explain your vin—your bloodline gift—further."

"Mine allows for my taiji to leave my form. I control it as it circulates out to a fine point and then return it back into my chakras to mitigate loss of energy. It's dense enough to protect me from blows and act as a weapon of whatever caliber I select." Shrugging, Caenrya looked down at the crescent indentations lining the soft flesh of her thumb. "I'm also capable of delving into the minds of those I connect eyes with. Depending on how strong the soul, I can entrap them indefinity or hold them long enough to eliminate."

"Have you been able to heal in the past using your gift?"

Unease halted her hand at the thought. "No. Never."

"The only explanation I could derive stems from the mechanism of the inner eight gates," Aya hummed, her face lifting as she grew deep in thought. "The Five Paths aren't achieved through such methods. However, it may be possible that the progression of a new gate allowed for your vin to further develop despite the lack of inner acknowledgment.

Did you recently experience any revelation that could contribute to a fundamental shift in your perceptions?"

"No." Caenrya scowled, feeling the shift the conversation had taken to be ridiculous. "I was furious at the time." It was none of Aya's business anyway.

A heavy note hung between them. Caenrya was on edge as the elder took her time to finally say, "Were you able to increase the power behind your visible taiji afterward?"

Her mind involuntarily remembered how she snapped against Two and how the cloak of energy enveloped further up her arms than she normally produced. Of how far it had impaled through the boy and into the tree beyond. "Yes," she chewed out, her index finger pushing the nail into her thumb once more.

"Have you ever experienced anything similar in your past, to the degree of sharply elevating your taiji abilities?"

Only once, Caenrya realized, had there been a time when something similar had occurred. She'd never forget the first day the daimyo had introduced her and Verina to the other kids, and the mosh pit that occurred the moment those iron doors had snicked shut behind him. With every new arrival, the pecking order was threatened, and each kid wanted to guarantee their number didn't increase by the end of that night.

Like crazed animals, dozens of them hounded Caenrya and Verina for hours. They'd circle for minutes, each taking a turn to dip in with a single punch before reeling back into the fray of bodies far beyond her reach. The sound of laughter, a glint of madness, and the thrill of their hunt propelled the hazing to a feeding frenzy when they discovered Verina's will to be weak. They craved the way she cried over Caenrya's raging attempts to fight back. It broke something integral in her core when Verina called her name between rasping breaths.

Then the sight of her sister's blood on the fist of a boy.

Caenrya's hand formed the seal she was taught before they were kidnapped, and the boy fell within the next laugh that escaped in the gathered crowd. Child after child fell before they even realized what had happened. The sight of blue formed blades around her fists, altering the laughs into screams.

She took a savage delight in tearing into several kids before the guards rushed in, separating the surviving forty into another room before she killed them all.

It wasn't until afterward that Caenrya was horrified at what she'd done. Even if there wasn't much choice in the matter. Even Verina was terrified... of her. It passed, but that expression was forever burned into Caenrya's mind.

That day was the first time she'd been able to wield taiji blades.

"Yes," Caenrya spoke somewhat distantly, her mouth working as she shook the vivid memory off. "I had to protect Verina."

"Your sister?" the elder asked. At Caenrya's confirming nod, she exhaled. "You've unlocked at least two gates then, both through anger. That's unfortunate." Skin crinkled between Caenrya's brows at that. "It'll be far more difficult to unlock further gates through methods of peace and meditation since you've gone down the path of anger. If not impossible."

Caenrya almost huffed. "I don't think I'll find any shortages of anger in my lifetime." *Or afterward.*

"It isn't a matter of *if* you'll cross into further gates but *how* you do," the elder emphasized. "With each passing of gates unlocked through anger, the paths of Awakening become vexing to progress through."

Throwing up a hand, Caenrya argued, "What does it matter? The gates, this seed nonsense, any of it? If I'm limited by what was given to me at birth, then why don't I solely focus on the Art of the Eight Gates rather than meditation? It's serving me well enough."

Aya shook her head. "The eight gates ultimately determine the power behind your taiji and how effective your Awakening is. The seed within your soul outlines your maximum aptitudes when each gateway is opened. With each one opened, your reserve of taiji increases, to put it in the most fundamental explanation." Meeting Caenrya's bemused gaze, Aya weaved her fingers together. "Everything is connected, from what we can achieve at birth to what we do with the gifts we are given. To excel as a shinobi, you must aim to open each gate through meditation and walk the Five Paths to earn what you are capable of. Without focusing on the Five Paths, you'll never unlock all eight gates."

A plain-robed lady refilled a steaming cup of tea beside Aya. The elder thanked her staff member, bringing the swirling green tea to her lips. Pausing, she eyed Caenrya. "You'll ruin your inner gates by unlocking them through anger. You'll never be able to backtrack, and you'll stunt your full potential." She sipped delicately, lowering the porcelain cup onto the spotless floor beside her cushion.

Gates. Awakening. Seeds. Caenrya reeled in her scattered thoughts. "For now, all I can do is meditate?"

"Begin," Aya said, assuming the sitting position of calmness and tuning out her surroundings.

Shutting out her vision, Caenrya drew in a deep lungful of air and meditated.

Well, she tried to for five irritatingly impossible hours. Nothing she did was right, from the distracting thoughts and little unintentional movements to the glares she attempted to sneak toward her elder. It was as if the old lady knew every thought racing through her mind and every twitch of her muscles as they protested from the prolonged meditation.

All Caenrya could think about on her walk back through the Citadel was how utterly defeated she felt. She adjusted a large amount of rather heavy texts in hand. Not for a second was she able to remain still, thought-free, and calm. The more she tried, the more she failed. With each passing hour, her teeth tightened a smidge to the point of her jaw aching whenever she attempted to relax. What only added to the anger was the fact that she hadn't the faintest clue where her lodgings were.

Attempting to weave through random roads proved fruitless. The blatant stares she accumulated had not gone unnoticed. Some were outright hostile, and while she certainly didn't balk from any, Caenrya couldn't understand why they were occurring. People kept glancing at her ears, the hair there tucked behind them. So, she stared at theirs, finding nothing remarkable but normal ears. It was dumb.

Caenrya untucked hair around her ears, covering them.

It wasn't until she stumbled through Riverside Square that she gleaned a better understanding.

Six younger shinobi were snacking on confectionaries. The black of their uniforms contrasted with the array of silken hues the common folk walked around in. The group huddled around a bench beside an enormous, marbled fountain littered with gold coins. One pair of black eyes squinted when she edged around the perimeter.

"Caenrya!" Owena called out with a beckoning hand. "C'mon over."

Hesitating, Caenrya hadn't the faintest idea of how to handle such a situation. It was obvious how much the raven-haired girl despised her, but if Caenrya learned one thing from her time under the daimyo, it was to never show the enemy her back. With caution, she crossed the bustling square, dodging passing residents as she analyzed the group ahead.

Niko, she recognized, his face downturned as Caenrya approached. The others all sported the telltale lithe builds of shinobi, a casualness that came with practiced fighters. In a second, she knew any of them could launch into action, their eyes constantly assessing. Based on their estimated age, they were all likely in the same class as Halden. She halted a purposeful six feet away from the nearest of them all, a rather short, spiky-haired girl who eyed her maliciously. However, this girl was still taller than Owena.

Their ears were all similar. Somewhat pointed. And easy to spot. Many here ensured they were easily discernible.

From where she sat, Owena cocked a brow as she jerked her chin at Caenrya. "This is the one I was talking about. Cadigan lost an eye defending this girl, who also happens to be the one who attempted to kill my father." She drew an expression of sympathy from the dark-haired boy who had an arm wrapped around her shoulders.

Shifting her stance, Caenrya's eyes flicked between each threat, repressing that pang of guilt that threatened to worm its way in. "Your father's condition was a complicated situation. I perceived him as an assailant, considering he invaded *my* mind first. I didn't hurt him, and both he and Cadigan hold no ill will against me." She knew not to reveal too many details, but it peeved Caenrya to have her actions misconstrued.

A rough laugh burst from Owena's mouth. "Of course, they'd tell you that. They wouldn't cross the shogun's will. I don't know what makes you special, but no one wants you here. Not Cadigan, nor anyone in that team." Hiking up her shoulders, Owena continued, "I'm the only one with enough guts to say it."

Words.

They were a new kind of combat she wasn't versed in, and they packed a different punch. Caenrya could discern how the girl's words rang true. Within a day, she'd managed to almost kill the entire team, and the sole reason she hadn't killed Owena's father was to hold his mind hostage in case the situation went south. Truly, the shogun's actions came across as generous. What was his true motive, and was the elder part of it all?

"Is she...?" One of the guys leaned forward, and his face lit up after reading the spines of the manuscripts Caenrya carried. "Oh man!" He laughed, gesturing toward the texts. "She's reading from the first-year academy books!"

The others snickered, Owena's eyes positively laughing at her. Caenrya's face burned, and her hands gripped the manuscripts tighter. Beside Owena, Niko raised his face to the sky, searching for something there.

"Poor girl. Brought in from the wild. So uneducated and oblivious." Owena picked at her nails, her voice turning singsong. "Out-side-r."

This was ridiculous. Why should she endure such treatment from someone who didn't know how lethal she could be?

The boy with an arm around Owena lazily grinned at her.

Raising a brow, Owena smirked at Caenrya. "Seems like you were allowed in for only one reason." She tapped the point on her left ear.

Ears. *Again.*

Yes, Caenrya's were far more pointed. And these people held such things in high esteem. Her mouth pressed into a line.

They cared about Elven blood.

Owena lowered her hand. "You're proving to be a remarkable letdown despite the advantage you should have. My clan is risking everything, bringing you into our fold. Your taiji isn't worth the space it takes up in your body."

Snarling, Caenrya dropped the books, and her right hand fell into the *zen* seal. Taiji erupted around her arms, her eyes rising to meet Owena's.

Shock slackened a handful of the group's faces, Owena's paling at Caenrya's lunging form. Pulling back her arm, Caenrya aimed for the girl's shoulder.

Out of nowhere, two palms shot out in rapid succession from the tunnel her vision had funneled into. Connecting above the center of her shoulder blades, they moved to sling her momentum with a smooth motion as her taiji flattered. Quickly adjusting her footing, Caenrya managed not to stumble as her speed took her a few steps past Halden's body.

It took even greater control not to lash out against him, and the need to punch anything became overwhelming. Caenrya's fists shook, and her lungs labored.

"Wild beast," Owena seethed behind her. Even Niko appeared discomforted by her presence. A sudden shift overtook Owena's features, and her mouth softened as her sight flicked to Halden. "Thank you for stepping in. I'm sorry you have to deal with such awful trash."

"Shinobi Creed: Shadow's Honor. Shinobi must operate with a code of honor, respecting the sanctity of life and avoiding unnecessary violence." Brushing past Caenrya, Halden stopped mere feet away from Owena. "This applies outside of missions, as you know. You should be ashamed of yourself. You are an ignorant child to demean others in such a way and to intentionally prod Caenrya to lash out." Wide eyes met Halden's blazing ones. His head turned toward the group. "We are not genin anymore. All of us are held to a higher standard than this. Our clan is on the brink of war with the Kriv Clan, and this is how you choose to spend the last minutes of peacetime?"

Halden's strong jaw ticked. "Disgraceful. Our ancestors would be mortified to see you now."

A part of Caenrya was surprised to see Halden's hidden metal beneath that controlled demeanor, the commanding undertone overriding Owena's previous influence over the chūnin. Many balked at Halden's presence, two having the decency to appear ashamed. Only Niko solemnly held his gaze. Owena's teary one grew frustrated as she threw off the other guy's arm from her shoulders.

"What does she have over you?" Owena asked through clenched teeth. The guy beside her glanced between her and Halden as if something dawned on him.

Caenrya wondered the same thing. Why had he gone to such lengths to stand up for her? There wasn't anything left she deserved at this point, so it had to be at his father's demand. Her back straightened. She didn't need a babysitter.

Pulling his shoulders back, Halden's face twisted into disgusted disappointment. "If you ever took the time to see beneath the surface of anything that displeased you, maybe you'd be less superficial and hateful toward the people you scorn."

Caenrya's lips twisted.

The fool thought he understood her. What a ridiculous notion.

If Halden gleaned even the slightest of darkness that thrived in her shriveled heart, Halden, too, would turn against her. Unable to withstand any of it, Caenrya picked up her books and retreated in the direction of her quarters. However, she soon spotted a familiar face in passing. In the nearby sushi stall, Ryu sat beside a girl who was chatting lively with wide gestures. When he saw Caenrya had discovered him, he shifted his head away.

But not before the flash of his guilt was noticed by her.

So. Even Ryu didn't think she belonged if he had witnessed the entire situation unfolding without stepping in. It seemed he still believed in all those foul words he shared behind her back.

Something in her chest ached as she left them all behind.

Chapter Eight

CAENRYA

Caenrya pushed through the crowded walkway. Halden's words after her were lost in the overwhelming voices within the square. Many of the younger citizens with unfriendly expressions gave her a noticeable berth. It only made her steps faster. Her heart raced from the deafening noise that crashed down on her. And when did the edges of her sight become blurred?

Caenrya's chest rose and fell quicker. Her legs all but ran up the stairwell to her apartment. Her shoulder roughly collided with the door as her free hand fumbled for the key within one of her many trouser pockets, the tremble unmistakable. A book slipped down with a thud. The blasted key got caught around anywhere but the keyhole. Everything pressed in around her, and her hand struck true at last. With a frantic push, she stumbled into her apartment, and the remaining books tumbled from her arm.

A foot nudged open her door as Caenrya's back pressed into a wall, her arms wrapped tighter around herself in the dark space. For a second, she saw the daimyo's face enter the room, his expression the one he bore when he lashed out against her.

It terrified her.

The ringing in her ears intensified, soon becoming the only sense her mind acknowledged until a voice distantly sounded. Over and over, words without meaning were said, and her ceiling came into focus. Her limbs were weak, and her eyes blearily blinked away the fog impeding her vision. First, she noticed the closed door beside her, each book she had carried stacked neatly next to it. Then Halden's hovering form beside her supine body.

Had she... passed out?

Grunting, Caenrya fumbled to sit up, a shock racing through her when he steadied her back with a hand. She pushed the arm away. "Go away," Caenrya snarled. Her neck strained. *Uncomfortable* was the mildest of words to describe how it felt to be touched by anyone.

"Look, I apologize for disabling your taiji," Halden said somewhat wearily. He leaned back into a sitting position and rested his elbows on his crossed knees. "But if you had attacked Owena, it would have been cause enough for her house to push for your arrest. Not to mention the attention it would have drawn."

Caenrya pushed her back against the wall, carefully observing him for any rash movements. "You are the type who dreams himself a hero for a girl in distress. You grew up in a gilded world, and I assure you, I'm the damned furthest thing from the girl you think I am. There is much to scorn. The things I have done in the name of survival... I can deal with girls like Owena. I am more than capable of handling myself," she retorted. Her body still reeled from the abating lightheadedness.

A brow twitched on his shadowed face, only the light streaming in from her opened windows illuminating his prominent features. "Why do you view yourself as such?"

"Because I've killed more men than you could even imagine," Caenrya ranted, her anger at his naiveness displayed across her face. "Because

I've brutalized others for sport, all in the name of a sister whose life depends on me. Because—" Her voice choked, her throat thickening. "I don't deserve to be saved."

There it was. The truth of it all verbalized for the first time. Caenrya regretted the words the moment she lost them, the creases in his face saying it all. He felt sorry for her. Bunching up her face, she glued her eyes to the lantern visible from the opened front door. "Leave."

"I don't think I will," Halden stubbornly stated, refusing to budge.

"I have several manuscripts to read through and meditation to practice. I simply do not have the time nor patience to waste on a petty squabble with a guy who has nothing better to do than to pity the refugee girl," she said, her voice low with anger. When he still didn't move, Caenrya had to refrain from launching at him. "I. Do. Not. Have. The. Time."

"The daimyo of Shikei won't kill your sister," Halden explained, those sharp eyes narrowing in on her distrusting ones. "For two reasons. I assume she has your vin as well, which is a valuable resource that will guarantee her life until we can move in. As you are no longer in his company, he'll require her to fill your absence. He knows your loyalty to her and also has the added advantage of being able to exploit that to regain your service. You have time, even if it may not be the desirable answer you wish to hear."

"You'll never understand," Caenrya said flatly. The slave mark on her spine twinged in response. "My time is limited."

Halden leaned in. "By what?"

"What is it that you hope to gain by being here?" she asked, turning the table on him. "You obviously have been pecking for answers. A spy for your father. So, what is it that you hope to hear?"

The corner of his mouth twisted at that, and his form became still.

"That I somehow hold the secret to dominating the contested lands? Or, perhaps, do you wish to send me back in to gather intelligence on your clan's behalf?" Her voice slowly rose, her distrust mounting. Deep and twisted, her laugh echoed in her very core. "Everyone always has a desire to use me. You people are no different, even if it comes in a gold-plated cage."

"What I want most is to help you," Halden quietly said. A note of sincerity rang in his voice. "If that means only helping with your training or keeping you from engaging in further trouble, then that's what I'll do. I won't lie. My father tasked me to learn of any information that could aid in our ongoing war with the Kriv Clan and your circumstances. I'll be blunt. I'd rather help you succeed than to keep up this charade."

But something in his bearing reminded her of another, and that train of thought tore her heart to shreds. She wiped it from her mind.

"I don't believe you." Caenrya's words were harsh against even her own ears.

Those steel-gray eyes redirected to the pillow she had moved to a corner of her room. A corner she slept in rather than her own given bed. "I despise politics. Even more so, I despise the notion of what this daimyo thinks he can get away with. Most of all, you need someone in your corner. I know a martyr when I see one, and I witnessed firsthand the aftermath left for those who suffered because of it."

Propping her head against the wall, Caenrya sarcastically asked, "And how have you suffered?" It was obvious he talked of himself.

His hands clenched, and a chilled breeze wafted through the dark room. People still ambled about below her window, all while Halden worked himself the courage to speak. The weight of his gaze pulled it to the floor, and the shadows obscured the distance in his eyes.

"My mother sacrificed herself when her team's intelligence proved faulty in an infiltration mission," Halden started. "They were to retrieve and interrogate a Kriv ronin who assassinated the daimyo of House Cadigan. On the night of the blood moon, nearly four years to this day, he was to be on a contract with an elite of the Kriv Clan and navigating through the Valley of White Sand. What was supposed to be a small operation ended up being a sabotage effort led by who we believe to be the same assassin."

With the dim lighting, Caenrya perceived the vicious twist of his mouth.

"They were outmatched, even with four exceptional jōnin to his three. This ronin was unlike any other, his capabilities ranging close to unfathomable with his fluidity of *kuji-kiri*—the nine cuts. Though, the strongest he excelled in was the void seals, going as far as to materialize realistic hallucinations with minimal strain on his taiji."

Kuji-kiri... otherwise known as the nine hand seals for taiji activation. Only one man could perform them all that she knew of, and only one who specialized in the void seal.

It felt as if a kunai had sunk into her abdomen, the awful realization stealing the warmth from her limbs. *Valen.* The one Caenrya feared more than any and the sole shinobi who was capable of keeping her in line at Shikei.

"My mother..." Halden cleared his throat. The pain was evident in his twisted facial lines. "She unleashed everything she had to derail the onslaught for mere minutes. The others took her command to retreat, leaving her to fend against a hopeless fate. In the end, she willingly gave her life for those three in her team, knowing she'd leave me and Ilias forever."

Her eyes were glued to his misery.

Grief, raw and untampered, lit his refocusing sight. "Upon their return, her team confessed they could have devised a way to bring them all back, even if scathed. But alive." His head lifted to her level. "But with her as team commander, they had no choice but to fall back and obey. Maybe they could have succeeded and withdrawn, but the alternative was the chance my mother wasn't willing to take."

"If it's any consolation, that man wouldn't have lost," Caenrya murmured, her expression softening a hair. "That was the only path to take against an opponent like him."

Stiffening, Halden asked, "You know of him? How?"

"If I was a slave, then he was the whip." Snagging a portion of her hair, Caenrya redirected her nervous energy into fiddling with it. "Valen is far superior to any I know, his Kū nature derailing mine every time he… practiced with me."

"White hair, shoulder length? A dragon tattoo across half his face?"

"Yes," she confirmed, unwanted images threatening to surface in the dredges of her mind. "Though the hair length always changed. He's been labeled as the Slayer of the Kuji-kiri, a man known as the Tenth Cut. A master of each nature a shinobi can wield. Thus, each cut that controls it through seals." She couldn't fathom how Halden's mother managed to keep him at bay, much less whichever ronin were with him. The power the woman must have wielded… "I'm sorry about your loss."

One of Halden's shoulders rose an inch before dropping. "It's been years, but at times, it feels like only days have passed." Serious-faced, he continued, "Learning more about this ronin would help, even if it's only what you can remember or what seemed insignificant at the time. We've never been able to identify him. Any help you can give would catapult our otherwise stale efforts."

That chill reached her chest, Caenrya's shriveled heart clenching painfully. Every part of her recoiled at the thought of reliving a single moment of that torture, much less sharing any of it with another.

Stinging, sharp rivulets of pain shot from her spine, the mark reminding her of where she should be. A place where she was being beckoned. Caenrya flinched, her back arching against the surge. In and out, she breathed it away. Within moments, only the aching remnants lingered along with a fatigue that ate at her bones.

Halden stood across from her, making for the door. Looking back over his shoulder, he mistook her reaction. "Take however much time you need. I understand you need it." He half-turned away from her before rethinking. "If you're due at Aya's residence tomorrow, I can help you familiarize yourself with the route again."

Caenrya nodded once and waited for the door to close behind him before moving.

Something shifted in her chest from the conversation. Knowing there was someone there affected by Valen too... Well, it was the first time she thought there might be something she had in common with someone.

With Halden.

The others, especially those young shinobi, were particularly infuriating and naïve. Halden mentioned his clan being on the brink of war, yet it wasn't a sentiment reflected in the state of the Citadel. No one appeared overtly concerned, and his peerage was more focused on ostracizing her than anything else.

It was childish, and it made Caenrya mad she could do nothing about it. Were people of her age this cliquish and immature? They were all close to her age.

Or... was she not normal?

Her heart tightened, and all she could do was clench a fist over it. She wished it were easier to blend in.

A shadow passed by her window, pausing outside.

Sighing loudly, Caenrya walked to it, placing her fingertips in the small groove of her window and sliding it open. A ginger tabby sat on a small wooden ledge between her and Wisteria Square, licking its paw.

A furry ear flicked, and Caenrya's eyes traced the feline's thinness. She turned to retrieve some slices of chicken stored in her refrigerator. As she stood, she saw the cat had moved inside the alcove. It waited on top of her desk, almost expectantly.

Shredding the chicken, Caenrya fed it small pieces.

A rumbling purr sounded from the feline as it ate. Three slices later, the cat head-butted her arm, pressing itself against her and flicking its tail. Caenrya stared at it curiously, raising a hand to pet it. But before she could, it darted back out onto that small wooden ledge, returning from where it came.

She closed the window, unsure what to make of the whole thing.

Falling asleep proved difficult once again, even after preparing for sleep and skimming through several pages of the shortest manuscript she was given. Somewhere far away, a dog barked at some disturbance. Nightmares plagued her throughout the night of a tattooed man. The cold sweat she awoke in only somewhat reassured her she was present and safe. That her corner of the room she had tucked herself into didn't have another within.

By the time Caenrya was dropped off the following morning, even darker bags dragging down her eyes, she struggled to maintain an alert composure. Though Aya's agitated countenance soon sent a nervous energy through her hands.

"I've taken time to reflect best on how to utilize our time wisely. We must make the most of our upcoming mentorship," Aya said, resuming her place of meditation beside the pond. "Within three weeks' time, the gathering of the five clans will take place. The Dagon house will be descending upon the Citadel like vultures, and it will become infinitely more tedious to manage their incessant probing. We'll work through every minute of sunlight, only pausing for necessities. From here on out, you must eat better, otherwise you'll be too weak to carry through my lessons. During your evenings, you are to study each text I lend you and ask any questions at the commencement of each day." A brow arched. "Any objections?"

Caenrya shook her head. She followed the elder's prompt and took her seat. Stealing a moment to steady her breathing, she focused on beginning her day's task.

Chapter Nine

CAENRYA

Every day became a constant source of frustration for Caenrya, her training amounting to a sore arse and a stiff back from the hours upon hours of sitting. The only source of relief for her constant itch to move was her occasional sparring sessions with Halden. While her mind wasted away on the endless hours of meditation, at the very least, her body could maintain some form of lethality. It didn't take long for her to notice the changes in herself each morning, the sharp panes of her face filling to a healthier shape. She soon required another set of shinobi uniforms, her figure becoming somewhat curvier with the small amount of weight she had gained in the last few weeks, some muscle included. For once, Caenrya stared at herself for a while, at the slight tan her skin acquired from the meditation sessions Aya held outside.

She was... different.

Better wasn't a term Caenrya would use to describe herself. The hours of practice hadn't amounted to much, and the pages of academy basics she digested only aided her in understanding that she practically knew nothing at all.

During this time, Halden had held true to his promise and refrained from further probing into her life. In exchange, she gave him tidbits about Valen whenever she could muster the courage. Nothing extensive, just his prominence in the daimyo's ring and his movement footprint. Valen mainly stuck like glue to Caenrya when she lived there, rarely leaving on solo assignments unless the daimyo required him to.

That flighty cat returned several times, gladly accepting her chicken and leaving with all due haste afterward. Caenrya knew it was there waiting for her when that slight shadow lingered on the other end of her window. Sometimes, she swore the tabby's orange and cream fur popped up at the edges of her vision throughout the day.

Otherwise, Caenrya noticed Ryu's complete avoidance of her, though she was grateful when Cadigan joined their sparring sessions. A part of Caenrya had worried the shinobi wouldn't be the same, yet the woman was in constant good spirits and had made the training more efficient. The only problem proved to be hiding her slave mark whenever it acted up. One slight twinge was the only warning before it activated, and she had to come up with a variety of excuses when one neared. At some points, she could discern the others knew something was occurring, so Caenrya limited the sparring sessions more in recent days. The pain grew to be unbearable, and her body was exhausted of energy afterward.

Meditation was the perfect excuse for her prolonged silence, and Aya never noticed as she recovered in the quiet. It grew more worrisome by the day, though, and Caenrya committed all she had to repress its effects on her.

"Focus, Little Dragon." A new pet name that always furrowed Caenrya's brow. At least the elder hadn't asked any intrusive questions thus far, but her nerves said it was only a matter of time to trade something of sustenance for knowledge. "Free yourself from negative thoughts and acknowledge your shortcomings. Only through this will you complete the Path of Self-Realization," Aya reminded for the sixth time that evening.

Grunting in response, Caenrya fought against a muscle twinging painfully in her lower back. She only tolerated this nonsense because the elder promised they'd train in Kū and taiji balancing tomorrow if Caenrya didn't complain throughout the last two and a half weeks. Besides, she wasn't convinced the meditation was of any use when it came to the application of the two yin and yang energy reserves. The manuscripts covered this in simplistic detail. The only thing required was to portion the two forces of yin and yang to the percentages needed for any one of the five elements desired to manifest. The only three cuts required for Kū were the *jin*, *sha*, and *retsu* hand seals, all easy to twist her hands and arm movements into.

Caenrya was itching to progress into anything that didn't require her sitting for hours on end.

"Hey, Grams. What's going on here?" a deep voice asked from nearby.

Only two weeks of being yelled at for twitching during such distractions had Caenrya rooted in place despite the urge to search for the owner of that interruption. The desire to assess a new potential threat was overwhelming.

"Osten," Aya greeted, the sound of his footsteps closing in toward her. "I wasn't aware you'd be arriving with the Dagon daimyo delegation."

A chuckle sounded, boots treading across nearby stones as they crunched to a stop between Caenrya and Aya. "As you're aware, the house has taken an interest in your protégé. I'm here to see history in the making," Osten disclosed, his voice lowering as if sharing a secret. "Formally, however, I'm here to attend my first clan gathering."

"Ah, I see. Hedin has officially declared you as his heir, then." A neutral undertone lined the elder's words, one Caenrya knew appeared when she was displeased.

"I know you don't care for him, but even you have to admit that you'd rather it fall into my hands than that of another Dagon branch," Osten pressed, his weight shifting.

The elder snorted. "Anyone else would be a worse-off choice indeed." Standing, Aya's voice turned a notch serious as she continued. "Caenrya, I do believe this to conclude today's training. It seems I have matters to attend to."

Caenrya opened her eyes. Stretching out to her feet, she took in the newcomer. Stocky with short, curly hair, Osten similarly appraised her with those dark eyes and features typical in the Dagon clan. There appeared to be a permanence to his slight smile, his relaxed posture relaying a friendliness she wasn't accustomed to around the Citadel. The blacks of his shinobi uniform were rich. Either it was a new set, or he rarely saw combat in any form.

Before she could get a word in to the elder, Osten held out a hand, his abnormally straight and even teeth gleaming in the fading sunlight. "Pleasure to meet you, Caenrya."

Reluctantly, she shook his hand once before releasing it. "And you," she lied, trying not to frown too hard as Aya left without a word. "Your uniform is pristine."

"Thanks." He winked, shifting his weight as if proud.

Caenrya's face crinkled. "That wasn't a compliment."

"Ah. A question without asking, then." Arching a brow, Osten was unaffected by her rebuttal. "I retired as a chūnin to delve into family politics. I'm wearing these today as I've been practicing some old tricks to stay current on training. After all, the most esteemed house heads always have a shinobi background. Few attend the Shinobi Academy, so it's seen as an acolyte to have had the experience, especially as someone from a major house. We are all forced to at least graduate from the academy before pursuing any other career. Minor houses don't hold their children to such standards."

Blinking, Caenrya couldn't understand why he thought she cared.

"Tell me about yourself," he prompted, his chin lowering in a quick dip.

Her frown grew deeper despite her efforts. "I'm a shinobi who trains under Aya Dagon."

Osten's smile widened. "Playing hard to get?"

Cocking her head, Caenrya thought back to the conversations she'd overheard among those of her age group. By the shinobi's demeanor, the rugged look he sported, and the way he was talking with her, she could only assume he thought himself a wooer. Without a word, she brushed past him toward the stairwell that led back down into the heart of the Citadel.

"I'll see you tomorrow, Caenrya," he called after her. "Looking forward to getting better acquainted."

Caenrya's nose bunched up, her steps hastening down the multitude of flights on the mountainside. By the time she neared the bottom, darkness coated the village. Lanterns were lit throughout the descending buildings, and her ears registered distant chattering. On the last stairwell, that all-too-familiar twinge shot through her spine. Panicked, she searched for a safe alcove to hide. The nearby trunk of an oak caught her attention, and Caenrya rushed to lean against it in preparation. Her hands shook, and her heartbeat was rapid in her chest.

Again? Already that day she'd had two episodes. That was one more than the previous day. It became alarming how rapid the progression had become, and before she could think of it more, the pain struck.

Despite every lash she'd received, every punch and kick she bore, and every mental attack, Caenrya learned to conceal her pain, as it only encouraged her attacker. But now, the razor-sharp rivulets became streams of agony coursing through her limbs. A cry of suffering escaped, and her eyes welled with unshed tears. Minutes passed without reprieve, something at the edge of her consciousness grounding her.

A hand.

It was shaking her shoulder, and the bleariness in her eyes was slow to adjust. The pain faded away, leaving her a shivering husk. Cold bark against her back and moist dirt beneath her became tangible. The words leaving the guy beside her were mumbled.

Swallowing, Caenrya gathered her strength and asked, "What?" Her voice was strained, and her dry throat made her crave water more than anything.

"Are you all right?" Osten asked again, concern etched across his face.

"Fine." Caenrya brushed it off, willing the unsteadiness to leave her. *Damn it*, she inwardly cursed. After weeks of carefully maintaining her debilitating condition, her secret was discovered by a guy she'd barely met.

Giving her a disbelieving face, Osten speculated, "I'd wager that you are not *fine*. I didn't peg you as one of those sorts who pose as such."

Glaring at him, she said, "I have occasional panic attacks. It's none of your business. Besides, why are you stalking me?" Perhaps if Caenrya could turn the conversation, he'd write it off and never mention it to Aya. She needed more time, and she knew she'd be able to push past it.

A cheeky grin split his face as Osten rocked back on his heels. "Being in my company does seem to have that effect on women." At her deathly expression, he raised his hands placatingly. "No need to get defensive. I, too, thought you were striking and may have been admiring you after you departed with such haste. After you were down for a while, I wanted to follow up and ask if all was well."

Her face grew hot at the blatant compliment, and her situation grew uncomfortable at a rapid pace. "Well, by all means, you can go now. As you can see, I'm not in need of assistance."

Crooking a brow, Osten smirked. "Then why are you still sitting?"

"You're obnoxious," Caenrya growled, willing her leaden body to struggle upward. Her knees were much wobblier than she would have liked, but she managed all the same.

"I think you fancy me too, which is why I'll advise you not to show any of your attacks to my grandma. She'll kick you out faster than my invitation was for a date," he quipped, rising beside her and clasping his hands behind his head.

Caenrya tried not to notice that his arms were indeed muscular.

"Would you allow me the opportunity to dine with you this evening? I know this outstanding ramen restaurant that I frequent when in town. It would be my pleasure to share the time with you," he said.

Eagerness flitted through his expression, not that it made any impression on Caenrya. Her exhaustion was bone deep. "No thanks. I have much to study and no time for frivolous things," she said, annoyance rippling off her at his presumption.

Swiveling on her heel, she threw every ounce of willpower into keeping her body moving smoothly enough, despite how the world teetered with every step. She ignored Osten when he said, "Another day then. I think the time with you would be worthwhile."

By the time she reached her apartment, there wasn't a need to force his dazzling grin from her mind as her body reached the point of complete exhaustion. She didn't even bother showering, electing instead to collapse in the corner and give in to the call of sleep. Within what felt like minutes, Caenrya awoke to yet another jolt of excruciating pain, the ends of each nerve frying within her body. Her teeth clamped on her arm to keep from screaming out in the dead of night, the tang of copper coating her tongue by the time it ended.

Panting, her eyes lolled toward the window to find a purpling sky, hints of orange lightening the edges. She waited several minutes before pulling herself together and forcing herself to prepare for the day. With the extra half hour she had, Caenrya took her time, delicately weaving between various flexibility techniques. She choked down a meal, her stomach roiling still from the last episode. Maybe it was irresponsible, but she refused to think of what the increased rate of episodes meant. Today, she'd focus on her lessons and get through them without incident.

Leaving her hair unbound, Caenrya set off on the familiar trek up the mountainside. As always, her ears were tucked beneath her hair, but somehow, others recognized her as rumors continued to circle about. Outsider. Wild beast. Other vile words and phrases all slung her way every time she set foot outside her residence. Those stones hit her each time. Her eyes kept low to avoid contact with any in the area. Already, she'd had an awful experience shopping with the stipend she was given whenever she needed to replenish her necessities. One store owner outright refused her coin, but when Caenrya didn't slink off like a wounded calf, they gave in, only to see her go.

When she crested the last flight of stairs, Aya and Osten were both sitting outside beside the large body of water. It mimicked the smaller one Aya had inside her home, with cushions resting around it. The spirit of a koi flashed out of the water, and the shimmering particles faded as it descended. Beautiful forestry surrounded the glen. Birds chirped in the nearby treetops. A wrinkled hand beckoned her forward. Aya appeared livelier than Caenrya had ever seen her in lilac silk robes.

"Caenrya," the elder greeted as her pupil took her seat. "Today we train with Kū, the one nature I believe you to have an affinity toward and one where I can guarantee you flourish." Regarding her grandson, she said, "Go watch over your aunt and uncle. I don't want them meddling further into my business while they are here."

For one instant, a flash of edged disappointment lowered Osten's face before he departed with a respectful bow. Caenrya observed as the door shut harder than necessary behind him. A small amount of tension gathered in the elder's shoulders.

Clearing her throat, she gave her attention to Caenrya. "From your readings, educate me what your knowledge extent is of yin and yang."

"The average body has two reserves of natural energy, yin and yang," Caenrya said, her eyes glazing as she visualized the images from the manuscripts. "Yin represents freezing, and yang boiling. It's a dynamic relationship that forms a variety of harmonized possibilities. Each element requires a different percentage of each reserve, an interaction called jiao."

"And what of Kū? What is that nature, and how is it reached through jiao?"

"Kū is representative of the mind—"

Aya sternly interrupted, "Wrong! That is a common misrepresentation that academics somehow perceive as acceptable for young minds. It's such a shame as it limits any who specialize in such."

Caenrya's mouth lowered at that, her fingers itching to weave seals and apply her knowledge.

"Kū is the nature of the void. It's a force beyond comprehension that encompasses the unknown. With it, a shinobi can wield countless talents, including bending light, warping of time, and even healing of the body," Aya recited.

An inkling of wonder lifted her spirits, and Caenrya's attention was devoted to every word uttered by the elder. Her mind was already spinning with that piece of information, and she was developing methods and ways she could use nature, the first and foremost being the possibility of removing the mark that plagued her so.

"Without a doubt, Kū is the deadliest of natures and by far the most extreme to master. For those who stray too far into the depths of the void and experiment with new methodologies and techniques, they sacrifice their lives in the process. However, those who dawdle and play it safe will never achieve the greatest one could achieve with such a gift." Intensity lit a fire behind Aya's dark eyes.

"I will mold you into a shinobi who surpasses me, and you will amount to the greatest achievement of my lifetime," Aya promised, her confidence overwhelming. "For you, I devote this precious time. I do not tolerate foolery, nor disobedience, as it will only result in your death or worse."

Caenrya was aware there were many fates worse than a quick end.

"If you swear to abide by every law I lay and keep my lessons only to pass on to your own protégé one day, then we'll begin now," Aya said.

Steel straightened Caenrya's back. The fire ignited a blaze within her. "I swear it. I'll do anything." Tilting her head, she couldn't help but say, "Though I already swore to abide by your rules."

Aya's chest lowered slowly, taking her time in an effort to not lash out. "This is no small matter. You will be pushed to the brink of death. The mind is not a nature to toy with, for you must straddle such a fine line to maintain your soul. You once said you wish to undo your past mistakes, and I, too, wish not to repeat some of mine. Therefore, I will cut you off the second you hesitate to obey any further training regulations I put in place."

Nodding, Caenrya grew even more excited at the prospect. She knew that anything thrown her way she could handle, and what others may determine an extreme was only but another opponent to crush.

"But first, I have a question for you," Aya warned, the underlying message raising Caenrya's haunches. "What pain is eating at you day in and day out?"

Remembering Osten's warning, Caenrya grew panicked. She knew if she exposed her weakness, the elder may end her apprenticeship. On the other hand, if she hesitated a beat too long or lied, there was a real chance she'd also be kicked out.

And that terrified her.

"What do you mean?" Caenrya asked carefully, stalling for time. All for naught.

"Your back. Often, I find you wincing at something or another. What is it that has been ailing you?"

Caenrya widened her eyes marginally. "Oh! I've been sparring often with Halden and Commander Cadigan. I'd be lying if I said I hadn't been injured a time or two or haven't pulled a muscle."

A moment passed as Aya considered her. During that long expanse of time, Caenrya swore her heart stopped beating. Finally, the elder said, "Then we shall proceed."

They started with their morning meditation, calming their spirits and listening to the sounds of nature around them. The rapid pace of her heart subsided, and the air soothed her as it left her lungs. For once, Caenrya was somewhat at peace.

"We'll be transitioning into the first part of what I'll cover on this day," Aya murmured, her voice low as they eased out of the mediation. "What is the final necessity to engage your taiji once balancing has been reached?"

Blinking, Caenrya adjusted to the midday sun. "A catalyst of sorts. The manuscripts were extraordinarily vague about that."

"Precisely, Little Dragon," Aya approved, her hands lying flat across her thighs. "The culture of the five clans is one based on secrecy. Never will you hear these words more than whispered to another, as every word holds vast power. Ultimately, these words change the outcome of every battle. That is, the language of the Elves."

Chills raised bumps along her arms.

"The Elven language is an ancient one. When intentionally used in conjunction with the practice of jiao—the balance between the yin and yang reserves—a shinobi can enact one of the five elements. The words are precious, more so than any fortune one may wield or even the worth of an entire clan," Aya said gravely, her eyes beseeching Caenrya to understand the importance. "There are common words that a majority of shinobi are aware of in each clan, but there are also select words so elusive that they are solely passed down through a single-family line. Centuries ago, when the Canecian people departed from our ancestral home, we retained much more of the complex language."

Aya wistfully sighed. "Alas, the words were forgotten or destroyed in the several power struggles that followed. All records were burned or sabotaged intentionally to weaken foes. Nowadays, they are ingrained into our brains. Shinobi went as far as to have adopted the practice of only thinking the word to perform ninjutsu rather than speaking it during combat to prevent any others from learning it. I could waste precious time spewing the slew of words I know of, but there are a few that take priority. First, be aware that practicing any of these words without my direct guidance can kill you. If you aim for something too complex, or a word that requires seven gates' worth of power to pull off, you will exhaust your reserves and die. Do you understand?"

Caenrya inclined her head, readiness making her impatient.

"We shall work on a single word at a time, and when you master it, you will move on to another. Each word must be memorized both the way it is spelled and pronounced. If you wrongly repeat the word with an additional syllable or switch a consonant, you run the risk of the meaning being altered and any risk of the new consequences that ability may have."

The elder leaned forward. "What will happen if you use a word above your skill?"

"I'll be dead." Caenrya fought to keep from sighing.

"And what if you mispronounce a word that has a higher demand of power to achieve?"

Caenrya's face grew deadpan. "Very dead."

"Good." Aya nodded, her face growing even more stern as she leaned toward Caenrya.

"For instance, if you accidentally say *balvany* instead of *balvan*, and you've only unlocked a single gate, you'll die attempting to summon several boulders even if your gate wields more taiji than the average person," Aya explained, whispering the Elven words.

"I see," Caenrya said, mostly to herself. Many things she'd gleaned over the years fell into place. An expanse of a puzzle finally pieced together. "If you knew the proper words, then anyone could utilize a similar bloodline ability to that in which I wield, or the shogun for that matter."

Aya's hand twitched, something dark passing through her distracted sight. With another heartbeat, the elder's face resumed a grave expression. "That line of thinking is perilous," she scolded.

Caenrya's face closed off in response.

"While it could be possible if our kind had the full extent of the language and a lifetime of skillful practice, it isn't remotely feasible. The number of Elvish words it would take to replicate the Arundel bloodline gift..." The elder shook her head. "Even trying to string together two words is dangerous since the meaning of one or both can be altered. An entire sentence would be suicide."

Confused, Caenrya recalled how Aaric was able to enter her mind when she was to be interrogated by the shogun. He was capable of something similar, at the very least. She repeated aloud as much.

"No," Aya countered, a strand of hair escaping her tight bun and fluttering beside her face with the light breeze. "You pulled him into your consciousness, entrapping him. Aaric can't maintain a space of alternate reality within any mind. His limitations rest with searching through memories, a feat *he's* content with achieving."

Scathing words. Caenrya decided not to delve further into *that* personal vendetta.

"For now, we'll cover *lávka*," Aya said, her tone still holding a tang of resentment. "This word and the proper jiao will allow us to pass words through our minds." Glaring now, Aya held a single finger up. "Be aware. Using this word with a faraway target will require more taiji, as it is with any elemental usage. Your texts covered this in the first chapter, but I will further emphasize that even a word like this can kill an idiot if they attempt to communicate with another halfway across the continent."

Straightening her posture, Aya arched both brows at Caenrya. "What will happen to you if you try using this word with me across the continent?"

"I'd be very, very dead," Caenrya said, keeping the sarcasm from her voice.

Aya peered at her. "What balance of yin and yang is required for such ninjutsu?"

Automatically, Caenrya responded, "As Kū is a neutral element, both yin and yang must be an equal percentage to achieve jiao."

"Which many cannot achieve as it is. Complete neutrality is near impossible between yin and yang. The two always wax and wane within nature. You must feel the cold and warmth within your soul to identify each." Aya pointed to the center of her chest, just under the sternum. "Then balance it equally before repeating the word within your mind and performing the *jin* hand seal."

The elder wove two hands together in an intricate dance, the *jin* hand seal displayed. *Try weaving the sign first.*

The words echoed in Caenrya's mind. She flinched, Aya's voice coming through with stark clarity. *Amazing.* A corner of her mouth twitched up at that, her hands miming the elder's.

Over and over, Aya had her relax her hands and repeat the gesture. After an hour more, it grew old, but Caenrya knew better than to question the technique.

The serving staff brought out delicious sandwiches while Caenrya was instructed to whisper the word between bites. Even with a mouthful of cheese, sourdough bread, dressings, and chicken, it posed no challenge for her. She almost snorted at herself when that particular thought crossed her mind, repressing it before her mind could linger into what once was.

They took a short break. When Caenrya felt the telltale sign of an upcoming episode, she claimed her need for a restroom. The whole thing passed, though her arm sported new bruises where her teeth had clamped down. The supple material of her leather shinobi bracers helped cushion the force, but Caenrya was still worried that some noise would escape from her episode.

When she left to resume her training, no one was any the wiser.

The afternoon ticked by with continuous practicing of the hand seal, word pronunciation, yin and yang balancing, and then the execution. The sun had begun to set when Aya permitted it at last, seeing as Caenrya had perfected the technique with ease.

Focusing on the elder, Caenrya did as instructed, repeating *lávka* when all criteria had been met. She sensed a string pulling her mind toward Aya's. Pushing out the word *hello*, Caenrya was pleased when Aya acknowledged receiving it with a small smile. The first sincere one she'd seen on the elder's face, and all because Caenrya was able to successfully accomplish her first task. It brought a strange feeling she didn't recognize, something that made Caenrya want to do it again to see Aya smile at her in such a way.

Caenrya couldn't remember a time anyone had looked at her so. With pride.

When Aya dismissed her that day, Caenrya raised her chin an inch higher as she crossed through the bustling streets of the Citadel. She wasn't a complete loss, wasn't worthless if she made progress. Even if it was small and such a trivial technique, it would help her retrieve her sister. It had to.

Even if the captured ronin who had taken Cadigan's eye turned out to be a dead end, his memory wiped of any crucial details before the mission as a preventive measure, it was her damned luck that the leader of that mission had known a full account of the assignment and had been trusted with the risk of his memory.

Caenrya vividly remembered him calling to his cadre, his words of warning to avoid making eye contact with her ringing like bells in her ears. If only he'd been the sole survivor...

It hit her then, with such force and suddenness Caenrya couldn't have anticipated it. Her back spasmed horribly, her body crumbling into a wall in an alleyway between various merchant shops. A guy backpedaled nearby when he saw who it was shouting in agony on the ground, choosing instead to turn around than to provide aid to the unwelcome clan intruder.

Not that she minded.

Nothing registered beyond the inferno of excruciation lancing through every cell of her body, even the cooling touch of the stone beneath her gone to its rage. Her diaphragm constricted, and her lungs were unable to function as she fell into a silent, indefinite scream. Caenrya didn't know when it ended, *if* it would end. All she determined was the pain somewhat abating. Enough for her sight to return fuzzily.

Only the force of a will that had been tortured endlessly, been through a crucible and survived, allowed her body to pick itself up through the haze and stumble through the remaining alleyways. Caenrya appeared inebriated as she picked herself off the floor, from the walls, and countless times along her trek. Her consciousness floated in and out, the single drive to return to her apartment keeping her from collapsing into a sobbing mess.

She didn't know when she arrived. She didn't even know if she was alive when she entered her room, but the worst of the pain had reserved itself for that very moment.

Chapter Ten

HALDEN

It had been days since he'd seen Caenrya, and he hated to admit it, but he far more enjoyed the time sparring with her than trying to attempt to speak with Ryu after what his friend pulled in Riverside Square. Halden tried to address that incident afterward, and much to his irritation, Ryu sided with Owena simply because he didn't believe Caenrya should be there. His friend confessed she didn't deserve such harsh treatment, but at the same time, she *was* an outsider.

They hadn't spoken since.

After Halden's father had suspended his team from assignments due to Caenrya's presence, it opened his schedule to focus more on whatever he chose. Eirea had been thrilled to help him hone a new technique he'd been working on. However, it didn't help. His thoughts were all over the place.

Between Aya's ominous message about his father potentially being moved against, Ilias's apparent power struggle within their house, a world-ending prophecy hanging over his head, and the root of all their trouble being a threat to herself, Halden felt the tension. On the bright side, Caenrya had appeared in somewhat better spirits within the last few weeks. The lack of news on her sister's whereabouts didn't help, but she had made some progress with Aya.

She certainly appeared better.

Halden caught the thought circling his mind as he left the training field, Eirea heading back into the Citadel ahead of him to meet with her visiting family. He was partially disappointed she hadn't shown up when night fell. All right, flat-out disappointed. Their occasional banter brought a semblance of light into his otherwise dreary days, and he supposed it helped she wasn't like his peerage.

With Caenrya, there was a lack of judgment for social misgivings, and he was comfortable openly discussing a variety of matters pertaining to his life with her. From his reluctance to accept his own station—his family was the most prominent out of each house in the clan—to how much he detested the drama associated with rank and social structures, she didn't belittle his opinions in the least. She simply listened, nodding occasionally and asking questions. He held to his promise, avoiding probing questions into her past and being grateful whenever she offered up small pieces of her life.

From all Halden had gathered thus far, it was apparent her past was far worse than he'd imagined that first day. It showed in the darkness that appeared to cling to her skin, an eerie shadow that followed wherever she trailed. The way her eyes regarded others, a general lack of care and distrust that somehow faded when they practiced at the training grounds.

Perhaps he should have been thrown by it, similar to Ryu. The notion of being in the company of a seasoned killer wasn't out of the ordinary for their line of work; however, many of his class hadn't experienced anything of the warring lands, himself included. To have someone among them with a background of surviving their time within—no, with a legend born from their actions—was almost unheard of. Only seasoned jōnin had such tales, many coming out with scars not only across their bodies but their minds. These figures were legends. Every clan had a handful of shinobi that were known across the land for their incredible skill.

To Halden, Caenrya was no different.

She was but a girl raised in the absolute worst conditions, fighting tooth and nail for survival. Fighting with everything she had for her sister. Shinobi were always at the bidding of their liege, making anyone who upturned their nose at her a hypocrite.

Sure, she wasn't of their clan. But there was a time when everyone living on the continent was of one empire. Before they divided into five clans. It may have been close to two centuries since, but if the clans could come to such a grandiose decision, then why not accept one outsider now? After some time, Halden was certain Caenrya would fit in, especially once they retrieved her sister and brought down the underground fighting ring.

It wasn't until Halden kept beside the Koi River long enough that he noticed the unusual flurry of activity. It wasn't unlike that day weeks ago when the spirits were atypically active. This time, they darted across his walkway, sparrows swooping low around rooftops and butterflies shimmering around the burgundy-painted rail separating the citizens from the ledge below. His gut told him something had to be amiss.

The ancestors were agitated. The only time he could remember it being to *this* extent was the day he learned of his mother's passing.

A tabby cat brushed his leg, meowing loudly. Halden stared at it for a moment, its jade eyes making contact before it bolted in the direction of Wisteria Square.

Without thinking twice, Halden ran through a throng of chattering kids toward a second-floor balcony. He gathered his taiji, leaping onto it before scaling to the rooftop. His chest constricted as he sprinted across the sky, flying as he maneuvered around the square. Swinging down into the second-floor hallway, Halden's stomach dropped when he saw her door open wide, the room inside dark.

Were the ronin back?

His hand rested on the doorframe, his eyes searching. "Caenrya...?"

When he heard nothing in response, Halden dared to step in. Flicking on the lights, it took but a second for him to find her.

Curled in on herself, Caenrya lay unmoving beside the bathroom entrance. Both of her bracers were discarded beside her arms. He slid to his knees near her, checking to see if she was alert. When he found her eyes closed, he gently shook her shoulder to no avail. He spotted a near-imperceptible rise of her chest and felt a weak pulse on the side of her neck. That was when he saw the blood.

Deep gouges down the sides of her forearms, the material pushed messily up to her elbows. The first thought that crossed his mind was of the prophecy and what the fallout would be if Caenrya were to die before she could fulfill it. That line of thinking made him grit his teeth, disgusted at himself for that being his initial reaction. Was he any better than the others who shunned her each day? Or his father, who saw her as a means to an end?

Delaying not a moment more, Halden swept her unconscious form into his arms and bolted out of the apartment complex. He dodged over-curious onlookers, knowing to make for the healing clinic with all due haste. Along the way, he couldn't help but berate himself the entirety of the winding run to the center of the Citadel. His genuine concern for her well-being was present despite the intruding thought of the prophecy.

Not once did she open her eyes, nor did she give any signal that she was okay. There wasn't any discernible cause, and it ate at him as he burst through the double doorway of the four-tiered clinic.

"Help us!" Halden called out to a female manning the entryway desk.

When a team rolled out a gurney, he refused when two attendants attempted to remove her from his arms. Instead, he gently rested her on it, and the staff maneuvered to help secure her. Finding the desk attendant, he commanded, "Request the shogun's presence with haste."

They knew who Halden was. The message would speak for itself when it reached Ilias.

With a confirming nod, the lady darted toward the messenger ward. As the gurney rolled down the lengthy hallway, he filled in the little details he was aware of. Naturally, they proved to be next to nothing.

Once they arrived in a room, several nurses and a healer swarmed Caenrya. Halden was forced to watch beside the entryway as they took her vitals and searched for the cause of her condition.

Only healers and medical shinobi wielded taiji to expedite healing. Nurses were regular people who assisted them, and medical shinobi didn't work in clinic settings unless there was a staff shortage. The latter would accompany teams on deadly missions.

The healer mouthed a word over Caenrya, a palm hovering over her as he searched for the injury. It wasn't until the nurses turned her onto her side that Halden discovered overlooked streaks of blood on her uniform. When a nurse lifted it halfway upward at the healer's behest, Halden's blood ran cold.

A myriad of scars were laced in a rigid pattern across her lower back, a runic symbol tattooed along the center. Not a single one of the cuts had been clean. It was as if a serrated edge had been hacked across her skin. Not a single stitch aided in the healing of them. The puckered skin and ragged lines indicated they'd reopened several times over the course of healing.

And they were *layered*.

It made him nauseous to think of how this additional piece of information fit into her story and what else lurked in those shadows her eyes masked.

The team tended to her wounds; all the while, Caenrya remained unconscious. It wasn't long before the shogun stormed down the hall, a pensive expression fixated on his face. Halden shared what little he knew, and the lead nurse walked up to give his input.

"There appears to be a slave mark, shogun. But nothing on the outside that would indicate anything is amiss."

"Have you determined the cause of her state?" Ilias questioned, his steel-gray eyes surveying Caenrya.

"No, but—"

Halden noticed it first. "She's waking." Crossing the floor, he stood beside her with apprehension.

Groggily, Caenrya opened her eyes, the light overwhelming her at first. A nurse explained to her where she was. The whole time, a war waged on her face. Halden heard the shogun's request for the staff to leave and procure a healer to repair Caenrya's arms. The entire time he registered the growing expression of distress.

"I have to go," she abruptly said, wobbling as she inched herself toward the edge of the bed.

Barricading the exit with his body, Ilias shook his head. "Not until you divulge the truth of what's happening."

Halden could see the quick rise and fall of her chest, those blue-gold eyes not seeing what was in front of her. He slowly maneuvered his hands to hook a finger on either side of his pants pockets, prepared to move in if need be.

"I don't have time," she stressed, the tone of her voice erratic at best. "I've tried—tried to wait. I thought I could." The words tumbled out in a grand heap. "I lied to myself, but I'm out of time and have nothing to show for it. I have to leave *now*."

Only a grunt escaped her when Caenrya slumped to the ground, her knees giving the moment she attempted to stand. He offered a hand, one quickly swiped away with the back of hers. It made his chest tighten when he saw the water pooled along the edges of her eyes.

"Caenrya, tell us what's going on," Halden tried, acutely aware of his father's keen scrutinization behind him as he kneeled beside her.

"I'm a damned fool," she rasped. Her trembling fist rose as she slumped against the bedside. She slammed it down against the floorboards again and again, until he caught her wrist.

It happened so quickly. The transformation. Tears streamed down her face, anguish splitting her expression. Her hand went limp, every part of her shaking as her fists listlessly clenched, only to be forced open repeatedly.

Halden was familiar with that despair. It was the same one he descended into when he learned of his mother's passing. One where he didn't know if he'd survive the pain that glazed over reality. If he even wanted to try. Seeing it in Caenrya was like viewing himself all those years ago, and he did the only thing he remembered brought a near-insignificant shred of solace to his broken soul.

A hand was all he could give, and she flinched when it rested on her shoulder. Halden stayed there, waiting for her to be ready. Ilias was silent, his own face portraying a tenseness Halden knew had everything to do with whatever prophetic words the ancestors shared. He questioned if this was in any way affiliated, and such a huge part of him detested the notion of setting Caenrya up for all of it. Especially seeing her in such an unraveled way when she was always in such control of her every movement.

"I'm dying," she whispered at last, making his hand slacken in shock.

If that were true, then what of their fates? Were the ancestors wrong?

"How do you mean?" Ilias asked, the undercurrent in his voice giving away he, too, had the same fears as Halden.

A breath shuddered out of Caenrya. The back of her head rested on the bed's frame as she met the shogun's demanding sight. "The slave mark."

Bewilderment colored Ilias's words. "What about it?"

Her voice was low when she responded. "Ninjutsu was layered with it, making it impossible to leave the daimyo's side for long without it warning me to return."

It hit Halden then, a brutal swing to his face. And it made him curse at himself for being so blind, so damned oblivious during the entirety of the last few weeks.

"I've lived with it but never experienced the warning more than a handful of times whenever I'd be gone," she droned, the only sign of her pain a drying trail of tears down her cheeks. "I thought I had more time. I tried to stay, to learn, and to wait as you requested. But it seems it will kill me soon enough for not returning to the daimyo." The scores down her arms... the blood. "My time is but grains of sand left in the hourglass, and I have to leave to find my sister before it kills me."

All those erratic behaviors. The grimaces of pain. Halden was an absolute fool for not piecing it together. "Even if you somehow managed to find her before our own clan did, you'd never escape. You'd rather return to that life than have shared this with us earlier?" Halden remarked, a hint of anger lining his tone. Those lifeless eyes didn't bother glancing at him. "We could have used these weeks to find a solution. You could have trusted us."

Caenrya stared at the bandages placed on her arms. "I can't trust anyone. Everyone dies or betrays me." Her lips pressed together tightly. "And you have it all wrong. I'd rather die than return to that life, but I'll be damned if I don't give everything I have, everything I am, for Verina."

Chills traveled down his spine. The realization of just how shattered she was changed his perception. Changed everything. "You won't make it."

"Then I die."

Her strength must have returned. The moment she finished that final jab, Caenrya roughly pushed him away, wobbling before the shogun, who continued to block her path.

"There may be a way to remove the mark," Ilias said, his brows lowering above eyes that whirled with a complexity of thoughts. "We have shinobi who specialize in markings, who may be capable of removing such ninjutsu."

Caenrya froze for a heartbeat, daring to allow the comment to wash over her before her fists balled. For just a second, hope made her hesitate before she shook it off. "I'm going—"

"Give us a chance," Halden interrupted, rising and meeting her challenge head-on. "Despite whatever happened in the past, you can trust us. We only want to help."

Caenrya lazily smiled, the gesture as fake as the lie that they only wanted to help. It wasn't the truth—at least, not in full. His father had an agenda, and Halden had loyally acted the part of a pawn.

"My entire life has never been mine. Not the days before I fell under the daimyo's wing and not now." Cunning and calculation flashed across those unforgettable eyes. "Your shogun has manipulated me since the day I arrived, tasking you to follow in his stead. You all but admitted that."

Ilias's head sharply turned to him.

"How can I trust anyone when all I ever encounter are people who only use me until dregs remain?" Caenrya's face twisted to the shogun. Her head tilted, spilling golden locks across her shoulders. "If I disobey, who will you kill to force my actions? Or are you the type to bring out the lash to make me heel?"

Every word tore at Halden, so much so he was at a loss for any words he could utter to reassure her. How could he offer a single warrior against a foe of a hundred strong? His words were meaningless. No action was possible that could undo the torturous years she endured.

"Caenrya, I swear I have no ill intent," Ilias reassured her, his shoulders forcibly relaxing to maintain a calm composure. "But you won't have the opportunity to see that truth unless you stay and wait for us to bring aid."

Time froze when she lifted a hand halfway to performing the *zen* seal.

Halden cursed, knowing this would end terribly.

As if struck by lightning, Caenrya collapsed in a screaming heap. Her back arched as if she were stabbed where her mark lay. Halden caught her shoulders before her head hit the ground, struggling to hold her steady as the nurses swarmed in through the door Ilias flung open. Halden could only focus on the excruciation contorting her features, feeling more powerless than ever before.

The slave mark.

A nurse inserted a needle into her neck, the staff carefully lifting her limp body and placing it on the bed once more. The screams echoed in his ears as he rose, his body paralyzed and eyes glued to her unconscious form.

My time is limited, she had said.

Caenrya would never trust any of them, and Halden knew for a fact Ilias would never let her leave. The graphite restraints he requested only sealed that fact, twisting Halden's gut in disgust.

That material was wretched, one of the few that absorb taiji. If a person used ninjutsu while graphite touched their skin, it would absorb the energy before it could be used. It was painless and effective. Their researchers couldn't figure out why or how it did, nor what happened to the energy harvested. Even Arundels couldn't see any taiji in the material. It was an empty space to their inner third eye.

When Ilias left, ordering him to report the moment Caenrya awoke, Halden sat in a chair they brought in as they wheeled in various tools and equipment. IV lines were placed, restraints locked, and a healer speeded the recovery of the damage to her arms, all while Halden watched.

Eirea was summoned, and Ilias worked to find a specialist to examine her mark and provide further information. Forty minutes passed, and the shogun's elite shinobi—the black-armored oniwaban—pulled for security around the healing clinic's perimeter as his father retrieved a retired shinobi by the name of Trenus. A talented merchant who specialized in shinobi-tailored scroll work and binding ninjutsu. When the man arrived, Halden spared him a second's glance before returning to watch for any sign Caenrya was waking.

During her induced sleep, she was serene. Her skin had tanned in the weeks she'd been here. He'd noticed she preferred patches of sunlight whenever they trained. Her face always raised in the direction of the sun when they took a break.

Halden knew there would be Hel to pay when she awoke.

If.

The thought worried him.

Several more minutes passed before Trenus determined it far beyond his skill grade, Halden bracing his mouth against his propped-up fist. The air was growing grimmer by the second, both Eirea and Ryu standing near him as Ilias came to a decision.

"Cadigan," Ilias directed, his tone dire. "I must ask of you a favor."

With a brisk nod, Eirea said, "Name it, shogun, and it will be done."

"Locate Aegeon in Centra Village and bring him here. Don't give him specifics, only enough information so that he knows his shogun is requesting his services on an emergency basis." A pause. Then a reluctant continuance. "If he refuses, promise him on my behalf that I'll grant privileges for his niece to become my apprentice for a year."

"Yessir," Eirea confirmed.

The shogun's exhaustion leaked through his tone, the burden of the prophecy weighing him down. "Leave immediately. Time is of the essence. Notify no one outside of this room, as this must remain confidential. Can I entrust this assignment to you three?"

While Ryu and Eirea had no trouble answering—the former appearing excited at the prospect of a highly important mission—the anger in Halden's gut continued to smolder. The room stilled as he stared down his father, unfurling himself from the chair. "This—" he waved toward Caenrya. "Isn't right. How do you expect her to cooperate after this?"

The shogun pinched his face in warning, moving past him to the exit. "One step at a time, Halden. I do what must be done."

After his father cleared the room, Eirea waved for them to move out. Halting at the threshold, Halden guiltily shouldered a glance back at Caenrya. "I swear I'm going to get you out of this," he murmured, a muscle feathering along his jaw. "I'm going to prove that you can trust me."

With that, Halden made to follow his team. A promise almost as empty as those eyes of hers echoed in his ears, his own self-doubt creeping past any fortitude he could muster.

Chapter Eleven

Halden

They traveled at a breakneck pace, Ryu and him not talking as they bounded through clan territory. For an uncomfortable time, they didn't even glance at each other as they glided along the hillsides. Eirea was on full alert, either ignoring their ongoing feud or immersed in the assignment at hand. Her short blonde curls blew back from the force of their speed. Hours passed as such. The only thing keeping Halden from wanting to fall asleep on his feet was the knowledge Caenrya could die if he did.

Centra was a day's journey by horse or half a day with the speed of taiji backing their foot travel. By the time the sun's rays lifted on the horizon, they could make out the edge of the village in the shallow valley.

"I don't want her to die, yanno," Ryu grumbled across from him.

Eirea kept her sight onward. She didn't want to interfere.

"When did you start caring?" Halden shot back, the fatigue heightening his frustrations.

Scoffing, Ryu glared at him from the corner of his eye. "Really? You know me better than that."

Halden leveled a look at him, the brisk air brushing through his hair in the otherwise still forest. Up ahead, Eirea shook out a hand, almost as if she wanted to turn around and bash in their heads. He could recall many times when she grew irritated enough with the lot of them to knock their skulls together. It almost made him rub his temple at the thought.

"You could try rather than siding with Owena and the others."

Halden struck a nerve.

"If you had bothered to stick around more often rather than hiding away with your books and taijutsu training with Caenrya, maybe *you* would have realized that isn't what I have been doing," Ryu provoked, an accusatory finger jabbing in Halden's direction.

Eirea groaned in annoyance, turning her head toward Halden. "Ryu's girlfriend broke up with him." At Ryu's disgruntled exclamation, she faced him, adding, "Halden misses you." Redirecting her sight forward, her voice became deep with warning. "You two need to sort this. Any discord within the team can lead to consequences should we not be capable of working in unison."

Well. So much for not wanting to stick her nose into things.

But she was right. And how had he not known about Ryu's breakup?

"What happened with Hina?" Halden quietly asked, chastised by their commander.

Rightfully so. Neither he nor Ryu were in the right, especially if Ryu had been reeling all this time from the end of his two-year-long relationship. She was exceptionally skilled and dedicated. Having unlocked six of the inner gates and capable of achieving a high mastery in three of the five elements, Hina Saito was a credit to her otherwise minor house.

Once a shinobi mastered one element, their jiao balancing became tenfold more stubborn to alter to different percentages of yin and yang. Halden had only accomplished two of the five, though his vin provided an enormous advantage with close-range combat. Even more so for scouting purposes.

"Hina passed the jōnin assessments," he said.

Clarity smacked Halden in the face, and his thoughts focused back on Ryu's situation. It only meant one thing—Hina passing the assessments first before any of his class. And it wasn't good. "You broke up with her?" Halden's mind internally berated Ryu for his idiocy.

Maybe Halden was to blame for discounting all the times Ryu grumbled about being incapable of being inferior in his relationship. It resulted in him leaving her the moment it became concrete.

"My father cornered me after it happened, all but saying I should to propose to her that night so he could secure her power in our bloodline," Ryu chewed out, his face working as his mind recalled the situation. "He doesn't think I'm capable enough on my own and won't stop shoving it down my throat every spare moment he has that Ren is far superior to anything I could ever amount to."

Halden's fists clenched at that, his jaw locking as he imagined decking the daimyo of the Sahkara house.

"There was even talk of disownment should I not heed his demand. I had to break up with Hina to spare her from my house," Ryu explained.

It was one of the worst punishments bestowed on any of a great house to be left without a last name and forbidden to return home. That person would be considered lower than any hailing from a minor house thereafter. For his father to even hint at such a threat... Well, it made Halden's blood boil at the fundamental lack of decency.

"That's absurd," Halden swore, his head shaking as they moved to bound around the dip between two hills.

"Yeah" was all Ryu said.

Sunlight glimmered on their lacquer-dipped armor as they crested one hill. A tiny pang of guilt gnawed at Halden's gut for presuming poorly of his friend. Despite his father being a piss-poor excuse of one, however, he couldn't comprehend ending such a perfect relationship based on that. He understood it was to protect Hina, but if Ryu truly cared for her, he wouldn't leave her to the circling vultures who would be eager for the chance to claim her potential for future generations. Not to mention Hina wouldn't want anyone else.

Halden told him as much.

Ryu objected, "What am I supposed to do, then? My father would demand too much from her if we were to become engaged at some point in the future. Hina is far too kind to withstand his plotting and meddling, and I wouldn't want to subject her to any of it. It's not fair to her." He threw his hand up in frustration.

The trees became sparse as they passed the waking wildlife, an occasional cloud shadowing the land below. Glints of sunlight caught on the blues and silvers ahead on Eirea's armor plates, her eye bright as it honed in on Ryu.

"With all I've ever taught you, what is of the most importance?" she asked.

"Don't be smart with you," Ryu huffed, the corner of his mouth turning down further.

An arched brow. "I feel like that one goes over your head daily."

Halden almost snorted at Eirea's statement. There was none truer.

"Never give up. I'm going to be disappointed if you permit your father to dictate such things. Be your own center."

It was a lesson driven deep within their bones throughout the last four years of their instruction. In meditation, every shinobi focused on the center of their being for calmness, allowing for the evolution of their yin and yang capabilities. Every shinobi relied on it for everyday living before entering the dangerous fray of battle or developing new ninjutsu techniques.

When they were to face an adversary, an unknown who could otherwise throw off their psyche and lead to failure, they were to rely on the steel formed within themselves after years of training. For if they could overcome such grueling days, they had every ounce of ability to see themselves through the next chapter.

"Hina is stronger than you give her credit for," Halden added, watching Ryu's brooding face. His foot snapped a twig, pushing off against the grassy earth. A sign that Halden was losing focus of his foot placement and surroundings. Internally, he chided himself for such carelessness.

Creases folded Ryu's forehead. "Yeah, thanks. I'm aware and then some."

Halden gave him a sideways glance. "I meant her backbone. She'd do anything for you, including standing up to your father."

"I remember when Hina went out of her way to get your favorite sake on your eighteenth birthday," Eirea chimed in with a knowing smirk at Ryu's reddening face. "The love note was enough to make the whole Citadel whisper about the two of you."

"Shut up," Ryu demanded, his eyes unable to meet theirs. But his head slowly bobbed, and Halden knew they'd convinced him.

Eirea's lips twitched, her chin rising at the nearing village. "Aegeon's family house is located on the outskirts, just beyond the auditorium. We'll directly approach it, retrieve his services, and make haste for the Citadel."

Halden and Ryu nodded, the urgency of the assignment pressing down on the group. Surveying shinobi on guard around the looming wall acknowledged them as they entered through the wide streets of Centra, spring blooming across the various shades of flowers and overhanging trees. Dawn cast shadows on the waking village, civilians ambling to and from their residences and setting up shop for the day. A trio of children grew excited as they passed, their high-pitched squeals and enormous eyes trailing Team Cadigan.

Only a scant number of rays fought through the looming buildings. Windows slid open to a temperate morning above. Chatter picked up when they neared the auditorium, and the village news board was stapled with a handful of newspapers by the local daimyo's page—Daimyo Beynon's page, if Halden recalled correctly. The local daimyo was a distant relative of Aegeon Beynon, the man they searched for. The territory thrived under the house's rule, with many of the residents eager to serve the daimyo and his residing family.

Centra Village proved a model to others in the early days of his clan's establishment. There were thirteen daimyo overseeing the twenty-nine minor houses. With each daimyo representing their individual house and lording over a vast territory of minor houses, it eased the shogun's responsibilities. Those living in each territory paid their tithes to the daimyo, who tithed for the Citadel's coffers. Coffers his negligent father ruled over and divvied back into the system how he saw fit.

At least his father was good for something. However, his handling of the entire prophecy situation was poor. It brought no small amount of anger to Halden at Ilias's earlier actions, Halden's train of thought almost blinding him to the vegetable-burdened shopkeeper he ducked around.

Twice now, Halden had been too distracted to keep his attention on task. He was no better than a child first entering the academy with such mistakes.

Shinobi Creed: Eagle's Vigilance. Shinobi must be perpetually observant to detect hidden dangers and openings for opportunities, Halden chided himself.

He straightened his armor as they walked into a narrow alleyway, lanterns turning the walls a shade of ruby. Artful imagery was painted on both sides, ranging from a cove of cherry blossoms to the sea separating from the rising tangerines and roses of the sun. At the end of the corridor sat an inlaid, single white doorway, elegant scrollwork embedded in sweeping patterns across the otherwise plain door. To Halden, it was clear the owner of the residence took great pride in his works of art, each sweep of the brush across the thick wood made by a polished and precise hand.

Taking positions on each flank of Eirea, Ryu and Halden stood statuesque as their commander's fist struck the door thrice before lowering. A prickling sensation struck just below the nape of his neck, and his gaze swerved toward the looming rooftops.

From the day he was born, his father had grand aspirations for his shinobi career. Toys a normal child might enjoy were replaced with kunai and any average sport with taijutsu training. While his mother had tempered his father's expectations, Halden wouldn't be amiss to say his skills were beyond that of his peerage.

He disdained the thought, but it was the truth.

So, when those hairs rose below his hairline, and his hand lowered to a tool pouch, Halden was prepared to engage any attacker. His forehead creased as he surveyed the empty rooftops, finding nothing but the shimmer of a passing spirit. Looking back at his team, no one had any reaction, carrying on as normal when the door hinges creaked open.

Maybe it was just the wind. Yet, his skin continued to prickle.

A spectacle-eyed man hunched over a palette of paint, a residue of varying hues splattered across his mismatched clothing. He appeared to lose balance on the bamboo tray momentarily, straightening with an irked expression.

"Yes?" Aegeon snipped, a thin smear of yellow bunching in his forehead creases.

With a fist over her heart, Eirea dipped her head in respect before responding, "I am Commander Cadigan, a shinobi under the direct authority of the shogun himself. Aegeon Beynon, your services are requested by Shogun Arundel with all due haste. It is a matter of grave importance."

The middle-aged man impatiently gestured for the commander to proceed.

"I'm not at liberty to discuss specifics," she said, "as the situation has been deemed high clearance."

Her tone took on a no-nonsense edge with that last sentence, the man giving them one appraising glance before turning into the wide gallery of artwork strewn across walls and propped against sporadically placed marble pillars. The floor was a mazed mess, almost as if the painter had reconstructed the room itself to be organized into a display of art.

If the art was symbolizing chaos, of course.

Mirrors and statues hung from ceilings and popped out from the marble. The sound of their boots echoed in a bizarre manner as the team trailed to where the artist rested his palette. Wiping his hands haphazardly across his outer robe, Aegeon shrewdly assessed Eirea.

"As of this moment, I'm occupied with a piece commissioned by Daimyo Beynon himself. Leaving a client empty-handed is awfully irresponsible for any duration of time, specifically for one esteemed within the community." A cunning glint crossed his dark eyes as his head tilted toward the massive portrait of a decorated man.

Eirea's demeanor subtly changed, the tell obvious to Halden and Ryu. The latter gave him a pointed wink, the words between them unnecessary. It was the way her lips twitched into her trademark smile, the way her chin rose so her eye peered *just* in between friendly and outright hostile at the artist.

Oh, man.

Their commander could be an absolute menace. Even Aegeon appeared off-kilter at the reaction. By no means was it expected, nor one he was accustomed to.

"The shogun of our clan has explicitly demanded your attendance in the Citadel. Should you defy such an order..." The artist's hand twitched. "Your daimyo would be understanding of the delay in his commission." Eirea's smile grew. "Likely not if the shogun has to summon him to inquire about repercussions one of his subjects must face."

The man's face blanched enough for Halden to glean Eirea's words had struck through the snake's attempt at weaseling high rewards.

"You'll be compensated justly for your services and returned as promptly as manageable," she informed him.

Discarding his robe with a wary glare, he replied, "I'll need time to sort my business. It'd be in poor taste if—"

With the speed of a bolt of lightning, Eirea drew a kunai from her weapons pouch and swiveled. Halden tracked the sharp point to a distant corner of the gallery. A pale, scarred hand snatched hers with ease. Spider-like, the figure moved around a column, smirking at the metal now being twirled in his hand.

"I was wondering when you'd make your appearance," Eirea said, her eye assessing the situation as her feet steadily moved between the man and the artist.

Halden and Ryu moved in unison, taking positions on either side of the artist. With a whisper of air, Halden activated his vin, searching the perimeter for additional threats.

Leaning casually against the marble, the tall intruder pocketed the weapon in his burgundy merchant robe, the glint of metal peeking from a fold underneath. Halden only saw the taiji of average citizens milling about nearby, returning his full attention to the man and facing him.

Only then did Halden realize who stood before him.

And it eradicated any sense of logic.

"You," Halden whispered, cold burning through his veins. It was surreal—the feeling of being disconnected from his own body. His feet were leaden, his arms impossible to move. He never expected this moment to come, never knew what he'd go through when he faced his mother's killer.

Silver hair fell to his shoulders, and sharp ears peaked on either side. Soulless, fear-inspiring eyes of the lightest blue stared at him, and for a second, the set of his face reminded him vaguely of Caenrya's mask. It was then that it sank into his bones. That girl was associated with this demon and even carried his mannerisms. She was *raised* by this man and slaughtered people with this man. A man who didn't appear much older than them.

What if she was there when this ronin murdered Halden's mother and had lied?

"Halden Arundel," Valen said, a contemplative undertone lining his words. His name. "I'll never forget that encounter with Enya Arundel. She had, perhaps, one of the most glorious deaths I've ever carried out. How her despair and anguish rose to the surface at her end was... breathtaking."

Before he could stop himself, Halden's face twisted into a snarl. His control snapped, and his body was shaking with rage. A single foot raised to make forward before a crucial element of his training froze him in his tracks.

The ronin realized his thoughts simultaneously. His perfectly straight teeth gleamed as the fly tumbled into his web. His eyes shone with vicious delight. Before Halden could react, though, three additional ronin stepped from different pillars, alarmingly close to where he currently stood.

How did I not see them with my vin? Ice ran down his spine.

Clad in black, they pulled katanas from hip-fixated sheaths. They remained still, their eyes trained on him as several more burst from the entryway behind him. Eirea gave the signal to attack. Ryu hopped beside Eirea, fending off the attackers with swings of his kusarigama. The blade of Eirea's katana matched another, but her form was sloppier than usual.

Her eye, Halden realized.

His commander had but weeks to adjust to the major alteration to her sight, not enough time to change her techniques and adapt to this combat level. Beside her, Ryu was struggling to spar against two ronin. He swung the chain wide to catch one's blade with the curved edge of his own and slowly spun the ball of the other to change the trajectory of a second katana.

The three beside Halden were still, waiting for the moment he turned his back to aid his team. Eirea shouted words muffled by the buzz in his ears, and Aegeon slowly inched further back until the wall brushed against him.

Should Halden wait any longer, his team could fall. However, if he neglected the artist, Caenrya would certainly die, and the prophecy would doom them all anyway.

Before Halden could decide, one of the ronin turned toward the artist, forcing Halden to leap after him. Another ronin moved to block him. Halden drew his sai and forcefully jabbed one into the man's abdomen. The ronin stumbled back into a pillar, shocked at the swift attack. Spinning on his heel, Halden wove the hand sign for water, *toh*, the Elvish words *vodná vlna* relaying in his mind as a wave of water blasted into the ronin chasing after the artist.

A smack was heard as the ronin went down, knocking him unconscious with surprising ease. The third ronin leaped on him, making Halden roll as the attacker fought to raise a kunai to Halden's neck. Flipping his legs out from under the ronin, he made to kick just as the ronin twisted out of his reach.

The second ronin stumbled from his pillar, blood dripping on the white tiles below as he joined the fray. Halden spun upward, sweeping the man back to the ground. His sai sang forward to meet the first ronin's kunai, his second sai slipping low to score across plated armor. With his next movement, Halden flipped through the air. He threw one sai into the exposed foot of the second ronin, and the man screeched. At the same time, Halden threw his second sai into the path of his other attacker's kunai. His second sai nailed the kunai into a painting across the room.

Across from him, Ryu skidded backward from a harsh blow barely blocked by the scythe-like portion of his weapons. His other attacker kicked him backward into the pathway of Eirea's movement. His commander had forced her enemy into a precarious position, and her arm arched for the killing blow. A blow that impaled Ryu directly in the chest between silk cords and two of the ribs that protected his heart.

Time went still as Eirea's face grew horrified. Her pupil fell lifelessly onto the ground beneath her. Her original target steadied himself, a cold bark of laughter escaping his lips as crimson pooled beneath Halden's teammate. Never once had Halden's commander faltered or missed a beat in training or combat. There was a reason his father enlisted her to command Team Cadigan from his own private forces.

Eirea was gifted in more than combat. Her intelligence permitted her to remain several steps ahead of her opponent at all times. It was a gift many shinobi only maintained rather than excelled at, prompting the shogun to promote her within his oniwaban at a young age as a strategist. More so, she was fiercely loyal, unshakable in the worst circumstances.

To see her leave an opening cracked something deep within his chest. The outcome of this predicament only left one path.

Steel cut deeply across her leg, white showing beneath the cut musculature as she crumbled to the ground with a cry.

They were going to fall here.

Fight, his subconscious ordered him. *Fell as many as you can, and maybe, just maybe, it will make a difference.*

Halden tore his sight from Ryu's glazed eyes, the pale, blood-splattered expression of shock forever ingrained into Halden's mind. With a roar of pain and fury, he directed his palms to the hurt ronin charging him again. Halden wove around the man with swift strikes, hitting each taiji point his vin lit up to block his attacker's energy. Pulling a shuriken from his belt, a steel star-like weapon, Halden tucked it between his fist before directing a final punch into the man's sternum. A crack resonated through his bones.

A ronin kicked Ryu's lifeless form out of spite. Eirea's limp leg dragged as she stood her final ground against impossible odds.

Nothing in his training prepared Halden for such anguish. His jaw shook as he clenched it. He faced the final ronin circling him. What was the point of all of this? Was every shinobi's fate sealed with a brutal ending?

They were sheep herded with the mentality of laying their lives down for their clan. They were taught emotion had no place on a battlefield. That it was *honorable* and *just* to die protecting the lives of others. What did his clan do for him that deserved such devotion and sacrifice? His entire team would be annihilated here, dooming Caenrya and his clan to some elusive prophecy. Why should he fight this outcome any longer?

His clan deserved to be wiped off the face of the earth for living in luxury and safety, only gained through the culling of their own people.

But why was he thinking such things?

Halden shook his head, his own thoughts warring with themselves.

Fight. Don't give in, that voice in his mind coaxed again.

Before his hand could inch toward his next shuriken, Valen formed a hand seal, resulting in a fierce gale of wind that thrust Halden airborne. Right into a column several feet behind him. Roaring wind made movement impossible. His entire body was glued to the marble from the force of it. Tears whipped from his squinched eyes as he struggled to free himself.

The building shuddered as if recoiling from the brutality. Artwork, statues, and tools flurried into the far corner as if a tornado had struck. Throughout it all, the ronin kept the wind streaming forward, Valen unfazed where he stood. Such an amused expression remained out of place on the ronin, something in the back of Halden's mind prodding him at the thought. With a word, the wind around Halden materialized into spiked chains. Agony ripped across his skin where it pierced him against the column.

There was a noise in the back of the gallery, drawing his attention to where Eirea fell beneath a katana propelled through her chest.

That voice demanded again that he fight and ignore the other sound dulled to his ears that echoed in the gallery. Halden struggled against the chains pinning him in place, cutting into his skin further when he thrashed. Pain throbbed in his head, and his thoughts scrambled as basic reason was discounted by his subconscious.

Nothing made sense.

Something was off.

This couldn't be reality.

"But it is," Valen whispered, the words carried to his ears clearer than the finishing whoosh of breath from Eirea's lips as she hunched over the steel. "Your weakness is unparalleled. Your capacity for surviving in this world is limited by the true players lurking in the darkness."

Valen removed his burgundy robe, leaving only trousers on his pale, lean form. Darkness whirled around the tattoos crawling across his torso, several depictions of intricate orbs oozing a black mist ingrained into his skin. Halden's mind recoiled. The voice that once propelled him faded to the truth of what was about to happen. He was useless. Fighting was pointless. Death approached him on bare, tattooed feet.

"You all are but mice in a field of circling hawks, unaware of the predators lurking in your midst. I'm not in the habit of consorting with such disappointing company, but even I must confess that my excitement is getting the best of me. Your people are stunningly ignorant of what transpires in the warring lands." Valen chuckled, his head shaking gently from side to side. "This has been years in the making, a beautiful crescendo that's nearing the apex note."

The ronin whipped a kunai from a pocket. The remaining gusts of wind separated around him as if he were in the eye of the storm. Drawing it close to Halden's face, Valen continued, "You know, I used to do this very thing with your new friend. My protégé." The sharp point dragged along his jawline, drawing a thin line of blood and an involuntary flinch from Halden. "I'd spend hours ensuring she'd hold up against torture. Eventually, I was encouraged by the lack of response to become innovative with my creative methods to win."

The kunai suddenly drew back, driving deep into his left shoulder. The cords in Halden's neck strained against the blinding pain and his resolve not to flinch. After the weapon withdrew from his shoulder with a sickening noise, it reburied itself in his gut, and Halden couldn't keep the grunt from escaping. The pain was worse than any before, and it had his vision darkening at the edges.

"I'm going to kill you," Halden growled, his rage bringing forth the words he knew deep inside he wasn't capable of carrying out. "Even if it's in the afterlife, I swear I will spend every second hunting your soul into oblivion." His words were raspy, but he forced the rest out. "If this is my death, then it's also your curse."

An oath had power with the spirits overseeing it. No matter the wording, the intention left a mark on the target for any who were superstitious. It wasn't sensible, he knew. But his team had been slain behind him in such a brutal way, and this man... this man has caused Halden and his father anguish for years. He had killed his mother and had tortured Caenrya. If the spirits could lend their aid to tormenting him, then it was a curse Halden wouldn't hesitate to invoke.

He struck some nerve, that smirk of Valen's lowering enough for him to notice.

"By the time we are done here, little pawn..." Halden's breath caught at that word, and Valen's smirk returned as he acknowledged the deep-rooted fear resting in the recesses of his brain. "Your mind will be fragmented beyond repair, and I fear your soul won't recognize the afterlife."

Slicing, cutting, jabbing... Hours transpired as the kunai carved every inch of him. Halden couldn't remember when his screams started nor when Valen's laughter tuned out.

CHAPTER TWELVE

CAENRYA

A void of writhing lava encircled her. Pain became a constant she couldn't get rid of. Caenrya discovered new shades of suffering that she'd never experienced before at a level that drove her insane in the crimson afterlife she floated through. She dimly recalled those final moments before it consumed her mind, an excruciating burn crawling through every cell of her body as she tumbled into eternity.

It had crushed Caenrya deeper than she'd ever admit when the shogun turned on her.

Perhaps Valen was right all those years ago when he instilled the lesson she couldn't count on others. The only constants in her life were Verina, their overlords, and the unyielding fact they'd never let Caenrya escape them.

Even when it meant she'd die instead.

Some part of her waited for Valen to come and retrieve her from the deepest pits of Hel, ones always created by him. It was another constant in her life, one where a bleak situation would finally make her give up, and he'd miraculously save her at the last second. It was potentially the worst form of abuse Caenrya could ever imagine, her sanity and body pushed beyond any natural limitation.

What that yielded, she wasn't sure.

Something infinitely broken, doomed to be shattered, only to be reformed in a new shape chosen by her captors. There had been a time when Valen recognized that she expected this, acknowledging that she was to rely only on him. It was a leash whose collar she allowed slipped over her neck, as it meant fighting another day for Verina.

Pain was a part of her, recognized as easily by her soul as her voice to her ears.

This clan... they'd never understand in their blissful ignorance. They had a bubble of safety where children grew up with love, care, and other garbage that turned their eyes from the truth of the world.

And it wasn't pretty.

Though for the first time in her life, Caenrya allowed a sliver of hope to wrap around her blackened heart. A semblance of calm had convinced her to ignore the destiny of death lingering about her. In reality, the only outcome of her presence here was death by the slave mark. The captured ronin who attempted to smuggle her back to Shikei weeks ago provided nothing of import, and her training thus far amounted to a single word passed between minds. Sure, her taijutsu had improved since applying herself with Cadigan and Halden, but that would never be enough to take on the daimyo or Valen. But that damned hope and need for something more kept her in the Citadel, even to a fruitless end.

The dream wasn't worth this outcome.

So Caenrya waited as her body tore apart, cell by cell. Waited for Valen to arrive or for death to claim her.

Chapter Thirteen

Halden

Halden opened his eyes, his head hung low. Noises echoed in the room, and his mind was unable to process any one thing. He wasn't sure where he was or how he was able to even think after all that transpired. Slowly, his eyes focused on his feet below, taking in the familiar chain wrapping his body to a pillar.

It took an absurd effort, but sluggishly, he inched his head upward to take in his surroundings. What Halden saw almost made him cry in despair.

"Not again," he got out through clenched teeth, his heart squeezing in his chest.

Halden didn't comprehend what repeating loop of Hel he was in, but more than anything, he wanted it *over*. On the floor again was Eirea, hunched over her knee before him. The artist was splayed across the destroyed floor. Unconscious or dead, Halden didn't know. And Ryu... Ryu was propped against a cracked pillar. Blood poured from a wound in his abdomen, and his armor was broken over his chest.

As for Valen, his amused face remained beside that pillar he'd first appeared by all that time ago. Almost as if he'd never moved.

"I can't..." Halden trailed off, his teeth chattering too hard for words to form.

A shushing noise echoed across the gallery floor, and the ronin's hand tapped the dragon's maw across his cheekbone. "You undoubtedly gave an ounce of fight after all, but now rest knowing your attempts were for naught."

More than anything, Halden wanted that escape of rest. A dreamless slumber to forget all that happened.

"Halden." A breathless voice sounded close by, and his face turned toward it.

An eye pinned Halden's fragmented gaze. Her shoulders heaved as she rose from the ground. Not a single injury had been laid on his commander, though exhaustion was evident in her tense features.

It made him question everything.

From the grimace Ryu's face now had to the lack of enemies in the gallery. Not even a scratch marred Halden. Everything was physically intact. Mentally, he struggled to reconcile what he saw versus all that happened.

"Don't look into his eyes again. You were under Kū ninjutsu," Eirea said, her words breathy.

Mind ninjutsu.

Everything he had experienced... was fake. Valen manipulated everything Halden perceived. He had realized the danger he was in the moment his eyes connected with Valen earlier, but everything thereafter had been too real to question.

Then the wind that buckled him to the pillar and the chains thereafter were Eirea's doing. The ronin he attacked was his own team. He confirmed it with a dart of his eyes. Water was pooled around the artist's body, silk ties shorn on Eirea's armor. But what really tore at him was the crack in Ryu's plate above his sternum and the deep wound in his gut.

A soft laugh sounded from the ronin. "It was but a minor trick made all too easy by his willingness to cooperate."

I did this. Halden could never forgive himself for turning on them, for he was too weak to realize the magnitude of the illusion placed on him and to break from it.

"Don't listen to him, Halden," Eirea grunted, her hands falling into the *zen* seal. "He's on a completely different level than any given rank. What I need from you is to recover Ryu and Aegeon. Fall back to where you must go to carry out our mission."

Just as his mother had ordered when confronted by Valen...

Eirea released the chains binding him in place.

He swallowed hard at that. "I won't leave you," Halden said, shaking his head in denial.

He couldn't. Wouldn't.

Looking at his commander, Halden could have sworn his chest was caving in. Eirea's steel will shone through her demeanor, and her eye was unrelenting despite the certain outcome her request would end in. She smiled at him, such a reassuring one that he had to grit his teeth to keep from tearing up. Even then, Eirea was putting them before herself. Yes, that was the duty of a commander, but it went beyond that.

Was this how his mother's team felt when she forced them to leave?

Eirea cared for them like family. She guided them to be shinobi, who excelled within their ranks but were more focused on maintaining the values that made their clan one of the greatest. She didn't order them to leave without ensuring to humanize it, to make certain that Halden knew this was her choice and she cared about their survival. It wasn't some cold demand that forced him to be resentful.

It made him feel unworthy.

Without a word, Eirea faced her opponent, and her shoulders squared against him. She kept her eye lower than his to avoid his mind techniques. "When have you known me to fail, Halden?" she asked, her hands holding the *zen* seal active as her mind uttered a complex string of words.

Light blazed through the destroyed gallery, a golden prism seen encircling the unflinching ronin when it died down. Halden had witnessed Eirea's barrier ability in the past, but nothing on the scale he now witnessed. Runes were etched into each corner, almost as if they were the thread that sealed every thick piece together. Raw power emanated from it, instinctively propelling him away. He'd never managed to break one in the past, and those were simple, translucent planes she'd summoned for their training.

Raising his chin, Halden put aside his thoughts and conflicting emotions to dash across the blackened and chipped floor. Evidence that a battle unfurled between the commander and ronin when he was unconscious. Though what it said that Valen hadn't moved an inch during it, Halden didn't want to know.

"Rest assured, I have no intentions to further pursue action against anyone of your group at the moment," Valen insisted, watching uninterestedly as the flesh of a finger sizzled when contacting the barrier.

"You don't have much of a choice," Ryu grimly muttered, rising with Halden's aid.

The ronin's mouth slowly curved into a grin in response.

Eirea's eyes narrowed a hair at Valen as she said to her team, "Leave now. Local shinobi should be en route and arriving soon for backup. I need you two to carry on with the mission."

Ryu waved him along, managing his footing fine without help. Turning toward the artist, Halden moved to protect his stout frame. All the while, his thoughts threatened to overwhelm his mind, the world dreamlike around him.

"I'll take my leave first if you don't mind," Valen said, his body dematerializing.

Wide-eyed, Halden pulled a shuriken out, scanning the gallery with his back to the scorched wall. Identically, Ryu retrieved his kusarigama, moving to guard the artist beside him. Carefully, Eirea surveyed the area. She searched for any distortion, any sound that might give away his position.

Within the next blink, Valen rematerialized beside the exit. His hands rested within the pockets of a robe he likely stole off a victim on his way there. "After all, I have an old acquaintance to reconnect with before she attempts to die on me." His eyes burned at Halden, chilling amusement palpable in the air. "I must express my gratitude for your participation in my little game. You were splendid to play with. I'd like to believe I have learned much from this."

Words wouldn't come to Halden, shame stealing them.

"You won't reach her," Eirea promised, her back straightening.

The ronin only gave that same smile as last time, the meaning clear to all present. As he turned his back—yet another bold move—Eirea released the barrier she vainly erected.

"Why let us live?" she called out, her stance poised with a false calm. Every second Eirea could stall was another second closer to the arrival of backup.

Without hesitation, Valen answered, "One could say I enjoy the hunt as much as the kill."

Chills ran down Halden's spine at that.

"Not to say, of course, that I've also been ordered to behave for the time being," Valen finished.

Whoever could control such a monstrous being... it struck true fear into Halden's heart.

"You sure like to hear yourself talk," Ryu spat out, raising a kusarigama in the ronin's direction.

Valen's thin lips curved further. "Your lack of tact may be your demise. Take care with your words, as little Halden there is frightened enough for the both of you. He hopes for my leave."

Self-loathing filled Halden at the truth in that statement. He turned his head away from his teammates.

"Give my regards to the shogun." With that, Valen whistled a merry tune and stepped out of the doorway, not even bothering to close it.

Everything Halden had remaining gave at that moment. He put his full weight against the wall, a tremor shaking his body. His calloused hands covered the sides of his head as if they could block out the demon. A feeble part of himself was fervently grateful for Valen's restraint, and that they wouldn't spend a further second in his company.

What Halden had done and what pain he'd endured, there was no coming back from that.

Hours of torture, only to be healed and cut up again. Skinned, torn apart, healed, and then enduring it all over again. It wasn't real, but in those hours, it was everything.

He struggled to breathe.

"Leave me behind," Halden croaked out, his eyes squeezed as shut as he could force them. "I'll explain the situation to Daimyo Beynon. Aegeon must be presented to the shogun without delay, and I'll only hold us up."

Before he could continue, a strong hand gripped his shoulder. That snapped Halden's eyes wide open. His body lurched from the contact as he raised a shaking hand to where Ryu's was a moment before. It made Halden want to crawl into a corner. How a *hand* could cause that much terror...

Such frustration and rage overcame him. He twisted to punch the marbled wall with as much force as he could muster. The pain barely registered in a body that still echoed with the agony of Valen's fake reality.

"Please." His forehead rested on the chilled stone. He couldn't meet their eyes.

A heavy silence hung between them.

Eirea contemplated her options. Finally, she said, "Ryu, remain back with Halden. Send an eagle to the shogun. Inform him of the ronin's potential threat and to tighten security. Once you've discussed the necessities with the local daimyo, seek healing and rest here for the night. You both need it before trekking back to the Citadel."

"The ronin is still out there going after Caenrya and may attempt another attack on you," Ryu protested, concerned for their commander's well-being.

Eirea shouldered Aegeon, sighing tiredly. "He's a problem for another day. For this one, he's retreated from attacking us. I'm not a betting person, but I'd wager his words were part of his ploy to agitate us." Flicking her eye on Ryu, she continued, "My order stands. Stick together and return tomorrow. Shogun Arundel will send a team to escort the two of you in the unlikely event of his return." She began making for the exit, her voice growing a notch softer. "Look after each other. All that matters is that we've made it this far, and the end is in sight. All will be fine this go around."

That reassurance used to bring a modicum of solace to Halden, but this time, the words fell flat to his ears. How he'd redeem himself and ever be able to face that man again he couldn't imagine.

Not even a minute passed after Eirea's leave when the daimyo's shinobi arrived to investigate the disturbance. Ryu performed the debriefing in his stead, and the two of them were escorted to the daimyo's residence for temporary housing after being seen by a healer. They were graciously given a guest room in the quarters reserved for visitors, an honor reserved for the daimyo's own shinobi or those he held in esteem.

Likely, it was due to the prestige Halden and Ryu's last names carried, and the tiny fact that his father was the shogun. Halden attempted the polite talk and gratitude expected of him and made for sleep at the first opportunity he could escape.

Ryu made true to his promise with Eirea, sticking close to Halden's side until the moment they slipped into two rather large separate futons. The sheets were of fine quality, smoother than his own. Chatter echoed below their third-story room, and the village activity slowly ebbed in the afternoon lull. A gurgle sounded from his stomach, but Halden wasn't able to get much down despite the chef's appetizing display of food.

Twenty minutes passed where they lay mutely, neither talking or attempting given the fitful sleep that would follow. It wasn't until Halden heard the rustle of sheets that one of them broke that seal of silence.

"We heard you, yanno." Ryu hesitated, fidgeting with one of the several pillows stacked beneath his head. "When you were under the ninjutsu." Another heavy pause, and when Halden didn't speak, Ryu asked, "What... what happened?"

There was only one other occasion in Halden's life when he was burdened with such terrible emotions, and that was after his mother had been killed in combat. In a sense, this had felt worse. Halden almost killed

Ryu had it not been for the armor shielding the worst of his attacks. Then, there was the knowledge they had heard him being picked apart, piece by piece, by that monster.

What pride did he have after that? There wasn't any to claim. Not for his failure and surely not for his weakness. During those infinite minutes of torture, Halden would have given anything for it to end. He would have given any secret, any part of himself, to stop that kunai from peeling the skin from his body.

All Halden said, however, was, "Hel happened."

Ryu's mouth formed more words, but Halden's ears were deaf to them, his mind reliving every single movement of that weapon against him. The expression of sickening satisfaction on that demon's face. Whereas Ryu eventually found sleep, Halden's mind spared no vicious punch against his soul.

Chapter Fourteen

CAENRYA

Reality and the afterlife mixed without discretion. At times, Caenrya swore she overheard conversations between the shogun and others, but other instances were far more unbelievable when she teetered into the world of the dead. During those dispersed times, she crossed paths with the ancestors, many sharing expressions of such sorrow that Caenrya simply could not bear it any longer. She'd plead for answers, but always to no avail. They'd always walk away.

In between the real and the dead, everything was excruciating. Every nerve flared with pain. Her body was being torn to shreds with nauseating slowness. Now, though, she could feel the pull of the afterlife beckoning her being. It was subtle, but Caenrya answered it willingly, as it always brought a semblance of a reprieve for her fracturing mind.

A part of her wondered if she was going mad or if this was the punishment she was destined to endure once she had left the world of the living.

The pull intensified, and mist cleared as Caenrya heaved onto a floor of growing grass. The contents of her stomach spilled, and the familiar warmth of the sun found her trembling back. A gentle breeze wafted away the smell, carrying hints of lavender and the sound of lapping water growing from an emerging lake nearby.

Gasping, Caenrya rolled to her side, her energy spent and head reeling. Eagles soared high above in the cloudless sky, the blades of grass tickling her cheek when she turned her head to a figure close by.

A woman this time, eyes of blue and hair that shone the brightest of brown. What caught Caenrya's attention, though, was the smile she wore instead of the pity others had glanced at her with. When the lady offered a graceful hand, Caenrya accepted it, rising to stand beside the sapphire-clad woman. The gauzy material drifted gently in the breeze, those piercing eyes searching for something in Caenrya.

Such peace resonated from within the woman that even Caenrya couldn't deny she became lighter than she had in... well, ever.

Caenrya didn't expect an answer but wanted to try again. "Why am I here?"

"To give you time to heal." The voice was song-like, a rich harmony of tones that were entrancing. "To save you from losing yourself completely."

Rocking back on her heels, Caenrya searched around at what could only be the ancestors' world. "My time there is over, is it not?" she quietly asked, taking in the lush beauty of her surroundings.

"Do you want it to be at its end?" the beautiful voice asked gently.

Caenrya nodded. Here, she knew such relief knowing her problems lay behind in the waking world and that there wasn't a single obligation she owed. Here, she knew she'd be content spending her days resting beside the crystal-clear water, observing and perhaps exploring forever.

The woman's hand grasped one of her own, warmth easing the rest of the lingering needle-like pains plaguing her body. "There is much left for you to accomplish. Your purpose lies in the world of the living. Your path is barely beginning to unfold."

"I can't keep going," Caenrya stressed, her brows pinching together. Releasing the hand, she took a distrustful step back. "Haven't I suffered enough?"

The woman's smile dimmed, and her eyes reflected that of the countless others Caenrya had seen. "There lies more ahead. And worse, I'm afraid."

Snorting, Caenrya crossed her arms. "You aren't doing a fantastic job at convincing me to return." Her stomach recoiled at the woman's words.

The serene expression returned once more, and her gaze was heavy with understanding. "Many would have already shirked from your fate, and none would continue past the point you have since borne."

"I think you need a revision to this pep talk," Caenrya huffed, turning toward the now-setting sun. The reflection was captivating as it glistened across the enormous lake, the hues far more intricate in this world than hers.

Walking forward, the woman paused when her back was to Caenrya. "You are the only one who can save our people and the only one who can bear the consequences of such responsibility without breaking."

Caenrya glared at the back of her head. That peace she found here was becoming rather allusive.

"Your heritage—"

"Do not," Caenrya growled, her fists trembling at the words that were to be uttered.

"As you wish," the woman hummed, turning her face to meet Caenrya's. "Then you acknowledge what is to come."

Lifting her chin, Caenrya rebutted, "I deny it. My only wish is to rescue my sister."

The woman's eyes switched between Caenrya's own, something infinitely clever and intuitive deep within the ancestor's gaze. "You aren't one to shirk your duty. I believe even you will be surprised to discover what lies within this." A hand rested over her heart. "Take assurance that your path isn't one tread within the dark, but rather, one that will lead to much of which you crave."

"I crave nothing but to remain here," Caenrya shot back, an arm gesturing to the surrounding wilderness. "Why can't I be left *alone*?" Such penetrating sadness enveloped that last word that even Caenrya couldn't deny the tiny part of her that recognized it wasn't her time.

"The balance of the world has been shifted. Nature requires balance, and the living have breached into forbidden places," the woman softly explained, her hands clasped in front. "I plead with you to give more. To suffer more. For if you decide not to, all is lost."

A scoff escaped her, and Caenrya had to restrain herself from releasing her temper. "Instead of being vague, why don't you start with being straightforward and explaining whatever big, bad people are doing that is supposedly causing the world to end?"

The woman only shared a sad smile. "I am prohibited."

"Naturally." Caenrya strode away from the disappointment, kneeling beside the temperate water. Her hand sent minuscule swells through a small radius, a curious beta fish nearing it. "Why would no one else here want to speak with me? Is my presence that tainted?" Much of her felt that way, as if she didn't belong or deserve such a resolution for her soul. However, she'd never admit that to this woman.

"When the living cross the thin veil between our worlds, only one of us may speak with the soul. Should they have uttered a word, I wouldn't have been able to speak with you."

Furrowing her brows, Caenrya stared over her shoulder. "Don't you all know the same things?" she mocked, eyes rolling at the idiocy of some ridiculous rule. "Why would it be important for you, in particular, to speak with me?"

"Yes and no, but that is an answer I have not the time to deliver," the woman said, sitting beside Caenrya at the edge of the waterline. "As for why me, I volunteered."

Caenrya stared harder, not understanding why she would.

"You see, I have a particular interest in the girl my son is frequently around," she said, a twinkle lighting up her radiant eyes.

Caenrya's widened at the declaration and her own obliviousness. It was as if a blurred film had been removed from her vision. The woman's elegant nose, curved mouth, prominent brows, and hair were so similar to Halden's that Caenrya inwardly questioned her own deductive capabilities.

The gut-wrenching guilt hit Caenrya with a force that made her shut her eyes. "I'm terribly sorry for what happened. You must despise me."

"I would never," Enya dismissed with such a lighthearted tone it squeezed Caenrya's heart.

Sitting back into the plush grass, Caenrya dug her fingers into the soil. "How do you not hate me?" She had spent most of her life with this woman's killer.

"I see you and who you are. You are too good a person to become Valen's shadow."

Caenrya met Enya's open expression, the words wringing that sliver of hope out of her. But she knew not to fall for it. It was always too good to be true.

"I must take my leave soon." Enya sighed, her face sinking with grief. "May I ask one more thing of you?"

"Besides that in which I apparently don't have the slightest choice?" Caenrya dryly remarked, her lips pressing into a line at the reminder.

Taking a moment to tilt her head, Enya tenderly asked, "Would you help Halden upon your return? I fear that I'm periodically unavailable when he needs me most. I want him to know that I watch over him and couldn't be prouder of the man he's become."

A questioning expression crossed Caenrya's face. "He seemed fine enough—"

"Valen found him."

Everything changed. Valen was near, and once again, Valen was going to pull her from the edge. Caenrya wasn't going back to the small stint of her life at the Citadel; that much was clear. Enya warned her there was much left for Caenrya to face, and it would be more difficult than she could ever imagine. Once again, she would return to Shikei only to scrape by as her mortality was pushed to its limits.

But Halden...

"Is he okay?" she asked, bitter at the fact she was forced to place her own predicament at the back of her mind to worry about another. How could she do much for Halden if her destiny resided back where she started? A knot twisted her stomach when she continued to think of Halden with Valen. How could she be concerned over someone who held no place in her life? She could only think of Verina.

When she glanced back at the woman, Caenrya was shocked to find she had gone. Every person and thing were gone, and the world slowly ebbed away into that endless fog clinging to her. The pull back to reality grasped her around the chest, a tight rope she couldn't shake, along with the return of the mind-numbing pain creeping back through her limbs.

Words echoed through that blissful world, barely reaching her before Caenrya succumbed to the torment.

I would have been honored to meet you. You have much that lies beneath that veneer you put forth. One day, they'll all see that if you learn to trust them.

Caenrya couldn't tell if the water in her eyes was from the physical pain brought on by the slave mark or if those words mended something fundamental within her.

Chapter Fifteen

CAENRYA

Everything spun around Caenrya, and her physical body was shifted with words being shouted in every direction. The pain of being jostled pulled her consciousness forth. An all-encompassing haze prevented her from doing much more than catching occasional words.

"Is it possible... remove..."

The shogun's voice. Caenrya distinctly recalled the timber of it.

Another voice, unrecognizable to her ears, said, "Time isn't on her side... I don't..."

Vertigo of the worst sort kept rolling through her, and her limbs were impossible to move. A static-like energy was applied to her mark, and the thought of anyone touching it sent her mind into a hateful frenzy.

Oh, Caenrya would enact her revenge if Valen didn't beat her to it. Did they know about his encounter with Halden or that he might very well return to collect his investment? She could only imagine the destruction left in Valen's wake, the countless bodies littering the place they held her in now. Without a shadow of a doubt, Caenrya knew he could do it. Valen would lay waste to this place, perhaps finding his only challenge in the shogun if Ilias managed to block his taiji. But even then... they had no idea of the beast that lurked beneath his tattooed skin.

"The oniwaban... surveying." The shogun was reassuring.

"Trying..."

"Messenger eagle..."

It was as if electricity struck her spine, sizzling throughout the cord and reaching every end of her with reckless abandon. It blacked out any semblance of alertness she'd gained, pulling her deep under into that cloud of foggy pain once more.

Time passed in an unrecognizable fashion. Her echoing screams quieted within the heaviness of the thick mist. Caenrya lay, half-curled, across a glass-like floor, panting and struggling to reel herself in after the last bout. How much longer could she take this? Already, it was hard to think. To breathe. Something foreign threaded through her, forcing her body to fight for life after it had long since given up.

"If you choose, you need not hurt anymore," a deep voice murmured, startlingly close by.

Forcing her eyes open was an enormous effort, but Caenrya did it to spite Valen with a rigid glare. "I thought we were far past you disrespecting my dreams." It was impossible to conceal the numbing fatigue that invaded her words, much to her annoyance.

A brow rose, his body lying on his side feet away with that same insufferable smirk. "Darling, if this is a dream, I'm concerned about your nightmares." Valen tucked an arm under the side of his head and assessed the shadows lurking behind her vision. "Perchance, are you ready to return to Shikei? Surely, you've shown the lord your displeasure adequately enough by now. I don't believe it to be a worthy enough quest for your life to be claimed in the act."

Yes, Caenrya wanted to say. *I'm ready to stop this endless cycle of torture.*

In her silence, Valen gleaned her thoughts. His other hand thrummed on the fake floor in front of his chest. He wore a strange burgundy robe, much unlike his usual kimono garb. "I'll be on my way then." He winked, and his hand flattened to push his body upward.

"No," Caenrya commanded, the warble in her voice discrediting the fire in her expression. "I will not be crawling back to you anymore. I'm done being broken and manipulated to your preference. You have no power over me now." That last part she'd ensure became true, no matter the cost.

If she accepted, countless lives would be lost. Innocent lives. While she didn't care for the shogun, she'd be weighed down by those others violently cast into the afterlife. Nothing would have changed, and Valen would only invent new methods of breaking her down. There was nothing to gain by going back other than more pain.

Caenrya had had enough, and she'd fight for something *more*.

Valen's face grew contemplative as he leaned his head on his arm once more. "You intend then to die?"

"Whatever it takes to stay away from you," Caenrya clipped, unable to do much more than the venom in her voice.

A soft laugh.

"My Nrya." Valen smiled, his hand patting hers. "You'll never be rid of me. Even if you happen to cross into the next realm, I'll only bring you back. If I've learned anything in my twenty-two years of living, it's that my target never escapes. Not even to death."

A shudder laced down her spine at that, Caenrya aware of the not-so-empty threat. His lips lowered into a line.

"While my heart only grows fonder, the daimyo grows weary of your lovely absence. Don't test him much more," Valen warned.

She grew nauseous at that. Such a fundamental part of her was terrified of this man, and it was becoming far more challenging to ignore her fear the longer he stayed.

"I see you've grown desperate for company," Caenrya deflected, knowing it ticked Valen off when she changed subjects. "You never could be satisfied with being the daimyo's lapdog. You wanted to take your resentfulness out on *me*."

With that, his hand gripped hers painfully. "Watch your back with your current company. You'll find that they are worse than me in many unpleasant ways. They will end up stabbing you in the back when you least expect it. You don't belong here, Nrya, and you know it. You belong with *us*. We don't need another repeat of Ten, do we?"

Caenrya couldn't breathe.

When his eyes narrowed on hers with forbearing promise, Caenrya couldn't help but feel the nauseating instinct he was right about it all. Before Caenrya could speak, however, Valen was gone. Her eyes grew heavy in the quietness of her mind. At some point, she registered her body lying on a cot, every muscle fatigued in her body. Everything felt *heavy*. The light above her was bright, her eyes tearing when blinking awake. Her mind was fuzzy, and her mouth tasted copper. It was far too dry for her comfort.

Blinking more, Caenrya managed to make out outlines that gave her the distinct impression she lay in the same exact room she'd passed out in. Only now, there was a second cot beside hers and two people too many in there.

Caenrya couldn't manage more than a garbled noise before coughing. That was enough to draw the man's attention, the figure rising to grab something on a stand beside her. Squinting, she could make out Halden's profile, though it was apparent something was off. The other man stood still beside the exit, geared up in a black version of the clan's armor with a black fabric wrapped above and below his eyes. The jagged wing emblem shone over his right shoulder.

That's when she sensed cold biting against the thin skin around her wrists. Graphite. They had her locked down on the cot.

A rush of cackling air escaped her mouth, Valen's words ringing true in her ears. Of course, he was right. Their knife of betrayal was centered at her spine, already making their intentions known.

Was the devil she knew better than the one she didn't?

No, that little voice said in the back of her mind. *It isn't. Valen was right.*

"Notify the shogun that she's awake." The shinobi dipped his chin at Halden's order, exiting with haste. Halden swept up a glass of water, hesitating before asking, "Would you like some water?"

His voice was rough, dark bags under each eye. Perhaps she previously would have had some shred of empathy, but now... *now...*

Something in her raged.

Plastering a tired expression on her face, Caenrya weakly nodded a *yes*. A shine glinted off the glass as it drew near her upraised position, and her hands worked in place. An audible crack sounded as she moved with practiced intent. She twisted and jerked her hands in one smooth movement. A scream of pain threatened to rip from her throat at the broken bones in her hands. A necessary evil to free them from those cuffs. Caenrya pulled both hands from the restraints, grasping the glass as Halden moved to pull back.

What he didn't see was the second hand snaking the key chain peeking from his pocket, continuing to be distracted by the fact that she threw the glass at his face as hard as her uncooperative body with two broken bones could muster.

"What the Hel?" Halden sputtered, wiping broken shards of glass carefully from his face to avoid further cuts.

By the time he opened his eyes, Caenrya had ripped every protruding tube from her body. Thankfully, they hadn't cuffed her legs. She didn't think her hands were capable of such movement in their current state.

Flipping a rude gesture at Halden's shocked expression, she bounded out the door without a second to spare. Betrayal never stung so much, despite every wall she put up to guard herself for when the time came.

Why hadn't she learned by now that no matter where she went, this outcome was inevitable?

Ducking low, Caenrya avoided the swipe of a shinobi posted in the hallway. Her white robes were cumbersome as she sprinted with all her might down an endless hallway. Staff scrambled out of her way, so many footsteps thundering after her that she didn't bother to guess what was nipping at her heels.

There wasn't time.

Blood dripped along her pathway, the roughness in which she pulled the tubes from her veins causing the wounds to leave a marked trail in her wake. A problem she'd have to address only when Caenrya made it out of this forsaken place.

Shouts sounded after her, the frantic pace of her heart thundering in her ears louder.

A sharp corner came up. Her shoulder slammed into the wall to slow her rather than wasting precious seconds with a jog around it. Caenrya tore off toward a large room ahead, two armored figures making their way toward her. Gritting her teeth, she steeled herself as her body launched through a window, debris raining around her airborne body. She rolled into a somersault. Her feet picked up the slack from the loss of speed the moment she had dirt beneath them.

Balancing her taiji, Caenrya propelled her sprint into swift bounds, racing down the dark and empty pathway in between two-story buildings. The footsteps were gaining on her. Caenrya was aware she had to change the course of her escape if she wanted to be successful. Her feet caught the edge of a slanted rooftop when she leaped for it, and her head tilted up to prepare for her next leap just as another figure landed across from her.

Another masked shinobi plated in black armor and the sigil of the blasted Duša Clan engraved in black over his sleeve.

There wasn't time for hand-to-hand combat, not to mention both of her thumbs were massively swollen and dislocated. Any hit to those and the pain would blind her and leave an easy opening for her opponent. Besides, the others were below her, moving to surround the residential area they occupied.

Caenrya's throat bobbed as she prepared herself for the influx of pain. Her hand sloppily forced itself into the *zen* seal, and her eyes teared. In her mind, she rehearsed the incantation of the Elven language. *Uvoľnenie darčeka*. Gift release.

Blue energy crackled at her fingertips. Her mind attempted a technique she'd only failed at in the past.

Spreading the taiji thin, Caenrya somewhat managed to push the energy outwards. Not in a point but a release of blunted taiji powerful enough to knock the shinobi down, his hands scrambling for the ledge before he found purchase. A whoosh of air passed by her side, another shinobi landing as she took off once again. With her vantage point, Caenrya could make out clusters of cherry blossom trees in a park ahead. An unfamiliar area to her eyes. She dropped from another building, bounding straight for the cover of trees.

Only two remained behind her, and the sounds were easy to distinguish within the calm of night. The others had to be closing ranks on either side. While under normal circumstances that wouldn't prove a problem, Caenrya's weakness was slowing her legs already.

A grunt escaped her lips as a figure dropped from the foliage of a tree, landing precisely on her as they toppled to the ground. Her senses were too muddied. Everything was more difficult for her to work through than usual.

Wrapping her taiji around her injured hands, Caenrya landed a powerful blow to the man's armor. The masked shinobi stumbled back as she stood, and her situation grew bleaker than she cared to acknowledge.

Three shinobi closed in from several directions, evenly spread to intervene should she run again. More footsteps approached from the south.

Her head turned to find Halden pulling up behind her. Then, a yellow sheen formed a dome over the park's entirety.

Trapping her there.

"Caenrya." Halden walked close to her, mistaking her stillness for acceptance.

Such coldness chilled her features as she raised a taiji-pointed arm toward him. His feet stilled a short distance away. "If you come any closer, I will not hesitate to take you down."

Hurt. So much *hurt* hollowed out her stomach.

"We don't mean any harm," Eirea said behind her.

Caenrya's arms were now outstretched in both directions. She shifted her sight every second, always moving, searching for any opening she could launch at to bring one of her would-be captors down. Eirea lowered the fabric below her eye, concern etched into her face. She wore the black plates, a color that confused her. Weren't they navy before?

It was a *lie*, though, all of it.

Caenrya tried to focus however she could on the situation. They were all spread out, one in each cardinal direction. Bushes blocked the path of one, another shinobi smoothly rounding a wooden bench to close in another couple of feet.

The commander's voice pulled her attention, a slight blurriness edging her vision. "You were given medication that helped with your pain, but it also thinned your blood, Caenrya."

A flick of Caenrya's eyes confirmed that she was, in fact, bleeding more than she'd anticipated. *Damn it all.*

"You need medical attention." Eirea's inner brows upturned in concern. "The shogun had worried that you may injure yourself or another given your condition. We never intended to force you to do anything you didn't want."

A sarcastic smirk crossed Caenrya's lips at that. "I don't intend to fall for any of this again." Her face turned toward Halden's pinched one. "No matter the cost."

At that, two shinobi launched toward her. Halden's voice called out for them to stop.

This was it, Caenrya thought. *The point of no return.*

Pouring every ounce of taiji into her efforts, Caenrya fully cloaked her arms as a defense, sharpening them into razor-like blades to kill with. If she was going out, it wouldn't be without a full display of her ability. Caenrya became the living weapon she was cultivated to surrender herself into, a whirlwind of deadly precision and bold moves. Their katanas glanced off her taiji, but she created a crossword of cuts with every offensive move she made.

Though she recognized they weren't striking to kill or maim, she refused to use any taiji against their would-be possession. In fact, they were rather weak attempts...

Were they waiting for her to tire?

Caenrya ignored the words Eirea spewed her way, not believing a single honeyed promise. Not even when her white robes glistened with her blood, her steps becoming sloppier. If it weren't for her taiji, she would have lost minutes ago. Ultimately, though, she wasn't coming out of this alive, was she? Not if she didn't want to be enslaved again.

Fevered thoughts kept twisting the thin semblance of trust she had in these people, almost to a point where Caenrya's mind warred with itself. Still, she kept moving in a dance long since embedded into her battle-weary bones.

Maneuvering low, Caenrya expanded one of her taiji blades outwards, impaling one shinobi below his spleen. With a grunt of pain, the man kneeled from the gaping wound, and the second swopped in front of him to parry another blow Caenrya aimed with her arm.

The ground shook beneath her for a moment before erupting into a chaotic array of chains. They snapped down around her, aiming to wind around her middle and pull her down. Gritting her teeth, Caenrya pushed against the force with her taiji, her strength ebbing with each gush of blood dripping from her arms. They shook, and the chains tightened with each centimeter her limbs gave up.

Eirea stepped closer, a hand keeping the *zen* seal active. Across from Caenrya, Halden dropped each sai into the dirt, his eyes not leaving hers. With an enormous effort, Caenrya heaved her taiji outwards, sharpening the form to cut through the tightening chains.

Audible snaps ricocheted through the dome. Caenrya's back straightened as her taiji reduced itself to only twin blades. Her blood loss severely cut down her stamina, and her mind frantically searched for any other possible option than the path she faced.

Though she wasn't given the opportunity. Halden made his own move. He ran to her, not a weapon bared or seal formed.

Caenrya raised a taiji blade in the direction of his heart. The message was as clear as the water in the afterlife. He would die if he continued.

Either daft or ignorant of symbology, Halden didn't alter his course. Then, he was to die.

His eyes were determined, his face set in preparation for what was to come. Caenrya didn't comprehend it, couldn't understand why he'd head toward such a pointless death. The shinobi had it all: family, friends, and a haven that wasn't attempting to use him until he was but ashes carried away by the wind.

What would he gain through this? Was it that he doubted her conviction or couldn't face his father if he allowed their prize to escape?

Feet above him, Caenrya could have sworn the spirit of an eagle soared by.

Just like that, the maniacal haze became abundantly apparent in her mind, allowing the logical part of her brain to realize what muddied her senses. Ice ran through her veins. During his invasion of her dream, Valen had snaked Kū ninjutsu into her mind. She was far too weak and exhausted to realize that momentary lapse when his eyes met hers at the end, spelling her into this spiraling state. Normally, she could sense it to a degree, but she hadn't realized it this time. She only had a second left to thwart the ninjutsu, a nearly impossible task that had her pulling everything she could muster from her will to not kill Halden.

Valen would have wanted her to kill them, and there was only one thing she could do to end it before she carried that mind command through.

Cursing herself, Caenrya shifted her taiji the moment it tore through the fabric of his shinobi robe. All at once, Halden barreled into her, the two hitting the ground hard. Immediately, her taiji dissipated as he disabled her chakra points with his vin. The cloud of ninjutsu interfering with her thoughts withdrew. Before she could recover, he grasped her elbows, pinning them beside her head as he hovered above.

She noticed the small cut above his brow. The glass she threw at him had done damage after all. A thin trail of blood leaked through his hairline, all of it but a foot from her face.

"Why didn't you kill me?" Halden asked, ignoring Eirea's presence as she carefully observed. The other two shinobi huddled to the side, one aiding the injured one. "You had a clean line to my heart."

Such conflict raged inside her that Caenrya couldn't form any words, and despised herself for the moment of weakness that led to this situation. Yes, a part of her seethed at the fact that the shogun clearly didn't trust her to stay put and locked her there with graphite. The other part, though, the part that pushed back against the ninjutsu, told her she couldn't do what Valen nearly forced her to.

Because she didn't want to hurt these people.

But she couldn't tell anyone what Valen had accomplished. Not only would they lose further trust in her, but she'd reveal her ties with him ran far deeper than they could have imagined. Even as black and wasted as those tormenting ties were.

"Your slave mark has been removed. You're not bound to your old life," Halden told her.

Caenrya's intake of breath was audible.

"We only wanted to keep you safe and to have the time to tell you that you're free. Before you grew unconscious, you were set on returning to your daimyo for that sole reason," he said.

Caenrya's arms relaxed, her ears not working correctly.

"You're free," Halden repeated, his eyes beseeching her to understand. Short locks of hair tousled free around his forehead. The tips were almost long enough to reach his lowered brows.

They had done it. Somehow, in some way, while she was unconscious. It didn't cross her mind that the pain was gone, and her newfound reality meant something different from what she had feared. She didn't have an incessant tug pulling her back to the daimyo. They told the truth. Perhaps there was room to listen.

Time to listen.

"You can choose now, Caenrya," Eirea said. Her hands relaxed as she tucked her thumbs into her belt. "Whether you'd be willing to join my team formally and permanently. You'd be an equal to your peers, and I'd only ask that you have more faith in us the next time it's tested." A shadow darkened her face. "I acknowledge that you were placed at an unfair disadvantage this time, and I swear if you accept my offer, I'll ensure nothing like this occurs again."

Caenrya's jaw worked, her face warring between anger, distrust, and longing. She wanted it to be true, but it was always a case of *this time*. "What if I don't join?" she asked, her defeat leaking through.

Valen's ninjutsu had only exaggerated her fears. Fears that had always been present.

"I'll speak with my father," Halden promised, his voice low. "If you don't want any part in this, then you can leave. One way or the other, I'll guarantee it."

A tense silence overtook the park, all eyes analyzing her next move. Except for Halden, she realized. His were different, Enya's words reflecting in the darkness that recently found purchase in them. Caenrya distinctively recalled how peeved they used to make her, always bright and calm. Naïve like the rest of them. Halden, in a sense, was everything she had wanted for Verina. To see those qualities in her sister's eyes... Caenrya had killed for her. Now, she saw some of what she experienced in them, a kindred scar that marred them both to the bone. It twisted her stomach to know that light had dimmed, but it was the ultimate effect this world had on the living.

Someone like that was perhaps someone she could learn to have faith in.

"Your mother saved me," Caenrya said slowly, taking care of what words she shared. The effect was immediate, however. Halden's body stilled above her. "You asked me why I didn't kill you, and the answer lies with her. She pulled me from the mark's effect into the spirit world when I fell unconscious, sparring my sanity when it grew to be too much. I would have given up otherwise." She worked her jaw for a moment. "I owed her, and... I couldn't deliver her message if you were dead now, could I?"

Well, technically Halden would have been able to receive it directly from her in the afterlife. Not that Caenrya would verbalize that. She didn't think Enya would be too grateful for that delivery method, and Caenrya didn't want to anger the ancestors. Above her face, Halden's expression fought with itself.

Without further prompting, Caenrya continued, "Enya has been watching over you, always remaining by your side. She's proud of the man you've become." Halden twisted his face away, but not before she caught the pain there. She wondered how much of that was from his mother's loss and how much of it was from the encounter with her killer. "She knows you'll get through the aftermath of what you've faced. And I know that you will too."

Damn empathy. It messed with her far too much for her liking. Best to shut up before she said something even worse. But then, a single tear fell to the side of her cheek, and Caenrya couldn't help it. She hated it when others displayed such emotion. She could deny it all she wanted to, but that sliver deep inside wanted to ease the anguish. Far too much of her own resonated with it. "And I don't regret hitting you with the glass. The situation was a real pane."

It was cheesy, but it was all her addled mind could come up with.

Something between a laugh and a choke burst from his mouth, and his head shook off the intensity of her message. It warmed the chill inside her. Leaning back, Halden tore a sliver of black fabric from his uniform, moving to wrap it around the oozing wound on her elbow. A different light than before reignited in those steel-blue eyes, not as bright, but it repressed some of the darkness lingering within.

Caenrya looked away. Her mind buzzed lightly from the blood loss. "You people are far too gullible. I could have leaped at this opportunity."

Snorting, Eirea leaned down to assess Caenrya's hands. Her brown eye peered at the damage. "I'd say we are decent judges of character. You never went for a killing blow and shortened the diameter of your taiji when running through Ren." That name sounded familiar. "All of your cuts were shallow. You had multiple opportunities to take a hostage—"

Caenrya grumbled something under her breath, almost insulted. Resting her eyes for a moment, she listened to Cadigan prattle orders. She could have sworn the breeze carried a handful of words with them, sounding along the lines of *thank you*.

Chapter Sixteen

CAENRYA

When it was decided she'd remain overnight for healing and observation at the medical center, Caenrya ensured her protests were heard by every ear in the radius. However, it wasn't long until sleep claimed the last of her energy, even though two others were posted within the confines of her temporary quarters. One was a black-robed, masked shinobi clad in black lacquer-dipped plates for armor. When she asked, they revealed how there was a rank above jōnin called oniwaban. It was the highest honor, save for the rank of shogun, that any immensely skilled shinobi could achieve. They only answered to the shogun himself. The other shinobi who remained behind was Halden. She wasn't quite sure how to reconcile his continued presence in the room or the fact that he'd been there for two nights already.

With the coming morn, Caenrya was informed of the shogun's absence; his presence was required for the monthly clan meeting held between the four established territories. He was to return soon, but thankfully Cadigan—Eirea—organized her discharge without issue. It was a tad awkward, all things considered, but Caenrya pushed through and eventually was led back to her own apartment.

As she stared into the back of Eirea's head, Caenrya found that a grudging respect had bloomed for the commander. She felt more comfortable around her and the others, though still out of place. Comfortable enough to use Eirea's first name after weeks of struggling between using the first and last.

It wasn't until they reached her stairwell that anyone said anything, the voice coming from her doorway. "So, are you with us or nah?" Ryu asked, crossing his arms on the railing above.

"I suppose. Yes." Caenrya nodded, uneasy with the barrage of stares that suddenly burned into her.

Ryu rapped his knuckles on the rail. "Then let's all go celebrate. There's an outstanding teppanyaki place in Riverside Square. My treat." At Eirea's raised brows, he defensively added, "I owe her one, okay?" A vaguely sheepish expression bled into his cheerful one. "Take this as my apology."

Eirea jerked her chin toward Caenrya. "An excellent idea, but let's give her some time to freshen up. We'll wait for you out here, okay?"

At Caenrya's nod, Ryu hopped down to join Eirea and Halden, winking at her amicably as she ascended the stairs. She didn't know what to make of it, electing instead to take a few minutes to gather a fresh set of clothes and rinse off. When she was dry, her long strands brushed through, Caenrya searched her back for that poisonous mark. She expected it to be present, but when all that remained was the pattern of scars, she couldn't do more than stare.

She was free. Utterly, entirely free.

Rather than wallowing in pity and self-loathing, Caenrya raised her head, staring deep within her own eyes. *I'll train harder than ever to get you back, Verina.*

Dressing in a short turquoise satin robe, Caenrya tucked the material into her black trousers. She wrapped the decorated belt from her hips to her waist, tying it off so the remaining fabric fell at her side. Over the long-sleeved robe, she put on a black half-sleeved overgarment. Sliding her feet into sandals, she made for the door when a square piece of paper caught her eye.

The edge found itself sticking from a textbook. Pulling it, Caenrya read:

I'll be watching.

-Val.

Her hand shook as she tore it to shreds, dumping it into a bamboo wastebasket.

Somehow, Valen had another sneak into her residence. A place that was near sacred to her heart. It was hers, and now it was tainted by the unspoken promise he left. One that told her she wasn't out of his reach.

Would she ever be?

More than a piece of her was too close to giving in to that pain and having Valen bring her back to the daimyo's side. Such agony could only be withstood for so long before even the strongest would crack, and Caenrya wasn't prideful enough to lie and say she could have lasted for more time. Even after a lifetime of pain and suffering, it wasn't something she could ever completely overcome.

Gathering herself, she locked the door behind her, falling in place beside Halden as they followed Ryu and Cadigan through the afternoon rush.

A bustling cross section caught them as they passed, one person bumping harshly into Caenrya's shoulder. A black head bobbed away, Owena's usual collection of shinobi huddled around her. Owena only narrowed her eyes as she passed.

Curling her mouth downward, Caenrya followed the team inside a flurry of an eatery. A table opened up for them in the back, and each sat around a flat, heated surface.

Noise. Too much *noise.*

It set her on edge. Even though she selected the seat with the back against the wall, Caenrya felt uneasy. When they asked for her order, she took whatever appeared first on the menu, wanting nothing more than to be done with it. Ryu spent most of the time talking about one thing or another, mostly focusing on how many more missions they'd be able to accomplish with a four-man cell instead of three.

It only made her think of Aya and the truth she'd need to divulge within the day. Caenrya's stomach sickened thinking of possible repercussions, not paying attention as a skilled cook performed tricks with the ingredients he prepared in front of them.

If it wasn't Aya, then her thoughts would stray to Valen and his oath. Every moment was monitored, that perhaps he'd been here all along.

What she needed more than anything was to become stronger. There'd be a day where they'd face off. Caenrya could sense it in her bones. As she stood then, there wasn't a chance. Not the most fortunate of opportunities and battle conditions would guarantee a victory, not when the man had two decades to collect the words of power and hone his ability with them. Not when he was obsessed with remaining at the top of the food chain, taking precise care to guarantee Caenrya knew it.

So. Months.

Caenrya would wait and train during those months. The shogun warned it would take time to find leads and organize a team, and while she despised the notion of leaving Verina in that forsaken place for another second, there wasn't a single thing Caenrya could do about it.

Months. Caenrya's fist tightened.

"What's on your mind?" Eirea questioned between bites, waves of her curly hair turning with her head.

After stabbing a chunk of spicy-flavored chicken, Caenrya sighed. "I need to speak with Aya after this."

"You can have the day to sort out things. Rest. Recuperate," Eirea said, eyeing each of them in turn. "Starting tomorrow, I expect each of you for morning training. We must not lose sight of maintaining our skills and bettering our capabilities." To Caenrya, she added, "You will be dismissed early, of course, to train with Aya. It's crucial that we have the mornings to learn how to integrate as a fluid team and to understand each other's cues in high-stress scenarios."

Caenrya took her last bite and dipped her chin in acquiescence. "That would be wise."

"I have my moments." Eirea grinned, leaning back with her arms crossed behind her head.

Summoning her courage wasn't easy, but Caenrya bowed her head. "Thank you all for what you did."

Across from her, Ryu's fork pattered against his plate, a mock gasp coming from him. "Food! Food makes you nice to be around." Caenrya's face burned, a deathly glare hitting him as Halden coughed after inhaling grains of rice. "I kid."

Ryu protested as a boot kicked him in the shin, Eirea's face angelic as she tossed Caenrya a pleased expression. "You're welcome." Spotting a new person had entered the room, she rose. "Well, I'll be taking my leave. I'll see you three at sunrise sharp. Training field B." With that, she went over to a tall, dark-featured shinobi, looping an arm around his middle.

Daven, Caenrya recalled. The commander of Team Pernelle, one of whom was Owena. It was obvious they were familiar with each other, the two feeding off one another's comments as they chatted.

There was something about the two of them that made her heart ache. Those little smiles Daven spared only for Eirea and the way his eyes were memorized by her. Eirea's face brightened considerably when he grew close, her mouth growing softer.

"I'll take mine as well," Caenrya said, rising and not glancing back at either as she thanked no one in particular.

Before they could catch up, she took to the rooftops to escape the ceaseless noise, her shoulders loosening a hair at the calm. It was far too loud in that crowded place. She finally felt like she could relax her shoulders. But her body was tired, her lungs working hard to travel.

Despite that, she was... content. Caenrya was free. Free of the slave mark that intertwined her destiny with that of the daimyo. Crossing the village was different this time, the pathways becoming more familiar. It was almost as if this was *it*. This was where she'd spend her days.

Would Verina want to live there too once all was said and done?

Would Caenrya want to remain there?

It disturbed her to think about those unanswered questions, and her mind pushed them back after finding an out-of-place shinobi sitting on the edge of the rooftop Caenrya needed to cross. The girl's shoulders shook as if she were crying.

Would it be rude to step by?

Caenrya certainly didn't want to deal with her, nor anything associated with her, but it seemed the ancestors had other grueling plans before she could leave.

The shinobi's face turned, her porcelain features blotchy from the tears. "I-I'm sorry." She sniffed, her long brown ponytail swaying as she wiped her eyes. "Don't mind me."

Caenrya was going to do exactly that, except for the small nagging tug compelling her from Hel knows where to say something. "If something is bad enough to send you to such a sorry state, then stop being a child and square up against it." Gathering next to the edge, she looked down at the black-clad shinobi. The girl looked close to her age.

"I don't know if I can," the girl said, her eyes pooled with water.

"There are few things in this world spilling tears over. Even if it's something worthy, don't let today have them. There will always come a time more terrible than now."

She nodded slowly, pulling her shoulders back. "Yeah. But this isn't something I think I can move past."

The shinobi glanced down at her fiddling thumbs, and Caenrya sighed. Heavily. In a way, the girl's mannerisms reminded Caenrya of her sister, and it twisted her gut. "You're a shinobi. You're only limited by your own standards." The way Caenrya said it made the girl blink as if an idea dawned on her.

The girl looked up through her lashes, a small smile quirking her mouth. Something Verina used to do.

Grief tugged Caenrya's heart. Caenrya jumped across before the girl could respond, bounding for Aya's endless stairwell to her home. She pushed the encounter deep into her mind, forcing herself to not think of it again. By the time she crested the hill, her lungs had worked overtime. Sunlight danced across the lush grass, greenery breezing across the wide space around Aya's home. Dew still clung to the edges of her curved rooftop, glistening with brilliance. A hare darted across the open space, and its tail fluffed as it disappeared into the sparse undergrowth of the forest.

Kneeling for a brief moment, she waited for the wooziness to pass. The blood loss had more of an impact than it should have.

It hit like a stone to the face.

If she opened the second gate of eight possible, then why didn't her vin heal her like it did when she was ambushed and Team Cadigan interfered? It was nonsensical, leaving her with more questions and nothing adding up.

Was it a fluke? Did she regress in her power?

Disturbed, Caenrya tucked away the thought to address later with Aya, raising her fist to knock several times. Footsteps shuffled forward, a member of her staff bowing his head before directing Caenrya to the study where Aya read. Passing through the meditation area, she noted Osten's focus as he let his mind waste away doing absolutely nothing. She did not comment, though, and continued passing through.

Look at her. Maturity was practically radiating from her today.

The staff member turned to leave, closing the thick wooden door behind them. Caenrya ventured ahead, marveling at the towering rows of books, their spines reaching upwards of nineteen feet. The air was filled with the comforting scent of aged paper and ink, while the hushed whispers of pages being turned created a symphony of knowledge. In the far corner, an inviting L-shaped cushioned floor was tucked against the wall. Passing through the endless titles, she approached Aya's unmoving shape.

The elder's hand turned another page.

"Good afternoon, Elder Aya," Caenrya said, lowering before the woman.

Before she had the opportunity, Aya swiftly held up a palm. "Don't bother. You are no longer my pupil."

Such harshness emphasized each word, leaving Caenrya kneeling with dashing hopes. Aya knew about her deceit and how Caenrya broke her most prized rule. Surely, the elder would understand her circumstances. She didn't have any choice in the matter. Never did.

But...

Lowering to her torso, Caenrya did a thing she'd never done in earnest.

Beg.

"Today, I've come here to apologize for keeping the mark a secret. I know what I did was wrong, and I'm aware of how imperfect I am. I won't bother with excuses, only that I swear on my very life and my sister's that I'll never lie to you again. From this day onward, I will work harder than any other, never complaining and never questioning any order given. I beg you to forgive me, to permit this one mistake so I will never make it again," Caenrya implored, her forehead an inch from the ground.

Nothing.

Still, Caenrya didn't move, listening as another page was flipped in Aya's novel. Then again. And again. Her neck grew stiff in the uncomfortable position, and her knees ached from the hour that had passed. But she stayed. Caenrya had no one else to teach her the art of the mind. She needed the elder's tutelage. How else would Caenrya defeat Valen, who'd long since mastered the elements of Kū, Fū, Ka, Sui, and Chi?

The elements of void, wind, fire, water, and earth.

At the very least, Caenrya had to master the void as it was the strongest her taiji could produce.

Two hours passed.

Everything ached fiercely from the stale position, but Caenrya knew she owed much more than this discomfort. She'd stay as long as she was required to.

Aya finally rose with cracking knees and paced for the exit. Over her shoulder, she called out, "I have lost my faith and trust in you. We are done." The disgust was evident in her voice, curling Caenrya's fingers where she kneeled.

The door clicked behind Aya.

Raising her head, Caenrya worked every ounce of restraint she had not to react, her nerves itching to explode. It didn't make any logical sense to her. She pled respectfully and wore her heart on her sleeve. Caenrya *needed* this. How else would she ever take down Valen? For minutes, she stewed there, burning a hole into the wall with her eyes. She rose to her height when a heavier set of footsteps entered the study.

"Not going too well?" Osten asked with sympathy, a hand scratching the side of his neck.

Caenrya made to depart before he clumsily tripped, tumbling into her and roughly landing them both on the velvet cushions below. Grunting in annoyance, Caenrya made to push him off at the same time his hands moved her head. She froze in horror as his lips grew closer, and his hand moved to grasp her thigh.

The door leading to guest quarters squeaked open.

Caenrya harshly flung him off, readying herself to punch him when she heard a squeal. Owena, Niko, and two others she recognized from that incident in the square stood by the door. Open mouths and expressions of disgust and shock plastered the lot of them. Cheekily, Niko turned and shrugged in their direction.

"Busted, I guess. We were having a good time," Osten roguishly grinned. He was quite the actor.

Owena's nose wrinkled, her mouth twisting in an ugly fashion. "You whore! Now you're getting it on with my brother too? What would Halden think?"

Osten and Owena were siblings.

It clicked, the ploy blatantly obvious, and it made her feel revolted. Every inch of her wanted to lash out, but Caenrya restrained herself from punching Osten the moment she became level with him.

Aya was grandmother to both Owena and Osten, so the unfolding situation all made sense. Owena poisoned Aya's view of Caenrya on top of the lie Caenrya was shortsightedly maintaining. Osten exposed her doubts, leading Caenrya to believe honesty wasn't the best course of action regarding the slave mark and telling Aya.

The two turned Aya against her. All because of what? That Caenrya was an outsider? That her ears were sharper than the Dagon child's?

Or...

Owena was jealous Caenrya was on Halden's team. Did the entitled girl have *feelings* for Halden?

It was only because Aya was near; otherwise, she would have laid waste to this group. No one touched her like Osten did and didn't sport at *least* five broken bones by the end of it.

Owena *would* stoop as low as hiring her brother to act the part and turn an innocent situation into some idiotic drama. How childish. She'd run her mouth and spout more nonsense about her throughout the village. By the gleam in those dark eyes, Owena thought she had won some major victory. For the first time, Caenrya wished she were at Shikei so she could place this arse of a shinobi in her place.

Frustration burned Caenrya's throat, and her knuckles whitened as she desperately tried to maintain a civilized demeanor. Because despite what she'd admit, the girl's words left dents in Caenrya's armor.

"If you have a problem with me, I'd be glad to take it out to the field and use our fists instead." Caenrya paused, cocking her head with a devilish grin. "Anytime, Owena. I'd be overjoyed to show you where you stand with me. And it won't leave you above ground."

The air changed in the study, Osten's face twisting with a serious edge to it. "Don't threaten my sister like that."

"I'll ruin you," Owena hissed, furious at the lack of reaction she wanted. "You will never be accepted here and never welcomed. You will never ever take what is *mine*."

Hers? *Hers?* What the Hel did that even mean?

Walk away, Caenrya repeated to herself, the effort exceptionally trying. Hand on the knob, she twisted it as she heard the next words leave the girl's mouth.

"You lost Aya's apprenticeship, and no matter what talk you spout around, someone put you in the medical wing for days. Obviously, you're not as tough as you claim."

Caenrya ground her teeth, every instinct warring with her rational mind to turn around and fight.

Sensing that she was finding purchase, Owena gleefully continued, "I'm going to find out who it was and dig up every secret you have to share with the world. By the time I'm done with you, you'll be running with your tail between your legs."

That dark part of her soul whispered to unleash her vin against Owena. It begged her to turn and cut her down. For one rage-filled second, Caenrya began to turn. If it wasn't for the staff member opening the door in front of her, freezing at the expression crossing her face, then Caenrya may have done something she'd later regret. But she pushed past the man, not bothering with any more until her feet found themselves sprinting between the trees beyond Aya's residence.

Caenrya couldn't *think*. The need to punch something devastated what little control she had at the moment.

Up the slope she went, bounding between trunks until a plateau of forestry spread out beyond her. An open grove sat to the right, the edge of it overlooking the Citadel below. Aya's house was cloaked by the slope of a hill and towering trees behind her. Further left into the foothills, Caenrya could make out the wall circling the village. She decided it wouldn't be wise to go much further than she was then.

Forming the *zen* seal, she allowed taiji to encapsulate her fists before throwing them into a pulverizing fury against every tree and boulder in sight. When thin trunks began collapsing to the ground, pebbles remaining in lieu of the large rocks, Caenrya formed her taiji into pointed blades to work on her form. She'd spin into graceful sweeping motions, visualizing decapitating the smug head from Owena's body.

Whereas Caenrya couldn't perform the pretty little flips and tricks Halden showed off during their sessions, she did incorporate some of the hand-to-hand maneuvers into her style to add variety. Fluidity was key, catching the opponent off guard crucial. By the time her chest heaved and her brow was slick with sweat, Caenrya had some semblance of logic return to her head. Attacking Owena, especially in front of witnesses, would never aid in her goal of reacquiring Aya's services. No matter how much the girl deserved it.

Plopping onto the ground, Caenrya sat as the world steadied around her. Her cheeks burned with rage and embarrassment. She'd been far too close to losing her last string of restraint. If she was to stay here for however many months needed to rescue Verina, she had to build a thicker skin.

Perhaps a half hour passed with her eyes staring at the sky above. Already, the itch to fight came crawling back.

And she was tired of the lurker shadowing her in the previous weeks.

Turning to a distant ahari tree, Caenrya shouted, "Don't you ever grow tired of lounging around all day? I could use a sparring partner."

When she received no response, she pursed her lips. "I'm almost offended that you think I haven't noticed I've been monitored for weeks now."

A black-masked figure rounded a tree's mossy base. His mask obscured most of his face, and he was most definitely a man judging by his tall build and broad frame—almost as tall as Halden but leaner. He didn't near. Instead, he leaned against the cedar trunk with folded arms. "If I may make a recommendation, try reshaping your taiji into a separate weapon from your body."

Caenrya furrowed her brows at that, sitting up.

"You'll have more mobility and minimize your chances of the opponent countering easy openings," he said.

Squinting at the shinobi, Caenrya asked, "What's your name?" She eyed the black lacquer plating covering his chest. An oniwaban, then. She supposed it was flattering that the shogun had his best shinobi monitoring her.

The man paused, thinking. "Ren, but you must tell no other. My assignment is confidential. I get the distinct impression you don't share much, though. Can I entrust you with this?"

Sniffing, Caenrya folded her arms back at him. "Well, *Ren*. I don't see any reason to do so, and unless you give me some other reason, I'll keep it. As for my taiji, it's not as easy as you make it sound."

"It never is," Ren cracked back, humor lining his words. "But you would have performed much better during your escapade from the medical clinic had you more movement at your wrist."

Ah, right. *Ren*.

That was the shinobi she took down that night. It peeved Caenrya that she knew he had held back along with the others. Her pride stung a bit, recalling that. "I don't—" *Have the time*, she was about to say. But... that wasn't true anymore, was it? There was no mark on Caenrya's back limiting her days. What stopped her from attempting to reshape her fighting style? What worked in the fighting ring couldn't apply to everything. That much was common sense. Maybe it was high time she paced herself to improve.

Sighing, Caenrya held out her hand, visualizing the pattern of a katana in it. With minor adjustments, she formed the shape fairly well. Streams of taiji escaped from her palm, flowing through the outline she limited it to. It wavered marginally around the handle she clung to, the process unnatural. Testing it out, Caenrya slowly etched through some basic sword-fighting forms she barely knew, feeling silly in front of an audience.

But the oniwaban was right. Already, her wrist was able to maneuver the sword better.

The moment her mind strayed from concentrating on the katana-like taiji blade, the form wavered. It reverted to what she had grown accustomed to. Her brow lowered, and her taiji strained to reform the sword into a plausible likeness.

The sound of steel exiting a sheath caught her attention; Ren moved across the field with a lengthy katana in hand. Lowering her flickering form of one, Caenrya wanted to throw it to the ground in frustration. All it did was fizzle out of existence.

Ren acquired a thick stick along the way, measuring it against the length of his katana before resheathing his weapon. Finding a similar matching stick, he tossed one through the air when he neared. Caenrya caught the wood with ease, sharing a bemused glance between him and the stick.

"Like this," he explained, holding it in front of him. Two hands grasped the base. Caenrya mirrored his posture and angled both feet in a fashion similar to his stance. "Tuck your elbows in further. Good."

He swept through exaggerated motions, eyeing her form and making suggestions all the while. "Remember to keep your knees loosened and your wrists from being rigid."

Clunking the edge of the stick into the ground, Caenrya gave him a face. "Unless I happen across a foe somehow deathly allergic to wood, I cannot fathom how this translates into a credible way of fighting."

Ren held out a single finger and took several steps back, falling into a defensive stance. Twirling his stick, Ren performed a variety of complex maneuvers that might have impressed her. Slightly. Switching to offensive postures, he wove together a precise attack that scored a single mark against a tree's bark when he landed it. A trundle of smoke rose from the contact, and his hand deftly returned another strike with similar results. Within seconds, he etched the letter *R* with such accuracy, and the skillful display captivated Caenrya.

"A skilled shinobi should be capable of applying their training to any tonki available, whether it be a kunai or a katana. For mastery's sake." Ren spun the stick on his return to his original position beside her.

Tonki—another word for a shinobi's weapon arsenal.

"A stick with the rough measurements of your weapon of choice is an excellent starting point to practice the forms. Once proficient with those, you'd advance to a bladed weapon to adjust your musculature to the added weight while maintaining that form proficiency."

Caenrya recognized the wisdom in his words and acknowledged the benefit of being capable of using a real weapon when taiji was unavailable. "I see."

Didn't mean she had to enjoy it.

"Besides..." Ren's upturned black eyes crinkled, a thumb jerking toward his katana. "Your taiji has the nasty ability to eat into steel. I'd rather not lose a good sword and prefer to stick with something we could both use."

Fine. That made her raise her chin an inch.

Chewing her lip for a second, Caenrya finally said, "Sorry about wounding you that night."

Reverting to a defensive stance, Ren only said, "Never mind that. It's nothing a medical shinobi couldn't fix. Now, attack me."

The guilt eased marginally, Caenrya orienting her mind to focus on the matter at hand. However, it didn't take long for her to sport several bruises. From a *stick*. Granted, Ren had a half foot of height over her, taller than anyone, spare Valen. A thought she roughly pushed away, especially when Ren's forsaken *stick* stung her shoulder without remorse.

Her nose crinkled in frustration all the while. Over and over, she'd try some new method only to be whacked in the arm or leg. It was remarkable—and not in a good way—how different using a stick was in comparison to her taiji blades. It made her subpar to how she ordinarily held up.

And the only change was the rigidity of her taiji to the multiple moving points with a stick. Caenrya focused on her shoulder and elbow with the blades, not once concerned over how her hand was positioned or her wrist. It was so drastic that by the time several hours had passed and the sun had begun to set, she hadn't made much improvement.

"This..." Caenrya waved around the stick. "Sucks," she complained, her breath hard to catch.

"You'll get there. With time, you'll see a drastic improvement with close combat," Ren reassured, tossing his stick into the undergrowth.

Caenrya sourly tossed her own stick, sighing through her nose. "Do you stalk me often enough to be my sparring partner, or is it someone different sporadically? I'd prefer to get somewhere with training, and it's fairly boring to be watching someone all day."

If she were going to be monitored day and night, she may as well put the stalkers to real work.

Backing up into the shadows, Ren only said, "If you'd like to continue, I'd be pleased to lend a hand."

Wiping loose strands of hair from her face, Caenrya watched as he disappeared back into the foliage, perplexed by the day she had.

Chapter Seventeen

HALDEN

Dinner was tense, to say the least, as this was the first night he and Ilias were home and eating together in, well, Halden couldn't remember. Months. A typical day consisted of Halden striving to be anywhere else when his father was home or at least asleep when Ilias returned in the late evening hours. It had been that way since his mother's passing. She was the glue that held them all together. She always had the right words to soothe arguments between them and convince Ilias to attend regular family dinners despite the extreme workload each carried.

The soft glow of lantern-esque lighting fixtures brightened the painted porcelain they ate from. Soft clinking of their chopsticks sounded whenever Halden distractedly fished for a boiled carrot. He shifted his knees on an ivory cushion. The color contrasted with the darker tatami floor. Gold-leaf, lacquer work, and intricate paintings adorned most of their walls. To his right, an alcove held various scrolls, vases, and decorative pieces his mother was once proud of, all artfully displayed on a polished wooden carving of a tree's trunk.

Outside a large, closed window, Halden could see flickering coming from the stone lanterns, tastefully paced between rocks and water features in their garden. The screens separating the spaces were painted with spring lilies, his mother's favorite flower.

Enya was the sole reason he sat at the four-seated dinner table. Her words, passed through Caenrya, made something inside him long for reconnection. Halden knew it wouldn't happen, that nothing would ever be the same. With each passing bite, his chest ached at the empty seat between them.

He needed something, though. Something to help him crawl out of bed each morning and to *try*. Those first few nights after returning from Centra Village, he couldn't face Ilias. Couldn't face the memory of his mom in the house. Halden thought the only option was to stay at the medical center, waiting for Caenrya to wake and explain away yet another of his father's mistakes.

Never would he have expected what happened next.

After that encounter with Valen, Halden could only feel worse about Caenrya's past. Watching Caenrya fight in that park was one of the hardest things he witnessed. It tore at him to see her wounded in the worst possible way by those who promised hope. He knew from the start she had no intention of coming out of that alive. It was only confirmed at that very last second when she attempted to turn one taiji blade toward her own neck instead of impaling the other through Halden.

Despite her at times frosty exterior and harsh words, Caenrya didn't want to hurt any of them, regardless of what was done to her. Halden couldn't fathom what she'd endured all those years with Valen.

And to still come out with the ability to care at all...

Halden was determined to help her and maybe, in the process, figure out how to move past his own demons. She'd helped him with rekindled hope after learning of his mother's words. Such a large part of him still felt worthless, but if he could accomplish this, then that meant he still had something to give the world.

The clinking of chopsticks against porcelain stopped across from Halden. "I should have gone to retrieve Aegeon myself," Ilias said with some hesitation, pulling Halden from his thoughts.

Gripping his chopsticks tighter, Halden peaked at his father. "We were capable of such a mission. We got him here, didn't we?" He scowled. Once again, his father was disappointed in his ability and in how he acted. Typical, especially during one of the few times they'd been alone in each other's company this year.

"That's not—" Ilias stopped himself, closing his eyes for a moment to lower his voice. "What I meant was you shouldn't have been placed in that level of danger. It's too soon." Breathing through his nose, Ilias opened his eyes and poised his chopsticks perfectly across his near-empty dinner plate. A few bites of broccoli-mixed beef remained beside his steamed rice.

An incredulous laugh escaped before Halden could contain it. He resented his father's implication, allowing some of that to enter his voice as he spoke. "You couldn't have predicted it would be that ronin. I'm not a genin anymore, and I am skilled enough to handle almost anything that comes my way."

"You can't *handle* that ronin," Ilias argued, anger rarely seen on him coloring his face.

A stab to the chest. "Of course, I can't!" Halden exploded, his chopsticks scattering across his half-empty plate. "You don't think I'm aware of that?" Extending his arm, he gestured to the hollow home. Paintings were scattered across side tables, a vanity, and cream walls, all painted and decorated by his mom. Her smiling face was on each one of them.

Ilias's features twisted, pain etching into every corner. His hands folded behind his neck, and his head hung between propped elbows. "I can't lose you, too. I just—" The patter of rain against the closed windows overtook the following silence. The air was thick with words unsaid. "It's been years, and I still haven't found out how to do this—*talking*—with anyone else but your mom."

Halden turned his face away, and his knuckled whitened. It was such a deep, scarred-over grief for them both, time covering it up with barriers prone to cracking again.

"When Cadigan gave me her report, I knew I let you down. I was reliving her death all over again." His father's head rose, a hand dragging across his forehead. "I'm sorry for sending you on that mission."

Still unable to meet his gaze, Halden only asked, "Then why did you leave for the clan summit? You could have sent Javan in your stead to give the monthly report and take note of the other clans' updates." He'd done it before, long ago, when she was alive. *Every* clan shogun did when circumstances prevented them from attending. "I was ashamed, a-and broken, and *you* weren't there," he stuttered, his chest feeling as if it were caving in. "You weren't there. *Again.*"

Just like when he threw himself into work after Enya's funeral, leaving Halden to fend for himself.

It was like Halden had struck Ilias, the way his father's eyes squeezed shut as if to blind himself from the impact. "I don't know how to do this right. Any of this," he quietly said, his remorse on display. "Throughout the academy, and when we were assigned to the same team, Enya was the only one who ever understood me. She was the only one I could share everything with and always far better of a person than I. I see so much of her in you." His father swallowed down the crack in his voice. "I'm afraid that I'm not good enough for you either."

Halden ran a hand down his face.

Opening his eyes, Ilias lowered his gaze to his clenched hands over his lap. "I'm going to try."

Halden had to wait a few seconds to ensure his voice would be steady. "I want you to be my father occasionally. Not my shogun and not the leader of the clan. Someone who treats me like a son, not like baggage or a disappointment." His jaw ticked to the side.

"You have my word," Ilias said, his shoulders loosening. "But know that I'd never ever consider you to be either." He rose from his cushion, bare feet pausing on the tatami mat. "Would you be willing to meet me halfway? I want to get to know you better, both personally and professionally. I think it is time you be dealt in on matters of our house and that of the Arundel daimyo." Ilias's elder brother.

The words Aya said a month ago when meeting Caenrya for the first time popped into his mind. *If you wish your father to not be deposed of, I encourage you to remove the shroud over your eyes and wise up.* His uncle mentioned something similar that same day, speaking of Ilias's tenuous position within the house.

Halden could do better, *should* do better, in matters of the clan. He'd never been inclined in the past, but he couldn't see how he could keep moving on his current path without doing so. Everything surrounding Caenrya and his team was a political mess. If he ignored his duty to influence the narrative, however he was capable of, then the ramifications could derail everything they'd worked for. It would be tedious and vexing, but putting forth this effort for his relationship with his father and that of his team was worthwhile.

With an agreeable nod, Halden said, "I can do that." He picked his linen napkin from his lap, dabbing his face twice with it before placing it beside his empty plate.

Maybe there was a chance of bridging the canyon between them, compromising now to start edging toward one another over the eroded gap. It would take time. How much, though, Halden didn't know. He was wary of his father's words, for they were often traded in lieu of the action demanded by the people of his clan. Nothing would change unless Halden tried.

Then, if his father let him down again, Halden wouldn't be to blame.

Once dinner was cleaned up, his father took a rare evening from work and relaxed into their L-shaped beige inlaid cushions. The downy material rose a foot from the floor, built into the foundation of the family space. Halden followed suit, passing the folding screen dividing the two rooms and sitting on the other end. He mustered the courage to start what could be another argument that would undo any progress they'd made that evening.

Sensing his son was about to speak, Ilias put down a historical novel beside a cup of jasmine tea on the mother-of-pearl lacquered table beside him. A twin to the table sat low beside Halden, a steaming cup of jasmine tea sitting untouched on top.

"I've learned much from Caenrya in the last few weeks," Halden said, the intensity of his father's gaze sharpening. He almost balked at the tongue-lashing that was bound to ensue. "I hesitate to share what I've discovered for two reasons. The first of which is the trust I'll lose with her should I parrot everything she divulges into your ear."

Ilias's face remained contemplative, listening expectantly. It was the next point, though, that could end badly.

"The second being that I disagree with the use of force against her," Halden said.

At the hardening of his father's face, Halden squared his shoulders, adamant that he got this out. "It led her to almost taking her own life when she broke from the medical facility. Your measures are only creating distrust, which is what she told you directly. If we are to earn her loyalty as one of us and trust her in turn, should we not strive to give her the opportunities to choose?" he asserted, his determination keeping him from balking.

Not once had he dared to speak to his father in such a way.

A single finger tapped once on the side table, Ilias's brow cocking at his son. "Being in my position requires sacrifice, shrewd judgment, and a critical balancing act. I don't expect to please everyone, but ultimately, I was elected to this position to determine what is most advantageous for this clan. I have to weigh every calculation against the costs and benefits, and this one pertaining to Caenrya is no exception."

Ilias's face tilted upward, his eyes searching for some answer alluding him. His next words carried a burdened weight. "I never wanted these responsibilities, and while I regret a scant amount of things throughout my life, how I handled this particular case is not one of them." Lowering his eyes, Halden noticed they softened with the quirk of his mouth. "Caenrya would never have confidence in anything that appeared too good, and the probability of her taking off the moment her mark was removed outweighed that of her staying."

Something dark flitted through his father's eyes before disappearing. "I may have positioned myself to be the villain of her story while she remains with us, but now she'll consider the entirety of Team Cadigan as her allies. I considered giving your particular mission to another, but you, Halden, are the only person I could trust enough to win hers by forgoing mine." He said it without bitterness, sipping from his steaming tea as Halden let the words wash over him.

Halden was stunned. Never *ever* had he considered that his father intended for Halden to deviate from his assignment. It was conniving.

Calculating. Clever. For someone like Caenrya, trust was near impossible to gain. It stood to reason one in her shoes would lean more on someone who discounted rules to help her specifically. Though a shade of shame flickered through Halden at the realization Ilias knew he wouldn't adhere to that given mission. Was his honor that lacking, or did he figure their personal boundaries would interfere?

Halden's tongue felt heavy. "I didn't realize you thought that little of me," he mused, his mind reeling from his father's words.

A delicate clink sounded from Ilias's teacup as he placed it on a saucer. Shaking his head, he said with an air of solemnity, "You have it wrong. I could only entrust this to you in particular because of who you are and your ability to remain faithful to your values. One of the many things I can only credit toward your mother."

A wistful note caught Halden's notice.

"I'm proud that I could rely on you for this assignment, even more so for the success you've accomplished within it. Any other shinobi wouldn't have secured her conviction, all but guaranteeing her leave weeks ago," he said.

The high compliment stirred something within Halden's chest, but another thought still nagged at him. "Does Cadigan know all of this?" At his father's confirming nod, Halden spoke his next thought quietly. "So that's why she'd been more hands off than normal." Normally, Cadigan would have been in their faces until an issue was resolved. Their commander was not known for subtlety when it came to managing such aspects of a team.

Their conversation lapsed into silence as Halden hunched over his knees, staring at his hands.

"I intend to step back henceforth, as any further pushing would only derail any progress." At Halden's nod of agreement, Ilias offered, "Join me next month for the Daimyo Assembly. The information I delegate from the clan gatherings will be of interest to you, and it would be well to know the changes among us."

While he may not have agreed with his father's mechanisms, Halden couldn't disagree with the results. Even if it was unsettling how cunningly Ilias plotted it all through. As for the assembly, he confirmed, "I'd like that." His eyes flicked up to Ilias's.

His father's gaze fell to the floor, his eyes contemplating some thought as he fiddled with a silver ring on his left hand. One he'd never once taken off. "I heard from Cadigan that your mother spoke with Caenrya." So quiet were those words that Halden barely caught them.

Leaning back into the plush cushion, Halden's mellow tone matched his father's. "Yeah. She..." *Saved me. Pulled me from the brink.* "Said some things I needed to hear." He wasn't close enough with his father yet to delve deeply into that emotional mess. Before Ilias could prod further, Halden switched the subject. "As Cadigan surely divulged, the ronin that confronted us indicated he had some sort of background with Caenrya."

Ilias's foot tapped the burgundy area rug in front of his cushion as he grew serious at the topic switch. "Has Caenrya mentioned anything of note about him?"

Halden inhaled deeply as his hands tightened. "The ronin's name is Valen. In a sense, he was her mentor for the duration of her time with the unknown daimyo."

His father was incredibly still, and his eyes were unreadable.

"He performed punishment on behalf of that lord, mostly tormenting Caenrya physically and mentally for years to break her will. He ensured she was loyal to them." Closing his eyes tightly, Halden said through clenched teeth, "I can't fathom how she survived it."

Neither one of them could find the right words until...

"Do you want to talk about it?" Uncertainty outlined the words, Ilias's posture grudgingly falling back into a forced pose of relaxation.

It seemed as if his father were about to leave the room at first, his bearing visibly shaken. Whether it was the news of Valen's role in Caenrya's life or the insinuation Halden made about those minutes he experienced under the ninjutsu, he didn't know which elicited the reaction. Regardless, Ilias stayed, reaching out for that olive branch Halden wasn't quite ready to accept.

"No." Halden breathed out the word, forcibly attempting to unclench his own muscles. "As the shinobi creed goes, we must represent a Titan's Endurance, withstanding psychological and physical pain. Train to endure both. I'll get past it."

Ilias respected his son's decision with an acknowledging nod but couldn't meet Halden's eyes. He planted his gaze on a small stain perceptible in the rug's corner. Days before she passed, Enya had wanted to cheer Ilias up during a trying time within the clan's inner workings. She swooped him into a dance, and their laughter reached Halden's room and drew him out in the early hours. He'd accidentally startled them, Enya knocking over a cup of coffee that they could never get out of the fabric.

Halden felt bad for ruining the moment, but a part of him had enjoyed seeing his father wave it away with a smile that had evaded him in previous days. Neither of them had the heart to further attempt the stain removal, it being one of the few reminders of Enya's mark within the house.

It was strange how the past could be haunting at times, but even more so how people would cling to those subtle reminders. It wasn't that they enjoyed the pain. Rather, it was a tribute of sorts. An unshakable gut feeling that they owed more to those who passed, and it was the only way to honor that feeling. It may not have been the healthiest way of coping, but it was what Halden and Ilias both acknowledged as theirs.

Switching to a lighter note, Ilias small talked over various topics, catching up on the more elusive details of Halden's goings-on. As the evening wore on, Halden eventually caved to making a cup of tea for himself, relaxing into the conversation with unnatural ease. Something had shifted between them. While he didn't want to delve into anything deep, it was enjoyable to have a real conversation. Nothing pertaining to his father's work, and only focusing on topics that both would have something to contribute toward. Halden believed it was a start. Much was left to work on, but that would come with time.

***

That next month flew by with incredible repetition. Training, almost all day, every day. Caenrya would join them for the morning hours, leaving thereafter to continue with Aya. She acted strangely about it all, almost as if she were withdrawing from them. Halden credited it to the newfound release from that horrific mark on her back. Anyone would need time to adjust, so he didn't needle further into how her hours went with Aya.

That morning, Halden tucked his black pants into his boots and cinched his black shinobi robe neatly beneath his belt. He finished wrapping his leather bracers over the long sleeves and fixed his short hair into place, noticing he was soon due for a haircut. The edges of his bronze hair were getting close to his brow when not styled. Besides the color of his uniform, the sheaths for his two sai and weapon pouches around his waist were clear indicators for shinobi.

It was dishonorable for any regular citizen to sport the appearance as it inadvertently made the claim they were to be regarded with the prestige shinobi earned. With the threat of fraudulent charges, citizens refrained from mimicking those who rightfully held the title.

When dawn crept over the horizon, Halden tucked the last of his sharpened kunai into a pocket. By the time he'd finished a hastily put-together meal of fried eggs, toast, and an orange, the sky brightened with vivid yellows and tangerines. The Citadel stirred as he made his morning trek to the training fields. Recent rain coated the village, the smell of petrichor heavy below the scattered gray clouds sweeping across. A robin's spirit fluttered on the edge of an upswept rooftop before swooping into the air below. Merchant stalls were rolling open in Riverside Square, and the smell of freshly baked goods wafted in with the natural smells of blooming flowerbeds. Children aided their mothers or fathers beside the Koi River, cleaning the previous day's clothes in the fresh water.

Ahead, Halden recognized a familiar figure propped against the side of the beet-red Riverside Bridge. She began styling her hair in a high ponytail, a black metal hair piece banding the hair together at the top. She braided it from there, tying the bottom off with that decorative metal, a style many female shinobi used. Halden knew she wouldn't admit it, but he could see how she was slowly adopting his clan's ways. She used to be conscious about her ears but now displayed them without a care in the world. Or perhaps she did it to spite anyone who dared to side-eye her.

That possibility fit in better with her character.

Caenrya's eyes closed as if she were drinking in the gentle noise of the slow-moving waters beneath and the happy chatter of those milling about. Her face was serene when he crossed his arms beside hers on the red railing. Stray blonde hairs wove an entrancing pattern around her low cheekbones and long eyelashes.

"What did you do to earn those bruises?" Halden inquired, eyeing the small collection of them on the back of her hands and one on the side of her face.

Sighing through her nose, Caenrya turned and strode toward the training grounds. "We are going to be late if we stick around," she said. Lines tightened across her brow.

Halden didn't feel quite up to being chastised for being nosey, choosing instead to walk with her through the well-trodden path. It made him reminisce about their first walk together about two months ago the same way. So much had changed since then but in such a short and drastic fashion.

In a way, Halden's perspective had matured. Sure, he'd originally wanted to be a shinobi, but only to gain the credentials required to delve into ninjutsu's research aspects. It fascinated him how taiji grew with a shinobi, even more so how a shinboi's intention could impact how a word of power was used. Despite each clan's limitations with what words they knew within their own houses, there was variability with each word that could be expanded into a different outcome.

With each assignment given by the shogun, Halden would play along and carry it out to expectation. They'd never left the clan borders nor faced the real threat of death as Team Cadigan had since Caenrya joined. It was easygoing most of the time with security details, investigations, and the like. Between each tasking, Halden had ample time to study techniques and the finer intricacies of ninjutsu.

But all that changed since falling under that mind ninjutsu.

Halden would have never expected that taiji element to wield such catastrophic potential, for it to be so *real*. Those minutes... it derailed anything he had once hoped to achieve. It was all pointless now. What effect would any of his research have against Valen?

Every fiber of his being wanted to decimate that ronin and to take his time in the process. His revenge wouldn't be swift, but it would be brutal. To achieve that, Halden recognized he had to gain strength and power. Strength, well, that would be found by furthering his aptitude with ninjutsu and taijutsu. More time would have to be spent meditating to progress on his inner gates of taiji. Even one more would greatly boost his capabilities. Caenrya may be willing to help him train against Kū attacks, thus rallying his defense for the next encounter with Valen.

As for power...

During the daimyo congregation that afternoon, Halden would sow seeds within the political community. He was the shogun's son, and that carried weight. That weight, something he'd always despised, would become his best asset. Whatever he could contribute, Halden would if it meant his father remained in power.

Should a new shogun replace him, the chances of that person's interests aligning with Caenrya's would be near impossible. More likely than not, they'd reject her presence, kicking her from the clan's territory to force her back into the warring lands. She'd become a ronin there, as any disgraced shinobi would.

The possibility someone would hire a ronin for nefarious dealings was historically high, leading the shoguns of each clan to outlaw them decades ago. Too many assassinations occurred along with pillaging, sabotaging, and even worse scenarios. The stigma with the term remained to this day, and if Caenrya left the clan after being there for so long, well, the Duša Clan would send every oniwaban after her to protect their own secrets and take care of her before she became a threat to the clan or others.

Every clan was honor bound to eliminate their own ronin before they disgraced the clan's name in the others' eyes, and Halden wouldn't put it past the next shogun to remove her before Caenrya could carve out a place within their clan.

Of course, Ilias would never let her become a ronin. Nor Halden.

The training grounds opened up ahead, and Eirea and Ryu discussed a matter beside a fallen log adjacent to the open sparring area. To Halden's right, Caenrya's eyes were glued to the largest cherry blossom tree next to them, each petal alive with a stunning pink shade contrasting beautifully with the dark brown bark. It was as if she drank in every fine detail, memorizing it down to the stem of a bloomed flower.

When she caught Halden watching, she grew defensive. "They are my favorite."

He nodded, a corner of his mouth hiking up as he looked elsewhere.

For Caenrya, that part of her appeared to remain the same. Her intensity when viewing the world was that of a person starved of it. Each sight captivated her, pulling her mind from the dark place it resided in. It softened the severity of her frown and widened her ocean-blue eyes enough that he could tell the difference when Caenrya was staring at a person versus a place. Halden was curious as to what she would have been like if she had never fallen into the Helish hole of Shikei, and if they would have ever met otherwise.

Since their first walk through this path, Halden discovered those chinks in her otherwise permanently present armor. Despite her best attempts, Caenrya was more than what she put forth for others to see. She was devastated when Eirea lost her eye in their rescue attempt. Ryu had hurt her when he watched as Owena and her friends tore Caenrya apart in the square. Caenrya's eyes lightened considerably whenever she returned from practicing with Aya, making Halden believe she enjoyed her time with a mentor who respected her. Though in the last month, they hadn't been quite as bright.

During that last stand she made after her breakout from the medical clinic, Caenrya upheld her demeanor with ironclad will. Halden saw what she was doing, playing the card of the martyr. He knew by then, by the words she shared after Owena's bullying and before Team Cadigan left to retrieve Aegeon, she truly wanted it to be over. The betrayal, the agony, and, worst of all, the self-loathing that almost drove that blade into her own heart.

It was what she had intended all along, never planning to escape. Halden wondered what transpired when she was unconscious. What had his mother said to her? Whatever it was, he believed it was the glue that pieced the edges of her broken heart to trust him enough to keep fighting. That stubborn part of her was what kept her heart beating, her chin held high despite every odd being stacked against her. It was the part of her that inspired Halden.

However she acted, Caenrya cared for them. Even Ryu when she thought him dead. Even Halden, whom she couldn't hurt. Even when she pretended not to want a team or friends. It showed when she made that offhanded comment to cheer him up that night when she fought them all in the park.

Heck, she even thanked each of them at lunch when Ryu treated them.

Though he worried about those bruises Caenrya refused to discuss, he worried more about what the other person sported. He knew the mark was gone from her back, a small balm to his growing confusion.

But Halden longed for a sense of normality for himself and sought to stop catching glimpses of silver hair and icy-blue eyes that didn't belong to any of the passersby. What it was that occurred could wait until he could breathe fine around bladed weapons again. More than a bit of apprehension made his hands jittery at the thought of resuming training with shinobi tonki, his stomach queasier than his pride would admit.

Not that he'd show it.

From this point onwards, Halden would strive to prove himself capable and would overcome the nightmares that plagued him since then. It was simply the first step. He could do this. He *had* to do this.

Turning toward them, Ryu clasped his hands behind his neck with a wide grin across his face. "Guess what?" he asked Halden.

Glancing at Eirea, Halden noted the satisfied smile. Her hand twirled an expertly crafted staff of durable make and delicate markings. Between Ryu's ecstatic demeanor and his commander's reaction, he gleaned something must have improved in his relationship with Hina.

"Have you two worked things out?" Halden inquired, Caenrya silently assessing the situation between them.

Halden knew only a handful of things made Ryu happy, one being a new shinobi tonki to add to his endless pile of equipment and another being with his team. The last, though, had always made a visible change in his personality.

His childhood sweetheart.

Ryu became a more tolerant and considerate person when he first informally dated Hina. The longer the two of them spent with one another, the more she was reflected in his attributes. Her kindness softened his temper, her responsibility tempering his carelessness. Together, they were head over heels for each other, and everyone firmly believed they would one day marry. It was the sole reason so many male shinobi had refrained from approaching her, though that didn't prevent the scant few who thought themselves more prestigious or ambitious.

In their society, it was commonplace to arrange marriages or marry young, all in the name of securing bloodlines.

"Even better," Ryu recounted, his eyes almost dreamlike as he continued. "My father, mother, and Ren were all at dinner when she knocked at the door. Hina didn't ask permission to enter when I opened it, which caught me by surprise." Halden too. Hina's manners could pale the most respected of elders. "She confronted my father, addressing the entire table when she told them her intentions."

Eirea's eyes shone as she rested her weapon beside her on the log, Caenrya appearing lost as she crossed her arms.

"Hina did apologize for her bluntness but told him she had no intentions of marrying now and would reject any forced proposal. However, she did add that even if I were to be disowned, it wouldn't sway her decision to stay with me. You should have seen the look on my father's face when his plans were ruined," Ryu cackled, slapping a knee as he hunched over with laughter. "When she was done, Hina couldn't help but apologize again in her typical fashion. But, Halden, I gotta tell you, I've never loved her more."

A smile cracked through Halden's face, slowly growing into a grin as his friend's story progressed. "I'm happy for you, man. I knew she had it in her."

Shrugging sheepishly, Ryu said, "I should have had more confidence that she'd be okay. Now I need to earn this second chance she's given me."

"Isn't that the truth, kid," Eirea snorted, waving away Ryu's protest and beckoning them to the dirt ring to begin their training.

True to her style, Eirea started off the session with a brief meditation to rid the mind of external distractions, having each of them find their centers and enter the state of mind necessary for focusing. For the next half hour, they stretched and warmed up with hand-to-hand combat, each pair rotating partners every three minutes. Academy students were being taught by instructors at the obstacle course nearby, one kid push-ing a leaping bound too far and smacking into a pole.

He wasn't envious of those days.

When Halden paired against Caenrya, he discerned the change in her fighting style. When they first sparred, her attacks were brutal in strength and blunt in direction. She threw everything she had into it, the wildness catching him remarkably off guard. She hadn't given him any chance of retaliating, and her swift strikes made up in power what they lacked in finesse.

Today, they were calculated and precise. Less viciousness and more cunning with each movement, integrating the way Halden's house uti-lized their opponent's force against them. It was by far more ruthless a style than any of his clan bore and much more effective than her previous style.

When they transitioned into team exercises, Halden's pent-up anx-iousness dissipated. He wouldn't have to practice with weapons this time around. Intentional by Eirea, he was sure.

They ran capture-the-objective missions where they slipped into de-fensive and offensive teams, the former guarding a rock to prevent them from theft. Each team would rotate after two attempts each, so every person had a fair shake with the commander and with each goal. No tonki were permitted since they solely focused on team building and mental exercises for surrounding incorporation.

Within the hour, every team member had thoroughly utilized the high ropes course to cross through different levels of the towering treescape, innovating creative methods of stealing an otherwise unre-markable rock. At some point, Ryu had snagged a berry or two to outline an angry face on the objective, the residue staining Eirea's hand when she tripped Ryu off the rocking log bridge and stole the rock. Afterward, she was adamant Ryu deserved to be thrown off for childish behavior.

All the while, Caenrya hung back, always observing as if she were trying to understand how they functioned.

How to belong.

When the sun signaled noon, they broke off for the day. With an ear-to-ear grin, Ryu bragged about the date he and Hina were having near the Ancestorial Shrine later that night. He'd spent the last evening fantasizing about the perfect picnic and left hastily after training to prepare.

Caenrya left so quickly and stealthily that Halden hadn't noticed until they reached the bridge. Ryu and Halden later met at their favorite ramen shop, enjoying a brief lunch before reconvening for further training. That part of the day was less fun without Caenrya, but it relieved Halden that Ryu had warmed up to having her on their team. Halden returned home late afternoon to clean up for the daimyo council and an early dinner. By the time he left, wearing a formal thigh-long robe and overgarment of his clan's shades buttoned down to his black trousers, not a half hour had passed.

The Duša Clan Temple was flurrying with activity on the first floor, representatives from each house meeting and greeting with pleasantries as Halden pressed upward to his father's office. Javan permitted his entrance, his father staring out the window with both hands folded behind his back. With a click, the kampaku closed the door behind Halden, Ilias's eyes bright as they turned toward his son.

His steel-gray eyes were alight with a fire Halden hadn't seen in years, and his words changed everything.

"I have uncovered the lead we've been waiting for."

Chapter Eighteen

CAENRYA

"Remember to keep those inches between your hands on the grip," Ren instructed, watching as her hands slipped within the last flurry of defensive maneuvers. "You lose accuracy if they are too close together, resulting in a hacking movement."

Out of breath, Caenrya only lowered her chin in acknowledgment, adjusting her grip accordingly. Ren leaped forward in a forceful attack with his wooden katana.

It surprised Caenrya he'd come prepared with proper training tools that day, though his reasoning was sound. The surrounding clearing provided scant few sticks durable enough for one session, much less consistent usage. Besides, sticks were typically for the safety of the children who learned first with them. As Caenrya had previous experience with her own form of weapons, Ren determined skipping that step would be permissible.

He detailed every aspect of the weapon, going into specifics on how only the back or side of the blade portion should be used for blocking to avoid excessive wear and damage. The last foot of the blade was not to be used for defense, if possible, since the metal thinned there, and it would be far more difficult to regain control and balance if struck. Next,

Ren went into proper form when blocking overheard strikes, correcting her angle to forty-five degrees with the sharp edge facing down. Side and low strikes confused her as the katana was to be wielded upside down, the position awkward with her wrists.

For *hours*, endless, famishing, and excruciating hours, Caenrya learned basic blocks even as her muscles screamed from movements and weights she was unaccustomed to. Taiji blades were weightless, and her style previously incorporated duel-edged sides and was uncaring of how they were struck.

Maintaining a real blade was far more tedious, but her dedication hadn't wavered an inch despite it. Caenrya would learn how to defend herself if her access to taiji was restricted again and never allow herself to be in such a defenseless state.

Before her arms gave out, Caenrya called it quits and returned the wooden katana to Ren's leather sheath. "Thanks," she huffed out, sporting a new collection of bruises that were sure to raise brows.

Well, not that she didn't already get enough stares, a majority outright hostile. Ren's masked face inclined in response as he made to distance himself once more, Caenrya watching in perplexity. What was the point of an eye on her at all times at this point? If it were for ensuring her safety against Valen or other ronin, then why remain lurking at such a distance?

She shouted after him as much.

"Shinobi Creed: Masquerade in Illusions. One must become fluent in disguise and manipulation, utilizing misinformation and psychological tactics to outsmart and mislead any foe." Ren called out as he spun halfway, "Should they act, it would be when you're alone."

Then, the shinobi corrected his position, resuming his subtle disappearance into the distance. Caenrya huffed in annoyance as the idea of anyone hunting her to that extreme was ludicrous. If Valen wanted to, she'd already be back within Shikei at the lord's beck and call. She knew, though, without an ounce of uncertainty, that the daimyo wanted her to return on her own terms. It went beyond that in which Valen shared during her slumber. The lord simply enjoyed the continuation of his role in this particular drama.

He enjoyed the groveling of those below, the power he wielded over each in his possession. Whereas Valen was easy to understand—pain and torment his only motivator—the lord had many faces he'd present, depending on the effect desired. Caenrya didn't believe him to possess any remarkable taiji capability, but the skill he wielded with words was unparalleled.

Something she never understood was why the daimyo commanded such power over Valen. There was a clear imbalance when it came to taiji. Perhaps Valen was paid well. Or maybe it was the satisfaction Valen got out of terrorizing children under a man who could materialize his dreams indefinitely and grant him immunity to do as he wished.

After all, what wouldn't a person do if it meant they could have all they wanted? People were selfish creatures, striving to whatever end to satiate their own urges. The daimyo wanted to be revered by all and feared by more. Valen craved pain and misery, inflicting it onto any in his path to fulfill that dark, insidious hunger.

It made her pick at a nail in anxiousness at the thought of his next move since her intentions of staying were clear by now. Valen knew who it was Team Cadigan sourced to remove her mark and knew she was free of any physical obligation to return. Maybe it was what the daimyo had sought all along: the ultimate test of her loyalties. What would she do when it was removed? If Caenrya returned, there was the possibility she'd be granted additional freedoms for garnering such trust, especially if she were to present intelligence of the Duša Clan's inner workings.

It made Caenrya wonder if the daimyo knew exactly how close Valen had come to killing her repeatedly and just how much absolute hatred she harbored for them. She always presented a neutral demeanor when dealing with him and the daimyo together, lest she endanger her sister.

Groaning, Caenrya began the tedious descent into the Citadel, refusing to glance in the direction of Aya's residence. Somehow, she'd have to regain the elder's trust and mentorship. Some gesture or another, but as for the how, she hadn't the faintest idea.

She couldn't bring herself to tell Halden or the others how she broke Aya's trust. Caenrya still felt too disgusted at herself for it. She couldn't handle it if they judged her similarly. The entire Citadel despised her presence already.

A ruckus sounded in the distance, grabbing her interest, and Caenrya peeled toward it. Her feet kept to the rooftops, an adopted habit considering the constant sneers she'd get if she stuck with the maze of pathways throughout the village. Using taiji, it was too easy to leap between the curved roofs. As with bounding, she sprung from each building. Then, as her feet connected with the next, she could use the natural energy to gain a foothold, sticking to the taiji gathered in the stone slate's composition.

Nearing a slanted edge, she perched there to overlook Temple Square. At least forty people strong cloaked in pure white robes kneeled on their knees, lanterns ablaze around the vicinity. In unison, the crowd chanted along with a single woman in front of the grand eagle statue. Regularly dressed merchants, artisans, and common folk in the stalls observed quietly around, tending to their businesses or fulfilling errands.

Caenrya's dust-coated ponytail braid swayed as she cocked her head at them, trying to discern the relevance of what was occurring before her. They spoke in a tongue unfamiliar to her ears, every pair of eyes closed in the unusual group as they swayed lightly to their somewhat musical verbiage.

The melody was melancholy, a desperation clinging to it like sap to a tree. Harsh edges of certain words softened to long drawls, the note resonating with something in her soul.

"It's best to leave them to their own devices," a feminine voice said, momentarily distracting Caenrya from the ritualist ceremony.

Taking in her commander's sudden appearance, Caenrya asked, "Who are they?" She looked up at Eirea's brown eye and the blonde curls that cusped her face.

Gesturing to her side, Eirea silently requested her to follow as she explained, "They claim to be the sole reason why any of us hold any connection with the ancestors. With every breath they loosen, they worship those who came before us but predominantly focus on those whose long-lost heritage gave us such *holy* gifts." She said the word as if it were silly.

Reluctantly, Caenrya fell in step beside Eirea, tearing her gaze from the crowd and leaping to the walkways below with the commander. She supposed no one would throw anything at her if Eirea was there, especially since the commander sported the shinobi uniform. "The Elves," she said evenly, gaining an idea of who those fanatics were.

Her eyes narrowed.

With a small smile, Eirea confirmed her suspicions. "We call them the Devout, a collective union of Canecians gathered from each clan."

Caenrya's brows bunched at that. "I thought inter-clan travel wasn't welcomed?" Turning a corner, she ducked her head below a particularly low-hanging string of drying clothes in the alleyway.

A man and his wife passed, though when his brown eyes spotted Caenrya's ears, they grew distrustful. With a quick motion, the man wrapped an arm around his wife's shoulders and didn't look back.

That ever-present stone weighed heavily in Caenrya's stomach.

"The Devout are the exception, as their mission to connect with the deceased requires constant movement. You see, each clan territory can connect to their own ancestors; however, those residing in that land cannot communicate with another clan's ancestors." Eirea moved into a small stall, pulling back the hanging curtains to place an order with the short man at the register.

Caenrya ducked her head under the curtains, the fabric falling back into place after Eirea released the black panes of silk. "Unless you travel there," Caenrya finished, somewhat understanding the bizarre concept. "Why's that?"

Stepping back from the counter, Eirea crossed her arms, her smile returning once more. "I'll have to give you a historical text that can help with understanding the background more in-depth, but for now, I'll skip ahead and tell you that each clan's ancestors exclusively walk with their own people in the skies above."

The man behind the counter offered a heavy-looking brown paper bag, bowing his head as Eirea thanked him. The commander returned to the alleyway with Caenrya in tow. Together, they strode by a gaggle of children chasing each other, their mothers eyeing Caenrya distrustfully all the while. A wafting scent of something sweet and fried drifted from the bag Eirea carried, her stomach clenching in hunger as her mouth watered at the tangy aroma. Hopefully, soon, she'd return to her quarters to dig up something.

Though her hunger was tempered by the newfound knowledge, Caenrya's mind contemplated how it fit in her picture of this outside world. "Why still would the Devout be granted such freedom? What's to gain for them and the clans that permit them free roam?"

Passing by the park, Caenrya couldn't help but see the marks marred into the grass from her short-lived battle a month prior. Her eyes picked out the spot where she had stood her final ground, and her traitorous mind recalled the ninjutsu Valen put on her, compelling her to act as she had.

A feeling of discontent shook her, but she was unsure of what was bothering her. She was restless, still uncertain if she made the right decisions that led to this moment. Would she only cause more pain this way, or should she have gone willingly back to Shikei almost two months ago when confronted by Two? The questions never ceased to turn her mind in dizzying circles, the very ground she walked on seeming an illusion soon to be pulled out from under her.

There lies more ahead, and worse, I'm afraid.

Enya's gentle words haunted her, warped her dreams and occasional moments of peace. After everything... how could it be that she was to suffer more?

"The Devout claim to gather wisdom between each clan's ancestors, sharing between the dead and living to help guide us all into an era of peace." Eirea softly spoke, as if she knew what battle raged inside of Caenrya, and she wanted to provide some distraction. "They offer the dead's words to the shogun and carry news between each sky of ancestors in exchange for their freedoms. They strive to unify all in this way of life, giving all they have for their mission. When the clans were under the banner of an empire, all ancestors were said to bicker among themselves, spurring tensions between the living. It was one of the many factors that broke it apart into what you see now."

Eirea shared a quick, humorous expression. "Even in death we still bicker among ourselves, getting even grumpier as the years pass."

The pathway ahead escaped into the surrounding forestry, massive columns of vine-covered stone meeting in a sweeping archway above. Beds of stargazer lilies lined the stone walkway between the interspersed columns, fireflies flittering around the low-hanging branches of leaves. A spirit of a fox shimmered within a sparse bush, and an owl sang in a nest far above.

"Our people call these the Moon Gates," Eirea said, nestling into a wide-swooping bench carved in the likeness of half a bird's nest. "The veil between the world we see and that of our ancestors is thinnest in the holy places of each clan, which is why you'll find more spirits to be hovering about nearby. You'll see the Devout coming here occasionally to meditate."

It was a soothing place, one that relaxed Caenrya's shoulders. Her legs tucked under her on the bench, and her back rested against the cool stone as her eyes discovered the countless stars hovering between the two moons in the night sky.

"Hope you enjoy sweet and sour chicken and sticky rice." Eirea pulled out two boxed containers from the bag, passing them to Caenrya with chopsticks and a napkin. She only winked when Caenrya expressed her surprised gratitude, and her eye glowed when Caenrya's eyes widened at the delicious fair. "It's one of my favorite shops to grab a quick meal."

With a small frown, Caenrya lowered the box of chicken, and her eyes absorbed the food before her. She imagined it to be the sort of meal her daimyo would have eaten at his own residence with gold chopsticks and the finest of silken napkins. It took time before she finally murmured, "We were only given the bare minimum at Shikei. Even then, I'd give Verina a portion of my rations every time. I couldn't stand seeing the hunger in her face, nor the way her bones stuck out as she grew up there. Even though I wasn't allowed to see her, the daimyo would have the guard pass it along for me. After some years, once I proved my worth, he incentivized me further by giving Verina extra comforts."

A cold laugh. "It worked," Caenrya said.

"How old were you both when you were taken?" Eirea asked in a tone not unlike her own.

Caenrya inspected the commander's bearing at that, determining what angle Eirea was working at.

Sensing this, Eirea said between bites, "You don't have to share anything you aren't willing to. I only ask to understand."

A pang twisted Caenrya's gut. She wanted to trust... to talk. Why was it so *hard*?

"I was almost eight. Verina was four. It was a year later when we entered Shikei."

There. She said it, somehow forcing it out with her constricting throat. Caenrya heard the intake of breath Eirea had. Anything further she might have said had gone with the guttering of her moment of vulnerability.

"She doesn't remember it then." Eirea hesitated, breaking up a rice ball with a chopstick. A brown eye glanced at her empathetically. "But... you do?"

Every second of it. Every bloody, gut-wrenching second.

Caenrya stuffed a piece of tangy chicken in her mouth, intentionally chewing instead of responding. She couldn't, for more reasons than the obvious. Though even if she wanted to, this wasn't a story she was willing to share. Not with anyone.

"I've heard that you've taken up the katana," Eirea attempted, trying for a lighter topic.

Her heart rate eased at the transition, and she worked to vehemently repress those memories as she continued the new direction of conversation. "It's been brought to my attention that I'm... stiff with my taiji blades. It would be smart to be seasoned with a physical blade anyway, and everything I pick up with that will translate with my taiji."

Eirea's whole demeanor shifted, her countenance lighting up like a bonfire after fuel was poured on it. Words poured from her mouth on the pros and cons of each weapon and why the katana was one of the absolute best choices to bring into battle. Occasionally, Caenrya would nod in agreement, sometimes string together a sentence or two. She preferred it this way, not certain what she'd say otherwise. Eventually, with full bellies and a lull in words, they both observed twin butterflies flutter past before dissolving into a shimmering light.

Chewing on her tongue, Caenrya pondered how to ask what was on her mind, settling for, "How—how is Halden holding up?" She couldn't yet muster the question of how Eirea was adapting with one eye. That culpability still clung to her like oil, making Caenrya writhe in disgust for what the commander had forfeited for her.

"I think you may know better than I," Eirea responded, her charismatic smile falling.

Drawing arms close, Caenrya huffed, "I don't know what you mean."

"The ronin was a large part of your past. Would you not know what he'd do to another?" she reasoned—not unkindly—with the patience to guide Caenrya to her own answer.

"Valen," Caenrya said, the name constricting her chest. "I'm familiar." An understatement. "But I only ask, as you know well more than I, how that sort of person would affect Halden in particular. Few held up at Shikei under his... training."

So many had died. Horribly.

"I see." Registering that bit of information, Eirea took a pause to think out her response. "Halden is a middle ground between you and Ryu. The latter wears his heart on his sleeve, while you are harder to crack than the thickest of vaults."

Fair assessment.

"On most things, I can easily read both of them, and this case is no different." Eirea leaned into the crook of the bench. "He could use a friend right now. Someone who can walk him past what this... Valen," she waved two fingers with a hateful wrinkle of her nose, "put him through."

"A friend," Caenrya repeated, her eyes raising back to the bountiful stars. "I'm not that."

Brooding, Eirea wrapped an arm around the lip of the stone nest. "You shouldn't undervalue yourself like that."

Without lowering her chin, Caenrya's eyes flicked toward her, somewhat annoyed. She had shared her unbiased outlook on the matter, not seeing how she was even remotely close to any other person beyond Verina. She couldn't be.

Nor would she admit she was convincing herself otherwise.

"You can deny it until your final breath," Eirea sighed, a corner of her mouth upturning as her head shook lightly. "But he's your friend, just as Ryu is."

Something buried deep within her mind rose to the surface, yet so did more memories Caenrya wanted nothing to do with. "And what makes you think that?" A bite hardened her words.

"Because you couldn't leave them to die that first battle."

Caenrya instead let Two get away, but only because he wasn't worth it. She tore her eyes away from Eirea, but her sight was unseeing.

"Because they put their lives in peril not once, but twice, to save you."

That was their choice, not Caenrya's. They were duty bound by their clan.

"Because you trusted Halden in the end and chose to live and fight another day with your team."

There weren't many choices left at the time. One of her hands gripped the stone bench with vicious strength.

"Because you cared enough to ask me how he is holding up," Eirea said, her voice barely audible against the array of crickets chirping.

Caenrya had nothing for that last point, and all she could muster was a glare in the commander's direction.

Pushing upward, Eirea rose from the bench, collecting the trash back into the bag. "Only friends try such things, such unreasonable and sometimes impossible things, to help one another."

"I can't afford to have friends. They are distractions, nothing more than loose ends to be completely cut off." Caenrya's teeth ached from grinding them together. *I used to have someone like that, and look what happened to him...* Caenrya's heart beat uncontrollably, her palms growing clammy.

"Only the most broken of people hope like you do, Caenrya."

She stiffened at Eirea's words.

"You try to mask it with all your might. You protect that kernel with your fierce words and isolated façade, using every tooth and nail to keep it from being extinguished. Despite your hardest attempt to believe otherwise, you've grown fond of us," she said.

Caenrya couldn't hear it anymore, rising to return to her apartment. Everything was a hurricane rushing through her, every wall she thrust forward crumbling as her emotions burst forth. She couldn't lose control. *Wouldn't.*

"You asked about Halden because you don't want him to agonize as you did, and only a friend would put another before their own selfishness."

"Stop." Caenrya sneered, spinning on her heel. "I have no friends and don't want anything of the sort. My *only* goal is to rescue Verina, and until then, I'll tolerate being here."

An empathetic expression crossed Eirea's face, and her feet walked past Caenrya as she said, "Don't comfort yourself with a lie, not when there is solace in the truth."

The sound of footsteps pulled Caenrya's attention before she said something she'd later regret. Her glare turned toward a familiar face and Ryu. The latter carried a wicker basket, his hand clasped with the curvy shinobi's hand.

"Ryu. Hina." Eirea grinned, propping a hand on her hip. "In the nick of time. I have a favor to ask."

Bowing respectfully, the girl Caenrya had found sobbing on the rooftop cheerfully said, "Good evening, Commander Cadigan. What can we do for you?" That's when she realized whose eyes shot daggers toward them. Her hazel eyes brightened. "Oh! It's you. I meant to thank you for helping me the other day."

Of course, the one good deed Caenrya did would haunt her in such a way. It was exactly why she didn't *help* people.

Ryu's eyebrows flung toward the sky at that. He peeked down at Hina. "*She* helped *you*?"

The audacity.

Caenrya was most offended at that, letting Ryu know as much with a face. Yes, it was hypocritical. It didn't mean she couldn't be offended.

"Hina, would you be willing to help Caenrya with elemental training?" Eirea asked before Caenrya had the opportunity to speak.

"I need *no* such thing from anyone—" Caenrya furiously started, a distant, terrible sound catching her ears.

Everyone reacted instantly, except for her. The others sprinted toward the source, the echoes of screams reaching them from further into the Citadel. In that moment, Caenrya had to face a choice: retreat with her rage and ignore the chaos ensuing or suck it up and prove Eirea right. It pissed her off royally that she'd hear about it later, but her instinct pulled her in line with her team and Hina.

Something deep within her, after all, didn't sit right with the idea of turning a blind eye if she had the option.

By the time they reached the park, civilians were running for their lives away from the direction of Temple Square. The primal fear among them leeched Caenrya's ire, and the blood splattered on every other person quickened her own steps. Eirea signaled for them to go airborne, and without hesitation, they bounded across the rooftops to avoid the clusters of people running for their lives. Screams of agony and absolute terror became louder than the beating of her heart, Temple Square opening to such a gruesome sight.

It was one familiar to her bones, something similar to scenes laid out before her by her own doing. Although this time, Caenrya could understand the perspective of those she'd left alive in her wake.

Snow-white shreds of robe littered the stone, some tinged with a crimson that contrasted heavily with the material. Chunks of flesh and splintered bone scattered throughout the entirety of the enormous square, red staining the ground as if it had poured a scarlet storm. Half a body was caught on the edge of the eagle statue. The tattered fabric remained on it, hanging as if from a flag of war. Some remained alive, begging for help, others huddled in complete shock behind devastated counters, pleading with the ancestors to spare them.

Nowhere could Caenrya see a hidden enemy. The area was empty except for the carnage and victims.

Hina immediately leaped into the disaster, Ryu following suit a beat behind her. Caenrya lifted a foot to follow, but a hand gripped her shoulder as Eirea said, "Make sure she returns safely."

"Let go of—" Caenrya started pulling from Ren's grasp before meeting his eyes. Normally, they were full of kindness and tranquility. It was as if a switch had flipped, merciless steel gazing back at her.

"You must return to your residence at once," Ren ordered, holding out a hand in the direction of Wisteria Square.

More than anything, Caenrya despised being treated in such a belittling manner. It felt childish when she was more than capable of watching over herself. Squaring her shoulders, she evenly held his sight.

"Caenrya, please," Eirea implored, her face decisive. "Return to your apartment. We do not know who or what caused this, and if you remain, it may garner the wrong attention from the citizens."

Caenrya stepped back as if struck, and her lips pressed into a fine line at that. The message was clear as day: they'd blame it on her. Already, they despised her presence; some were outright violent, throwing things at her or pushing her around. It wasn't fair.

"It could even be Valen's doing. We need to assess and regroup before bringing you near this," Eirea tried further explaining. It showed on her face she knew what damage it was causing, and she was sorry for it.

But it was too late. Caenrya's ears were deaf as she turned to bound across the rooftops, Ren closely tailing her. It wasn't long before another black-masked oniwaban joined him. The village was alive with panic as they traveled away from the destruction. All around, shinobi were being called into action. Black-clad figures raced past her. For every one of them, the anger in her heart beat louder.

They may as well order Ren and this other one to join them for all the good they would do against Valen. No one can beat him. She glowered.

Rage smoldered in her chest, and her fists itched for a fight. When her apartment door slammed behind her, oniwaban stationed themselves both in front of it and at the rooftop above her rear window. Caenrya twisted her shower handle to the hottest setting it could manage and stepped in the sweltering heat. It burned her skin to the brightest shade of red, but it paled in comparison to the inferno beneath it.

Only the most broken of people hope like you do.

What complete and utter nonsense.

CHAPTER NINETEEN
HALDEN

When Ilias said those words, it froze Halden in his tracks. His mind wondered if he misheard, for it was certainly too good to be true. But at the same time, disappointment rose with the realization of the lead. Caenrya would get her sister back, but then she might not linger afterward. It only made sense she'd want to return home to the place they were stolen from, and that wasn't here. He'd expected another four months from the estimate his father provided, not scant *days*.

Could he convince her to stay? Would she be willing to?

"Come," his father beckoned, waiting until Halden sat before his desk. "We've secured a merchant selling illegal wares along the border of the warring lands. With enough persuasion, he confessed to having stock in the underground fighting rings within that territory."

Halden's fingers curled. "By stock, you mean people like Caenrya?"

With a curt nod, Ilias confirmed his suspicion. "We negotiated a deal of sorts, where he brings in a new fighter, and we begin scouting from the inside for further leads that point us in the direction of this unknown daimyo."

A creeping vine of apprehension crawled down his spine. His mind picked apart his father's words, gleaning a terrible premonition. He turned in his seat, fingers digging further into his knees. "You intend to send her back," Halden accused, his face incredulous.

A sideways glance. "Not alone, of course. Unfortunately, Caenrya is the only one who can easily and correctly identify our targets. We cannot proceed without clarification on who we are set to ambush, but also must take extraordinary care to refrain from exposing ourselves," Ilias disclosed, his eyes going distant as his mind scrutinized the possibilities. "The informant claims he can ticket in one new fighter and justify two guards to oversee his dealings while attending a single fight. We'll have to construct the perfect execution team, skilled enough to withdraw should they be exposed but discrete with their profile as to not be recognized. Caenrya will have to be disguised in the role of a guard, but as for the others..." He trailed off, a hand tapping on the desk along with his thoughts.

"Caenrya isn't ready," Halden cut in, his features set with the determination of his assessment.

Blinking away his thoughts, Ilias faced him with a frown. "The merchant doesn't have a reservation for another six months. The fighting rings apparently change location, cost for entry, and status requirements per monthly meetings. He is remarkably low on the totem pole, but we can work with this." His father's brows drew together in contemplation. "Is that enough time?"

Caught off guard, Halden's mouth opened, then closed. A hand rubbed his brow, the pressure growing there. "Maybe. Should be. I don't know," he blew out in frustration, standing abruptly.

"What is it that makes you believe otherwise?"

He didn't want to say it, but the possibility existed. "What if her sister is there?" Halden asked, pacing back to the small library of books on the far side of the office and back.

Ilias slowly nodded, running a hand over his trimmed beard while saying, "We have several months to change that outcome and to guarantee one favorable to our plight."

It wasn't a comfortable option for Halden.

"Does any of this correlate with the prophecy?" Halden had to know if some of his father's logic had been impacted by the sentence looming over them all.

His father shared a tight-lipped smile. "Everything pertains to it. Only time will tell if this engages the next foretelling and who the balance will lay in favor of afterward." He sipped on his classic jasmine tea, placing it half empty back on the table afterward.

Swallowing, Halden's back tensed as his mind fashioned various imaginary outcomes. None were good, for anything ending as such seemed impossible. "Have you informed anyone else of this prophecy?" He had to know and wanted to see if he could be included in the finer details of what exactly threatened them all.

"No," Ilias said, his tone hardening. "If anyone were to find out, specifically Caenrya, it may devastate the one chance we have of surviving, as slight as it already stands."

Halden's stomach grew leaden at the implication.

"I trust that what I've already shared remains exclusively between us, not a word to be uttered to any other. Of this, I'm afraid I must be clear," his father said.

What about this prophecy would change his actions? Was it dire enough that knowing would alter their paths from their destined ones?

"It does and will continue to be so," Halden promised, the weight of it settling further on his shoulders. He stilled, turning to stare into his father's serious eyes. "I want to be on the team for this mission."

Ilias leaned back, and the lines on his face tightened. "It's too risky sending two faces that Valen, among others, may identify. Even if we disguise you both with ninjutsu, the chances of being caught increase fivefold. The smartest course of action would be two oniwaban accompanying Caenrya. They far exceed the exceptional talent observed in jōnin and have seen what evils lurk in that land. At the very least, I could justify this as a jōnin-ranked mission. I never once have sent a chūnin into the Kriv Clan territory."

Glaring at the ground, Halden worked his jaw. He understood. But...

Straightening his spine, he stared steadfastly at his father. "I may be far from the capabilities of an oniwaban, but I'm not far from that of a jōnin. If, in the next six months, I can advance to that rank, will you give me permission to join the infiltration team? It would be best to have someone she trusts to have her back *there* of all places."

He put every ounce of his determination into that question, his eyes portraying his resolve. Halden had slacked on trying to further his shinobi career in previous years, but he was confident he could reach jōnin within that time. He mastered the first three paths to Awakening, and the last two had been stunted by the loss of his mother. For a long time, he wallowed in self-pity, not attempting to progress in meditation or unlocking gates.

Now, though, he only had two paths left: the Path of Cultivation and the Path of Awakening. He mastered two of the five taiji natures, leaving only one to master. He was close to perfecting his water yin and yang balancing. Six months... Halden could do it.

A grave glint entered Ilias's eyes, but he sat silent for some time. Contemplating. Finally, he said, "If you can achieve the rank, then I will allow you to join the team. Six months may not be enough, though, to master what you must. I will not allow the examiners to go easy on you should you meet the requirements for testing."

Halden couldn't help it. He lowered his chin, a determined smile crossing his face. "I wouldn't expect anything less."

A new kind of chill spread across his skin, one that spoke of something final. One born of a life-changing resolution. The kind that would be sought to fruition, no matter the cost.

Ilias stared hard, nodding once. "Then it's settled." His eyes analyzed Halden for a moment more, respect lingering there.

A knock pulled them from their conversation, Javan signaling the shogun's designated time to leave for the Daimyo Assembly. Halden moved, pushing back the upheaval of thoughts circling his mind, and proceeded after his father to the assembly chamber.

It was a grand room of three tiers, marbled stairwells running down between the five-foot gaps. Already, the thirteen daimyo of the major houses sat on plush cushions at the bottom tier, a person of their choosing behind each on the second tier for recordkeeping purposes. A handful of apprentices sat eagerly on top of the third, their backs to the oval gold-encrusted wall encompassing the lantern-strewn room. A single cushion, doubled in size and embroidered with gold around the royal blue hue, sat at the end of the first tier.

Ilias strode for that one, the people in the assembly standing respectfully with heads bowed as Javan and Halden passed through, only steps behind the shogun. Halden sat on the third tier, overlooking the room's entirety, Javan doing similarly a tier below. His mostly bald head shined in the low light, though his plaited black hair fell to his lower back. At the bottom of the assembly room, Ilias remained standing as the others lowered themselves in unison, hushed and awaiting the shogun's report of the monthly clan gathering.

Even Halden had to confess Ilias knew how to command attention, his bearing unwavering as he spoke with an eloquence reserved for such matters of importance. It was a brief recap, as many of those present had attended the gathering, but it was necessary for those who hadn't and to assimilate that information into adjustments throughout their clan.

When it came time for the daimyo to give their territory reports, Halden couldn't help but lean forward when Daimyo Beynon rose. After all that had occurred in his home village with Valen, he wondered what he would detail to the others.

Halden waited for the shoe to drop as Daimyo Beynon detailed his expense and tithe reports, commenting when concluded on how his house's textile businesses were increasing prices due to a shortage of a certain fabric being imported from the Dych Clan. Once resolved, he assured that he'd lower the cost to the previous amount, but for the time being, they had to ensure the livelihoods of the minor houses in his lands. Without another announcement to share, the next daimyo stood to deliver his own accounts.

Impressed, Halden anchored his eyes toward his father's sitting form, thinking of the negotiations made behind the scenes that guaranteed Daimyo Beynon's silence. Turn by turn, each daimyo shared their reports, various concerns raised about the influx of embargos on the Kriv Clan the other four clans had voted on during the gathering and how that would impact their own territories. While the remnants of the Kriv Clan warred against both exiled ronin and separatists from the other four clans, going as far as to reengage dangerous threats and offensive actions against every clan, their precious gems, glass, spices, and wheat were banned from trade.

Alarming accounts rose with increased Kriv patrols and stray ronin by the border territories, two separate daimyo claiming sights of a large beast lurking among the fringe of their lands. All the while, Javan annotated every detail in shorthand within a journal for the shogun, his hand moving furiously with the pace of words shared over the course of several hours.

A graying daimyo stood up, the last major house to be represented at the assembly. Steel-blue eyes shone with cunning as Halden's uncle, Markus, quickly ran through the reports of his house, one known for the academic works of progress that were disseminated throughout the clans. With a recent scientific discovery leading to a remarkable scope that could clarify images at vast distances, their house had led the industry with new inventions. Hunger shone in the eyes of another daimyo, as if he were devising how to get his own hands on something with that marketability.

As the assembly heard the conclusion of his report, many heads turning back to the shogun, Daimyo Arundel cleared his throat before addressing the collective group. "If I may voice one concern of my house, we have a most regrettable grievance."

An array of murmurs spouted forth, the shogun silencing them all with a single hand. "Proceed," Ilias said, his tone level.

"Many of us have become aware of the continued presence of one who does not fall under the umbrella of Devout," Markus began, addressing his kin daimyo with a dramatic sweep of his hand. "Respectfully, Shogun Arundel, we are befuddled as to why we are harboring an exiled ronin when such matters are forbidden within the Treaty of Clans."

Gritting his teeth, Halden maintained his composure at the barbed attack. He could envision how to redirect such a distorted version of events without proclaiming the prophecy. Even pulling the barb out would cause damage, no matter the excuse.

Of course, his uncle would wait until today to turn the tables against his father.

Across the room, Halden made out the slight smirk on Daimyo Dagon's face, surely siding with Markus at his niece Owena's behest. The raven-haired shinobi detested Caenrya for one reason or another, and Halden knew she was close to her uncle. A quick survey of the room showed few unperturbed by the bold accusation, many outright critical. Only Daimyo Beynon appeared unfazed, even somewhat defensive of the shogun.

Rising to his feet, Shogun Arundel clasped his hands behind his body. His posture was open and unbothered. "I'm afraid I must correct an imperative mistake in your question. The girl in question is a refugee, and one not hailing from any clan. By our own doctrine, the Kriv Clan remains as half of the population or less that the territory consumes. Others living in the warring lands are clanless, a separate, rising entity that intends to overtake the territory. Furthermore, she was never recognized nor established as a shinobi or ronin in any territory of the collective lands; therefore, she does not fall under the constraints of the Treaty of Clans."

More than a few were shocked by the shogun's statement, Ilias having withheld that crucial piece of information to determine who would turn against him before the verdict was out. It was clever but also alarming, the percentage who leaped at the opportunity.

Though Markus... Markus was livid and embarrassed, his face paling before the assembly. "I see, Shogun. Regrets for the confusion on my behalf, though I must know, where does this *girl* hail from? She obviously has been gifted from generous bloodlines. It would not fool anyone to assume she is from mere common stalk in the warring land's clanless faction."

Halden's muscles tensed. To speak out against a shogun was akin to committing a crime. A punishable offense. His uncle had kept matters between the family until now to his knowledge. Was Markus testing his father's limitations?

"Since when do I answer to a daimyo, Lord Markus? Do check your tongue before your misplaced approximation of rank and power leads you to disrespect your shogun," Ilias reminded, the soft command in his voice unmistakable.

The effect was anything but soft.

His brother tried to fish a shark, and his pole snapped as a result. It was a glimpse beneath the waters, only rising near the surface to flash his teeth as a blatant display of authority. Everyone in the room acknowledged it like a whip to their backs, straightening and wiping any expression that may have been construed as rebellious. They almost forgot who led them, just for one precarious moment.

Only one of the clan's strongest shinobi could be worthy of the title of shogun, and Ilias had never been bested in a formal challenge. Such disrespect would beget two results. One, the offender could publicly apologize for his actions. Or he could challenge the shogun for his title, testing him in combat. Should the challenger fail, he would be stripped of all titles and power. However, if the challenger won, there would be a reelection.

Markus wasn't strong enough, and he knew it.

Tradition dictated then that Markus fall to his knees and beg for forgiveness or else his honor would be tarnished and that of his direct family. Perhaps even to the degree of severe punishment, should the shogun deem it so.

Halden forgot who lived under the same roof as him, and the absolute rule he held over the clan. Within the past few years, he viewed him as a poor father, neglecting his son for work and duty. He never saw Ilias work beyond the public appearances and office work. It was shortsighted, Halden now realized, of his previous perception. There was much his father had to balance, and he was just beginning to see the surface of it all.

With a second's hesitation, Daimyo Arundel lowered to his knees to ask for forgiveness, Ilias overlooking the action as if it were beneath him. All present knew the daimyo hesitated too long, showing his displeasure blatantly. While the shogun would be within his rights to punish Markus, Halden knew his father wouldn't. Ilias wielded power with a humble balance, but that charity could be perceived as a weakness by those who sought to challenge him. It concerned Halden.

The shogun's voice rose as he addressed the assembly. "I shall only state this once, only to prevent further *confusion*."

At the hint of anger, Daimyo Dagon lowered his head marginally, unwilling to further test their shogun. Halden questioned if his father had ever executed his authority in such a way, the daimyo seemingly caught off guard by his countenance and exertion that demanded obedience in its entirety.

"This girl is under my personal protection, a request made to me by the ancestors themselves," Ilias warned. Outright gasps escaped two daimyos and an apprentice at the declaration. "I dutifully follow the will of those before us and will not abide any inquisition against the wisdom of our ancestors."

Halden was astounded, then impressed beyond words, by the craftiness of his father. Not only had he managed to put his uncle in place without grave offense to the other daimyo—somehow managing to secure his veiled threat against all—but he made any further attempts against Caenrya an act of treason. It was forbidden to dishonor those who walked above. It was grounds for execution if made public.

And he knew exactly which daimyos were involved in this small act of rebellion. Their shared glances spoke more than their words did when Markus rose to challenge Ilias. One peek at Javan's notes confirmed it for Halden. The kampaku recorded those who expressed dissidence.

Ilias would not tolerate any curiosity about her origins or place within the clan; his only concern rested with the perception of the other clans. Halden began envisioning where that trouble could lie and even predicted his uncle's mechanisms wandering toward that pathway next. Flexing his hands, Halden itched to discuss it with his father, and ideas formed to counter his uncle's next move.

Murmurs of *Yes, shogun* echoed throughout the chamber, Ilias analyzing the display of reactions before him. "There will be no further discussion of this topic until our ancestors deem the change necessary. For now, let us place our whole and undying trust in them and press forward with their guidance."

The chamber echoed with confirming words of assent, Ilias finally ordering Daimyo Arundel to return to his seat. From there, he began addressing every concern lifted by his people, proposing incredible solutions to every problem raised. Efficient and simple, but given in a way that revealed the intricate nature of the mind that contrived all of it. Pleased expressions met the shogun's all around, the methodology of his words chosen, tone used, and mannerisms performed resulting in the image of a ruler any would lay down their lives for.

Halden had never been stirred in such a way, had never realized what his father was to these people. Hel, the other month, he almost threw a fist at the shogun when he ordered Caenrya to be cuffed. Shortsighted.

Incredibly so. It all clicked together why Halden was treated with such reverence by the citizens and why his peerage was in awe of him.

The man before Halden was why. He only hoped he could live up to the legacy.

By the time the assembly was dismissed, Halden was prepared to ask Ilias what their next steps would be. But before they could do much more than crest the second-floor landing, oniwaban were racing to them.

Never a good sign.

Halden's mind went straight toward Caenrya, envisioning all sorts of terrible things that may have occurred. Had Valen fulfilled his promise to them, raiding the Citadel to retrieve her? She'd all but confessed she didn't hold a candle to his flame, guaranteeing her loss against the ronin should he have made an appearance within the village.

It made his heart rate quicken, a sickening weight clinging to his gut.

"What is it?" Ilias questioned, a tense hand beckoning Javan close.

"A beast has appeared in Temple Square. It appeared from thin air and is slaughtering our people," an oniwaban swiftly reported. "It's something we've never seen before. Nothing resembling any animal or creature known to us."

Immediately, Ilias's bearing became that of a warlord's, power exuding from him and his following orders. "Send both vanguards two and four from the oniwaban reserves to face the threat directly, one and three to guard the Citadel's perimeter. I'll lead the reserve from any Arundel forces to mark the enemy's location and tail should it attempt to escape. Summon Eirea Cadigan to capture this beast alive, if possible. Alert the oniwaban on Caenrya's detail to confine her to her quarters for the time being. Send two additional members to guard her quarters."

Halden stood, tuning out the flurry of confused voices from the council as his father barged out of the Duša Clan Temple. Without waiting for his own orders, he followed the shogun. Calmly, but with confidence and efficiency, Ilias continued to delegate tasks to disseminate medical relief. The oniwaban departed with haste to enact his shogun's demands, Ilias beckoning Halden as they moved to bound through the Citadel to reach the square.

"When we near," Ilias began, speaking to his son this time, "we must assess and leap in where the difference could be made. If I order you to retreat, do so without delay."

"Yes, Shogun," Halden acknowledged, addressing his leader rather than his father. Now that he knew Caenrya would be safe, Halden could push aside his fears to focus on the matter at hand. Clearing his thoughts, sharpness edged his battle-ready mind, his eyes taking in every detail as they neared the square.

But as they closed in, only the sound of distant wailing within a chilling silence reached his ears, a few oniwaban falling into rank as the scene opened up before them.

It was...

Clenching his fists, Halden refused to let the horror of it sink in. Rather, he honed in on Eirea, Ryu, and Hina across the square as they applied basic medical assistance to those in need. The commander passed words to Ryu as she crossed the cobblestone to intercept the shogun.

"Shogun," Eirea greeted, a fist clenched over her heart.

Without returning the motion, Ilias demanded a rundown of intel, directing the oniwaban in the vicinity to assist with medical attention.

"The few who survived claimed an enormous beast to have ravaged the square, appearing out of thin air and disappearing in a similar manner," Eirea grimly reported, her features tight. "It had the mashed appearance of a humanoid mountain lion with characteristics of a bull.

It moved to slaughter with speed unparalleled to our own shinobi that happened to be within the vicinity. None survived who faced it."

Blood... so much blood. Gouging claw marks stood testament to its presence. Buildings were devastated around.

"Halden and I will scout the area until it can be determined that this beast isn't within our village." Turning toward the arriving reinforcements, Ilias divvied up the shinobi into teams for scouting, each party taking one Arundel to aid with taiji marking.

It was fortunate a few shinobi traveled from House Arundel to accompany Daimyo Arundel to the assembly. Their vin was perfect for this crucial undertaking.

Eirea was left in charge of the scene and would organize the medical teams upon arrival. True to his word, Ilias left with Halden as they claimed the sector Eirea determined the beast to have escaped into. Each other team scoured the Citadel, advising civilians to return to their respective homes and questioning the ones who may have spotted the *thing* leaving.

All to no avail.

Hours of tedious hunting proved unfruitful. Every other team encountered the same result. It was as if this beast really had appeared and dissolved out of nowhere... which only left room for confusion. If the reports from outlying territories indicated this particular beast's presence, then surely it traveled on foot.

But how had it gotten past the Citadel wall? Could it use taiji similar to shinobi, allowing it to scale over?

The wall was warded to indicate passage of anything of remarkable taiji, which every being held within their bodies. Not to mention the dozens of shinobi posted along it, always patrolling.

By the time a disaster area was set up at the medical center for those displaced due to damages, and the scant six survivors were given care, Halden was exhausted from the adrenaline leaving his body. It all happened so quickly, leaving no clue as to what this beast was or if it would return.

A majority of the victims were reported to be the Devout. A small gathering of their people happened to be worshipping in the square when it all occurred. Not much more intelligence could be gleaned from the survivors, the carnage and brutalities paralyzing many as they attempted to escape to hide in whatever crevices available that could provide some semblance of protection.

The night was wrapped up with a miserable air. Security tightened throughout the Citadel for the indefinable future. Halden barely slept that evening, the cold bite of a pillar behind his back plaguing his mind as the sharp tip of the kunai danced across his skin. Many times, he awoke in a cold sweat, hearing Valen's laughter. The morning brought about nothing but more weight as his father's presence was noticeably lacking in the wake of the unnamed attack.

Many teams, including his, were assigned to regular patrols, alternating for short breaks as the square was being rebuilt. Caenrya wasn't permitted near Temple Square, instead utilizing the time to continue her training with Aya throughout the days.

Meanwhile, Halden trained with his vin, pushing the limits of his duration, seeing all with it during each scouting route. His body was trembling by the end of each passing day, and his knees were shaky as he collapsed into his bed. It was more than he'd ever pushed himself, his line of sight increasing as he expanded his consciousness to visualize the taiji in every leaf, squirrel, cloud, and person within two hundred meters at a constant pace. If he pushed in a single direction, Halden almost reached four hundred meters, a distance that surpassed a handful of his cousins within the house.

Eirea intertwined training with their patrols in the following week, including brief spells of zazen to continue down the Five Paths of Awakening. It had become infinitely more challenging for Halden to find his center, obstructions stemming from the nightmares Valen forced on him, preventing any true semblance of peace. This proved to be far more aggravating than he anticipated, for he was close to completing the fourth path—the Path of Cultivation—thus freeing himself from any worldly ties to emptiness.

Now, though, Halden struggled to reconcile the fact that something fundamental was broken despite his previous confidence he would continue without issue. He pushed the thought away, hoping that ignoring it over time would aid in healing—or, at least, that by pretending, he could trick his mind into peace. He had less than six months to become a jōnin.

But he still caught the occasional flash of Valen's face hiding around an oak tree or at the corner of an opened window. It sent his chest into a beating frenzy, his ears ringing as Halden strove to regain control of his senses.

Over that strenuous week, the daimyo congregations left for their respective territories with extra protection provided by the shogun. Caenrya remained confined to her quarters or out training with the Dagon elder, not crossing paths with her team due to their varying schedules. Eirea was indirect with her answers regarding Caenrya's training, and the vagueness raised Halden's suspicions. Something was amiss.

With how fatigued he'd been by the end of each day, Halden hadn't mustered the energy to attempt a visit to Caenrya after their workday concluded. If he were honest with himself, he'd also accept the fact that he didn't feel worthy of doing so.

Since that encounter with Valen, Halden could empathize even more with Caenrya's history. Though it was such a meager, scant amount of time he endured, and she had undergone *years* of it, still managing to come out better than he had. Which made him weak and such a pathetic excuse of a man that Halden could only imagine what Caenrya thought of him.

Time, it seemed, would not lend its aid to his plight.

Chapter Twenty

CAENRYA

Caenrya was mandated to steer clear of Temple Square, so that she did. From the crack of dawn to the rise of the moons, she practiced with the katana. Today, Ren provided several bamboo targets, instructing her on methods of attacking, many of which Caenrya was familiar with. Informally, of course, as she learned from years of finding out the hard way in the ring.

Whereas her taiji blades would cut with ease, physical steel required such practiced accuracy and precision that Caenrya still struggled to move the blade without changing the angle of the blade as it cut through bamboo. When she claimed it to be impossible, Ren simply wielded his own blade and seamlessly chopped through a grouping of six bamboos tied together. Then, he showed off with several swifter strikes, each shaving but centimeters off the top with such skill that Caenrya couldn't help but glower.

Horizontal, vertical, and angled strikes all required something different of her, a most trying endeavor that had her catching her teeth grinding of their own accord.

"Ensure that your dominant hand is closer to the guard while performing the strike from below," Ren instructed, demonstrating with his own blade. Pausing at the end, his dark, upturned eyes met hers as he held the position. "Always end at the chest so the sharp side of the katana remains facing upward. This will be an excellent transitioning point to flow into another cut, depending on how your opponent reacts and their level of skill."

Again and again, Caenrya repeated the movement until it was passable, taking a break only to eat a packed lunch. When the afternoon arrived, she returned to wooden sword fighting, Ren deeming she was still far from any combat with steel. With each swing, Caenrya threw her anger into it, Eirea's words still pestering her.

It was the fact Eirea was *right* that shook her.

Don't comfort yourself with a lie.

It was the way, the *only* way, to prevent more tragedy. Despite what Enya had told her, there were some things Caenrya could control, fewer things she'd suffer over. These little lies were all Caenrya had, the only thing she could cling to. How else could she bear what was to come, her inevitable destiny?

There is solace in the truth.

No. Not even a modicum. Should Caenrya accept what she truly knew deep, deep within, she'd cease to exit. Her soul had long since been fragmented, and if it weren't for these precious lies, how would she ever manage to continue?

There was a time when she felt more freely and trusted somewhat. That only led to one of the detrimental turning points that careened her into the monster she'd become and the monster she would remain to rescue Verina.

Her sister weighed heavily on her mind, blame still hanging from her as a ripe cherry would a tree. Caenrya couldn't bring herself to sleep on the futon mattress, tucking herself into the corner each night and staring into the darkness until sleep pulled her from the waking world. With the next attack, almost a week after the first and in the same exact place, Caenrya had all but been forbidden from public dawdling.

The attack was identical, though only one perished. It was mostly confined to physical destruction, furthering the previous damage it enacted on the square.

Whoever the unfortunate soul was who left her groceries each week did it in a punctual manner. When she traveled directly to the newfound training area, Caenrya noticed the lack of civilians who traversed through the Citadel. Shinobi regularly monitored the walkways, and shutters were closed on storefronts normally booming with activity in the early morning rays. By the end of the fourth week, another ambush occurred. Though as for the where, well, it alarmed the populace.

Riverside Square.

Always, this so-called beast would materialize from the ether, tearing into any innocents in sight without a soul left to witness. It learned from its first mistakes, leaving no survivors to gather data on it and making a point to demolish everything in sight. Its power was immeasurable, tearing into every shinobi stationed nearby and obliterating metal with ease. Its intelligence allowed it to evade the shogun's constant vigil, appearing in the exact opposite location of Ilias and dissolving into the air just before he could arrive.

As if it were toying with them all.

For the clan, it was the absolute worst nightmare they could envision, their terror keeping them all isolated within their residences.

For Caenrya, it was simply another day.

To that point, she continued to train with the katana, avoiding Team Cadigan at all costs. Even when Halden knocked at her door one eve, even when he kept returning every other day to pester her when she ignored him over the last few weeks. Even when Ryu had left a boxed lunch of mouthwatering teriyaki over steamed rice, and when his girlfriend, Hina—her soft-spoken voice somehow managing to reach through a door—apologized for any offense she may have caused when Eirea asked her to aid Caenrya.

Even when Eirea herself asked to speak one morning before her practices.

Caenrya's anger hadn't dissipated one bit, the unfair aspect of being forbidden from wandering the Citadel entirely pissed her off. More so her so-called *team* was out on patrols, and Caenrya was restricted to limited movements with a guard over her shoulder at all times.

The only bright aspect was Caenrya dramatically improved with the katana over the month, moving on to the steel blades Ren supplied at last. While her muscles screamed, she refused to balk from the added weight to her movements over the course of every day. Stamina, strength, and skills all improved day-to-day, and Caenrya finally gained the fruits of her labor.

The oniwaban still kept to himself, rarely uttering any words outside those required for training. In a way, Caenrya was glad for it. What did she have to share otherwise?

When the early evening stole the sun from the sky and the stars greeted her eyes, Caenrya made her descent back into the village. She paused at her door, her hand lingering on the chilled metal before she backtracked. There'd been something she'd had her eye on for some time, and she thought it may be time at last to supply her own equipment for these training sessions.

Most storefronts were outright shut, but some still operated behind closed shutters. When Caenrya padded down a walkway, no others in sight, she turned a corner leading to Wisteria Square just below her apartment. Across from her window was a weapons shop that still permitted customers. During these turbulent times, the owner made a small fortune off the common folk's worry over this beast.

Knocking, Caenrya took a small step back and waited for the lock to turn. Several pairs of eyes warily watched as she entered past a worker, but the silence was music to her ears as she made for the wall of katanas on display. She ignored the person with a hateful sneer and the other one who pulled her child behind the counter. Caenrya only had eyes on the display of beautiful metal works before her, unsure of which to purchase with her given allowance. They all appeared similar, with slight differences within the guards, handles, and blades. At the top, a collection of ornate katanas gleamed, the notion of jeweled weaponry immediately turning her nose from them.

The middle contained an interesting assortment of engraved blades, the purpose unclear to Caenrya. So, her eyes lowered further to the bottom blades, each more ordinary than the previous. The handles were bare, the guards thin, and the blades uneven by a slim margin. Frowning, Caenrya shifted in her boots, reluctant to purchase anything she was unsure of.

Customers navigated toward the purchase counter, their voices whispering within earshot malicious words. *Why doesn't the shogun sacrifice her to the beast? That's why it's here. The ancestors couldn't be clearer.* And. *There's been talk of the pointed-ear one being the summoner of the beast. She delights in our deaths.* And. *We could try to take her out now. We'd be doing the clan a favor.*

That was when the mother shushed her husband, pointing to their child frightened beside her leg.

Biting her tongue, Caenrya turned to leave. It was painfully obvious everyone had moved from hating her to outright plotting against her.

What was the point of *anything*? Why stay in a clan that would kill her in the end?

A shine caught her eye when she twisted away from the wall, a single katana propped on a cushion above a glass pedestal. A small etching was written in a plaque below, reading: *The blade that cuts only what must be.* The handle was black-wrapped over diamond-shaped openings of gold, the guard slim but strong. Caenrya leaned forward, inspecting the razor-sharp edge and fine-line mastery of the make.

This was the one. She knew it in her bones.

Turning, Caenrya made to request them to hold it when the tip of a blade met her throat. A trembling man stood at the other end of it, and the rage in his eyes pulled his thin lips back. "You don't deserve to be here, eating our food and taking the lives of our kin," he spluttered out, the thin edge warbling.

Before she could do anything, a firm knocking sounded at the door, pulling the man's attention. The woman quietly begged him to withdraw, the child sobbing at her leg. Swearing, the man backed off, holding the katana in Caenrya's direction all the while. "Leave," he seethed, gesturing once toward the door with his weapon. "Before I make you."

Doubtful.

But she wouldn't say as much, for if she did, Caenrya would surely start a fight. That would only confirm the clan's perception of her, even if it were already true. Really though, it would eliminate any opportunity for growth with the katana and taiji as she'd be exiled. She wasn't sure if that were something she'd be willing to lose yet.

Caenrya exited the store with loud footsteps, slamming the door behind her while glowering at the unfamiliar oniwaban outside of it. "I know," she growled before he had the opportunity to lecture her about straying outside her allowed pathways.

The man disappeared back into the night, leaving Caenrya to storm across the otherwise empty square and round the corner to her residence. Climbing the stairs, she heard the shuffle of steps before her eyeline crested the top. Her feet stalled on the last step, and her mind cursed at her for the luck she was having.

"What do you want," Caenrya said flatly, meeting the heavy steel-gray gaze that didn't balk from her own.

Halden leaned against the frame in gray and black silk robes, his bronze hair glinting in the lamplight as he jerked a thumb toward her apartment door behind him. "Wanted to stop by and see how your training was going." The tabby cat she'd been feeding for over three months wound around his legs, creating a figure eight.

Traitor. She glared at it.

Then she looked back at Halden. There was much to decipher, between the forced nonchalance of his tone, the hollow edge to his expression, and the strain in his shoulders. Caenrya was beginning to realize a trend in her behavior with the weakness she exhibited around others when they displayed their own. Despite it, and damned to it, she unlocked her door. Caenrya sensed his hesitation after walking in to turn on the lights, giving him a face that clearly read *well?*

The tabby darted in, ready for his daily chicken treat.

Closing the door behind him, he removed his sandals, and Halden pressed his back against the wall. "I've seen this cat around a lot. I didn't realize you adopted one."

Snorting, Caenrya shook her head, moving for the refrigerator. "She adopted me. It comes and goes as it pleases. A *cat* has more freedom than I." She glowered at her chicken as she fed shredded bits to the purring cat.

"Does she have a name?" he quietly asked.

Caenrya huffed, suddenly feeling self-conscious. "No."

Opening the window, Caenrya watched as the grateful creature headbutted her once before leaving on the infamous ledge outside. Closing it, she removed her boots and turned at last to face Halden.

His eyes went to the purpling bruise on her cheekbone, to the splayed array of manuscripts along her alcove. Back to the bruise, perturbed by its presence. "Is it happening again?"

Concern. He was... concerned for her. Over the mark that was no more.

"No," Caenrya softly said, crossing her arms and waiting for him to get to whatever it was that kept bringing him to her doorstep.

He nodded, blowing out an *okay* before turning to leave. But guilt crawled from her bones, eating away at the ice she shielded herself with.

"Why do you keep returning every week?"

The muscles in Halden's arms rippled below his silken sleeve as it rose to grip the back of his hung neck. A moment passed, and Caenrya was a second away from giving up that meager branch she stretched out. Finally, he faced her, agitated. "Don't you care about any of us?"

Caenrya's lips pressed into a line. She wasn't sure how to answer that, something at in her chest preventing her from doing so. Something fragile. Something she couldn't afford to break else she might never be able to recuperate from the damage dealt.

"I don't get it, Caenrya," Halden quietly spoke, his jaw clenching. At her persistent silence, he made a noise in exasperation. "Why do you refuse to acknowledge all of us? We've been trying, and you push us away at every turn."

Her eyes hardened, and her will forced her shoulders square.

"Give me the reason. That's all I want." His voice was edged with defeat, and his feet stepped forward across the tatami mat until hers backtracked several steps to compensate.

Halden witnessed the flicker of dread across her face before she could hide it, his own twisting into something that Caenrya had to turn her back to. She planted her hands on the desk to steady herself against the swarm of damned memories that kept threatening her.

"I care about you," Halden admitted, uncertainty almost undermining his statement. "Which is why I won't let you distance yourself from us. From me."

Those words... Caenrya put every ounce of strength she had into freezing in place, for if she moved a single muscle, she could very well lose every ounce of self-control.

"I'm not leaving. Not until you tell me why," he said.

It was respectful, the way he said it. Accepting and trusting as if whatever words she told him, he'd remain there. He wouldn't turn tail and abandon her. That's what he silently said, and with it, Caenrya couldn't help but recall that vulnerability he showed the night she escaped from the medical center. The way his eyes were lost, as if he were searching for that reason to live, too.

"You don't have to go through anything alone anymore. I promise you that, Caenrya."

Such gentle words. Caenrya knew he meant it. Believed it. And it killed her because it was happening all over again. This, she realized, was no better than Hel.

Her chin trembled from the force of hysteria that was close to overwhelming her. Her fingernails scraped against the wood of her desk. Caenrya's mind whirled for a way to regain control and fix this before it ended like that one time... just two years ago.

Breathing shakily, Caenrya took advantage of the minute he patiently waited through—true to his word. As for Caenrya, she knew what must be done, what must be said. It would be one of the most horrific things she'd ever done, but it was the only way to save those around her.

The truest form of loneliness wasn't being abandoned or ignored. It was having to push others away to give them every fighting chance at surviving. Otherwise, she may ruin their lives, too, when they inevitably get caught between Valen and herself.

A shallow laugh escaped her lips. Caenrya's shoulders moved as her laughter coldly bubbled around her. She turned toward Halden, folding her arms across her chest with a lazy smirk crossing her face. At the tilt of her head, she could see the immediate effect she had on him. Both of his pupils dilated, and his body went rigid at the reminder of who mentored her.

She knew he saw those icy eyes and silver hair, the mask of his mother's killer.

So close. She was too close to breaking her act, but it had to be done. With a final condemnation of her soul, she drove the stake home.

"I've never met someone so pathetic. You're a child who pines over what he thinks is *good* and *noble*. If only a few minutes with Valen can make you piss your pants, what in the world could possibly delude you to this extent that you think you have a fighting chance?" Caenrya cooed, the smugness she portrayed contesting heavily with the self-hatred she internally harbored. Especially when she witnessed her words strike hard and fast, like an asp to his throat.

Tilting her head to the other side, she forced her hand to pat her arm casually. "The type of man you are is simply tragic," Caenrya said, sharpening her gaze. "I've said it once, and I'll say it again. I stay only to use your clan for my sole purpose of rescuing Verina. Nothing. Else. Matters."

She stepped once in his direction. Eirea thought they were friends. Caenrya had to break that assumption with all haste.

"I don't understand why your mother's sorry for you. This world isn't for the weak and useless. Perhaps it's a good thing she isn't here to see you fail worse than she did."

Despicable. Unworthy. Loathsome.

Caenrya was all those things, a bane on all of those who tried to lend aid. The only way to preserve the goodness of others was to protect them from the worst of it. She only wished it didn't hurt so damn much. He flinched, driving the nail deeper through her heart.

Her smirk fell a fraction when Halden's expression recovered, pointedly making a show of planting himself on the edge of her unused mattress. "You can say nothing worse than what I already have to myself," he said, his tone pulling at her. His face fell toward his fidgeting hands, and his voice barely reached her ears. "A lifetime of nothing but bleak prospects can make anyone the worst shade of themselves. The things you do and say as a result only make it that much more impossible to forgive yourself."

That smirk of hers lost its edge when his eyes met hers. Caenrya failed, and try as she might, Halden was dead set on his resolve. It was aggravating. Why couldn't he leave her be? She didn't want them to die, any of them.

Especially him.

Halden's expression was assertive when his face lifted, and his broad shoulders pulled back. "Stop this."

Everything was silent as her chest constricted, Caenrya fighting an internal war in which she had no idea what side she was on. It was hard, so damn *hard,* to try to push him away any longer. She longed to have the privilege to rely on another again but was terrified of the repercussions. Her eyes burned as she ran her hands over her forehead, brushing back stray hairs.

"I've already forgiven you. There's nothing you can say that I wouldn't," Halden said, his sight burning into hers, stealing the last ounce of resolve she could muster.

Biting into her tongue, Caenrya lowered her hands, an inferno of anger churning in place of the self-hatred and horror eating away at her. "Why are you people so impossible?" she shouted, gesturing wide with her arms. "Why are you so Hel-bent on dying for someone who is *nothing?*"

The anger felt so good to let out. Her anger at the luxurious lives these clan people led. Her anger at Team Cadigan's camaraderie and the lack of repercussions from it. Anger at herself for wanting it all, despite her sister reaping a continued life of slavery. But most of all, her anger at a man who'd give it all up for *her.* A person so unfit for such a gift.

A slight scoff sounded from Halden, his calloused hands closing into fists. "I'm Hel-bent on living to see the moment where you realize there is something worth living and fighting for beyond that of your sister. There will come a time when we do rescue her, and then what? Do you think your life ends there?" Notes of anger crept into the velvet of his voice, growing and growing as he spoke.

Her mouth opened, then closed. A flush spread across her cheekbones. "I don't have time to worry about what comes next. That's a boon people like me don't get."

"We bought you time!" His dark brows narrowed. "Through bloodshed and our own, we've given it to you—"

"By almost dying!" Fury filled the fire in her chest, burning all reserves she typically held in strict check. A warble slunk into her next words. "I don't want anyone to die because of *me*."

Pristine black silk flickered in her room's lighting as Halden shifted his stance. The hard panes of his face softened marginally, but his voice was unrelenting. "We won't. The entire clan is behind you in this endeavor, and my father will ensure we rescue your sister without fail."

Flashes of dead bodies, smells of rotting iron, echoes of broken promises, and the fading light of a person's last second in the world all overwhelmed her at once.

It peaked to a crescendo—the fury, aching sadness, and so many *regrets* when she said, "*Everyone* does." Her voice cracked, and her throat grew too thick for her to speak anymore.

Bone-tired and defeated, Caenrya leaned into her desk chair, turning her head away from him as she couldn't stand the disgrace of what she had spewed at him. It didn't even matter if he had forgiven her, for she already felt redemption was a long-alluding concept she'd never be able to comfort herself with. Maybe, though, maybe she could offer this one explanation and allow him to run for the hills while there was still time.

Maybe honesty would be her saving grace and, more importantly, his.

Swallowing, she got out, "Valen will kill you if he learns that..." Her voice caught, her throat thick with emotion. Taking a moment, Caenrya steadied her words. "If he learns that I care for you too. He will go to the very pits of Hel to destroy anything that I grow close with, only sparing Verina to keep from losing me completely."

A dangerous sharpness entered Halden's oncoming words. "What has he done?"

It was the crack that broke the dam, everything coming back with alarming sharpness. Caenrya's lungs hitched, and her eyes squeezed shut as her mouth moved. "Out of all the children in Shikei when I first arrived, there was only one I eventually took enough pity on. At the cost of Verina and I's future, I never allowed myself such weakness before then. He struggled in the fighting black-sights, a coined name for the underground fighting rings. As we grew older, his punishments became more severe. The daimyo swore if he lost his next match, he'd be put out for slaughter."

Hands clenching around themselves, Caenrya pressed on her mind, reliving every second. "I... helped him. Secretly. Over the course of several weeks, he improved remarkably. He won the coming match and the next. This went on for two years, and for those years, I had a friend to lean on."

Everything hurt in her chest, an ache so deeply buried she'd forgotten just how raw it was still as it surfaced.

"A younger girl was brought in, so terrified and hurt that we took her into our small circle. I only had weeks with her before his next match approached." Such devastation clawed at Caenrya, leaking into her words. "I never realized that it was all part of Valen's game."

Close by, Halden shifted, the noise drawing her slightly from the pull of the crushing, agonizing waves of memories shifting through her mind.

Caenrya bit her lip for a moment, separating herself however she could to avoid the emotion of it all. "Valen waited all those years for one slipup, one thing he could punish me for above the rest. I—we—held hands for but a foolish moment around the others. I didn't want to chance it, but Ten was insistent. Determined to show where he stood in front of the scared girl. Determined to show that, even in a dark place such as Shikei, there could be hope. The night before the match, Valen pulled the boy and I aside. He somehow saw that brief moment we had held hands, and it was over. He forced me to choose between the boy and Verina, choosing one to kill."

"You chose Verina," Halden murmured, his voice unrecognizable.

"No," Caenrya answered, meeting his shocked gaze with her broken one. "I couldn't choose. I had grown too close with Ten, and it cost him everything. Valen dehumanized Ten's mind, hours passing in *our* world as he stripped Ten of all reason and emotion until he was but a husk. Two and Three held me back the whole time. I couldn't do anything if I wanted Verina to remain unharmed. I was forced to watch every minute."

She got out, "We both know time passes differently in the mind. Valen tortured him for *weeks* in his mind."

Caenrya's head slowly moved side to side without her being aware, the scene fresh in her mind. "Valen let Two and Three finish him off with such brutality, but there wasn't anything left of Ten to feel it." The chilling cold hands of Valen haunted her shoulders, the very place they were when Ten was murdered. "They knocked me out after that, and when I awoke, I—I was in a coffin," she gasped, the space more claustrophobic than it had been a moment before.

The room spun on a teetering axis, a rotting stench filling her nose.

"Ten's corpse lay beneath me, and for days, I screamed for help, for anything."

Her teeth chattered, and both of her arms wrapped around her tightly. Caenrya dimly recognized Halden's expression of horror and the unnatural stillness he stood with.

Licking her lips, Caenrya told him, "I tried everything to get out." The broken nails, split forehead, bruised knees... all resulting from her attempts. "But the only thing that worked was a bone." Ten's. "I could only split the wood apart enough with it to claw out above the layer of sand." Meticulously, she had to shuffle the sand to the bottom of the coffin to avoid being buried alive. "When I finally managed to get out,

Valen was there to bring me back. By the time I arrived back at Shikei, the girl had been sold to an awful lord with a reputation for the unseemly, and the only remains of Ten were the stains on my clothes."

Clothes she was forced to wear for days, but the final screams and expressions of pure agony tortured from Ten lingered much, much longer. And what she did in that wooden coffin to get out...

For her sister.

How could she put this fate on Halden? On any of them? At least with this... he should leave her be.

"All of it was a cruel lesson to only trust him. Only rely on him. Him, and second to him, the daimyo. I was no one else's," Caenrya whispered. Such humiliation ate at her, her weakness, and what she allowed to happen. What she *did* to survive.

You belong with us. We don't need another repeat of Ten, do we? Valen had said to her, the threat crystal clear. It wasn't Ten who stood in front of Caenrya now, but the man Valen threatened.

Forcing her knees to lock, Caenrya swayed lightly as she stood, incapable of looking at anything else but the floor. "Please leave. Leave and understand that I can't do that to anyone else," she said, wanting nothing more than to be done with this disgrace.

Her voice was hollow, but her mind wasn't. It echoed with Valen's promise of killing Halden.

Halden moved, but not toward the door. Strong arms pulled her in close, his chin lowering to rest on her shoulder. Caenrya's eyes shot wide, and her entire body stiffened at the gesture.

"I'll never leave you, Caenrya," Halden's voice rumbled gently in her ear, the words shattering her last semblance of control.

Tears pooled in her eyes, her lower lip trembling from the welling emotion. This was the first time she'd ever told that story, no one else comprehending the extent other than Valen.

Halden only held tighter, Caenrya allowing her forehead to press against his warm chest as she struggled to process his words. That promise. One sob racked her body, the whole thing incomprehensible to her.

Her shoulders shook harder, both of her arms squeezing across her chest as she leaned into Halden. How could anyone willingly stay with her after hearing that? Who could bear the consequences of such a thing?

But...

Some aching part of her lightened at his words. Felt less isolated by the comfort of his strength. Caenrya selfishly wanted this all to be true, but she knew what repercussions would come of it.

"Valen will—" Caenrya started, a hiccup cutting off her sentence.

"We'll deal with him. Somehow. Someway. You belong here now. With us," Halden reassured, his scorn for the ronin evident in his tone.

You belong with us. Valen's cold words sent a shiver down her spine. Did she?

Desperately, Caenrya wanted what Halden said to be true. She wanted to stay with them. Wanted the nightmares to end. But Enya's warning hung heavy on her chest, and Caenrya knew more would be asked of her yet. A pestering nudge claimed it would be their lives, but surely Enya would warn her if the cost was Halden's life.

If he were to be spared, then Caenrya could let this play out... for now.

Sometime later, her sobs calmed, and the room stilled from its previous spiral. Her arms slackened, and a part of her wanted to return the embrace. The beating of his heart reverberated in her ear. His warm chest drove away a plaguing chill that lingered in her. Her shoulders loosened, and without knowing it, she had leaned further into him. For a handful of precious seconds, she cherished the feeling of closeness and security.

Caenrya had forgotten what it was like.

But she couldn't force her limbs to move around him. It was embarrassing to be so vulnerable, and she felt exposed. The natural urge to retreat reared its head. Pulling back, Caenrya solemnly met his concerned gaze as she glanced up. There was so much to say but nothing she could voice.

Pulling his hands to his trouser pockets, Halden's face appeared troubled. "Thank you for telling me. I know that wasn't easy."

It was hard to get the words out, but these she could manage. Barely. "I'm afraid I took the coward's way out for too long," Caenrya said, much to her chagrin. "I'm sorry. For the words."

"You have nothing to apologize for," Halden swore, agitated where he stood. A muscle tightened above his jaw. "I just—"

Caenrya cut him off. "I know." Her face tightened. "There's nothing to be done about the past. I only hope to avenge Ten. One day." Before Halden could speak again, she added, "For now, I want to call it a night. I'm exhausted."

At her tone and the slouch in her shoulders, Halden's expression loosened. "I'll head out then," he offered, stepping backward a few steps before shifting in the direction of the exit.

"Halden," Caenrya called out, watching as his head turned to her from the outside of the apartment. "The next time you knock, I'll do better at answering."

A small smile pulled at his lips, and she could have sworn something changed in his eyes as his chin inclined in acknowledgment. The door shut behind him, leaving Caenrya alone. The ghost of his arms loitered around her, along with a strange buzz in her veins that she wasn't sure how to categorize. Her fingers grazed the skin on her forehead, wondering at the warmth that still lingered there.

All she could think about was that hint of a new emotion she felt when Halden's eyes held hers... and how she didn't dislike it.

CHAPTER TWENTY-ONE

CAENRYA

A cool breeze gently caressed her long strands as they danced in the air behind her. She stood beside a breathtaking temple of gold-leaf and marble artistry. The sound of rustling leaves and distant birdsong filled the atmosphere as the scent of roses mingled with the fresh, earthy fragrance of the temple grounds. Gold silk wrapped around her frame, the burnished hue matching the thin rim around the blue of her eyes. It fell in the traditional kimono way, the bottom of the dress brushing against the dirt between the endless rows of rose bushes. Every direction she made out was a flat expanse, the sun rising in a gorgeous canopy of color beyond the indistinct boundary of land and sky.

A person stepped near, warm air teasing her ear as the man spoke. "I missed that delightful fire in your eyes."

"And I miss the dream you've interrupted," Caenrya shot back, pulling in a smooth motion away from Valen. "It was rather pleasant, just getting to the best part where I put a katana through your eye after you placed that ninjutsu on me."

A cream blanket appeared below where Valen made to sit in a sophisticated kimono of sapphire and gold, the space around it clearing as a glass of wine materialized in his cupped hand. "See, no one else gets me the way you do, Nrya," he grinned, toasting her with the ruby-red contents before sipping from the delicate glass. "Not to say that it doesn't wound me at times, but I do surely enjoy the bite."

Caenrya only glowered. "What do you want?"

Elevating his brow, Valen's eyes relished some card he held tightly. "That's hardly what you should concern yourself with. Are there not other matters you'd much rather ask about?"

Verina.

"What have you done with her?" Caenrya stepped closer, her face promising violence.

Valen only shrugged nonchalantly, never once breaking eye contact with her. "Nothing yet. Though I will share that his royal daimyo-ship has taken more of a hands-on approach with her of late."

Ice ran through her veins, and her face became colder than any snow that could fall. "What has he done?"

Patting the blanket beside him, Valen laid the glass down on the other side. "Come. Enjoy the field with me if you're to attempt a coup on my time with you," he said, regarding her as she stiffly obeyed.

"Now tell me," Caenrya growled. She despised his off-putting requests, and the relish he took in small manipulations.

"Let's do an exchange of sorts. I ask you a question, then you may take a turn, and we each answer honestly," Valen offered, his tone magnanimous.

Little alarm bells chimed in the back of her mind, for the timing of everything was all too convenient. Had he somehow known what transpired that evening between her and Halden or simply guessed at her growing attachment to the team?

His track history with such exchanges never ended without some form of torment. Threats against her sister, a lash with the whip, or psychological manipulation were among his favorites. However, if she refused to play his game of choice, the outcome would be much worse by the time she attempted to do so. Valen once threw her in a chamber of water, locking the lid until she caved. When Caenrya refused, she blacked out, only to have him drag her out and wait for her to recover. Within minutes of regaining consciousness, she was thrown back in with reckless abandon.

Over and over.

It scarred her permanently, and her fear of swimming in deep waters forever lingered.

Not taking a chance of repercussions, Caenrya grudgingly agreed with a nonverbal nod, waiting for him to speak first. She only hoped it would have nothing to do with them. Her team.

"How is it without the slave mark?"

Caenrya's brows furrowed at the unexpected question, trying to decipher if his expression of curiosity was sincere or if it was some long game he was laying a foundation for. When the ronin pulled another drink from his wine, she dryly said, "It's been a relief to not have an anvil hanging over my head at every given moment. Freedom suits me better than slavery."

An appreciative light entered Valen's eyes, the smile growing a hair. "I can attest to that claim. You look different in almost every way." He surveyed the surrounding fields, his dragon tattoo starkly marking his side profile. "Alas, it is wistful indeed. It cannot continue to be."

Caenrya's heart thudded, and the rise and fall of her chest slowed to maintain a careful demeanor. "My question now. What is the daimyo's newfound interest with Verina?"

"He seeks one talented in the arts of Kū with an inclination toward the *sha* seal. Fate has it that your little one has a budding talent for the healing arts and has rocketed into his favor for it," Valen distractedly told her, his eyes back to drinking in every detail of her stressed expression and her glowing hair bathing in the sun's rays.

Before she could stop the words, Caenrya blurted out, "Then she's okay? Physically, mentally...?"

Grinning, Valen winked at her with those too-straight, gleaming teeth of his. "It's my turn, is it not?" At her pointed scowl, he proceeded. "How do you find it is fitting in within clan society?"

Another odd question.

Why not ask about what their plans were or what her intentions were? It made no sense, this cat and mouse tit for tat. Unless... he somehow knew everything. Perhaps the daimyo had spies within the clan's ranks, easily gleaning this information and delivering it into Valen's wicked claws. He had someone leave that note after all. Caenrya wouldn't doubt that for one second, but couldn't understand what he'd stand to gain by playing this particular charade.

"You already know I don't," Caenrya replied, planting a palm on the deliciously soft fabric beneath her. Her eyes narrowed on his, searching for some clue as to his motive. "I don't fit in, nor do they accept me."

An unusual twist turned Valen's mouth, something flickering within his elusive eyes. "I don't care to flaunt it, but I've warned you in the past how they treat people like us."

Like us.

Did Valen have history within a clan? In the years of his presence, Valen never once gave any inclination as to his upbringing and had already been employed at Shikei when she arrived. It made her wonder if there was any merit to knowing what his past may hold or if it could give her a lead to destroy him with.

Moreover, it disturbed her at how this kindred fact remained true. Or was it? Caenrya *did* have Eirea, Ryu, and Halden. Not everyone despised her presence, though her actions certainly hadn't helped.

"Verina has and will remain unharmed, for now. Return to me," Valen requested, his visage growing serious, along with his normally flippant edge. "People like *them* do not deserve our efforts, nor the glory we reap or the power we harness."

Caenrya remained silent, unsure if she wanted to prod at him when he switched into such a state. Her breaths were coming faster and faster, and her body leaned as far as she could from him.

"Together." Valen's brows lowered at her. "I vow it, when we are together again, I'll ensure you remain free of the mark. We can serve our daimyo and make every enemy of his quake at the devastation we'll leave in our wake. Verina could join us, free as you and I." His pale hand swirled his glass of wine, the liquid catching the light over and over.

Raw emotion seized her chest, and Caenrya slowly withdrew. "I can't trust you after all you've done. After the *years* of anguish and pain you've inflicted." Her voice was low with wrath and promise. "I will never be a number in his collection again. Nor yours."

Valen's face went stone cold, his chin rising. "I assure you, you'll regret that."

With that, Caenrya rocketed from the corner of her apartment. Her chest thundered harder than the storm raging outside her window. Opening it, she embraced the wind against her clammy skin. Her lungs filled fast and emptied faster.

What did it mean that Verina had the daimyo's favor? And for healing of all things?

The daimyo always had a staff at his beck and call, including a small team of proficient healers. It made no sense to Caenrya, other than he was attempting to slight her, but that would require her to be jealous. A thing she was not by any means. She had only concern for her sister.

Then there was the threat. A fairly blunt one, by Valen's means. It meant there was something grand in store, as he took pride in his subtler plots. And that meant Caenrya had to prepare the only way she knew possible.

For the remaining hours of the thundering night, she devoted every single second to her readings. Caenrya poured through scripts on taiji balancing for every element, ideas formulating in her head. When the waking world rose for the day, she already had her training blacks on and her hair in a high ponytail-braid, bounding across the rooftops of a forlorn village. Even she had to admit to what devastation this beast had caused. Everyone remained locked inside their homes, only going out to brave the world when supplies were needed.

The normal overhanging sound of laughter, the passing of coin, and footsteps yielded to the frenzy of gusts a storm blew in, rain falling in lighter sheets now that the worst had passed. The smell of wet grass rose in the air, and her foot splashed in a tiny puddle. With the visibility reduced, Caenrya could make out Ren's shape as he trailed her, cresting the hill as she stilled in the center of her groove.

Drops fell down the sides of her face, mocking the tears she shed the night before. But today, Caenrya would guarantee there'd be no further reason for sorrow. She *would* overcome her own limitations to emerge as the threat Valen and the others dreaded her to be.

Ren wouldn't interfere unless she summoned him if the past weeks were any indication. There wouldn't be time for swordplay for Caenrya required something far more powerful than the tip of a blade for what would be coming. So, she calmly folded into the full lotus position, allowing her soul to rest in meditation to prepare herself. It would take one word, only one, to bring him down. A single word of power Caenrya once heard spoken in a previous life, and one she could never share with another.

One that, in the wrong hands, could bring down an entire clan.

In the back of her mind, she heard Aya's voice. *What will happen if you use a word above your skill?*

It was a gamble, sure, but at this point, there was no viable alternative. Caenrya had to protect those in danger from Valen, knowing Halden wouldn't back off even with her attempts to persuade him. Aya wouldn't train her, so it was time she took matters into her own hands. When her mind was at peace with her decision, her body tingling with anticipation, Caenrya climbed to her feet, facing the nearest tree.

In unison, both of her hands formed into the *retsu* hand seal, one that activated the dimensional Kū variation, and balanced the jiao between yin and yang accordingly. Once she met the right balance in her taiji, both of her eyes honed in on the center of the bark ahead. The mid-sized ahari tree reached far above her, leaves blowing furiously in the wind. When Caenrya felt confident, she uttered a single word in her mind.

Krútit.

The drain on her taiji was immediate. The gasp that left her mouth was inevitable, and her body seized as the strain took every ounce of taiji she could offer. Ahead, all that summoned forth was a translucent mirage, taiji not yet properly formed.

And all that raced through her mind was that she had made a terrible mistake.

Caenrya didn't have enough in her reserves to form the ninjutsu properly. Only a frail shadow of what it was supposed to be appeared. More alarming was the continued drain on her energy, as if it would pull every drop from her to finish what she had started. A choking noise escaped from her mouth, her body slouching as she fell to the dirt. Her hands were frozen in the seal, the bargain made remaining until she provided the taiji required or died trying.

Distantly, Caenrya recalled that warning from Aya.

Death. That's what happened to those who used a word above their skill.

Stupid. Stupid. Stupid.

Ren dropped to her side, cursing when he figured out what idiocy she was up to and swearing more when there was nothing he could do but watch.

Caenrya couldn't breathe, a force beyond their world tugging at her very soul with all its might. Her neck strained, every fiber of her body violently shaking as the ninjutsu stole away her life as recompense for overreaching.

This was it.

Her vision was fading, and her heart rate slowed into a fatal trance. Being on the ground, unable to breathe or move, felt eerily similar to all those times Valen kept her underwater. Her body was at the point where it began giving up, her lungs easing into defeat and mind slipping into numbness.

Rain drenched her useless form; Ren shook her shoulders, yelling unheard words into her ears.

It would be easy, too easy, to give in again. For the last, final, time. To let her soul rest in a peace long since eluding her. Caenrya could avoid this awful destiny the ancestors placed on her, handing the reins to others who hadn't suffered as much as she.

Even Verina was enough if what Valen said was true.

But now, *now*, Caenrya had a life to strive for. A home to fight for. People she didn't want to lose. A man who swore he would fight with her, too.

She wasn't alone. Eirea, Ryu, and Halden made sure of that. Had gone through such trials on her behalf. She owed them this fight.

A final memory surfaced in her mind. Arms around her and a face that held strong for her. One that pushed aside her attempt to leave this world before, pleading for her to stay. Because he saw something in Caenrya that was worthy. To Halden, she meant something.

She had found her people.

Caenrya wanted to *live*.

At that critical realization, something blazed open in her chest, a buzz that laced through every atom of her body. As soon as it erupted through her, almost every newfound drop of taiji immediately dissipated. Caenrya's lungs fought for air, her palms separating as the ninjutsu faded. Rolling to her back, her lungs worked furiously, making her hyperventilating as her mind struggled to reconcile just what the *Hel* happened.

"You're okay," Ren breathed, pale as a ghost as he lifted his finger from her carotid.

"Holy... Hel," Caenrya whispered, the words taking more out of her than she could have imagined.

Everything was a dead weight on her, and the act of moving her eyes and blinking was challenging. Not once had Caenrya ever experienced this degree of complete physical exhaustion, not even after being on the run from enemy would-be assassins in the Towering Wings Pass back in the warring lands.

It took a second, but Caenrya managed to get a glimpse of what became of her ninjutsu.

Three feet from the roots of the tree, the rest of the trunk was shaved off.

Twist.

That was the word of power she used, warping the fabric of this dimension and cutting the trunk clean in two. It twisted the space of her ninjutsu as if she had pinched a sheet of fabric and twisted everything around it, warping it in the direction of her pull. While she didn't know what happened to the remainder of the tree, she could only imagine it tumbled down the steep slope on the other side.

And that little action took everything she had. What a letdown.

As for when Ren swooped her up, Caenrya honestly couldn't tell. Though something about his exposed face bugged her, seconds passing before it clicked. His mask had been pulled down. His face was familiar to her. The thought peddled around her mind, comparing those she knew against what his face reminded her of. But no matter what she came up with, she couldn't place the similarities. It nagged at her as the oniwaban moved down the hillside.

Things blurred around her, rain streamed into her eyes, and she distinctly recalled the sound of several voices before she decided to take a small nap.

After all, hadn't she earned it?

Chapter Twenty-Two

HALDEN

Halden was set to murder someone, but not any random person. His mind was intently focused on the silver-haired ronin. A man Halden grew to hate more than he ever thought possible. For Caenrya to share that one tiny slice with Halden, and for that single story she shared to send her into such a state, he couldn't fathom what else she had survived.

At first, Halden thought he understood some of what Valen wrought on her, but after hearing that... Well, he never wanted to hurt someone as bad as he did him. Livid barely described it, and if he could, Halden would take on Valen this second for all he put Caenrya through.

It all made perfect, awful sense.

Caenrya kept them at arm's length due to the trauma of her past. All this time, Halden could sense there was something that made her extremely reserved and short with them. Never, though, would he have imagined it to be to that extent. Even worse, he had a sinking feeling that was only one of many pages in her story. No matter how dark or twisted it was, he wanted to know when she was ready to share. He'd be there for her when the time arrived. Always.

That night, Ilias reluctantly set out for the monthly clan gathering, leaving only with a minimized protection detail. His usual entourage remained at their house estates or within the Citadel, every oniwaban on rotations to weed out the beast's location. Rumors circled that the beast was a spiritual being materialized by the wrath of the ancestors as punishment for harboring an outsider. Others claimed it escaped through the folds of the underworld for no reason at all.

The former, Halden was certain, were rumors stemming from his uncle's mechanisms.

But the fact remained its attack patterns were odd for a beast. It appeared only during the evening, staying for scant seconds and leaving no trail in its wake. The only evidence was that of gouges left by its claws or fangs, the litter of fallen scattered maliciously across the area. It began raiding nearby homes when the people grew too cautious to wander outside, occasionally claiming a victim or two before oniwaban honed in on its location.

Rumors emerged of the beast's name, many calling it Hel's Harbinger in the whispers people dared to utter about it.

During the day, every team within the Citadel spread out to search every nook and cranny for any hint that may lead to a discovery about it and to offer a small sense of false security to the population there. Many retreated to other territories within the clan, whether they were in the same house or had any familial ties, to avoid being a tally on the harbinger's death list. Thus far, only the local areas of Riverside and Temple Square had been targeted, every block slowly vacating around it. Oniwaban and jōnin alike were stationed around each, swarming the locations during the nighttime hours.

His father had many sleepless nights spent in those areas.

It would materialize as far from him as possible. By the time Ilias would show up where it had been sighted, for now it was impossible to miss the sinister aura it exuded, it would disappear back into nothingness. It infuriated his father.

Every time it was reported, it was either a fleeting glance, loud screech, or other destruction people spotted. No one gleaned a clear look at the beast, nor did they want to. It would be a death sentence. Ilias's vin couldn't pick it up, which drove a stake of true fear through their hearts. It was utter chaos, and Halden could sense the grim air in the Citadel as Team Cadigan trekked back from the northern wall.

The rain soaked through their uniforms with ease, rolling down the plating of their royal blue armor and muddying the ground below. It was one of the few times Halden could appreciate the benefits of taiji balancing with nature, the grip between both stabilizing as they bounded down the steeper ends of the hillsides.

"Why can't you tell us?" Ryu complained for the third time, referring to Halden's conversation with Caenrya the previous night.

Eirea scowled at Ryu, her voice purposeful as she said, "For the same reason I don't run around telling people what Hina said to you between patrols yesterday."

Like a wildfire, Ryu's face blazed with embarrassment, which only raised Halden's curiosity. "What did Hina say?" He smirked.

Ryu muttered incoherent words under his breath, Eirea picking up his slack by explaining, "It was a lovey-dovey proclamation."

"Hey," Ryu loudly protested, even his ears burning a bright shade of red.

Snickering, Halden could only smile as his foot dodged a protruding branch. "Caenrya will tell you in her own time. I think things will be different from here on—"

A scraping crash reverberated down the hillside, the noise echoing up to their location. All amusement was leeched from them, leaving only the tense awareness they might have discovered something bad. It ran through each of their minds, and the look shared between them was somber with understanding.

The beast could be ahead.

Eirea took the front, Ryu and Halden at her five and seven. Scanning with his vin ninjutsu, Halden focused on the plateau below. His extended vision barely caught the mark of a shinobi, the person's taiji blazing in contrast to that of an average person. By the prominent amount emanating from the shadow of the being, Halden could only assume it was either an oniwaban or a credible threat.

He filled in Eirea, Ryu listening intently as they crossed the open grove the person ran from. Only a bizarrely torn tree was evidence of the shinobi's presence, spiral-like indentations carved into the stump. Caught between two other trees on the downward slope was the trunk, with similar markings on the base.

"Which direction?" Eirea demanded, her eyes searching for evidence of the shinobi's presence.

Halden pointed east, describing what he could discern. "Toward the Duša Clan Temple. The person is edging around the Citadel's perimeter."

They chased after their target without delay, hard-pressed to catch up with the distance lost. Halden gave quick updates as they bounded through the thinned forestry and pouring rain. The figure began slowing as it turned toward a new destination, curving toward Temple Square. It only increased the tension between Halden's shoulder blades, the others feeling similarly, judging by their locked jaws and tight faces.

What if this individual was a summoner of sorts, compelling the beast to attack there?

Then, much to their confusion, the person slowed into the medical center, entering through the first floor. Halden and his team followed suit, knowing the probability of their fears actualizing was slim.

Halden's heart stopped in his chest at the sight.

Sodden, an oniwaban, carried Caenrya's limp form to the reception desk. Her arms dangled below her, the taiji that resided in her virtually untraceable. This entire time, Halden could only discern one single person, and for her to have gone unnoticed...

"What happened?" Eirea questioned, her tone commanding as she recognized the same elements Halden had.

Halden could barely blink as the oniwaban turned, Caenrya's unconscious face pale before him.

The oniwaban Ren—Halden was numbly shocked to recognize—reported, "She attempted unknown ninjutsu that was above her taiji capabilities."

"But she's alive?" Ryu half-asked and half-said, his confusion evident along with his concern. Something like frustration lingered there as if he blamed his brother for the accident.

"Only because of her simultaneously opening a gate of power. Otherwise, she'd have died," Ren hastily explained, moving as one of the staff waved him to an open room.

She almost died? What training was Aya putting Caenrya under? It was ridiculous the elder would force her to such an extent, senseless that she'd almost kill the person she swore to guide. The gnarled tree trunk... what was she practicing? Halden hadn't seen anything with that sort of remnant, and it made him question the integrity of what the elder was instructing Caenrya to do. In his mind, he replayed various ways of telling her *exactly* how he objected.

As they brought Caenrya to a room, the staff requested they stay within the waiting area as the halls were already backlogged and flooded with residents seeking shelter or medical care from the harbinger attacks. Sitting beside Halden, Eirea was unnaturally still as she peered at the hallway, waiting for Ren to return with a more thorough explanation.

When he did, Halden barely noticed the twin wooden katanas strapped to Ren's back, more concerned about Caenrya's condition. Halden stood abruptly and had more than an edge of irritation in his words. "Explain how this happened."

Ryu's brows rose a fraction at the tone, Eirea not flinching in the slightest as she held the oniwaban's gaze. Her voice was even when she spoke, with the respect only fellow oniwaban could have for one another. "I have thus far appreciated the continued updates on her daily activities, but I am confused as to how this happened when she isn't receiving instruction from anyone of note in regard to taiji."

That was a surprise to Halden, which reflected on his face as he turned to his commander.

Ren's eyes narrowed above the fabric of his mask. "I haven't any idea of what ninjutsu she attempted nor where she gained the verbiage for it."

"Can you describe what it manifested as?"

At Eirea's request, Ren closed his eyes for a moment before answering. "The girl performed the cut of *retsu*, the hand seal for dimensional ninjutsu. I can only assume the art to have been an ancient one due to the nature of how it occurred. The fabric of reality itself spiraled in a fold of space where she focused, similar to water spiraling down a drain, and when the ninjutsu was completed, it churned the tree within the dimensional space it occupied."

An appreciative whistle came from Ryu, who leaned back on the tan padding of the bench they rested on.

Ren continued, "As for where the word or words could have originated, there is only one within the clan who may have an inkling."

"Aya," Halden assumed, taking in Ren's nod of confirmation. "But you said she wasn't training with her or anyone. How long has that been going on?"

Eirea stood with a sigh, rocking back on her heels as she took the response from Ren. "Caenrya lost the apprenticeship after withholding information from Aya almost two months ago. Since then, she's been dedicated to her studies and that of the sword arts." At Halden's look of frustration, she added, "I, too, am doing what I can to ensure she takes her own steps when she's ready. Until then, it was her business."

All those bruises she'd collected then were from hours of training with Ren. For some reason, it didn't sit right with Halden. Not one single bit.

"Well then," Halden said tightly, bracing his hands on his knees. "She couldn't have received the knowledge from Aya on... whatever ninjutsu that was."

"It would remain best to wait and hear from the girl directly," Ren concluded, lowering his chin in agreement. "I'm to resume my—"

Ryu waved a hand toward his elder brother. "Wait, wait, wait. So how long have you been assigned to Caenrya's case? Because you never told me," he accused, appearing peeved he just found this out today.

A sigh.

"You know as well as I that I'm not to discuss assignments within this position. Shinobi Creed: Silence is Survival. Oniwaban are to remain confidential about their assignments, especially when an enemy may use your identity against you." Ren shared a sideways glance with his brother before addressing their commander. "Cadigan, I must return to my position."

With a nod, Eirea released a troubled sigh as the oniwaban made down the length of the hall where Caenrya was being cared for, rising to her own feet. Halden reluctantly followed as they set back to have lunch before resuming their own duty. He swore to himself he'd later return to check on her condition. For now, Caenrya was okay.

The lack of good sleep wore him down. His eyes were dryer than sandpaper, and the need to blink repeatedly was overwhelming.

They worked in silence, each burdened by different thoughts. For Ryu, Halden knew he was bitter that his brother had once again claimed more valor than himself, their rivalry likely to never end. Eirea verbally mused over the possibilities of the unknown ninjutsu with Halden and who may have shared the word or words with Caenrya.

Halden mainly stressed Caenrya's condition, never having seen any shinobi with such remedial amounts of taiji keeping them from the brink of death. Every living being contained the energy, though only those with blood ties to Elves could have the chance to wield it and harbor more of it. Compared to where Caenrya had now, a wood ant had more taiji in its chakras. It was not a reassuring thought in the least.

A part of him was stung she hadn't shared the termination of her mentorship with Aya, but after what he'd already gathered from her, he couldn't hold on to that hurt for long. He was sure there was a deep-rooted reason why she hadn't.

Caenrya cared for him. Worried about all of them.

That was what was important, and Halden had the distinct impression things would change for the better within the team dynamics. However, not much could happen until this harbinger was caught and eliminated. There'd been several attacks since it first appeared weeks ago when the Devout gathered. It was not promising that no one had gleaned a clear up-close sight of it and lived to report the tale. Since the oniwaban had been posted and Ilias had been actively patrolling the sites, it would only materialize for a matter of seconds, leaving when the first threat approached.

Many speculated it was fearful, but Halden knew the truth.

It was almost as if it were biding its time, learning from the previous attacks before reengaging. Unfortunately, with nothing to go off of, only time would reveal more about its motive and patterns. Every team scouring the area was discouraged, some slightly fearful that they'd be the ones to cross that monster and fall to it.

But that was the duty of the shinobi. To lay down their lives to protect their clan and honor their ancestors. When that was threatened, they had to act.

No one else would.

When night fell, the sun sinking far below the horizon, any sense of security fled with it. The village became a ghost town once more except for the shinobi returning home or starting their shifts for the evening patrols. As Halden passed by, he acknowledged them with a tense nod, Eirea addressing them by name and sharing her scheduled whereabouts if needed. Ryu trailed, silent and wary of the darkness lingering in every corner as they made their way to visit Caenrya.

Only the oniwaban tucked into those shadows, obscuring themselves and remaining undetectable to all except those with Halden's sight skill set. It interested him being able to discern that, observing their particular movements and tucking that information away for his own use if he had an assignment where being untraceable could be of benefit.

When they returned to the center once more, the crowds of people had calmed for the night, hushed as if noise would draw the beast their way. A tall man escorted them to her room, and an oniwaban Halden didn't recognize was stationed outside when they arrived.

It didn't take long for them to confirm Caenrya still wasn't awake. The machine reading her vitals had abnormally low values. Eirea softly told him that was expected after experiencing the near depletion of taiji, and it would take time for her to recover. Her chakra points were overworked, and the damage required time to heal before taiji could be replenished. She promised to share any updates she received in the coming days, reminding them both to keep positive. The worst was behind Caenrya.

Even Eirea was lackluster, though, when saying it. The dreary atmosphere of the Citadel was wearing even her normal cheerful countenance. It wore at all of them, making Halden even more exhausted when he returned to his empty home. As he cleaned up and made to warm some leftovers, he couldn't shake the feeling the situation would become much worse before it got better.

CHAPTER TWENTY-THREE

HALDEN

Every opportunity he could, Halden planned to visit the medical facility. Before meeting with Eirea and Ryu, he checked with the front desk workers only to find nothing had changed. Hours later, when the afternoon had slowly arrived, it worried him she still hadn't woken. The team wanted to join him when they completed their checks, returning to the medical center after a takeaway sushi dinner from one of the few remaining shops open.

During the evening, the center was active once more, with people milling about the right side of the multi-story complex. Staff were distributing meals to those displaced by the harbinger attacks. The front desk insisted only one person may visit any patient at a time to minimize congestion.

When offered it, Halden took the first visitation, his long strides carrying him down the wing for those injured. It didn't take long to spot her room, for Ren stood statuesque outside the doorway. With a nod, the oniwaban opened the door, permitting Halden access and closing it behind him.

Still, Caenrya hadn't wakened, not so much as stirred in her deep slumber. She appeared peaceful with her tanned face smoothed and relaxed. A nurse came in to record her vitals as Halden took a seat beside Caenrya, releasing a tense sigh as he all but collapsed onto the cushion.

"Were the healers able to work on her chakras?" he asked the nurse.

The woman gave him a soft smile. "They did what they could, and her chakras will heal. Now it is up to the ancestors to determine when she wakes."

Once the lady left, sharing a quick nod of respect with Halden, he couldn't help but close his eyes out of pure exhaustion. Hours of running about did that to him, especially when straining his vin to the limit throughout each day. Halden was spent, wishing the day would come when the beast would be captured.

A piercing, shrill scream sounded through walls.

Halden's adrenaline shot up. A swift sweep of the room showed nothing out of sorts, Caenrya remaining as she had been and nothing out of the ordinary otherwise. When a second shout sounded through the walls, the door burst open from the hallway, Halden rocketing to his feet with his sai singing from their sheaths.

Katana out and poised, Ren sharply gestured toward Caenrya to a sprinting nurse. "Remove her from the machines *now*," he ordered, the lady making haste to do as he said despite the fear reflected on her face.

Halden's blood pounded in his ears as he navigated around the woman. Did Valen finally hold true to his word?

It was drilled into every shinobi to prevent taiji depletion due to its lasting effect on the body. It brought such a vulnerable state that any shinobi who reached such incredibly low levels was sure to fall in combat. Every opponent pushed for their enemy to waste all their taiji if they proved equal in physical combat, leaping at the opportunity to finish off all who succumb to it in a fight. With a team, it was drilled into them to cover any member who was weak, as the enemy would surely target them first.

Right now, Caenrya was the perfect target if Valen moved to secure her.

Both Ryu and Eirea rounded the corner, the latter glancing once at Caenrya as the woman worked to bandage the puncture mark of the IV. Ryu was wide-eyed, and his knuckles whitened at his sides.

"We move to the Ancestorial Shrine?" Eirea asked Ren, her left hand lingering close to the staff tucked away on her back. At his nod of confirmation, the commander turned to fill Halden in. "The beast has struck again in Temple Square, but this time, it's moving in this direction."

Halden's lungs constricted at that.

"We must move. Oniwaban are already holding it at bay. Our primary assignment is to guarantee Caenrya's safety, and the shrine is warded against evil spirits. It's our best bet," she said.

Halden nodded. It was all he could do as he focused on stamping out the rising wave of fear that swelled at the new development. Ren issued orders with precision, his voice unwavering. When the nurse backed off, Ryu hoisted Caenrya's limp form into his arms, running in the center of Ren and Eirea as Halden scoured the perimeter for the harbinger.

They had to force their way through panicking masses, many civilians fearing for their lives as they insensibly sprinted in every direction. Scared words and loud noises echoed throughout the halls, making everything else indecipherable as they finally reached the exit.

Outside wasn't much better.

Streams of residents bolted from their housing, shinobi evacuating the area with all due haste. Children wailed as mothers frantically ushered them away, fathers cradling babes in the dark evening.

Veering from the masses, Ren directed them to the rooftops, only taking a moment to slow when the outline of a shinobi leaped toward them from an adjacent building. An oniwaban, judging by the appearance of his mask and bearing, but it was the state of him that froze Halden's feet.

"Rainer," Eirea said softly, her lips pressing into a firm line to keep her shock at bay.

His tanto blade was cracked in half as it hung from a limp arm, black eyes glazed from his lifeblood splattered across his shredded body. Thin ribbons were all that remained of his taiji, even that force flickering and ebbing. A deep, gushing wound bled under his shaking hand as Rainer struggled and failed to apply enough pressure.

"It killed everyone," Rainer said in a wet breath, the words striking something deep within each of them.

The oniwaban. The harbinger must have slaughtered the other two stationed at Temple Square, only Rainer escaping to deliver his warning with his dying obligation. If three shinobi of his clan's highest shinobi rank couldn't fell this beast, no one stood a chance.

The oniwaban slumped forward as Eirea caught him. Reiner's mouth listlessly moved as his eyes glazed over. Grief pulled at Eirea's face as she listened to Rainer's final words, Ryu similarly cracking beside Halden. Only Ren remained infallible, prepared to lay down his own life if necessary for his duty.

"It's coming," Rainer gargled. His body succumbed to blood loss, and the light in his eyes dimmed.

Three oniwaban dead.

And it was coming.

For them.

Ryu swore, Ren signaling toward the shrine.

Without hesitation, Halden tore after his team and Ren, their formation tight. "Still no visual of the beast," he said, his chest heavy from the death witnessed and forbidding situation.

As his body went airborne between buildings, Halden noticed a bizarre movement of taiji to his left. Normally, the particles of airborne energy drifted in scattered patterns along with the wind, dispersed and free flowing from the bodies they originated from, whether wood, stone, or animals. Now, they parted around a vague void, the empty gap spreading with a speed Halden had never witnessed before.

Before Halden could utter a word, that void collided straight into Eirea's blind side.

No, no, no.

Ryu skidded as he landed, face horrified as he watched his commander disappear through the wall of an apartment. Halden gritted his teeth, released his vin, and blinked away the sight of natural energy to gain a physical visual—his own feet landing beside Ren.

It was sadistically mesmerizing in its appearance.

Two back-bent and sore-ridden hind legs scrambled from the collapsed building, a slick sheen clinging to the leather-like skin surrounding the mass of pure muscle and horns. Around each appendage, tiny blades in the shape of scythes protruded multi-directionally, the two prominent horns gleaming like steel above its maw of tri-rowed dagger teeth.

No sight of Eirea.

His commander would never be defeated that easily. Right?

The image of Reiner flickered in his mind, the death of three oniwaban pressing into his thoughts.

The creature pounced onto the pathway, and the cement shuddered under its incredible weight. For a second, it appeared to regain its senses, nose in the air as it turned in their direction.

All will be fine this go around, Eirea would say.

His chest squeezed the air from his lungs.

"*Run*," Ren snapped at them, hand gliding into the *zen* seal.

Halden hated this. Despised splitting the team in any manner, especially when one was down. They were taught to never leave a fallen man, dead or alive, but only after the success of the assignment was assured. As an oniwaban, Ren outranked all of them, making his word absolute law.

Even though everything in him despised himself for doing it, Halden raised his foot to follow. Before they could so much as sprint across the rooftop, however, the harbinger launched.

With a *toh* seal, Halden formed an enormous whip of water, slamming diagonally across the spikes lancing down the beast's spine.

It barely had any effect. The water split as if it met metal rather than skin and bone. Faster than should be possible, the harbinger lunged for Ryu and Caenrya, his teammate attempting to throw himself to the side before its claws had the opportunity to find purchase. Ren's form spun in front of the beast, swiveling with dual katanas—one aiming for the soft skin between the claw projections and the other moving to deflect the trajectory of the other arm.

Neither had the opening to contact, for the harbinger's spiked tail whooshed forward and lopped off the oniwaban's left arm. But the man didn't so much as blink. Halden saw why in the next second. Ren had created a duplicate of himself with his vin, and his actual body was hidden in the monster's shadow. Both of *his* arms were intact.

Ryu fell to his side in the nick of time, and Caenrya hit the sloped edge of the rooftop panes. The claws of the beast screeched as it turned, one limb collapsing a segment of the roof beneath it as it scrambled. Taking advantage of the moment, Halden cast the seal for *pyo*, summoning a sharp gale directly at the harbinger. With a precise movement, he flung his body around, launching a sai with all the force he could muster. The weapon raced toward the monster's throat with the wind's speed boost. It was the thinnest part of the beast, and—

And the sai glanced harmlessly off.

Impossible.

Halden had practiced this move hundreds, no *thousands*, of times. Every single time, the sai would impale rock, wood, or anything it touched with more force than any person could aggregate. What did that say about the monster's skin?

It was impenetrable while being impervious to ninjutsu.

That's when it screeched, a mind-numbing, bone-shaking noise that had Halden collapsing to his knees, the other sai clattering down and falling onto the pathway two stories below. But he couldn't help it. Even his hands against the flesh of his ears were incapable of containing the pain that had his mouth open in a soundless scream of agony.

When it stopped, the world teetered around him, his ears ringing violently in the following silence. Two more Ren clones attempted a series of striking maneuvers against the beast, nothing gaining even a millimeter into the depth of the hide. Even fire couldn't leave a scorch mark.

Three other Ren duplicates summoned lightning, the electricity raising all the hair on Halden's head. The power was incredible, mesmerizing, and deadly. Blue light lashed across the night, originating from the sky hundreds of feet above their heads, cutting deep into every shadow imaginable as it lanced forward. Even the sky itself trembled from the impossible force of lightning, the electricity in the Citadel flickering as it struck the beast.

A wave of pressurized air blew past him, and he squinted against the force.

The power of an oniwaban, Halden thought, awed.

Blinking, he was sure it would have struck true, but when it slid off the beast, plunging deep into the building below, his jaw loosened. Ren summoned more lightning, regaining its attention when it swiveled toward Ryu. Each strike would have obliterated any living being, but against the harbinger, they glanced off into the surrounding rooftops.

Mini explosions threw shockwaves around them all, Halden's arms raising to bar the flying stonework from hitting his face.

For every clone Ren Sahkara summoned with his vin, a technique Ryu employed countless times over the years, the beast tore through it with reckless abandon.

With a deep shudder, the remainder of the roof began to fold inwards from the carnage of battle. Ryu missed the slight dip of the panes next to Caenrya's body, that part of the roof precariously close to collapsing. He couldn't hear Halden's shout over the deafness of their ears. Ryu was creating his own duplicate with his vin, attempting to throw barrages of both ninjutsu and taijutsu attacks beside his brother.

Caenrya was about to fall over thirty feet to the ground, and Ryu wouldn't notice in time.

Halden didn't waste a second as he threw himself forward, catching her slipping body as the edge gave way. They went airborne, falling two stories before the ground met them. Twisting, Halden's shoulder and hip took the brunt of the landing as they rolled twice, a pop sending electrifying pain down his dominant arm.

Dust and debris was flung into the air and scattered around the stone, Halden's back shielding Caenrya from the worst of it. His body throbbed with pain, muscles braced as the wreckage settled around them. The ground vibrated with the battle waging on top of the next building complex. Ren and Ryu fended off what they managed to with their vin.

Yet his ears still rang, the noises coming through muddied.

Halden knew he had to obey Ren's command to run, so he began to rise to his knees with a hacking cough from the cloud of dust he inhaled.

A shifting foot caught the fringe of his attention, and Halden discovered a heart-wrenching sight. A sobbing girl, no older than seven, tucked behind a strewn potted plant, stared at the sky above.

Halden followed the direction, finding the last of Ren's duplicates being torn to shreds above. Ryu kneeled beside the edge of the crumbled roof, and his brother assessed the situation between strikes against the beast. The oniwaban peeled his mask down to his neck, giving a severe expression to Halden as he mouthed two words.

Leave us.

Halden's throat closed, but an order was an order. So, he wrenched his body upward, using his last good arm to haul Caenrya's weight along with him. Even as it tore at him to leave Ryu behind along with Eirea. Even as his chin gestured for the nearby child to follow.

Halden gritted his teeth, pushing every emotion raging war deep, deep down.

That's when the harbinger went airborne one last time, sewn sockets where its eyes should have been pointed right at him.

Chapter Twenty-Four

CAENRYA

Caenrya couldn't understand why everything was faintly ringing around her, why everything hurt throughout every cell. The ground swayed, bouncing close then far with a jolting movement. A tiny child's hand gripped her own limp one, blotchy face slick with tears as she cried.

Something crashed at her side, wood, bamboo, and stone exploding as a large object collided with a nearby building. A shockwave shuddered through the air with the debris, chucking into them with force as they were all flattened to the ground.

Caenrya's back skidded against the stone, the kid colliding with... Halden?

Blearily, Caenrya blinked several times, the ringing in her ears dimming to background noise as the surrounding area sharpened into focus. She was in a wide walkway between residential housing, but the building in front of her had collapsed on itself, dust coating every particle of air and concealing anything beyond.

Halden shifted beside her and grunted in pain. His arm beneath her head slid away gently. It was difficult, but Caenrya could make out his expression beneath a coat of dirt, see the determination that picked him up. Those steel eyes flicked toward a massive being pulling itself from the shattered walls, glass, and frames of windows scattered to high Hel around them. She attempted to call out to him, but her throat wouldn't work properly.

Carefully, he let go of the child's hand, and his words barely reached Caenrya's ears. "I'm sorry, Caenrya, to do this to you after all I promised."

Rising to his feet, he reached out with one hand and jerked his other arm in a strange motion to relocate it. A hiss escaped his mouth as his hands wove into a seal she couldn't see. A monster of unimaginable mass shook itself out, gorged eyes honing in on Halden's words.

"I didn't mean to leave you." Such sorrow enveloped his tone...

The beast stepped toward Halden, Caenrya's mouth forming the word as she forced it out.

No.

At that, Halden's head swiveled. His eyes were somewhat relieved to see her awake, but he was mostly dismayed she'd witnessed what he was about to do. Within the same movement, the beast halted, its head adjusting to where she lay instead. Halden noticed that in the next beat, and his features pulled into a snarl as he resumed his ninjutsu before it could attack her.

The beast pounced, claws outstretched toward Caenrya's eyes. It came so fast she didn't have time to gasp, not even enough for her to process what was about to spell her death.

The child's scream pierced the air, and the head of the beast twitched mid-leap.

As Halden's chest rose, the creature within feet of her, yet another thing startled Caenrya.

Chains whipped from the ground, as dark as obsidian, and wrapped the beast from horned tip to spiked tail. With force, it pulled it in a direction away from her, securing it to the ground without an inch of room to give. The ground shook from the collision.

Behind it, Eirea's hand held the *zen* seal, one bloodied thigh wrapped tight with a makeshift tourniquet. Her face was a picture of rage but not directed at the beast. "Halden Arundel, I swear to the ancestors. *Put your damn hands down now!*" she yelled, her voice shaking with pure wrath.

As Halden obeyed, visible relief etched into his slouching shoulders, the beast began disintegrating before them. Everyone stared, every muscle tense as it disappeared into the air. Eirea's chains fell flat upon the cracked stone below. Caenrya somewhat managed to lean up. Every cell in her body ached fiercely, a burning sensation coursing through her chakras. Her eyes were heavy, and the need to sleep was overwhelming despite the adrenaline that raced through her thudding heart.

On the rooftops, Caenrya made out Ren's hunched form crouched beside the ledge, Ryu breathing hard and shell-shocked nearby.

A hiccup sounded from the child beside Caenrya. The girl's eyes were as wide as saucers, staring at the spot where the beast had been moments ago. Caenrya grimaced as she slowly maneuvered her legs into a sitting position. Her head swayed, eyelids rapidly flickering as she clung to consciousness.

Halden stepped toward her, concerned. He opened his mouth to say something. But he never had the chance since Eirea's hand angrily gripped the front of his shirt and pulled him in her direction.

"You are forbidden from using that ninjutsu while I am your commander. Using that during this point in your training will permanently cripple your chakras, or worse, kill you as you may not have the taiji capacity for it yet," she seethed, the anger uncharacteristic for the woman. Even Caenrya felt cowed by the force of it. "Do you understand?"

"I understand," Halden quietly said, the weight heavy in his words. "But I cannot promise that if anyone on my team is about to die."

Everything stilled for a moment, Caenrya's breath catching at the moving devotion that showed in him.

She knew what ninjutsu they referred to—a sacrificial type, forbidden, so powerful that it could claim your very life to wield. Halden's family must have had a sacred technique passed down through their lineage. One that would surely make the world tremble if unleashed.

And for her, he was willing to take that chance.

It made her knotted up inside, a tang of bitterness mellowing the sweet. It wasn't what she wanted: to finally let them in only for their lives to be sacrificed for hers. It hurt much more this way.

For a moment, Eirea didn't move, her eye assessing Caenrya and her charge. She inhaled deeply and furrowed her brow. "You idiot." She pulled him into a tight hug, every bit the older sister he didn't have. "I'm thankful you all are okay." Eirea stepped back and shook her head. "You guys scared the Hel out of me."

For once, Ryu had no smart commentary, and his face was blank as he leaped to the ground beside Ren. He stumbled a step before Ren steadied him, Ryu slapping the hand away the second it touched him. Annoyance briefly shone in Ren's gaze before he left Ryu alone, crossing toward Caenrya.

That's when she saw his mask pulled down and the similarities between Ryu and the oniwaban—the square faces, straight eyebrows, and high cheekbones. It clicked then he must be Ryu's elder brother. Ryu only mentioned a brother once but never explained it further. It was shared in such a way that Ryu didn't appear to be close to his sibling, so Caenrya let it be.

The way they interacted with each other was familiar in the way of siblings, their mannerisms and slight reactions making Caenrya long for what she had with Verina.

"What happened?" Caenrya winced from a sharp pain in her chest. Her hand pawed along her ribcage, her white robes from the healing clinic dirt-streaked. It felt as if she had broken ribs along with a deep ache akin to bruising all over her body. Then there was the fatigue, already coaxing her awareness back into the dredges of sleep.

"We became the only surviving shinobi to fight the beast," Ryu muttered, disheveled and burned out as he went to check on the little girl's well-being. He smoothed his face, putting on a brave smile for the terrified child as he asked her questions.

Something shifted in Caenrya's perception of Ryu.

Ren's tone was slightly irked when he said, "Show some respect for the fallen."

The younger brother only pressed his lips into a fine line, Ryu attempting to ignore him as he wrapped a small bandage he kept in one of his tool pouches on the child's scraped hand. His hands were careful as he murmured encouraging words to the child.

"The beast appeared this evening, leaving Temple Square in a beeline for the medical center," Eirea explained, favoring her non-injured leg as she limped toward where Caenrya sat. Curls escaped her bun, dusted with dirt.

Halden's face was shadowed as his eyes took to the ground, heavy with more than the near-death experience they all just had. He pocketed his hands with the relaxed indifference he customarily carried himself with, feigning calmness when she knew he felt anything but. Sheathing his own katana, Ren closed in on the spot where the harbinger had disappeared, running a finger over the ground where it had lain.

"Three oniwaban gave their lives to try to defeat it, but they failed," Eirea said. The pain of losing her previous comrades was evident in her eyes, but she held herself with confidence. "One managed to deliver a message that it was close, and so we moved for a safer location."

Three oniwaban. Caenrya's stomach grew queasy at the thought, knowing if it hadn't disappeared this evening, they all could have been next. Oniwaban, she'd learned in the last few months, were revered. To become one, well, there weren't criteria like the other ranks. It was rumored they had to be near the capabilities of the shogun to even be looked at. They had to have had an extensive history with jōnin-ranked missions, an incredible success rate, and a high count of enemies felled.

If three had died...

Granted, the oniwaban were handicapped. They couldn't obliterate the Citadel and harm civilians in their attempts to destroy the beast. Their full prowess could only be carried out within the confines of a battlefield.

Who else could withstand a chance of defeating it when every parameter was rigged for them to fail?

"It followed us. Me," Caenrya said quietly, culpability falling squarely on her shoulders.

"We don't know that," Halden abruptly cut in, the fierceness in his face pulling her from that spiral.

He knew what she was thinking, the blame she harbored for any ill happenings. And she could only lower her chin in response to that, unable to deflect that guilt so easily. Caenrya saw the way its attention snapped toward her when she spoke, knew it wasn't coincidence that Valen's threat predisposed this.

What would they say if they learned about her encounters with Valen and his warnings?

Eirea moved to speak with the child, comforting her with a genuine smile and mild words. Walking toward her, Ren motioned for Ryu and Halden to follow him.

"We'll be returning to the healing clinic promptly." Keeping his voice low, Ren traded words with Eirea, planning to lead her team back while she returned the child to her family.

Kneeling, Halden outstretched an arm, the black material along it torn and streaked with dirt. Her hand automatically reached out, then hesitated. She didn't want to be a burden, though she knew Halden didn't see her as such. It was hard to reconcile, but she forced her hand to close that gap between them. Her legs trembled as Caenrya attempted to stand, one of her arms looped over Halden's shoulders.

Before she knew it, Ryu slipped her other arm over his own. His face was pointedly forward as they began their trek back to the center. "So," he drawled out. "I hear you've opened another gate, and it saved your butt."

Caenrya recalled that raw power coursing through her, such a brightness that she was certain she'd never experienced before. A fractured sense of pride warmed the chill in her chest. She opened a gate of power, one of eight. "I've decided that I'm done giving up. I'm going to fight for every day, and I refuse to let my past doubts haunt me any longer. That's what opened it."

Huffing, Ryu side-eyed her. "About damn time. My arse is tired of saving yours."

That caught her off guard, and Caenrya was unable to help it. The corners of her lips twitched up, something like happiness budding inside her at what she became a part of. A team. A cadre of her own that pulled her from the pit of loneliness she no longer had to bear alone.

Ryu glanced away, but not before he shook off a slight smile of his own.

"Thank you both," she murmured, the ground swaying slightly as they picked through debris.

Halden's shoulders were strong beneath her arm, and his calloused hand rested against her shoulder blade. His face, as dirt-crusted and serious as it was, warmed at her gratitude. Something deeper flickered in the depths of his gaze, sending a nervous butterfly into her stomach.

There was still a world of healing to go, a universe of acceptance and repentance for her past deeds. But this was a step forward—one of many Caenrya would journey through, and for the first time, with those who would take those steps with her.

Chapter Twenty-Five

CAENRYA

It was hours before everyone was able to be inspected for injuries, before Eirea came back with the news she was able to return the child to her family. The Citadel was in complete chaos, a majority panicking now that the harbinger had strayed from its normal method of operation. Now there was a distinct possibility it could appear and go anywhere. No one was safe, no matter where they fled.

Before she could do much more than take a few bites of a beef and potato platter, Caenrya fell into a deep sleep. Knocking on her door pulled her from it the following morning, sunshine making a path from the hallway's open windows into her room as people filed in.

Ren waited beside the door for the answer to his question, everyone else standing beside the empty white wall adjacent to him. *What exactly were you doing with that ninjutsu?*

Caenrya eyed the closing door, the second oniwaban leaving as Ren's shift had since begun. "I overheard the word once, long ago. It's as simple as that. I didn't know what it would entail in terms of taiji required," she said, pushing a boiled egg around the plastic breakfast plate Eirea brought in.

It was taboo to ask others about words of power, for it was insulting and ill-mannered to the clan folk. Caenrya could see the curiosity but was thankful they held this bizarre custom for the first time. She had to take better care with such matters. Words carried more weight than anything else in the shinobi world.

"Take caution with that ninjutsu you performed," Ren warned, his arms crossed. "Something of that magnitude could cause permanent damage to your chakras if you use it again. At a minimum, you could attempt it only after more ninjutsu training and opening another gate before your body can manage that level of power."

Caenrya nodded in agreement, unwilling to endure more days of being bedridden. It was more irritating than the way Ryu was currently chewing on a stick of dried meat, and that was *very* annoying.

"You'll need to be relocated in the coming days," Eirea said, the declaration making Caenrya frown.

Caenrya asked, "What's wrong with my place? It's as safe as can be."

Shaking her head, Eirea squinched her face. "On top of your home being within the perimeter of Wisteria Square, which could be a location the beast appears next in, your residence has thin wards that wouldn't stand a chance against a monster that ninjutsu barely affects."

Halden's face twisted as he hovered close to her. "Where else besides the shrine would be safer? She can't live on a bench, even if the area is tightly wrapped in protective ninjutsu barriers."

Caenrya had lived on worse. She almost said so.

A knock startled all of them. The door opened before any could give permission to enter. An aged voice echoed in the room, Aya sternly meeting Cadigan's surprise-lit gaze. "She'll reside with me until that ugly thing is dealt with." Before anyone could protest, she proceeded with a finger in the air. "My home has been guarded by the highest caliber of ninjutsu for decades, and while my age reflects on my wrinkled skin, it has not dulled my ninjutsu capabilities even the slightest of fractions."

A spark of hope flared in Caenrya's chest at the offer. Would this mean Aya would teach her again? Had she been forgiven?

She lowered her chopsticks.

Ren lowered his head respectfully, saying, "I concur that would be the best course of action."

"The shogun will return by the evening. Until then, I see no better alternative." Eirea inclined her chin, observing the Dagon elder with a cool look. "Do you intend to mentor Caenrya in ninjutsu once more?"

Tucking her hands before her silken daffodil robes, Aya lowered her sight to Caenrya for the first time. It was unreadable.

Caenrya fought the urge to turn away.

"That all depends on her. May we have the room to speak?" Aya asked.

Everyone moved to give them privacy, Halden reluctantly leaving last with a final glance of apprehension toward Caenrya. When the door clicked shut, Aya clucked her tongue. A disapproving glint entered her dark eyes as she took in Caenrya's state.

"The Arundel boy is smitten with you," Aya observed with distaste, her body gracefully folding into the chair beside her cot.

That was not what Caenrya had expected to come out of the elder's mouth. A slight redness crept over her cheekbones, but a kind of nervous energy swam in her stomach. Pushing it aside, she rested the plate on her lap, leaning back into the raised backing of the white bed.

"I meant every word that day," Caenrya said softly, referring to when Aya rejected her mentorship.

The elder rubbed her chin with a critical expression. "There are worse houses to marry into. As far as this cohort of shinobi is concerned,

Halden is perhaps the most advanced among Hina and Niko. He certainly has the most potential. Niko hails from a respectable house, but not one as prominent as the Arundels."

Caenrya's face grew redder, and her lips pursed as her mind wondered at what the elder was getting at. The woman had an agenda. Was she attempting to lay on the embarrassment as a punishment?

"You'll have to be courted soon, though. Females with great potential are sought after with a vengeance by every house within the clan. You'll be pestered to no end," Aya clucked, a thin brow raising. "The house will expect you to bear children with all due haste since bloodline is status within our ranks. It guarantees the best shinobi upbringing or acceptance into any school of choice for children. Sharper ears beget power and prestige in any line of work. Your pedigree will be something men will fight over. Possibly to their deaths."

Caenrya's left hand gripped the white bedsheets.

Pausing, Aya's eyes sharpened as she struck her main point. "All of your training will be wasted, words of power shared with you rendered as coin to sell to the highest bidders within your new house. You'll amount to nothing more than a trophy if you pursue this route henceforth, and your life will amount to the accomplishments of your heirs."

Ah. Caenrya's mouth curled with distaste. *Ahhh.*

Aya wanted assurance that she'd pick up the elder's mantle, becoming a legend who wielded taiji in the name of the clan. Caenrya could respect Aya didn't want to waste time on a protégé who would amount to nothing in the shinobi way; she only wanted to prove herself to be the pupil Aya desired.

Aya wanted to mold a shinobi destined for greatness, but more importantly, one who would not only chase such heights but lay down their lives to seize them.

"It's an utmost respectable position for any individual but not for any I train. I must have your entire focus and your word that you won't pursue any distractions until you fulfill your calling," Aya pressed, the lines harsh across her face.

A shiver found itself crawling down Caenrya's spine.

"If you want my word, you have it," Caenrya promised. Her forehead pinched as she pushed her near-empty breakfast plate across a small table beside her. "But what do you know of my calling?"

Her time in the ancestorial world rose in the back of her mind, the words of warning sparking dread in her stomach. All she knew was the ominous warning Enya had shared. Vague, nonsensical words that doomed her to some fool's errand. They loomed over her daily, always making her question what Caenrya would lose next.

Now, more than ever, there was much to lose. While she felt grateful for the boon, she was terrified to lose who and what she had grown attached to.

The floor creaked as Aya shifted forward, her dark eyes guarded. "I have read between the lines of the divinations those above have sent to us. For years, I knew of the discord rising between the living and dead, the balance between our worlds being violated." Gnarled thumbs intertwined on her lap. "Decades ago, neigh on forty years now, I was bestowed a dream by the ancestors. One where my own path was laid out before me. Henceforth, I was to lay down my tonki to take up the mantle of mentor. To find and raise the soul who'd become blessed by the spirits to restore balance."

Who'd *become* blessed? Was that in reference to the time she spent in the spirit world? Caenrya could discern how one could perceive such things, but it didn't sit right with her.

"I once thought it pertained to another and made the critical mistake of training someone else for naught. It's been years, and I've learned from my ill choice. I knew, without a shadow of a doubt, that you were the one chosen by those who walk in the sky the day you showed up on my doorstep. The ancestors have since spoken with you, only confirming what I already knew to be true."

Caenrya couldn't help it. "Then why did you send me away? I begged for forgiveness, and devoted myself to be your apprentice," she said bitterly, thinking of the weeks wasted where she could have flourished from ninjutsu growth.

Shaking her head, Aya pointed an accusatory finger at Caenrya's heart. "You weren't ready to fight for your life and destiny. Not then. You had to undertake and overcome that journey before I could proceed."

Shame colored Caenrya's face, for she knew the elder to be right. She hadn't been ready for the war constantly raging inside her, sending her reeling in too many directions. There was much for her to learn and accept, forgive and conquer, both within and outside the perception of the world she once clung to.

"Forgive me, Elder Dagon," Caenrya said, lowering her head respectfully. "I see that you are right. I'm..." Her mouth worked for a moment. "I'm being spun in endless circles, and I don't understand what is being asked of me at times. What this destiny entails. I had only wanted to rescue Verina."

"Forgiveness has already been given," Aya said, her voice softening around the ragged edges. "But I cannot give you those answers."

Caenrya's neck slouched toward the bed, and her eyes closed to the frustration of the unknown fate she'd been tasked with. If anyone truly wanted to help her, then why withhold such crucial information? It would only aid in the time she had to prepare.

Caenrya knew she owed the ancestors of this clan. They had saved her life when the mark would have crushed her. She owed her team as well, for they had nearly laid down their own lives time and time again. It was a debt Caenrya had to repay, one she'd manage to do while recovering her sister.

"But..." At Aya's next words, Caenrya's eyes opened and lifted. "I can give you every tool you need to succeed. Should you be the blade that cuts into our enemies, I'll be the hand that guides you. Sharpens you into the finest edge. So, when the time comes, none will stand the slightest chance."

Whatever it took, Caenrya would do it.

"For the last time, the only chance you have remaining, will you obey my rules?"

When Caenrya nodded, her eyes blazing with resolve, Aya called for the others to return and packed her things with all due haste. They trekked back to her apartment, pulling her textbooks and necessities to deliver to Aya's residence. Ryu managed to complain the whole climb up the switchbacks of stairs, keeping his voice just low enough Aya nor Eirea heard ahead.

Caenrya had thought *she* complained a lot.

Relief found Caenrya when they arrived at the guest quarters, all empty of the Dagons who currently despised her. While her temporary room was smaller, the artwork of fanciful nature paintings and elaborate woodwork had a mellow air she appreciated.

Everyone disbanded then, returning to their daily duties, save for the elder. Her wrinkled face gave Caenrya a sour expression.

"Meditate," Aya barked at her, and without hesitation or reluctance, Caenrya gratefully complied.

A new sense of peace drifted through her when doing so, the sounds and light of the world more astute to her senses. Everything felt... right. The tatami floor beneath her. The tranquility of the pastel green walls closed in around her. For hours, she enjoyed the task, which no longer was redundant and silly. She could sense the taiji beginning to renew within her, the ache running along her veins stinging slightly less.

Over a dinner of steamed veggies, savory steak, and roasted potatoes, Aya struck up a conversation on the events of her gate opening. By the time Caenrya recounted every aspect, save for the word itself, the elder was picking apart her story sentence by sentence.

Aya said, "That was your first gate, then."

Caenrya confirmed with a nod, voicing the one question that pestered her still. "Since it seems so, I don't understand how my vin has fluctuated over the years. It helped me recover from a paralysis toxin once but never healed me in the past. It had grown stronger another time but didn't require a gate to awaken."

Polishing her plate, Aya neatly folded her hands. "You lack control over your taiji, a skill gained through proper training over years. Taiji, in its raw essence, holds potential over every element. Given what you've shared, your vin is fundamentally leaning toward a jiao of healing, and when you concentrate, aids you in battle. You subconsciously drifted toward that balance in the fight where you healed. Once mastered, I'd wager that you'd grow capable of unconsciously healing while fighting. As for the fluctuation in power, that's a simple matter of will. Perfect your consistency, and you'll find that you will expect the same results with maximum potential each time you engage your vin."

"I see," Caenrya distantly said, her mind absorbing the information.

She'd been cocky in the past about her ability, always flaunting it to hold power over the others in Shikei. While Caenrya didn't blame herself for that, as it was necessary for survival, it gave her a sense of humility to realize it now.

Stranger was it, when she awoke mornings later, that Caenrya realized she'd been within the clan for over four months. Four months, and everything had changed.

Except for the cat. She followed Caenrya there, often lounging on Aya's roof until the elder caved and had her staff arrange for a cat bed to be placed in Caenrya's room. The elder was superstitious, believing the tabby feline to be a sign of good fortune.

Caenrya thought the creature simply had a chicken addiction.

It was still a struggle to walk, Caenrya's legs burning after prolonged use, but it was a relief to manage moving about by herself. Aya had assigned meditation and several texts to study since any usage of taiji would only regress her condition.

The elder gave her a thirty-minute tongue-lashing before sleep, Caenrya swearing up and down to never attempt a word of power again without the logical confidence she could pull it off. But in the back of Caenrya's mind, she was pleased she had succeeded in what Aya deemed a jōnin-classed ninjutsu technique. With another gate opened, Caenrya was sure she'd be capable of practicing it again one day, hopefully soon.

The Path of Self-Realization.

One of five Caenrya believed she could master, one where she acknowledged her own faults and suffering, proving she could go beyond those limitations. During her morning meditations, she'd focus on identifying each and every fault. A lengthy list, if she cared to admit it. Her mind would absorb it, then process it, knowing they were barriers to her ultimate goal of Awakening. This carried into afternoons, until Aya would instruct her to turn over pages and annotate key principles to learn.

Five days flew by that way, Aya refusing to allow Caenrya any visitors until she could prove herself dedicated to the regime.

And she was.

Every tiny doubt flew from Caenrya, assured she would become the shinobi Aya expected her to be. It cleansed the dirt from her skin, and she recognized there was more to her than Valen forced her to believe. There was strength in finding her center, a trust that everything may end up well in the end.

When the next morning arrived, Aya pulled her early from her meditation, instructing her to go outside in her shinobi robes and practice in the fresh air. Caenrya followed her instruction, confused as to why she gave such vague orders. But when she opened the door, Caenrya found Ren meditating beside the pond. As the door clicked shut, he stood with a cloth-wrapped object in his hands.

Greeting him, Caenrya hesitated a few feet before the oniwaban.

"This is for you," Ren said, his chin dipping toward his outstretching hands. "Elder Aya determined it was time to continue with your sword skills, and I saw to it that you can learn with a blade of your own."

Caenrya slowly unfolded the cloth to find a familiar sight. "*The blade that cuts only what must be*," she recalled reverently, blinking before shaking her head. "I cannot accept this." The price flashed into her mind, and it was steep.

"Unfortunately for you, it's a non-refundable item, and I have far too many in my possession already."

The blade inched forward.

Relenting, Caenrya took the scabbard, drawing the gleaming blade in a smooth sweeping motion. "It was the only one that stuck out to me," she confessed, admiring its masterful quality. "How did you know?" Out of the corner of her sight, she made out his eyes, squinting in amusement.

"Simply put, it's my job to know such things." Ren shrugged it off, drawing his own blade.

With a hum, Caenrya returned the weapon to its sheath, clasping it into place along her hip. Gratitude welled in her. "Thank you." They were heavy words, ones that stung her eyes for a moment. "May I?" She gestured toward it, and her eagerness to wield it in practice showed.

With a nod, they fell into warm-up stances, flowing through each numerous times. The weight nipped at her muscles, fatiguing them quickly. The taiji depletion affected her stamina to a degree. She pressed on, eventually transitioning into mock battles. Caenrya relished the stretch in her body, the power behind the blade. It was pleasing when Ren gave his nod of approval, her progress remarkable with the weapon.

It certainly helped that she had experience with her taiji blades, but Caenrya had to admit this was much more challenging. Besides, it didn't help that she'd been incredibly inactive for too long, her body suffering the effects. And Ren had been more than acquiescing when she asked if he could teach her more about the clan. She just didn't think it would be *during* practice.

Caenrya's arm swooped up, blocking a downward cut.

"Explain the Shinobi Creed: River's Dance," Ren said, his voice purely instructional.

Grunting, Caenrya swiveled to deliver a glancing blow he easily blocked, almost as if swatting a fly. "Shinobi must represent adaptability and strategic flexibility."

Ren feinted, stopping his blade beside her neck.

A frown crossed her face. Caenrya reset with the oniwaban, sweeping with a precise uppercut the moment he cued her to start.

"Elaborate." Ren blocked, his blade blocking in a diagonal arc.

Pinching her brows, Caenrya said, "We must be as fluid and—" Ren's blade distracted her, but his side-eyeing reminded her to proceed. "And adaptable as a river with the ability to think dynamically in changing situations. Flexibility in tactics is crucial during a fight."

His eyes crinkled above his mask in approval. Right before cleverly moving in, disarming Caenrya before she could blink.

"Again," she said, pressing her mouth into a line before falling into a starting stance.

Ren nodded once.

After a midday meal, Caenrya transitioned into ninjutsu practice with Aya. They settled into meditation, eventually alternating into Kū techniques. They began with the footbridge ninjutsu, speaking between minds to further detail new words of power Aya was to share.

She covered the two key differences of hand seals, both *jin* and *retsu*, and which words fell into each category. *Jin* pertained to the senses and capabilities of the mind while *retsu* pertained to the wonders of the dimension. Healing fell firmly into *jin*, a hand seal Caenrya now formed. Her eyes were trained on a torn leaf, Aya instructing her to heal the split with the word *liečiť*.

By night's fall over the Citadel, Caenrya had saved a handful of leaves, all sadistically torn in the name of ninjutsu practice. It was clear why Aya had selected to alter her training toward this path, as it showed the distinct difference control made. Only one leaf was halfway closed, the rest only somewhat mended. Each had a slight variation in progress, the control over the taiji as it worked varying. It frustrated Caenrya her control was shaky at best, but the change slowly became more precise as the night went on.

Crawling into her bed's sheets, Caenrya's lids closed with relish as the day concluded, and she felt vastly more accomplished than she had previously. She was making tangible progress, and even though her body was numb with exhaustion, every second had been worth it.

A furry body crept near her stomach, wrapping itself into a tight ball before Caenrya could protest. Sighing through her nose, Caenrya allowed the creature to sleep beside her. It wasn't long until she fell asleep.

She opened her eyes to a stunning grand waterfall cascading down the valley before her. Caenrya took a moment to transfix the details of the gorgeous view before searching for the culprit. The man was sitting on a swinging bench. His kimono, this time, was a fine burgundy that matched the tight satin kimono falling with decorative ribbons around Caenrya. For once, she could see an edge of tiredness lining his features, though his trademark smirk was glued in place.

"Stunning as always, Nrya," Valen purred, his eyes drinking in the disgust clearly written across her crinkled expression. "Oh, come now. Why must you look at me so?"

Her toes curled in the grass beside the cliff, the dewy, chilled blades as real as if she were truly there in the ranges of majestic mountains. It was the only tolerable aspect of these invasive dreams, everything else making Caenrya want to punch somebody.

Namely, the ronin who lounged in front of her.

"Don't you have something else better to do? Like sending your beast for a nice supper elsewhere for a change?" she growled, hating how the dress revealed her figure a *tad* too much.

Valen's lips pressed slightly as if he were smothering a laugh. "Did you enjoy it? I thought it entertaining."

Her limbs grew deathly still, and her face was a picture of absolute contempt. "There is nothing remotely entertaining about innocent deaths. It's sickening, and I can promise you, *Valen*, that you will regret this."

By her tone, Valen should have been able to tell she meant it. It was one she hadn't used in a long time. Any repercussions had long since been unworthy of such rebelliousness.

He took a moment before sighing wistfully. "I crave the sound of your voice. Not as endearing as it would be in person, however. It's been far too long since I've shown you where you stand within the ranks. You've grown far too bold. I plan to plea my case before the daimyo for permission to extract you since you've grown soft and content. Maybe I'll acquire some additional recruits for Shikei. That little clan of yours has plenty to spare. The number of fighters here has drastically reduced since you've left. These useless kids don't hold up to my training as you did."

That was it. The final straw.

Flipping Valen a crude gesture, Caenrya leaned backward over the cliff's edge, watching with a semblance of satisfaction at the horror on his face as she fell. The wind whistled beside her ears, and the drowning roar of the water below calmed her mind as her body fell into that meditative-like trance. Down and down, her body parted air as her long strands whipped into a frenzy around her. Her heart calmed into a normal rhythm as her eyes opened to a roof over her head.

Chapter Twenty-Six
HALDEN

That smile. When Halden saw it, his breath caught. It changed Caenrya's face, the sincerity of it, and ancestors be damned if he didn't want to see it again. It was—she was—entrancing. Everything had tuned out in that moment, and her face sharpened to him in stark clarity as they had walked back to the clinic after the harbinger attack. Despite the absolute chaos his life had become since she arrived, Halden knew something finally had come from it.

That smile.

It stuck with him throughout the coming day, only fading when his father returned from the clan gathering. Ilias had already been briefed on the attack before he opened the door to his home, but he again requested every detail from Halden.

The shogun's eyes were dark, drinking in every provided scrap of information about the harbinger and Caenrya's close call with ninjutsu. Ilias approved of the latter's temporary lodgings with the Dagon elder, relieved Aya had initiated training her once more. It concerned them both that the beast didn't appear to harbor any taiji. It only left more questions than answers. In exchange, his father detailed the clan meeting, emphasizing that Markus hadn't attempted anything—as of yet.

But.

No other clan was plagued by a demonic beast as they were, the typical struggles clinging to each of them instead. Stray ronin attacked a seaside village in the Carov Clan, apparently fleeing into the depths of Verg Clan's territory. Nothing of which concerned the Duša Clan, not when the harbinger wrecked their own land.

Due to the loss of Devout within their territory at the hands of the beast, other clans were clawing at Ilias for answers, especially when the possibility was thrown out by the Dych Clan that it may stroll into their own territories if left unchecked.

Which would show two things.

One, the Duša Clan was far too weak to deal with such a trivial matter and would open them up to vulnerability to the other clans' machinations. It wouldn't be the first time one clan attempted to steal land from another, going as far as to claim their resources as well. Two, they didn't provide enough protection for the Devout, who were supposed to have it freely. Since they failed, it would be an offense to the ancestors, remaining Devout, and other clans if they botched eliminating the beast and providing proof of such action.

That would leave them open to retaliation.

It was a stressful position to be in, to say the least. Ilias was hard-pressed to show something, anything, by the next clan meeting. It would not be good news to disseminate at the Daimyo Assembly.

When they gathered the coming day, everyone was skittish. Many had sent representatives in their stead, terrified of the monster lurking within the Citadel. Most of the news revolved around people fleeing to their house's territory or family homes, the time flying by extraordinarily fast due to the lack of participation. Ilias shared what he gathered of the harbinger; for some, that was enough to convince them of progress toward its capture.

Wisely, Halden's uncle refrained from involvement, keeping a low profile after the catastrophic repercussions he almost faced during the last assembly.

The oniwaban were regularly updated on Caenrya's progress. Aya distinctly told off Halden's entire team the first day they attempted to visit, stating they were overbearing hens who needed to flock elsewhere. Otherwise, Halden would have only three things to focus on: his training, his assigned patrols, and the procession for the fallen oniwaban.

Rain fell from the sky that day in a fine mist as shinobi, family, and friends gathered for the funeral of the three deceased. Even the spirit animals were mellow in nature, their movements small and grieving. It was, perhaps, the lowest Halden had ever seen the Citadel hit, every face scared and suffering at the loss. What hope was there if no one could leave as much as a scratch on the harbinger?

That day, his father took it upon himself to join every single evening shift, routinely alternating between Temple and Riverside Squares each night. If anyone stood a chance against the beast, it was the shogun. Before, he'd patrol frequently, but now he was steadfast in his oath to spend every waking moment of the night protecting his people. It rose spirits within the shinobi community to see him investing more time, many growing confident the harbinger's next attack would be its last with the further increase of oniwaban present. His father had pulled many from their missions to guard the Citadel. Halden was more concerned than ever for him. With each passing day, his father only had meager hours of sleep between his daily duties and his nightly taskings.

It was enough to wear down the toughest person, not to mention the enormous responsibility he owed to protect his clan from the other vultures lingering and waiting for him to fail miserably. Halden understood Ilias's request to keep the upcoming assignment into the warring clan's territory secret, for it was far too early to risk any of that information leaking. Though today, Ilias had promised they would share it with Caenrya at last.

There were only four months left before they left for the Kriv Clan's underground fighting rings. Four months for Halden to prove himself worthy of the rank of jōnin.

When they crested the hill, Halden's eyes immediately found her.

The sunlight lit her hair a brilliant shade of gold as the braid whipped around her in a serpentine motion. Her limbs moved with a grace few could hope to master as she wove patterns with her katana against an invisible foe. Her dark, narrow brows lowered with focus, brilliant eyes sharp as she completed a complex maneuver, ending with a downward block and offensive uppercut. With each heavy gasp, Caenrya kept moving, never stilling as the metal curved and struck into each enemy she pictured.

Observing in the role of teacher, Ren caught her attention before showing another technique to attempt. Nodding, Caenrya repositioned her feet, wiping the sweat from her brow before whirling into action.

The oniwaban shifted his focus to them, respectful and alert as he moved. Bowing, Ren sheathed his katana as Ilias and Halden approached. Caenrya completed the maneuver before lowering her blade. Her guard immediately shot up when the shogun closed in, and Caenrya did not utter a word to either as she distrustfully eyed Ilias. Halden didn't blame her in the least, for his father wasn't the most forthcoming of individuals, especially when navigating the field as he'd been for months.

Ilias had given her many reasons to distrust him.

"Sahkara, Caenrya," Ilias politely greeted, his face directed at the oniwaban. Gold flashed in his topknot, and his brown hair gently waved about his shoulders. "May I have a moment alone with her?"

Caenrya sheathed her blade, the fabric of her shinobi robes crinkling at the elbow as she rested a hand on the pommel of her katana.

"Yes, Shogun Arundel." Ren bowed, leaving to allow for their privacy.

When he was out of earshot, Ilias addressed Caenrya, "I've discovered a crucial lead at last. We will move forward in four months' time to secure further intelligence on the whereabouts of your sister through a merchant who reserved access to a pit fight then."

The impact was immediate. Her eyes were a flurry of emotions, and her hands fell limply at her sides. "Why not now? We've already waited four months too long."

Halden brows tucked together at that, not expecting the apprehension that had Caenrya biting at her cheek, nor the way her eyes emptied of emotion by the end of it. Something had her reacting in such a way because Halden expected her to light up when this news was shared.

His thoughts curved around possibilities while his father explained the situation in detail. When he divulged the nail-biting part, where Caenrya would be entered in a fight to provide any insight to the players of the underground ring, her eyes grew clouded, nostrils flaring as she inhaled deeply. The tips of her fingers inched closer to her palm, her chin lowering as she picked apart every word the shogun said.

"Who else?" She abruptly cut him off, a sharpness to the words. "Who else is going with me?" There was an angry undercurrent to them, almost as if she suspected already.

Silver and blue silk robes swung with the wind behind the shogun, the fabric curling around Ilias as if providing reassurance as he said,

"Halden as the fighter and Ren Sahkara posing as a hired ronin along with you."

Halden blinked at that, pleased that his father believed him capable of achieving the jōnin status before the mission commenced.

"No," Caenrya refused, her mouth twisting. "Not Halden."

Though Halden was shocked at the news, he didn't show it. He refused to, especially when facing Caenrya's rejection of his company on the assignment. Even Ilias was taken aback, his eyes crinkling.

"Why?" Halden asked, his arms crossing and voice darkening a shade. "I have as much a right as yourself to go."

"*Exactly*," Caenrya said, her own voice becoming harsh. "For you, this is personal. There is no forgiveness for letting one's emotions get the best of them inside these places. For someone like you, you'll be ousted the moment you are escorted through those doors, specifically at your age. No person above the age of ten hasn't already experienced the underground, and with your history, that place is a catalyst for you to lose it in. You'd only be a hazard to the operation."

The words hit harder than any punch Halden had endured in his years of training, every muscle attached to his jaw aching as his teeth ground together at the sense her point held. Despite it, he wanted more than anything to go—to be there for Caenrya when she revisited her past and to protect her however he could from the repercussions.

To be a part of the team that brought down Valen in the end.

Turning toward Ilias, Caenrya insisted, "Let me go with Ren and the merchant. We don't need an additional team member. It only adds risk when there is much to begin with. *No one* in Halden's peerage would hold up on that stage." Inhaling deeply, her eyes were fierce. "Let me fight instead. I'm the only one with experience, and I'll know how to blend in."

"The merchant himself insists he must be present. He didn't care for the idea of two undercover ronin along with a fighter following him in," Ilias said, watching as Caenrya confirmed that first bit with a nod. The merchant absolutely had to be present. "I cannot allow anything less than a full team to enter such premises. Would it be reasonable for a fighter to have a merchant and two ronin escorting them? Or would it be conspicuous otherwise for the merchant to have two fighters in his arsenal and one guard?"

Caenrya turned her sight toward the flicker of a nearby spirit, and her voice grew reluctant when she finally spoke. "Somewhat, depending on the status of this merchant. Those who have a reputation pull a larger crowd of ronin and acquaintances to observe their own fighters, while others either go solo or with a small collection of ronin or acquaintances. The higher echelons are all intimately familiar with each other's status, fighters, and associations. As long as this man isn't known, he could reasonably pull in a couple of newcomers and a single unknown fighter without raising a red flag."

Staring down, Caenrya ran her tongue across the bottom of her canines. "Two fighters, at our age, will get us caught. Two ronin escorting him would be nothing too suspicious, but if you want to maximize your reach for information, it may be best to have Ren pose as an acquaintance to converse with other onlookers." Narrowing her brows, she peered up at Ilias with those deep blue eyes. "He will need an iron-clad backstory."

His father nodded in agreement. Halden watched as Caenrya's eyes flicked over, narrowing on him.

She propped an arm on her hip. "You hypothetically could have another undercover shinobi act as a ronin. As you've mentioned, this merchant is low status. I doubt he'd be capable of hiring two." Her words were weighted.

"Then allow me and Ren to attend as his ronin and acquaintance, respectfully," Halden proposed, not balking from the displeasure Caenrya stared at him with.

Nodding slowly, Ilias looked between them, something flickering in the depths of his eyes. "We can arrange that. I'll contact the merchant and entice him to acquiesce to this development. It's crucial that shinobi with the vin of the Arundel and Sahkara houses accompany you. The combination of bloodline gifts will greatly increase your odds of success. For now, let us all prepare how best we can. I expect your training is progressing?"

"At this moment, it appears to be stilted," Caenrya muttered, her dislike evident toward the shogun. "I'd like to resume if there's nothing more to discuss."

It would have raised serious brows if anyone else spoke to the shogun in such a manner.

"Not at the moment, Caenrya. I'll leave you to it." With that, Ilias turned to depart, a heaping pile of paperwork remaining on his desk to address before he took his nightly shift at Temple Square.

Stepping toward her, Halden made to say something before she twisted away, ignoring him. Ren returned to the small clearing, and a door closed behind Aya's approaching figure. At the clear dismissal and gathering crowd, Halden only shook his head in frustration and followed his father's steps down the steep stairwell.

As he said a brief goodbye to his father, his feet bounding toward Eirea's meeting point for daily patrolling, Halden's mind spun from the interaction with Caenrya. She was utterly infuriating at times with the frequent shifts between hot and cold, and her demeanor was rarely honestly portrayed. Today had been no different. The intention behind her words was clear, but the reason was shrouded. Halden wanted answers on what had changed since she had learned about this plan and why she was yet again pushing him away.

Sure, he could comprehend how he may not be best suited for this particular assignment given his history with Valen. But Halden was a shinobi through and through. He'd be more than capable of handling the aftermath of the fighting ring and whatever atrocious dealings the underground thrived and teemed with.

Throughout the patrol, Halden pushed himself harder than ever within the limitations of his visual vin, taking every spare second of his breaks to weave through his forms with the dual-wielding sai.

By the time his shift was over, he had collapsed into his bed, uncaring that he hadn't eaten dinner or cleaned up. The exhaustion drove all logic from his mind.

The following night passed in the blink of an eye and a flash of vivid memories. When the alarm rang from his clock, his hand fumbled a few times before accidentally knocking it from his futon's side table. Cursing, Halden rolled over to grab the damned thing, slamming it down on the dark cypress wood before running his hands down his face.

Exhaustion still clouded his mind, body aching as he readied himself for the day. He moved slower than usual, and by the time he reached the training grounds, he wasn't surprised to see Eirea and Ryu waiting already beside the entryway of cherry blossom trees.

What did surprise him was the second shinobi team on standby beside them.

Commander of Team Bedevere, Naja, stood sternly beside Hina and her teammate, Finn Langley. Impatience was written across every stretch of the tall woman's face, and her dark almond eyes narrowed on Halden the moment he came into view. Her deep voice traveled to Halden's ears as she spoke to Eirea. "We must be off if we are to make it in a timely fashion."

Hina sheepishly smiled at Halden, sharing a small wave before whispering something into Ryu's ear. Shrugging, Ryu quietly responded before returning his attention to Halden's arrival. At Halden's confused glance, he said, "The shogun has requested every team's presence, from those recently having graduated to those about to disband and lead upcoming teams of their own."

Ah.

Ilias had mentioned nights prior that he was going to gather the shinobi for a brief gathering to regroup. This must be what he had discussed over dinner.

With a nod of welcome, Eirea led them through the training grounds, academy students gawking in awe and longing all the while. Each itched for the day they'd graduate to the rank of genin, able to undertake assignments and stake a name for themselves in the shinobi ranks. This morning, it appeared they were being instructed on taiji grappling, balancing their own with the wood of trees to scale easily in the likeness of a gecko.

Ryu slowed his steps beside Hina, the pair falling back to Halden.

"How is Caenrya doing?" Hina asked softly, genuine concern lining her hazel eyes as she glanced up at him. Ryu leaned in when Halden answered, also wanting to know.

"She's back to training," he said.

"But not with your team?" Uncertainty creased Hina's face, making it clear to Halden she didn't want to tread on any boundaries.

With a heavy sigh, Halden said, "Not for some time. She is apprenticing with Elder Aya Dagon to train in Kū."

Understanding flooded Hina's face, warming her features. "Well, should she want any assistance with the other elements, please do let her know I'm more than happy to help with what I know."

They crossed through a narrow twist of trees, Halden trying for a slight smile despite the rock in his gut. "I'll pass it on."

The mixture of cherry blossom and ahari trees gave way to the gathering field, a wide-open grassy knoll teeming with activity. Over thirty teams in full, making the count over a hundred strong by the time they joined. Varying ages of shinobi milled about, conversing about their patrols or what they suspected the gathering to be about. Even full-fledged jōnin congregated along the edges of the group, all ones in the shogun's service without a team.

It was strange to see the fresh handful of groups, the genin no older than thirteen and still starry-eyed about it all. Looking back to Eirea as she spoke with Naja, Halden recalled the first encounter he and Ryu had on graduation day.

Every newly promoted genin was awarded a set of armor and assigned a captain, but when their names were called to line up with this beaming shinobi, Halden grossly underestimated just how much of a bad-arse Eirea was. It wasn't until their first serious assignment years ago that Eirea's previous identity of oniwaban was accidentally shared with them.

A ronin whose partner Eirea had removed from their clan a decade ago had hunted her down, promising revenge when ambushing them all during a setup escorting assignment. The ease and skill she displayed that day had awed Ryu and Halden, who never again doubted her smile concealed the deadly oniwaban within. Eirea was still very much the same person and easy to her frequent grins. But she had nearly sacrificed her life numerous times for them, even giving up an eye to protect her latest charge.

As for Ryu, well, he was still immature and had a way to grow in that sense. Halden couldn't deny his strides with his vin, a rare ability to form working duplicates with any natural material his taiji touched. In the academy, he'd barely be capable of holding a duplicate for mere seconds and a girl's attention for mere minutes. Nowadays, he was as loyal as could be to Hina and his team, even stretching out his neck in the path of a shuriken for Caenrya despite not knowing half of what Halden did. He rose from the bottom of the class to a respectable shinobi, aiming for heights Ren managed to achieve.

Halden had since recognized the privilege of being a shinobi and what it truly stood for. What he'd sacrifice to continue being and honoring. It was a terrible burden to bear at times, between the near-death, heart-stopping moments and waking up to view the world as it was, but there was nothing else he'd rather become than the one to walk in the steps of those who fought for this generation to exist.

For the next unborn.

When his father emerged from the tree line, the crowd of shinobi falling still and silent out of respect, Halden squared his shoulders with resolve. Hina's eyes were wide with admiration, Ryu stealing glances at her when she wasn't aware.

Shogun Arundel began his speech with words of gratitude for their hard work and dedication, lifting the spirits of many listening. Then, he delved into darker topics, recounting all they had since gleaned of the harbinger and what they could expect going forward. It brought confidence to all that the shogun himself was making rounds at night, determined to handle the beast himself to spare any further loss of life.

Then.

"Beginning today, we mark a distinct change in each team's training initiatives."

Everyone's attention was snagged by that, curiosity palpable in the light spring air.

Ilias's gaze flicked between teams as he spoke. "We will continue to roll out patrols but decrease the amount necessary per daylight hours to permit time to increase every shinobi's skill through rigorous training. You may have noticed the board posted in front of the training ground entryway this morn."

Halden surely did, now connecting the dots between its appearance and what his father had proposed to him.

"There will be taskings assigned to every team present here today by six a.m. daily. Each team will be given one according to current skill and capabilities to be read only by the commander's respective folder attached. Some will find them exceedingly difficult, and I will not sugarcoat it for any here."

A pause had the crowd on the edge of their toes.

"You will be pushed further, expected to reach higher. Now more than ever, our clan requires the strength of our shinobi, and your generation will be the upcoming hope to preserve our legacy."

Eyes shone, and chins inched upward. Everyone recognized the solemnity of the moment and knew it would be a turning point they'd never forget.

"By now, assignments have been posted, and expectations are high for each of you. I ask that you give every ounce of will you have to them, for there will come a time when life-and-death situations demand even more than you realize you are capable of," Ilias promised, his voice strong and inspiring despite the gravity of his words. "In our line of work, we lose people. Perhaps the one standing beside you at this very moment."

Halden didn't dare glance at Ryu or Eirea on his other side. They'd been close far too many times. Around him, a heavy note hung about as teams shuffled where they stood, taking in what they were fortunate to have at the moment.

"We don't have the luxury of being the protected, but we have the gift and privilege of extending it to thousands more through the very blood we ourselves lose in the heat of battle. You all once swore to our clan to protect and serve, and I ask once more, will you uphold that oath until you lay down your sword?" Ilias boomed, his voice rising with the passion radiating from his words.

Every shinobi let out a resounding, *Yes, Shogun*.

With a decisive nod, Ilias concluded, "Our ancestors shine upon you all, and I am without doubt each of you will honor them in return."

Dispersing after his leave, every commander led their eager teams toward the board. Eirea purposefully held back to let other teams pass through first. By the time they reached it, every folder had been taken under each commander's name. Hina sadly departed with a wave as her team bounded off to complete their assignment.

When Eirea pulled theirs, a twitch pulled at the corner of her mouth.

"What is it?" Ryu impatiently demanded, fingers drumming over his thighs.

Folding it neatly, Eirea placed the paper into a pocket. "Remember those jōnin back at the clearing?"

"The ones without teams?" Halden asked, distinctly remembering the way they spread out in a purposeful manner around the coagulation of teams.

Eirea mm-hmmed, proceeding to ask, "How many were there?"

"Seventeen." They were too obvious to not discern, and a shinobi must be aware of their surroundings at all times. "They are part of our assignment?"

It only made sense. Halden knew there were more jōnin in the shogun's employ than that. He'd just assumed the rest were on duty.

An impressed grin. "We are to hunt them down throughout the Citadel."

Ryu threw his hands up in exasperation. "That's mainly going to be on Halden since I don't have freakish ball eyes."

"You have duplicates," Halden reminded, amusement sounding in his voice.

"What's the plan?" Eirea prompted, resting a hand on her hip as she watched their minds formulate a plan of action.

"I will search with my vin as we move about the Citadel while Ryu navigates his duplicates in areas where I can pick up taiji markers," Halden said, his mind devising the most efficient method to sweep the entirety of the village. "We'll begin at West Gate and clear through the center until we reach East Gate."

Quirking a brow, Eirea asked, "Are you confident you'll be capable of scanning through the entirety of the Citadel along the way? Our boundaries are limited to the confines of the inhabited and frequented portions within our walls, and our time is limited by a six p.m. deadline. All targets will be outside and alone."

At Halden's assurance, Eirea continued, "All right. I'd like to tack on additional challenges." At Ryu's disapproving groan, her voice only rose. "Halden, I'm tasking you to start remembering the taiji markers of individual shinobi outside of our circle. There will come another day, much like when we chased after Ren and Caenrya, when it would be of great benefit to know if the person is friend or foe."

Reading taiji was akin to reading novels. Each one he had in his collection was written by a different author, a factor made clear by the tone and voice of each work. Taiji was no different. Every shinobi had key tells with distinctive characteristics. For example, Ryu's was similar to a beehive, blunt and at rest until provoked. Whereas Caenrya's was constantly shifting, with a sharpness to the edges.

It wasn't an easy ask. Most shinobi of the Arundel House weren't adept with it until they were in their jōnin years. Halden inclined his chin, acknowledging his assignment.

"Ryu, I want you to increase the duration of your duplicates with consistency. The longer you can hold on to each while multitasking will be crucial when faced with a larger collection of assailants. Let's aim for this first, and then you'll strive for additional duplicates when two are mastered." Eirea ticked off the last of her fingers. She pocketed her hands and turned down the trail leading back to the Citadel. Head over a shoulder, she gave them an expectant look. "Well?"

Ryu and Halden streamed through the forest and alongside the Koi River until they arrived at the western edge of the village. There, they began the tedious task of hunting down their seventeen targets, an assignment made easier by the lack of common folk wandering the streets.

Halden worked to differentiate markers showing throughout the village, some being residents inside their respective buildings or others teams scouring the Citadel for their own assignments. One marker, a splitting taiji that seemed to cackle above a sloped rooftop, rested suspiciously in place. With a hand signal, Halden directed Ryu toward that location, his teammate sending two duplicates up there to confirm.

When Ryu himself held out a confirming thumb, the team made their way up, scaling a wall and leaping from a second story to the roof of a third. A man sat up there, reading a novel in his shinobi blacks. Halden had seen him quite a few times passing through but never had the opportunity to speak with him.

They took a moment to familiarize themselves, Halden learning that the jōnin, Cato Pernelle, was Daven's older brother. Eirea had already been well-acquainted, judging by the fact they shared a brief laugh about an inside joke before departing.

When afternoon arrived, they managed to secure every jōnin's location except for the last. Nearing the eastern gate, Halden had picked up on a cluster of markers scattered within the treetops, a sight that made him wary as they approached by ground. One was Hina, the other two presumably Naja and Finn. The marker across from Hina was dimmer than her, which made Halden assume that was Finn while Naja hung back further along the path.

Halden relayed as much to his team. Eirea pulled further to allow them to assess the situation. At the signal of Halden's hand, Ryu sent a duplicate forward to test the waters, both of them acutely aware the other team's assignment could very well be to ambush other roving teams.

When a shuriken spun from Hina, Ryu's clone swerved just as the edge of a point scratched through the fabric on his shoulder. Finn shot from a concealed branch high above, twisting into a powerful kick with the bottom of his heel that made to connect with Ryu's head. It landed with an audible thud; the duplicate slammed into the ground beneath Finn, a preemptive *whoop* sounding from the shinobi before he realized his mistake.

One, he had no visual on the remainder of the team. He acted too soon.

Two, the duplicate *poofed* into a puppet of wood beneath him.

Three, that he was vastly outmatched.

Ryu and his second duplicate leaped from the foliage behind him, weapons drawn and eager grins across their faces. Across from Ryu,

Halden gripped a branch on his upswing, landing deftly beside Hina as he knocked her second shuriken from the air with a sai.

Hina's hands moved with practiced speed—a gale of wind fiercely throwing him toward the ground below. Halden controlled his fall and nimbly landed on his feet, immediately leaping backward to dodge the ball of fire that split against the ground where he had been but a heartbeat before.

With surprise on his side, Ryu had effectively constrained Finn before the shinobi had a chance to fight back. Finn's face shone with disappointment as he sat beside Ryu. Turning toward Hina, Ryu grinned a wild thing. "Sorry, Hina, I think we got the jump on you two."

"Yeah." She smiled, twirling a shuriken in one hand. "But I think I can still put up a good fight."

Before Ryu could say anything more, several shuriken rained down in rapid succession, one almost impaling his duplicate while he threw himself into a sideways roll—careful to not cut himself on his own weapons.

Halden knew her weakness was hand-to-hand combat through the numerous instances they had sparred at the academy, only needing to get close enough to use his vin to disable her wide range of ninjutsu. With a shared glance between him and Ryu, they leaped into action. Ryu ordered his duplicate far, effectively surrounding the tree his girlfriend stationed herself in.

"Sorry in advance." Hina winced, her hands reaching out, palms down as they lowered beside her middle.

That's when Halden saw it for the first time in Hina. Taiji from nature slowly flowed into her limbs, her stores soaring, and her capabilities expanded beyond the slight boost the energy would lend for speed, strength, and regeneration. Eirea rarely extended the need for the

Awakening state, but Halden knew she aimed to wipe out her enemies whenever she used it. As for Hina, she was new to the ability, and all Halden had to do was shake her enough to jolt her out of it.

Rezat.

Halden's hands were already forming the wind seal, a blade of wind incredibly honed and sharp that it cut through the branch Hina stood on as if it were butter. Launching off, Hina landed just as the three assailants made to strike. Hina sidestepped and pulled her katana for a graceful block, spinning to knock Ryu's clone into him before rolling to avoid Halden's sai. Her ponytail swung wide around her, and the katana tucked between her arm and side as her hands performed another seal.

A fire ring blasted outwards, taking out Ryu's duplicate and violently throwing Ryu and Halden backward into the ground. Lurching forward, Hina drew the katana low to force Ryu into surrender when Halden threw an arm wide.

The shine of his sai flicked across the small space, Hina's eyes widening as she spun in the nick of time to avoid injury. Ryu's hands fell into a *kai* seal, and a thin bolt of lightning shot from his hands toward Hina's feet, barely nicking her left one. It was clear Ryu had no intention of harming his girlfriend, but Halden gave him credit for the fight he put on anyway.

Bingo. Hina lost focus and disconnected from the Awakening state.

It seemed her heart wasn't entirely in it either.

Jumping into the fray, Halden began an aggressive assault with his sai. Hina managed to deflect each attack despite the limp in her foot and Ryu's kusarigama entering the battle. It was an ebb and flow of exchanges, with Halden moving forward when Ryu stepped back and Hina working hard to keep either from landing a single blow.

But when Ryu threw his whole weight into one final attack, Halden took advantage of it and jabbed Hina's right shoulder, blocking her chakra point from delivering taiji to her hand. Without any vin capabilities, Hina would have to rely solely on her sword until her chakras recovered.

Within a handful of maneuvers, they managed to trip her up, successfully thwarting the ambush attempt.

Clapping sounded behind Halden as Ryu offered Hina a hand—one gratefully accepted with a breathless grin. Finn complained about happening across the *one* team that would have spotted them in advance, but his commander snapped at him in response that his foot was visible the entire time. Eirea only winked at Halden and Ryu, resuming their own assignment with haste.

Chapter Twenty-Seven

CAENRYA

Coming weeks came and went all the same way, a new focus clearing her vision with each proceeding day. Soon she may see Verina again. Until they left for the next underground fight, Caenrya would pledge every spare moment to training. It wasn't long until her katana work became decent, taking to sparring with Ren blade to blade in normal rhythms. The elder encouraged her meditation, and the calm transitioned her into ninjutsu practice every time.

Even that tabby cat tested her meditation state, crawling on her lap and shoulders during it. Aya was quite impressed that Caenrya was able to ignore the feline.

Before Caenrya knew it, a month had passed in such a way. Only three months left until she'd set out back into the warring lands once more. Several times, her team had visited to check in on her. Aya had stuck to her side like the tabby cat did every slumber, either ensuring Caenrya didn't stray from her training or perhaps a slight overprotective, Caenrya hadn't a clue. Probably the former, if she had to guess.

More than a small nagging thought pestered her throughout each day, and her mind worried over useless nonsense about the upcoming assignment. She could handle it, no doubt, but Halden...

She didn't want him to see that part of her life.

Even though it wasn't the worst, not by far. But any part of her past felt dirty. Tainted. Showing that to someone she held in regard only made her dread it. Halden had only recently transitioned to viewing her as a peer rather than some victim. She despised the way he and the others had seen her when she first arrived, neglecting to notice the strength she bore within.

Possibly more distressing, Caenrya feared what would happen if their presence was revealed. None of them would escape, not with the top-class ronin the underground hired for security purposes. It would be a bloodbath. Only Caenrya would survive to be sent back to Shikei. There was a chance, as slight as it was, that Valen would get ahold of Halden and Ren first, leading to—

Exhaling, Caenrya forced aside the detrimental thoughts, her taiji wavering in front of her.

"Focus," Aya snapped, whacking her with a stick.

It was light, but that didn't stop Caenrya from scowling harder as her taiji slipped completely. "I can't focus when I'm being struck." She put everything she had into keeping the bite from those words.

"You'll face much worse in combat, Little Dragon," Aya scoffed, leaning back into her cushion.

Stars gleamed through the fading light above, Caenrya ignoring the fireflies gathering above the lily-padded pond beside her. Some of them had previously distracted her, the spirits of fireflies blinking into existence with the living. Shadows moved in the distance as Ren was relieved from his shift, a different oniwaban nodding at Aya before drifting into the tree line.

Silken ivory robes fell below Caenrya's hips, moving with her outstretched hands. The flexible material of her navy-blue trousers creased as her taiji formed a shield before her. A tiny string of taiji connected her hands and the large barrier before she consciously disconnected it, satisfied with the quality of the taiji hovering before her.

Sweat beaded on her forehead as Caenrya kept it in place, slowly moving about the grassy lawn with sweeping motions as if she wielded a blade in her hands. Aya would occasionally call out a direction a new imaginary foe appeared, requiring Caenrya to adjust accordingly and move the shield wherever the new attack was coming from.

The concept sounded easy.

It wasn't.

The damned taiji shield would flicker if she lost attention to its shape or moved it too fast, only making her question whether she'd ever be capable of producing taiji katanas when she progressed to that stage of training.

"All right, that's enough for now," Aya called out, rising with a faint pop in her knees.

Groaning in relief, Caenrya wiped her brow and disconnected her taiji, her breath heaving from the exertion of the day. It said enough that she could barely do much more than take steps to the house, trailing behind Aya in a haze of fatigue. But before they could do as much as turn the knob, a thunder of footsteps sounded behind them. Caenrya twisted her head and watched as her team bounded over the edge, hastening toward where she stood beside the elder.

Frowning, Caenrya took in the twist of their mouths, the edge of their eyes.

Eirea spoke first. "The harbinger attacked again."

A punch to the gut.

The guilt had accumulated to an immeasurable amount over the past months. Somehow, in some way, Valen had orchestrated this beast to attack innocent people. She had thought since her last dream of him invading her personal space that maybe he had stopped at last. Why then, after another month, had he decided to act again?

"How many were injured? Anyone we know?" Aya asked, her voice unusually mild. She clasped her hands, lines creasing beside her eyes.

The tabby cat leaped to Caenrya's shoulder, wrapping its tail around her neck for balance.

"None," Ryu said, his expression perplexed. His gelled hair was slightly disheveled, though he raised a hand to comb through it. He eyed the cat tentatively, reaching out to touch it.

The feline swatted his hand twice, startling Ryu as he swiftly withdrew it. Ryu scowled at the feline.

Caenrya was beginning to like the animal. She blinked, tilting her head away from the cat. "Was it caught? Deterred?"

They became dodgy again, Halden's heavy gaze said more than the others. Despite not losing anyone, the beast had to have done something catastrophic enough for the entire team to race to Aya's doorstep.

The commander folded her arms, one brown eye and one gray one staring at Caenrya. It was only a recent development that she forwent the eye patch, showing the scarred eye to the world. "The beast destroyed your apartment, Caenrya," Eirea said, her face unnervingly solemn without her natural smile.

Blinking again, Caenrya's frown deepened. "Well, it's not like it was precious." There had to be more.

But deep inside, her stomach sickened at the loss. For the first time, she had something of her own. A place she could call hers, with belongings inside that she memorized every inch of in fascination. Now it was gone. In so many ways, it hurt to have that first space of hers desecrated.

At least the cat had followed her. Caenrya would have been guilt-ridden if something had happened to it.

Halden rubbed behind his ear, flicking his eyes toward Eirea before speaking. "It left a message scratched into the remnants of a wall."

That's when Caenrya's lungs froze in her chest, real fear striking her. Valen must have left a condemning message for her team to be in such a state. Perhaps she should have been more straightforward about her past or maybe even those dreams she had with Valen. Depending on what the ronin shared, Caenrya might not be able to recover from the trust she'd lose.

"Out with it," Aya demanded, her face lined more than usual with stress. "We haven't all day."

"I'm Two," Eirea said, her eyes searching Caenrya's for a reaction.

No.

No. No. *No.*

Her face paled, a hand bracing against the cypress wood of the house.

Valen had done it, had accomplished what she truly feared on a scale unimaginable. It was much worse than Caenrya could have predicted, wishing that the words scored into the ruins of her apartment were anything but that.

I'm Two.

Two had lived, after all, all those months ago. Then, he'd been sent as an offering, but now his presence was punishment. A harbinger indeed.

Of more to come.

Enya had warned Caenrya that the balance of nature had been warped, and she had a sinking realization this was but one piece of the puzzle. An inkling of what lurked beneath the surface. It terrified Caenrya to think of the danger being left behind if she were to retrieve Verina and run as she originally intended months ago. Eirea, Ryu, Halden,

Aya, Ren... all of them wouldn't hold a candle's flame to Valen and the daimyo's mechanisms.

What should she do?

But perhaps the ultimate question was what *could* she do?

"What does this mean?" Aya questioned, her face no-nonsense as she addressed her pupil.

Her hands fisted, her will forcing Caenrya to get her act together. *Later*, she promised herself. *Later I will devise a solution to this mess.*

Out loud, she spoke to no one in particular, "At Shikei, every one of us had a number. It was a barbaric system intended to keep each of us at the other's throat, never knowing when we'd slip in rank and lose favor. Those at the bottom had a tendency of being sold into... something worse than fighting as a slave, or they would find themselves six feet underground."

Too many. With Verina at the bottom, Caenrya committed atrocities to keep that from being her sister's fate.

Caenrya could almost see her now, Verina's sweet smile as she played with Caenrya's braid. She gasped in absolute joy whenever Caenrya would return from a particularly grueling task with a wildflower or small toy she'd been able to acquire in those first years.

Those hopeful eyes always squeezed Caenrya's heart, the essence of happiness somehow returning for those brief and dispersed moments. Caenrya felt Verina's breath when she fell asleep on her shoulder one night, relived the devastation eating at her when that metal door creaked in her cell and Caenrya's time was at its end for that month.

If there was good in this forsaken world, it was found in Verina's soul.

No matter how many months they endured, Verina would always cherish those moments with Caenrya. It made it all worth it to have her sister's love and adoration. Caenrya always strove to ensure every speck of blood was scrubbed before visiting, any trace of what she'd become left at the door whenever she entered the makeshift bedroom. For scarce minutes, she became the sister Verina craved, the one she once was before they were spirited away from their family.

A tapping of a foot sounded. It withdrew Caenrya from the endless pit she almost spiraled into, every bit of it tearing at her chest. "Two had been my only true adversary, the rest not as concerned with my rank as One. He failed that day when our daimyo sent him with the other ronin to find me. I believe the beast is how he was disciplined."

"You mean to say that he somehow summoned this monster?" Ryu asked, disbelief etched into his features.

Shaking her head, Caenrya corrected him. "Two *is* the beast."

Shock crossed each of their faces. Aya, however, appeared disconnected from the conversation. Eirea shuffled in place, gazing distantly as her mind toyed with the possibility.

"How is that possible?" Eirea asked, her eyes unseeing as they narrowed on the wall behind Caenrya.

"Through the most despicable of transgressions against the teetering balance of life and death. A wrong against every law of nature that sanctions ninjutsu," Aya breathed, something dark lurking in her tone. "They have done the unspeakable, tearing the very core of taiji from a living being and warping them into something unrecognizable."

Horror lowered Ryu's jaw, Halden's face appalled by the revelation. Only Caenrya folded her arms, turning away to distract herself from the reality they faced.

"Do you know if it's possible to recover from such a thing, Elder Dagon?" Eirea solemnly asked, her good eye clear with understanding. She knew the gravity of the situation and was aware of what it spelled for the clan.

Rubbing her gnarled hands together, Aya lifted her face to the sky as if taking in her last glimpse of the untamed beauty. "I believe the time is upon us that we must fall to our knees and beg the ancestors for forgiveness and guidance. Our civilization will crumble within the coming years otherwise." With that, she left them out in the chilled air, taking comfort within the confines of her home.

"But... it's only one beast," Ryu got out, his face tinged with desperation. Even the young knew an awful reckoning was nigh when the elders of their clan caved to the sight of it. "We'll find a way to take it down. Your father is after it now, right?" Turning toward Halden, Ryu's face fell further when he saw the way Halden's head twisted away, his own eyes closed as he processed the newfound knowledge.

Eirea sighed, placing a gentle hand on Ryu's shoulder. "If there is one, there will be more. The odds of that are great. Every enemy they capture could be turned against us in a similar manner. Without a working knowledge of how to destroy something undefeatable, I'm afraid we are stuck at the drawing board."

Something straightened Halden's shoulders. When his gaze rose, so did a strength within. "We'll find it. Our ancestors haven't abandoned us." His eyes found Caenrya's, the burn of them raising her own. "I have faith in them. In us."

Caenrya got the distinct impression he knew the information she lacked. The confidence otherwise would have been foolish, and Halden did not strike her as one burdened from such an affliction.

"As do I," Eirea agreed, thrumming her fingers along the belt of her black robe. "I must report these findings to the shogun. I'll see you all tomorrow."

The commander left, banking in the direction of the Duša Clan Temple. Ryu muttered something about finding Hina, giving a distracted wave before departing. Halden hesitated, taking a step away before glancing back at Caenrya.

Aya, for once, gave them privacy. Even the tabby decided to sunbathe, leaving them for Aya's roof.

For a second, they stared at each other. Alone. Caenrya's eyes masked the shame and sorrow she knew her presence had since caused, but Halden's swam with questions unasked. She sensed it, the drive behind his pause. She gestured at the pond and heard his steps padding behind hers. It was so quiet in those few short seconds as they folded themselves onto the cushions. The water across the pond didn't so much as stir as her eyes grazed across its mellow surface. Caenrya waited for Halden's words.

When they came, she wasn't quite prepared.

"When you spoke with my mother back then," Halden began quietly, elbows resting on his thighs, "did she say anything else?"

Caenrya chewed on her tongue for a moment, thinking about how to respond to such a complicated question. "She was concerned for your well-being is all. Had some unfounded idea that I cared."

A corner of Halden's mouth quirked at the small jest, his eyes held down with a hint of sadness. "Was she... did she seem content?"

It tugged at something she had long since remembered—the loss of a parent. In what could have been eons ago, Caenrya, too, had wondered the same things. "Enya was at peace," she said, her eyes watching his expression from the corner of hers.

It was dangerous to allow herself this time, to be this close with him when what lay ahead surely would go awry. There was only one she owed everything to and should entirely focus on. But her thoughts were betraying her, whispering to her that there was another now. A few others, but one out of the bunch she cared deeply for in a way she couldn't allow.

Halden lowered his chin, and the knot in his shoulders loosened. "Thank you. It makes a difference knowing that." Working himself the courage, he reluctantly asked, "How did you manage all of those years with Valen?"

Caenrya's expression hardened. Both fists balled tight over her knees, and her eyes grew fierce as she met Halden's searching ones. "I grew to view it as the game he claimed it to be. A game you'll lose if you play. A convoluted, never-ending cycle that allowed him to mold everyone to his expectations. He always knew best how to manipulate us through every pain imaginable. Physical and mental."

Halden's eyes were locked onto hers, his chest stilling.

"You refuse to let him change you. You hold on with every bit of will you can muster to the only thing you cherish above all else, and the essence of who you are will follow. That's how you win without him knowing he never stood a chance," she murmured, her face softening. "It's how you survive while playing along, waiting for that one moment where you can run."

Those piercing gray eyes of his flickered, a decision made in his mind. Halden nodded slightly, the movement near imperceptible if Caenrya hadn't been paying such close attention. "I—" His voice cut off as a door briskly opened at the house's entryway.

A butler gestured for Caenrya to return to Aya's residence.

While she had the courage, Caenrya faced Halden as they rose from the ground. "Don't go on this mission to the warring lands." She kept the words even enough, despite the needling urge to plea them.

A half smile rested on Halden's lips, and his eyes brightened with an emotion she couldn't identify. "Did you make the same request of Ren?"

Bemused, Caenrya furrowed her brows at him. She didn't understand why he'd ask such a thing. Did he want her too?

"Didn't think so," Halden said to himself, pocketing his hands. Something made him grin in a lopsided fashion. Louder, he added, "That's why I'll be going despite your best attempts to the contrary. I promised I wouldn't leave you after all."

Something stirred in her chest, something she pressed down, down, down.

With a wave of his hand, Halden walked the endless descent into the Citadel, leaving Caenrya in a web of conflicting thoughts she wasn't sure should be untangled.

She'd have to devise a method of keeping him from going. There had to be a way to convince Halden and keep him from it all. However, it was frustrating how dedicated he was.

In the meantime, Caenrya had to figure out how to bring Two down. He was her responsibility. She had the opportunity to kill him months ago but didn't regret sparing his life to save Halden and Ryu's. The only regret was she hadn't been faster when fighting Two. Maybe the people here had a right to hate her. It was her fault for many of their deaths and all the destruction left in her wake. Which was why she absolutely had to bring an end to this before another was lost. With how spread out the attacks had become, she possibly had weeks to prepare, but that wasn't a chance Caenrya was willing to take.

Not when she decided not to wallow in self-pity any longer. It was time to rise above it and do something.

She had to open another gate of power.

It was the only way. With how far she had come with the first gate, Caenrya was confident another would lend her the strength to easily survive attempting that dimensional ninjutsu again. Taiji elemental ninjutsu had no impact on its hide, but twisting the very space it resided in *had* to be effective.

At least, she hoped.

***

In the coming days, it was all Caenrya could think about. Her mind replayed the brief encounter she had with Two, recalling every tiny, even insignificant, detail possible. When meditating though, Caenrya poured everything she had into focusing. She could almost feel it within her bones, envisioning that energy released through her chakras once more. Further and further, she pushed herself with the katana and taiji sessions, urgency propelling her in each.

For the next week, Caenrya couldn't help but worry the harbinger would return soon. The dread crawled into her waking moments, consuming her thoughts in her dreams. To her frustration, her meditation hadn't progressed opening her inner gates, but during the late hours of night, a second's worth of memory woke her during a nightmare.

One of many she'd recently had.

A child's scream and the beast's head ticking sideways as it leaped at Halden.

Two had appeared to be in pain for that brief moment, the claws on each appendage flexing. He no longer had eyes, but the method in which he found his targets was a combination of sound and smell. Sound must have been a larger irritant considering the way Two reacted when Caenrya spoke out loud that night.

The harbinger was dead set on Halden, leaping for him at first. When Caenrya talked, Two's head immediately twisted toward her as if she were the true target all along but couldn't pinpoint her other than by traces of smell that lingered on each shinobi present that night.

Sound.

Sound was Two's weakness, and ninjutsu may work only internally. That's why Valen cut out Two's eyes, to prevent her from entering his mind.

Like a shot of adrenaline, Caenrya rocketed from her room that morning. The tabby protested with a loud *merrrrww* as it was flopped to the side of the bed.

She looked back at the tabby, its fur fluffed ridiculously. "Sorry," she said, wincing. She forgot the feline was there, giving it a few pets until it forgave her. "I'll be back."

Caenrya raced into the dining room, still dressed in night robes. A cup of steaming tea rested with a faint clink on a porcelain plate, Aya frowning at the head of the table with a book splayed across the oiled cedar wood.

"I think I figured it out," Caenrya said, slightly breathless. "The beast's weakness."

At Aya's expectant expression, Caenrya recounted her experience with Two. She went into every ounce of detail she could share from start to finish. From there, she worked up a feasible plan, one she'd share without delay if Aya thought it doable. But when Caenrya described just *how* she planned to get rid of Two...

"Too risky." Aya shook her head, her eyes clouded as Caenrya kneeled on the cushion to her right.

"It's our only chance," Caenrya protested, her eyes widening at the blatant denial. "I'll be the first to admit that it isn't ideal, but Two—whatever it is—will continue to raze the Citadel unless I use that ninjutsu."

Snapping shut the book, Aya's swift change to anger almost had Caenrya flinching. "I'll only say this the once, Little Dragon. If you chance it, you will not ever be capable of using taiji again. Your recovery took far longer than the handful of taiji depletion cases I have witnessed, and half of those ended in the permanent loss of the chakra points guiding taiji."

Her palms grew clammy at that, a shiver coursing down her spine. Caenrya hadn't realized just how fortunate she was.

"Your path has barely been tread. Far too soon for it to be abandoned. Open another gate first, and then perhaps we can reassess." Sharp eyes flicked down her robes, unpleased with the attire.

Deflated, Caenrya dipped her chin before turning on her heel. The entire time she readied herself for the day, she couldn't help the surge of frustration at the wave of uselessness overwhelming her. Breakfast was silent that morning. Aya only shared that she'd notify the shogun of Caenrya's observations to determine whether something could be implemented to exploit that weakness.

It was the best Caenrya would get, it seemed.

Katana training had her sweating in the warm sunlight within the hour. Ren held back less and less with each proceeding week, striking with more lethality and maneuverability than she was accustomed to.

An oniwaban, indeed.

As he indicated for their practice to conclude for the day, Caenrya couldn't help but be proud of the small beads of sweat gathered on Ren's brow.

She was improving.

"If I may," Ren started, sheathing his katana in one fluid movement. "You struggle yet with the first of Five Paths?"

Caenrya nodded once, working to repress the tiny flare of frustration at not being able to achieve progress in that way. During the time spent with Aya, Caenrya knew she had to become more forgiving of herself. She had to accept progress as it came and not become wrathful when it was dangled in front of her unobtainable. It would only hinder her growth in the long run.

Ren's dark eyes were intense, his left hand casually resting on the pommel of his katana. "I believe you're close to passing the first path, but there is one thing I've witnessed that may be prohibiting your success."

Her interest peaked at that. Laying her katana on a cloth to be cleaned, Caenrya straightened her back. "Any insight would help," she admitted, knowing she would never have gotten this far without the aid of others. And so, she listened with rapt attention.

"You're not acknowledging a fault of yours." Ren's brow pinched, a finger tapping his head twice before lowering. "You withhold truth not because it is necessary, but rather, you don't want to confront the inner turmoil it is associated with. You fool yourself into being blind against it, not realizing until consequences are born of your inability to be more honest with yourself. Such things will lock your path to self-realization. Take it as you may."

Firm words but delivered in a humble way.

Opening her mouth, Caenrya was about to protest, but as it settled over her, she saw the reality. She closed her mouth and stared at the swaying blades of grass, clouds in the sky casting shapes upon it. She nodded her head slowly, finally meeting Ren square on with her eyes. "Thank you. I'll work on that."

She could have sworn his face moved into a smile beneath that mask as Ren turned, leaving for his hidden post.

***

Caenrya retrieved her cleaning tools from Aya's residence, choosing to enjoy the weather before it grew too warm. Cleaning and maintaining her blade proved a calming transition into the afternoon. She mulled over Ren's words, taking them to heart. She analyzed everything. Her reactions to the clan and they to her. The decisions of her team, the words they spoke and actions carried out, and the truths she hadn't shared.

Some truths Caenrya acknowledged the base reason she refused to share. She faced her regrets and swore to do better, especially to Eirea. Eirea sacrificed her eye, believed in Caenrya from the start, and even put up with her attitude when trying to help. She owed her best to her commander from here on out and would not let that sacrifice go in vain. It opened her eyes just so—enough to see more of who she was and how that affected her more than she thought.

However, one thing in particular stumped her.

Caenrya recalled Halden's words. *Did you make the same request of Ren?*

When Caenrya hadn't responded, Halden had continued.

Didn't think so.

Why had *that* mattered? She furrowed her brows.

That's why I'll be going despite your best attempts to the contrary. I promised I wouldn't leave you after all.

Why hadn't she thought to tell Ren not to go?

Well, that part was easy. Caenrya didn't want Halden to be near Valen or to see the dark place she had lived in for too long. It would be bringing a person to witness her biggest disgrace firsthand. It would be... words couldn't describe how awful it would be.

For Ren to be there, well, it wasn't ideal. But she wasn't as worried about him.

Blinking, Caenrya stared at her reflection in the polished katana.

She imaged those steel-gray eyes staring back, the light in them as if he won something.

She recalled the first time he worried over her in the forest, right after they defeated the ronin who had drugged her. Halden had helped her sit and checked her for injuries before anything else. He stood up for her that other day at the fountain when Owena and the others were being beyond idiotic. Every time there was a side to take, he sided with her. Supporting her. Sacrificing for her.

Both of them had suffered in ways so similar yet in methods so different by the hands of Valen. Without a doubt, Caenrya knew Halden wouldn't balk when they faced him again. He wielded a silent strength that only flourished when his circle of friends grew. When he had more to care for, he became everything a shinobi stood for. Halden wouldn't leave her to fend for herself.

She deeply respected that about him.

Yet as Caenrya tried to push him away at every turn, he wouldn't be dissuaded. The idiot ran at her, somehow confident she wouldn't spear him with those taiji blades when she broke from the medical clinic under Valen's ninjutsu. Deep down, she couldn't do it, even under powerful mind-controlling ninjutsu that egged her to fight against them all. Something dangerous broke through, turning that blade before it was too late.

Even after sharing what happened to Ten, Halden only bucked down his resolve. His will was steadfast, and his oath to stay resonated inside her empty chest like a music note echoing inside a bell.

Halden stayed with her every night in that clinic and had almost used a forbidden ninjutsu to sacrifice his life to save hers when the harbinger was on them. He almost *died* for her, and... and...

So had Eirea. So had Ryu.

That terrified her.

Caenrya had too much to lose now. Before, she had one purpose, one source of strength. Now, she had much more at risk. No one was more terrified than she at the thought of losing it all.

The harbinger was here because of her. Every soul that perished, and every soul that continued to risk their life, was because she remained in the clan. Initially, she would have used these people to get her sister back, thinking they were only using her in turn anyway. But these people had wormed their way into her once shattered heart. A place she used to only have room for her sister but, by some twist of fate, had grown to include more.

Caenrya wouldn't trade any of it. She wouldn't regret opening that small corner of things she valued to include them. She just prayed to the ancestors that they didn't claim those treasured pieces that filled the holes in her heart.

Rising, Caenrya placed her blade into the sheath across her back. Her eyes burned as she looked at the wooden stairwell descending into the Citadel.

Did you make the same request of Ren?

No, and it was because she didn't care for Ren in the way she cared for Halden. All those times she felt something catch her breath, steal her attention, and constrict her very heart around him, she repressed it. She didn't want to confess there were more emotions she was capable of experiencing or that they were okay to have.

It had been traitorous of her to allow herself to feel such things when she had let her life revolve around one person for so long. She clenched a fist over her heart, the storm of emotions threatening to overwhelm her. Admitting that to herself was more terrifying than anything she'd ever faced before. With a heavy pause, Caenrya swallowed hard and made for Aya's home.

Tons of torn leaves littered the dining table, a clear message as Aya read her book. Caenrya got to work without complaint. Even the elder had to admit her control had since improved, the mending of each leaf smooth and without defect. When it came time to revive the taiji shield later that afternoon, the edges were firmer, and the taiji was evenly distributed. Moving about proved easier when the shield followed, shifting in directions the elder called out.

Aya asked her a question per lesson, though every answer involved recalling what was taught. Caenrya was grateful for that. By the time she slumped against her futon, her body was spent. But her mind still reeled, restless and grasping for more.

Caenrya folded her legs and assumed a half-lotus position before hopping into the shower that night. Exhaling out negative energy, she focused on inhaling calmness. The sound of crickets hummed in the night outside, and the occasional call of an owl broke through.

When she reached the state of stillness, Caenrya was at ease with herself. Thoughts would sporadically float through her mind. She acknowledged them but allowed them to pass through to remain in the trance-like zone. It was shocking how many of them were truly welcomed to her, the positivity rare in her mind.

It reminded her of how far she had come since arriving there all those months ago and of all she would learn in the coming years.

Years.

Caenrya couldn't deny it any longer. The truth was unveiled from the meditation's serenity.

She wanted to stay, to have the last of her family thrive alongside her. Caenrya envisioned it as clearly as the waters in the Koi River all those weeks ago when she watched the families play and clean within them. Verina would love the atmosphere and could easily fit in with anyone. Whereas Caenrya was distant and reclusive, Verina shone with her charisma. Caenrya could easily see Hina being a close friend of her sister and Eirea pulling Verina under her wing.

All Caenrya had to do was remove Two's stain from the clan and rescue her sister from Shikei, an enormous undertaking, but she wasn't alone in this. The Citadel would be a haven where Verina could pursue whatever life she wanted. Perhaps something in agriculture since she absolutely adored flowers growing up. Even when she was a toddler, Verina would always giggle and smile when given beautiful wildflowers.

Possibly more remarkable, Caenrya saw a future for herself in the clan. A future where she could carry out missions for the betterment of the people. Where she could have friends and family. She wanted to stay and grow with Team Cadigan. Caenrya missed the members more than she would have thought. She wanted to make Aya proud and have the people of this clan accept her.

Without a shred of doubt, Caenrya knew this would be their home. And for two sisters who had gone so long without, the thought affected Caenrya deeply.

But it pierced her very soul when she acknowledged Halden was a big part of it all, and those feelings for him somehow sprouted despite her being so damaged in the past.

Caenrya rolled out her shoulders, a hint of a smile tracing her lips at what the truth unleashed. Not even Valen himself could stop her, not from defending her newfound home and certainly not from bringing down the entire Hel-damned underground.

The path forward was open.

CHAPTER TWENTY-EIGHT

HALDEN

After a day of sparring with several jōnin—utilizing only innovative methods to secure a win—Halden and Ryu were absolutely winded. Even Hina was unusually deflated from the constant intensity with which they were being pushed. Her demeanor lacked the usual lightheartedness as they wove through the Citadel walkways.

"We are having chicken tandoori tonight if you'd like to join me and Ryu at my family's table, Halden," Hina kindly offered, knowing how Ilias's absence would be missed on the remainder of Halden's birthday.

While it wouldn't be the first time Halden had done so, it usually only reminded him of what he'd lost whenever he visited Hina's house with Ryu. Whereas his was nearly empty daily, Hina had siblings and grandparents living within the walls. Never was there a quiet moment, always alive with music and chatter bursting at the seams.

It was such a homely place, the Saito family hosted new guests every other day.

Regardless of his own troubles, Halden accepted out of politeness and his friendship with both Hina and Ryu. These days, there was enough turmoil and grief lingering from the beast's constant attacks. He'd push aside his own doubts and be grateful for the time he had.

A shift in Ryu's smirk had Halden eyeing him warily. It was one he frequently wore when he was about to instigate something. "So. When do you think you'll ask Caenrya out for a date?" Ryu winked, Hina beaming next to him as they walked hand in hand.

Halden shook his head but couldn't help the corner of his mouth that rose a fraction. "It's something I'd consider only once everything has settled," he answered, falling back a couple of steps as they turned a sharp corner toward the Citadel's western edge. "Both she and I are dedicated toward our goals at the moment, and I'd rather not chance losing focus of what I aim to achieve in the meantime."

If things weren't so dire, then perhaps…

He shook his head slightly.

Once Caenrya had Verina back and the harbinger was taken out, Halden would consider it in earnest. Right now, Caenrya was entirely fixated on the upcoming assignment, and he respected her priorities. He had the distinct impression that once her sister arrived, Caenrya would let her guard down easier, relieved of the guilt preventing her from living her life. Halden looked forward to meeting Verina and was eager to return to some semblance of a normal life that included them.

"I think she's good for you," Hina hummed, her pale skin bright under the lamplight. "You've been much more driven since she arrived."

"All in an attempt to impress her, I'm sure," Ryu joked, thumbing his nose with lightheartedness in his eyes. Hina squeezed his hand, her face clearly saying *don't antagonize him.*

Halden's hands rose. "Maybe you're onto something. I—"

A loud crash sounded far behind them, echoes of screams reaching their ears. They swiveled in the direction of the disturbance. With the dark sky looming above, they knew what they would encounter should they pursue the noise. Despite it, the trio sprinted through the Citadel in the direction of Wisteria Square, Halden engaging his vin to glean a better view of what was before them.

Mere blocks away, he witnessed that similar gap in space that pushed aside taiji, the area racing across the square.

"It's the harbinger," Halden called out, his heart racing faster than his legs moved. He expanded his visual ninjutsu, searching for others in the vicinity. "My father is already coming from Riverside Square. Several oniwaban are circling it now to engage."

Ryu didn't speak, his expression saying enough in response. He was terrified and rightfully so. The last encounter was far too close for comfort, and without any solid method of bringing it down, there wasn't any guarantee they would come out of this alive.

Long brown hair swayed around Hina as she turned her head. "We must do what we can to aid the others," she said, her hazel eyes unwavering with conviction.

It was mirrored in Halden. For this time, there was a chance.

That chance became known within the next second, explosions in the air and loud colliding sounds circling the entirety of the town without delay.

Sound.

It was what Caenrya relayed to Ilias and the entire shinobi force throughout the day. Other teams disseminated the crucial intel throughout the village, ensuring every citizen knew exactly what they must do when the signal was given. Noise, as much as they could produce, and earplugs.

They leaped above the outside ring of buildings, taking measure of the scene before them as they adjusted their earplugs.

Halden ignored the brilliant array of fireworks above them, following the sound of every pot, pan, stone, and everything dense colliding with a similar object around them. Like wildfire, the action spread throughout the Citadel, every person bravely putting themselves in harm's way for the sake of their clan.

Four oniwaban encircled the beast, closing in on its shaking form. Every inch of it violently thrashed as if that would shake off the noise. The tail seized in random directions, steel whipping from every shinobi around it.

Caenrya was right. It worked.

With everyone dawning on the same realization, people began shouting with wild abandon, windows being thrown open and people sticking out to get closer as they made noise. It gave Halden chills as he drew his sai and gave Ryu a renewed sense of confidence as they dropped onto the stone below.

The moment the first weapon connected, all Hel was unleashed.

That inconceivable silent wave erupted from the beast, barging through the earplugs every person wore in the vicinity. However, this time, it didn't bring Halden to his knees. It only made his teeth grit at the fierceness of the soundless noise that stabbed into his brain.

However prepared the shinobi were, the civilians weren't, though.

At that horrendous screech, many retreated back into their dwellings, covering their ears and terrified of the monster outside. Only fireworks continued to blast overhead, the people in charge of firing them a safe distance away to prevent interference. With the noise created severely impacted, the harbinger managed to regain its footing.

That's when everything went awry.

Even hindered, the harbinger viciously lashed out at the nearest oniwaban. The man leaped back and narrowly escaped the reach of its claws. Another went in with a brutal strike, the tail narrowly missing her and pinging a third's weapon across the square.

With practiced movements, each oniwaban attempted to land a blow on the beast in turn, coordinating every step with expert precision. Every time steel met the beast's hide, it merely glanced off. Hina and Halden joined the fray, doing what they could with distracting taiji attacks whenever the monster would gain an edge on another shinobi. Ryu sent in dummy clones to absorb killing blows, the tax of his vin already causing him to sway on his feet.

Everything failed.

"Back!" an oniwaban to Halden's right shouted.

Without a second to spare, Halden danced back, a spike whooshing by their faces.

Only one idea surfaced in Halden's mind, which was the riskiest of them yet. For every muscle the beast moved, Halden ingrained its sporadic patterns firmly into his mind in an attempt to anticipate its actions as best he could. He prepared himself for a last-ditch maneuver and shouted his plan to Hina.

It was clear she didn't like it. Not a single bit. But they both knew the outcome of things if they continued. Several oniwaban were already haphazardly cut up and down their bodies from narrow escapes as they took the brunt of the harbinger's attacks.

Hina responded with a grim nod of understanding. Her hands moved at a dazzling speed between three hand seals. Wind, water, and flame all danced into a mesmerizing spiral, impacting the beast squarely on its head. What would have killed anything else only threw the beast sideways, momentarily stunning it as Halden went airborne.

Mustering all his taiji, Halden landed on the harbinger's side, both palms flat across its back where its heart should have rested. He sent a silent prayer to the ancestors and tried the stupidest thing he could ever have thought up.

His vin pushed out his taiji into the beast, and for that split second, what he saw made his very soul revolt in horror.

Every chakra point was corroded beyond recognition, and the core where taiji normally stored itself alongside the heart had been obliterated. Halden could not destroy the beast for whatever demon morphed a human being into this monster stole everything that made it alive. It was an abomination that shouldn't exist.

"Halden, watch out!" Ryu screamed over the fireworks, a red explosion popping overhead.

The light illuminated the spiked tail marked for his head, a brutal swing that would lop it clean off. Even though Halden leaped, his body already suspended in the air, the beast recalculated the trajectory swifter than he thought possible.

The last thing he saw was his father's petrified face as he crested the rooftop across from Hina.

For once, Halden regretted how their relationship had suffered in previous years. At the missed opportunities Halden had with him. He supposed it was in a person's final moments of clarity that they recognized such significant things. Maybe he should have expressed more of what he truly felt to Caenrya before it was too late.

It all moved in such slow motion that all Halden could hope was it would be quick.

A dazzling blue-tinted taiji shield appeared in front of Halden's body just as the spike closed within inches of his eyes, sparks flying as it glanced off the floating taiji. Bounding backward, Halden could barely do more than breathe at the narrow escape. The beast screeched in rage. With his vin still engaged, he watched the shield before him dissolve into a cascade of sizzling energy. It didn't take even the blink of an eye to find the source.

It shone brighter than any star.

She outshone the moons, her taiji an exuberant force radiating from the rooftop above him. Caenrya's stores had exponentially grown, the energy blazing inside of her. It was night and day, a pebble in a stream versus a boulder damming it, from where her taiji began to the massive well it had become. It almost paralleled his father's, a feat Halden hadn't seen another close to accomplishing.

She had opened another gate. And this was only her second?

Beside Caenrya, Eirea summoned chains of steel to wrap the beast once more. His commander gritted her teeth against the strain, the harbinger violently thrashing against the metal encapsulating it.

It wasn't going to hold.

Ilias, upon realizing the same, signaled for the shinobi on standby to reignite the noise by any means necessary. He formed the hand seal for water, an icy prison warping from the bottom of the harbinger. Ice crawled up its limbs, capturing it along with the metal chains collapsing the beast to the ground. The oniwaban retreated several paces, Caenrya ignoring his command and leaping into the square beside the monster.

Stay back.

Those two words sounded in his mind, the voice Caenrya's. By the expression of shock on everyone's faces, she must have projected the command to everyone in the vicinity.

For an incredulous moment, every eye was on her and the beast. She walked closer to it, shinobi hurrying to reignite the onslaught of distracting noise once more. When his father stood his ground, observing what unfolded before him, Halden knew exactly what he was intending.

Ilias waited to see if Caenrya could bring it down.

Whether for the benefit of her prowess or for his people to witness, Halden wasn't entirely convinced. One thing he did know was that he wouldn't leave her to it alone. Without delay, he released his hold over his vin.

Halden's feet moved within the next second, Eirea on his heels with the same idea. It heartened him to see Ryu and Hina close in on the other side, similarly set to aid Caenrya when the time came.

As the tension escalated, Caenrya murmured some unheard words to the harbinger. Her blue eyes weren't kind, but there was a resolution that conveyed her words carried weight.

Then it snapped.

Ice shattered around its feet, most of the chains breaking around the harbinger. Fast as lightning, the maw of the beast reached for her. Matching its speed, Caenrya drew her katana from her hip, taiji expanding across the fabric and metal until it reached a sizzling point at the tip. Inhuman swiftness accompanied her strike, the collision between taiji and razor-sharp teeth causing the beast to recoil in shock and pain.

With the radiating blue light from her taiji, Caenrya's face was outlined to all as a grim smile confirmed her suspicions. Suspicions that Halden's eyes grew wide at.

The harbinger was physically harmed by taiji, the very thing it lacked.

Enraged, the beast swung through two remaining chains, the ground trembling from the cracking force. Yellow fireworks cast a glow as everyone in the vicinity leaped into action despite Caenrya's order to stay back.

A good team would never let one of their own fight alone.

Hina and Ryu threw shuriken and kunai at the monster's gaping maw, a sharp point digging into the rotten flesh of its tongue.

Eirea's hands flung out a seal with haste, the earth beneath each clawed foot crumbling under the beast and climbing up each leg to secure it into place. Meanwhile, Halden summoned a raging storm of wind onto the crown of the harbinger, the roaring funnel crushing it slightly toward the ground. His nose flared, and he sensed his taiji rapidly depleting from the immense power poured into the attack.

Before he could second-guess whether he'd be enough, a stronger force of wind danced with his, Ilias's might combined with Halden's. Halden's father dipped his chin in his direction, pouring his taiji into the storm that forced the harbinger down.

Halden's eyes stung from the force of the gales ripping through the area, but he gritted his teeth and held firm. Both of his hands were steady as he held his taiji in check with the wind seal.

Clanging, sirens, piercing whistles, and every sound imaginable scoured the square, the beast shriveling inwards in torment.

The wind whistled through them all, Caenrya's braided ponytail cascading behind her as her hands formed the *retsu* seal over the katana's handle. What happened next captivated all around the perimeter.

Color, flesh, and the very space itself warped around the beast's neck, twisting as if Caenrya pinched it and flicked her wrist.

Halden's eyes widened, the power of the ninjutsu surpassing nearly any he'd witnessed before. *This is the power of mind ninjutsu*, he thought in amazement.

That awful screech emanated from the harbinger, a last-ditch effort to condemn them all as its head separated from the remainder of its body. It collapsed into a lifeless heap, the head rolling twice before coming to a stop feet from Caenrya.

Upon releasing the ninjutsu, Caenrya's body sagged from the enormous taiji consumption. The noise ebbed from the square, an awed silence blanketing it all.

And Halden immediately saw why.

The spirit of an eagle materialized over her head, lowering until its feet rested on her shoulder. The one where the emblem of a jagged wing rested on her shinobi robe. A faint glow emanated from the spirit, highlighting her sharply pointed ears. It only meant one thing.

A blessing from the ancestors.

Every soul in the square followed his father's cue, bending a knee in honor of the ancestor's message. Oniwaban followed suit, and the citizens who previously scorned her now stared at her with near reverence.

Halden kneeled, proud and fascinated by the person who stood before him. Someone he knew the imperfections of and the resounding bravery and enduring spirit beneath. Gone was the image of the scrawny girl who rejected the notion of their clan, replaced by the prophesied savior of their people—the sole shinobi against the approaching calamity.

Ilias's eyes gleamed with victory, a fire blazing as what he sought to accomplish came to fruition at last.

As for Caenrya, her eyes were guarded as the eagle flapped its wingspan. The spirit lurched into the air, breaking apart into a fading shimmer above them. The poise with which she stood and her confidence in the return of her blade into its sheath all spoke volumes. There was an edge of reluctance to her face but a declaration of defiance in the way she lifted her chin. Caenrya was the picture of a shinobi who unwaveringly accepted a duty with a heavy heart, knowing fully well it could cost everything.

His heart skipped a beat.

Caenrya knew of the prophecy.

Did she find out when Enya visited her? Did she know that he knew? Was Ilias aware?

What *exactly* did Caenrya know?

As everyone rose on the shogun's lead, Caenrya warily stilled as Ilias approached. Fireworks had yet to rest, an oniwaban sending a messenger eagle to the crew shooting them off as the medical staff arrived to tend to the injured shinobi. Eirea unraveled her vin, the chains dissolving back into the earth far below.

Having only now seen the array of shinobi across every rooftop and scattered through every walkway, Halden knew the news of this evening would spread like wildfire through the Citadel and beyond. Every team retiring for the night was present, every free jōnin and oniwaban on patrol for the harbinger lingering to witness the shogun's words. This was the turning point in the clan, and going forward, everything would be different.

Halden knew the truth of that in the marrow of his bones.

"My clan," Ilias said, addressing all within earshot. "This is your moment of victory. Never before have you united in such a courageous way, trusting each other with your lives in the face of an unspeakable foe."

The shogun tactfully placed a hand on Caenrya's shoulder, the one where the eagle had rested but moments ago.

"Tonight, our ancestors have indoctrinated a new bloodline into our clan, one blessed to accomplish great heights and take up the mantle of protecting the flame that burns within our hearts." Inclining his chin by a margin, Ilias's eyes shone as Caenrya reciprocated the gesture. He pulled away, and his voice boomed across the foundation of the Citadel. "Tonight, after suffering long months of facing this harbinger, we usher in a new era of strength unfounded in previous generations. We have been mauled at our core, pushed past limitations invading our family hearths, and we will wake on the morrow even stronger for it. Our foes will see this, and they will quake where they bend the knee. Other clans will see this, and they will respect the ruling lion within their dens. For we are the Duša Clan."

Cries of resonating approval escalated from the gathered clan members, clapping and the stamping of feet reverberating throughout the ancient bones of the land. When Caenrya's eyes locked onto Halden's, he saw the fire of his clan echoing within them. He knew they'd be successful in undermining the nefarious dealings of the underground. Knew without a sliver of doubt Verina would soon be welcomed into their clan. Whatever prophecy the ancestors dangled over their heads would amount to nothing in comparison to the promise they wielded.

And so Halden grinned as his voice joined the roaring fray, a canopy of azure fireworks flooding the brilliant night sky.

CHAPTER TWENTY-NINE

CAENRYA

Caenrya sat in front of a mirror in Aya's residence, wincing as a hairdresser poked and prodded her long hair into a sophisticated curled updo. She almost didn't recognize the young woman in the mirror.

Teal silk caressed her shoulders, exposing her collarbone and wrapping around her torso in a crisscross pattern. Long, loose sleeves hung from her arms, gold silk pulling in her waist further. The material she was swathed in was embroidered with stunning golden lace, edging every end the dress had and bleeding inward. The women tending to Caenrya's hair adorned it with pins resembling dragons, their serpentine bodies wrapping around her head.

With the faint traces of makeup they had applied earlier, Caenrya was shocked at her appearance. She appeared older. More mature. Beautiful.

Completely different than how she'd ever pictured herself.

By the time she was ready, Caenrya couldn't tear her eyes off the image she presented. Did that make her vain? A small smile appeared on the person in the mirror.

No. No it didn't.

Caenrya rose, squaring her shoulders, and left the home.

Aya silently meditated beside the koi pond. As Caenrya shut the door behind her, she noticed a stocky boy leaning against the wall mere feet away.

Osten.

Further back, Owena and Niko quietly talked with each other, just out of earshot.

"Before you tell me to go screw myself," Osten said, raising a hand from his crimson robes, "I wanted to apologize. I owe you one and have owed you this for a long time now."

She stood there, waiting. She wouldn't let him off the hook that easily.

"My sister and I didn't like you after you attacked our father." Osten saw the look on her face. "Okay, we hated you," he corrected with a sheepish expression.

At least he had the decency to look ashamed.

"But we weren't given the full truth, and we were angry. Owena more so than I. She took absolute joy in being the only female everyone paid attention to. In her world anyway." He ran a hand through his curly hair. "She concocted the petty plan of me trying to woo you, and obviously, that didn't work as intended. You're a tough one to crack."

Caenrya rolled her eyes at that.

A small smile crinkled Osten's. "It was vastly immature. I realized it when our father explained the situation further with the shogun's permission. It couldn't have been easy being mistaken for an enemy when you only wanted asylum from the warring lands. Your reaction was warranted. I apologize for my shortsightedness. You're a credit to shinobi in this clan, and I'm grateful to have you added to our ranks."

A knot in her shoulders loosened at that. But before Caenrya could say anything, Owena walked forward.

Her eyes honed in on Caenrya's, Niko following behind her. "Caenrya, I'm sorry for spreading unfounded rumors about you and setting you up with my brother." Her words were sincere, even as her face showed she disliked them. "Clearly, our ancestors have welcomed you into the clan. I'm not one to defy their decisions. So, I'll be seeing you around, I suppose."

Niko gave a respectful bow of his head, saying, "I'll be proud to work alongside you as a fellow shinobi."

Caenrya let the moment linger. For months, she had endured people shunning her, throwing things at her, and calling her names behind her back and to her face. Now, the ones who started it all were owning up to their actions.

Apologizing. To her.

Such a stubborn part of her wanted to turn away from them both, but Caenrya knew doing so could ruin any chance of being accepted by her peers. Something that mattered more than ever before. "Thank you. I accept your apology. Both of yours," Caenrya added, glancing at Osten, who shot her a wink. She gave him another face. He held up his hands in mock surrender.

Owena held a hand out in front of her, inspecting her polished nails. "But just so you know, I'm still a far more prestigious shinobi. When it comes to being the most renowned and sought after, pedigree matters." With a sniff, Owena left for the stairwell, Niko in tow.

Yeah, she didn't forgive Owena—not yet. Caenrya's mouth formed a line, annoyance furrowing her brow. Pedigree—how absurdly ridiculous.

"She's only mad there's real competition in her class of shinobi now. She needs a rival to humble her out some." Osten pushed off the wall, folding his hands into the pockets beneath his belted robe. "You look great, by the way."

Osten followed after his sister, and Caenrya was left behind with a weird mix of emotions. Gratitude, exasperation, and something like contentedness shifted like grains of sand in her hand.

"Let's be off," Aya said, her voice cracking through Caenrya's mind. "We don't want to be late to your ceremony now, do we?"

A smile crept across Caenrya's face. She couldn't help it. They were accepting her formally, everyone in the clan. It brought a new emotion she hadn't quite experienced: giddiness.

The feline sat on the edge of Aya's roof, waving its tail.

She thought back to Halden asking if it had a name.

Bless, Caenrya thought to herself. *I'll call you Bless.*

Bless flicked her tail sharply as if in approval. Caenrya knew the cat would be there when she returned.

They set off, winding down the stairwell and walking through the streets of the Citadel.

Spirits fluttered to life around her, birds swooping above her head, critters scurrying around her feet, and felines walking alongside her. People of the clan gathered at their windowsills, at the thresholds of their doors, and along the sides of the walkways to cheer as she passed. They threw things around her, but this time they were cherry blossoms instead of spoiled food.

She blinked and blinked. Hard.

There was only one person who knew cherry blossom trees were her absolute favorite kind. And in that moment, she couldn't help the well of emotion that threatened to rock her off her feet.

Halden had remembered.

That one day, months ago, when he caught her staring at the breathtaking blossoms on their way to train as a team. She had been defensive letting that vulnerability slip, but now it meant the world that he took that moment and tucked it away into his memory.

Further into the Citadel, Caenrya and Aya walked. They passed the bridge leading to the training grounds, the place where Caenrya had fought Ilias when she first agreed to stay. Her eyes crinkled in that direction, remembering how firmly she believed she'd win. The Koi River brilliantly ran beneath, shimmering fish leaping from the waters before disappearing into the air.

They walked through Riverside Square, Caenrya's eyes wandering to the teppanyaki place she'd eaten with Ryu, Halden, and Eirea after they saved her from the slave mark. It cemented her as a part of Team Cadigan. Next, they ventured through Wisteria Square, Caenrya's eyes wistfully marking her destroyed apartment. Though it eased the pain to see repairs already being made. She hoped to move back in soon. A surprisingly large chunk of her heart missed that space that was hers.

They breezed through Temple Square, her path littered with blossoms. Repairs were completed in that sector, though lanterns were hung in remembrance of the lives lost by the harbinger. They floated on strings around the eagle statue in the center, portraits of each person and letters engulfing the circumference.

Everyone and everything were healing slowly. Repairs would take time, and people trickled back into the Citadel. She bore witness to it with the smiles and cheers freely given.

After bypassing the healing clinic, a pang of regret haunted her as they walked through the winding park where she thought she'd die after Valen's ninjutsu altered her thoughts. Images of that night flashed through her mind, but none more pressing than the one of Halden saving her life. He knew what she had planned somehow and put his life on the line yet again to convince her to stay and fight. The memory of his face over hers... Caenrya would never forget it.

Not too far away, she had her first encounter with the harbinger. Two. She'd awoken to Halden standing before her, fearlessly facing off against the beast. Ryu, Ren, and Eirea had all put their lives on the line to watch over her after she depleted her taiji.

Caenrya swore she'd never put them in such a position again. She'd grow stronger and more capable than ever. From now on, she'd be the one to defend them. That was the funny thing about having more to lose. She could view it as a burden, but Caenrya chose to view it as a blessing. A blessing she'd gladly defend but not to the grave. Not anymore. For she'd soon become a force that would bring a reckoning to any who dared to harm these people.

She wouldn't lose.

The brief image of an eagle took flight from the branches of an ahari tree, people cheering beneath. Pink blossoms fluttered all around her as Caenrya and Aya passed.

Ahead, a stone pathway led to the nearby forest. Beside the archway hanging over it, Ilias, Ryu, Eirea, and Halden all patiently waited. Numerous others gathered nearby, a few faces she recognized. Hina, Daven, Niko, Osten, Owena, and Aaric.

And they all bowed their heads respectfully as she approached.

Caenrya felt it was only right to return the gesture, even if Owena's face spoke of wanting to be anywhere but there. Caenrya surmised Daven was responsible for that, especially when he and Eirea shared a swift, happy exchange of smiles.

But her eyes became focused only on Halden afterward.

He wore silk layers of the deepest black, highlighted by designs that reflected with the color of his eyes. Short brown locks were swept to one side, styled in such a way that only accentuated his strong jawline and cheekbones.

He looked handsome. His mouth was quirked into a smile, one side higher than the other in a faint smirk. Both eyes were alight with admiration as he met her gaze.

Hearing a throat being cleared, Caenrya's attention was dragged to Aya. The elder grabbed her arm, giving her pupil a strong squeeze. A broad smile crossed her face, those stern eyes radiant with happiness. "I am proud of you, Caenrya. Overcoming what you have is nigh impossible for most."

Caenrya had to blink hard at that.

"You were a *complete* urchin at first."

A laugh escaped Caenrya's lips, the corner of her mouth hitching up.

"But it is an honor to welcome you into this clan," Aya finished.

"Thank you for seeing something worthy to take in," Caenrya quietly said, silver lining her eyes.

Aya lowered her chin, stepping back to join her grandchildren.

Halden's hand rose when she neared, opening to reveal a final, perfectly formed cherry blossom.

Caenrya couldn't help it. An earnest grin overtook her face. She couldn't remember the last time she'd done such a thing, but it felt right. Natural. Small butterflies fluttered in her stomach, and a warmth even a fire couldn't produce ignited in her chest.

Steel-gray eyes widened a hair at that, Halden's head shaking for a moment as if to clear his thoughts. "I—"

"Remembered," Caenrya said, accepting the blossom with a grateful nod.

His voice lowered a fraction. "Congratulations, Caenrya."

"I can't wait for all the trouble we'll get into," Ryu cut in, leaning an arm across one of Halden's shoulders as he waggled his brow.

Eirea snorted. "How about taking some time off to recover?" She gave him a stern glare out of the corner of her eye. Blonde curls cascaded around her heart-shaped face. "Staying *out* of trouble."

"I believe that to be wise," Ilias said, moving in. "Come, Caenrya, and let us officially introduce you to our ancestors."

And so Caenrya took in her team. *Her* team. She smiled and said, "Thank you all for bringing me in and not giving up on me."

"Don't mention it." Eirea smiled back from where she stood behind Halden and Ryu. She patted both on the shoulder. "The knuckleheads and I will await you when you return."

Ryu frowned. "I'm not a knucklehead." His face exasperated as he turned to Caenrya as if expressing, *Eirea. Am I right?*

Halden tilted his head toward the pathway before her, his eyes saying it all.

The cape on Ilias's shoulder billowed in front of her as she trailed behind him.

Spirits darted to-and-fro, some leisurely basking in the light that radiated from the clear sky above. Leaves whispered with the breeze, lilies swaying at both sides of the path. The stone Moon Gates passed overhead, and the bench where she and Eirea had eaten dinner all those months ago appeared. It was a time she'd reflected on greatly.

Only the most broken of people hope like you do, Caenrya, Eirea had told her.

It was true. Her entire life was lived on a single hope. A hope that two sisters would have a happy life in a place they could call home.

Caenrya had committed unspeakable atrocities in the name of that hope and had endured impossible lengths of suffering to achieve it. Even at her weakest points, that single thread withstood it all.

An oniwaban stood beside the bench, his mask pulled up above his nose and hood lowered just to his brow. Ren.

Caenrya nodded at him, smiling slightly. His eyes crinkled back, and she knew he returned the gesture. She owed him much. Not only had she grown in skill but as a person. Without his truth, she would have never accomplished reaching one of the Five Paths, and with it, opening her second gate. He was a quiet soul, but she appreciated the silent camaraderie he provided during their lessons.

As the path gently curved, it led past several more benches. Fireflies gracefully danced around the gates along the way, casting their enchanting glow on the vine-covered stone. With each step, the air carried the soothing scent of earth and vegetation. As the final turn approached, a dense canopy of trees embraced each other, creating a sense of tranquility and seclusion. At the entrance to the cove, a majestic Moon Gate stood, exuding an air of anticipation.

Ilias stilled, clasping his hands in front of him. His bearded face tilted forward, eyes solemn. "This is where I leave you, Caenrya. May you walk forward with the blessing of the ancestors."

Hesitating, Caenrya peered at the lingering darkness beyond the final gate. "How will I know what to do?" Worry tightened her brow.

"You'll know when the time comes."

Thanks, she wanted to say with more than a hint of sarcasm.

The nerves were speaking, but Caenrya lifted her chin and walked forward.

Step by step, she crossed into the darkness, only to find that dangling foliage had covered the entrance. Brushing it aside, Caenrya's eyes grew wide at the stunning sight.

A pool of water glowed with a captivating luminescence, casting a mesmerizing shimmer of blue-green hues. Within it, a stone rested at the bottom, appearing no larger than her fist. The trees surrounding it enveloped the entire space with lush greenery, creating a sheltered haven. The air was filled with the gentle rustling of leaves while the faint light filtered through the dense canopy above, casting a soft glow on everything below.

A cool mist clung to her face as Caenrya kneeled on the cushion of grass around the water. Clasping her hands on her lap, she closed her eyes to meditate. It felt right.

An eternity passed before someone spoke.

"Caenrya," A soft voice greeted her.

Caenrya's eyes snapped open. A woman was kneeling across the pond from her. "Enya."

"On behalf of the Duša Clan ancestors, I welcome you to our people," Enya said, her voice soft and kind. Her eyes were positively radiant as she lowered her chin.

"Thank you," Caenrya said, her eyes searching around. "Are you really here?"

Enya stood, motioning for Caenrya to follow the trail of her shimmering lavender robes. As Caenrya obeyed, she gasped. Her form, her spirit, left her body in a translucent shimmer. She stared at herself for a moment, completely unsettled.

"When you are ready to return to the waking world, all you need do is to return to your body," Enya explained, her head turned over her shoulder.

Uncertain, Caenrya said, "Good to know."

They walked through the foliage, their bodies passing through with ease. The shogun had walked away from the Ancestorial Shrine, meeting Ren back near the bench and talking in low whispers.

"Normally, we'd speak within the comfort of the shrine," Enya said, her words overshadowing the conversation the two were having in the waking world.

Caenrya didn't miss Enya's brief expression of love when gazing at her husband. That glimpse, something fundamental that transitioned the line between the living and dead, touched her.

"Though, this is a particularly special occasion. You're the first person foreign to our clan to walk with the ancestors, and as such, we wanted to introduce you formally to our own skies."

Caenrya followed Enya as they approached the courtyard that opened up to the park in the Citadel. She couldn't help but gasp. Thousands of shimmering figures dotted the enormous space, the forms of the living scattered throughout. Spirits of animals stood with solid forms among them, acting as normal, calm wildlife would.

"Caenrya."

She turned to face Enya, whose cool hands grasped her own.

"My people are your people."

The shimmering ancestors bowed, Caenrya's mouth slightly parted at the collective gesture.

"We rest our fate, and those of the living, in your hands. Know that you'll never walk alone, and you'll always have a place in our skies." Enya's face was warm and welcoming, that of a mother.

Unshed tears prickled the corners of Caenrya's eyes.

Leaning forward, Enya placed a gentle kiss on Caenrya's forehead. "You have our blessing."

"Thank you," Caenrya whispered, gently squeezing Enya's hands. Her gaze shifted to the mass of ancestors around her. "Thank you, all."

One face in the front caught her complete and utter attention.

Rainer. The man who died defending the clan from the harbinger. Who said never to trust her at all. "I'm sorry," Caenrya said, her voice heavy. Rainer had lost his wife that fateful night they ambushed her.

Guilt, untampered guilt, ate at her—

Rainer peaked up from his bow and met her remorseful gaze. He nodded once, squeezing the hand of another who stood by him.

Serillia. His wife.

"Rainer doesn't blame you. He knows what we all do and has long since realized the misjudgment he held for you," Enya said.

The man smiled lightly, straightening as the other ancestors did. Serillia pressed into him, an adoring expression lighting her face as Rainer turned his growing smile toward her.

Caenrya's eyes burned as she released that guilt, hearing the truth in Enya's words.

"Let us return. After all, the living aren't meant to stray too long in our skies."

Caenrya turned from the masses of faces only to see Halden speaking cheerfully with Ryu and Eirea. Ryu smacked Halden's back a couple of times with a palm, laughing at a joke. Halden blushed slightly, much to Eirea's enjoyment.

Enya pulled her attention to her with a mischievous twinkle in her eyes. "You also have my blessing for *that* as well."

Warmth crossed Caenrya's cheeks.

Ilias and Ren were discussing security matters when they passed by, invisible to their eyes.

"Can anyone visit you or any of the ancestors in such a manner?" Caenrya asked, distracting herself from Enya's implied permission and what that entailed.

A knowing expression crossed Enya's face, but she went along with it with good nature. "Anyone is welcome to our shrine, but many rarely wield the ability to cross into our skies to speak with us. Those strong in the way of taiji and nature have a more powerful link with the ancestors, but we, too, must acquiesce to speak with the person seeking us. Even then, most can only sense our presence."

They entered the shrine, Caenrya hesitating before returning to her body. "I see."

"Unfortunately, our time has come to a close." Enya sighed, kneeling in her original spot across from Caenrya. "It has been a pleasure speaking with you, Caenrya. Thank you for protecting my clan. Go in peace."

A sudden, blackening exhaustion had her knees buckling, and Caenrya kneeled where her body rested. A strange chill laced through her spine, and when she blinked, Enya was gone. Staring at her hands, she found them to be her corporal ones.

Caenrya felt different. Her eyes wandered across the serene shrine once more before leaving. Every step was weighted, and she couldn't help but replay all that transpired over and over. Light filtered through the leaves above, and her feet made it mere steps before a sight completely froze her entire body.

Fear immobilized her, sending her heart thundering into a frantic rhythm.

Outside of the final Moon Gate was a silver-haired figure, the dragon tattoo a stark contrast to his white robes. Lethality emanated from every edge of the man, and his icy eyes peered into her soul.

"Nrya," Valen greeted, his posture casual despite a maddening darkness lingering in the depths of his expression. "I've longed to see you in the flesh. Well," he smiled to himself, "face-to-face, I should say. I've been closer than you could have imagined countless times."

Dread held a vice grip on her throat. Her mind frantically ran through a list of options to *get out of there.*

"I'm, rather unfortunately, not here to deliver good news," he said, his feet moving to circle her. He was impossibly silent as his boots treaded the path, not making a sound as he passed beside her. "A mere inconvenience has happened to me recently."

Caenrya moved as fast as lightning, her right hand a split second away from making the *zen* seal before Valen grasped the hand roughly. He pinned it behind her, swiveling with impossible speed. Before she knew it, he'd locked both hands behind her back in a painful position.

She gritted her teeth and refused to give him the satisfaction of making a noise as agony threatened to snap her joints.

"As I was saying," Valen murmured into her ear, his breath warming the back of it. "It seems the daimyo has a new favorite, and it's no longer you."

Caenrya's jaw trembled, her mind thinking the worst.

"I'm here to give you one last warning, my Nrya. Verina isn't the person you remember. There will come a time when you'll regret staying with this clan. The reckoning is nigh upon you."

"In what way?" she asked, her voice shaking. When he didn't answer, her stomach grew nauseous. *"In what way?"*

"There's still hope." A heavy pause. "If you leave now, you may be able to repair the damage dealt. Should you elect to say, I'm afraid you won't ever get her back." His voice carried a note of amusement. "After all, I know how much you care about such trivial things."

Caenrya forced herself to reason. He was playing her—he had to be. But with Valen, there were always games played. Was there a half-truth wrapped up in all of this? Her brow furrowed, and her chin lifted. "And how does this inconvenience you? I would think my return would be anything but."

A gentle laugh. "The inconvenience lies with the little brat turning on me. She thinks she has more power than I do since she wields the daimyo's attention and temporary interest." His head backed away. "It's bothersome. I'd rather have you to deal with than that runt."

The pressure on her wrists released, and as Caenrya whirled to attack, his body evaporated. Was this...?

"Verina is in danger, Nrya. But not of losing her life... rather, every semblance that formed the girl you once knew." Valen's last words washed against her with looming menace. "I. Want. Her. *Gone.*"

Gasping, Caenrya's eyes burst open to the shrine once more, and a deep chill settled in her bones. She violently shivered as she stood, running her hands against her silk-clad arms.

It wasn't real. It was just another ruse of his.

Something rang true in Valen's words, however. Something haunting.

Caenrya slowly exhaled.

Verina wasn't dumb. It was entirely possible she was buying time, taking up Caenrya's visage and playing any leverage she could wield to better position herself in Shikei. It could be that Valen was trying another tactic to scare her, and while she despised admitting it, it worked.

But.

Now she wasn't alone. Caenrya had a whole clan working with her to rescue Verina and a team she knew she could trust with her life. She wouldn't act blindly, not when she knew the only way forward was with those already beside her.

Less than three months now and they would enter the savage chaos of the warring lands.

Caenrya stepped out of the Ancestorial Shrine, relieved to find the space clear of any threats. She repressed the shock of seeing Valen unexpectedly and straightened her shoulders. She walked down the curving path, making eye contact when Ilias and Ren spotted her.

Caenrya would rescue Verina. Soon, they would embark on the first mission to go undercover in the warring land's fighting rings. She would go in again without hesitation, knowing it would bring them a step closer to finding her sister. She'd see Verina soon, and no manipulation from Valen would get in her way. After all, only the most broken of people hoped like she did.

But only the most devoted brought hope to fruition.

Chapter Thirty

VALEN

Opening his eyes, Valen blinked several times, clearing the ninjutsu from his mind. A ghastly tint discolored his pale skin from near exhausting his taiji reserves. Amid him, dancing flames cast a mesmerizing glow, ensconced in swaying dragon-clad lanterns. The chamber was adorned with intricate wooden panels, painted with scenes of war-torn cities. The air was filled with the faint aroma of musky incense. Soft light filtered through the paper screens behind the cushion where he kneeled, casting a warm glow on the polished tatami mats. The sound of distant harp-borne music echoed through the room.

Annoying, pestilent, maddening...

Valen's eyes rose toward the daimyo whose presence commanded respect and authority in his throne of solid gold.

My lord, my chain, my liege...

"My daimyo," Valen cooly said, lowering his chin an appropriate amount. "The idealistic fools mistakenly believe the prophecy proceeds according to their wishes. One has been accepted into their clan. They rally against us."

He itched to tear them all apart, to bathe in their blood for turning Nrya against him. The sins they had committed, Valen would never forgive.

Must kill, tear apart, bathe in their blood...

Nrya was his to control. The daimyo had many in his arsenal, and Valen wanted *just* one puppet to manipulate. The daimyo vowed he would be her handler, and to have waited this long with no results... to not be allowed off his leash had eaten at any semblance of control he had.

Valen's breathing became labored, and his vision flickered in a red haze.

The faintest impression lingered at the back of his brain, a breeze against the obsidian wall of his mind. It pleaded to be free.

Eyes as black as the darkness in his soul fell on Valen, the weight behind them curving his broad shoulders.

When the daimyo spoke, his every word echoed in the chamber. "I was hoping sense would return to the girl before now," he said, the underlying tone rumbling his displeasure. His bejeweled hand thrummed against the solid gold carving of a dragon's head. "It would seem all sense has entirely eluded her."

"It has," Valen hissed, his lips curling. Every finger dug into the silk of his blood-red kimono. "They have rinsed her free of our teachings and bonds. Those shinobi twisted her mind, manipulating her to fulfill their prophecy. No longer does she consider us maker and master, and we have the houses of Arundel and Dagon to thank."

At that, the daimyo's nails dug into the gold. One cracked, a thin trail of blood leaking from the force. Though the daimyo didn't react, his face remaining otherwise impassive. "What have I told you?"

The danger in those cold words rinsed goosebumps down Valen's back. "Apologies, my daimyo. My hatred got the best of me."

Faces, so many faces, flashed in Valen's mind. Each one he'd soon brutalize.

Kill them, kill them, kill them, his thoughts cooed.

The daimyo's square jaw tightened, the action nearly imperceptible. But Valen knew him well, more than any other. He was furious, raging at Nrya for not returning despite all the peace offerings he sent. Enraged that Valen's ministrations hadn't brought her back. Livid that the clan thought they had won.

Even the note he had one of his minions leave in Nrya's apartment didn't work, so he had that so-called home of hers laid to waste.

Even if they didn't comprehend the size of Hel that was about to be unleashed on him.

"I take it my creation didn't work as planned?" a soft, innocent voice asked behind him.

Valen bit into his tongue to keep from reacting, iron spreading through his mouth.

A blonde girl strode by him, prim and composed. So at odds with the feud Valen fought within his own mind to control his impulses. "Shall I make more then?" Verina's angelic eyes gloatingly met his.

The thing about angels... They didn't belong in this Hel. Valen wanted to pluck every feather from her wings, to send her tumbling into a brimstone abyss and be damned for eternity. Valen wouldn't risk the daimyo's wrath, but he couldn't help his fingers twitching as he imagined the scene playing out.

"They will have as much effect as the first one," Valen growled, rising to his feet. He towered over the wraith of a girl, though she wasn't concerned in the least.

A light guttered out in her large ocean-blue eyes, pools of water collecting at the corners as Verina turned to the daimyo. Her dainty hands whitened as she collapsed them before her ivory kimono. "She's truly not coming back then."

Pulling back his shoulder blades, Valen leveled himself with the daimyo. "Such it remains unless I receive my leave to retrieve her. My daimyo, I woefully believe it is high time to take matters into our own hands. The longer we wait, I fear we'll never reclaim her." Valen narrowed his eyes, all eight gates of unlocked taiji tingling through his limbs. "May I have your leave to retrieve One and raze all those who stand in my way?"

Destroy, obliterate, annihilate...

Such a heavy pause lingered in the dreadful air. The daimyo stilled, his gaze still lingering with traces of anger as he searched Valen's face. Then, his upturned eyes swept to Verina's crying ones, softening.

The daimyo straightened on his throne, pulling his shoulders back. Inclining his chin, he only said, "You have my leave, but do not lay a finger on those who I've claimed for myself."

A wicked, cruel grin spread ear to ear on Valen's face. It was time to send for his closest allies and bring the Citadel to its knees.

This would be particularly *delightful*.

THE END

If you have enjoyed Blood and Betrayal, please leave a review. I enjoy hearing back from you, even if it's a kind word or two. Feedback inspires me to continue writing the next book. Keep turning those pages for a sneak peek into another book!

Author Notes

Firstly, thank you SO much for reading Blood and Betrayal! It's been a dream of mine to write a book since I was in middle school. I never thought I'd accomplish this feat, and I'm so thankful for your support in reading my second published work. My first book was written in 2020, and since then, I've enjoyed every moment of my writing career. Blood and Betrayal was written at the beginning of 2022, and since then, it has undergone the journey to where it is today. It will be the second in a line of many books to come!

When I'm not lost in my writing world, you can find me hanging out with my amazing husband and our super lively 3-year-old German Shepherd. They are my world! I play tennis for fun, love diving into video games, and there's nothing better than a good hike. Especially in someplace stunning! I've recently moved to Washington, and let me tell you, it's gorgeous out here. So, that's me. I'm just living life, enjoying the journey, and hoping my stories find a little corner in your world too!

I'm thrilled to share that the sequel, Spirits and Sorrows, is coming along great! If you'd like sneak peak chapters and other fun updates along the way, join my mailing list to stay in touch. If you have any comments or questions, feel free to reach out via my email bookinit@shblodgett. com. I try to respond to every person! I also have an expanding Discord page you can join through my website's member page. I hang out there often! In the meantime, please write a review on Amazon. Every review helps boost my book and reach new potential readers. Plus, it lets me know you want a sequel!

I'm so grateful and appreciative of your support. I hope to share my next story with you soon! If you'd like to explore more about my work, connect with me on social media, join my Discord community, or find direct links to my books and website, check out my Linktree below.

https://linktr.ee/s.h.blodgett

WORLD BUILDING GUIDE

(AND PRONUNCIATIONS!)

- Taiji: tai – jee

  - Taiji is the natural energy within all living beings and materials. Within people, taiji has a network of paths similar to the cardiovascular system

- Yin and Yang

  - These two components form the "heart" of taiji. Both are central reserves within a body that have unique attributes for the magic system. The energy flows through chakra points throughout the body in a way similar to that of veins. Yin represents freezing energy, and yang represents boiling energy. The balance of the two reserves can be willingly shifted by a person, altering the energy's elemental affinity

- Jiao: gee - yow

  - Jiao is the act of balancing yin and yang in order to perform ninjutsu. Different percentages of yin and yang change the nature of one's taiji to a new element. There are five elements that a person may use through proper jiao: earth (chi), water (sui), fire (ka), wind (fū), and void (kū)

- Ninjutsu: nuhn – joot – soo

  - Magical conjurations cast by a living being through three crucial requirements: taiji expenditure, a hand seal, and an incantation in the Elvish language. When all three are done properly, the taiji will leave the reserves, travel through chakra points, and perform magic.

- Kuji-kiri: koo – jee – kee – ree

  - The nine cuts, otherwise known as the nine hand seals required to conjure ninjutsu. They are intentional, dance-like movements with the arms that release one's taiji. When a person moves their arms, it in a likeness of cutting the air, giving the nickname "the nine cuts." Each of the nine cuts is attached to an aspect of an element. The nine cuts are as follows: rin (earth), pyo (wind), toh (water), sha (healing), kai (fire), jin (mind void), retsu (dimensional void), zai (releasing ninjutsu), and zen (vin activation)

- Vin:

- A rare case where a person has a third reserve of energy next to yin and yang. This bestows a person a bloodline gift that can be passed through generations. The ninth cut, zen, and an incantation allows a person to activate a unique ninjutsu (or multiple) that would otherwise require a rather large or impossible combination of Elvish words to create

- Elvish words

  - The third requirement for ninjutsu casting. Along with the hand seal (kuji-kiri) and taiji balancing of jiao, one must use a word of purpose to give the final details to the magic being cast. For example, if a person balanced their taiji toward a water element, used a water seal (toh), and said the words vodná vlna, a wave of water would be created. If they changed the Elvish words to bič, it would create a whip of water instead

- Zazen

  - Meditation that allows a person to unlock different gates of power through long durations of practice

- Art of the Eight Gates

  - Unlocked through Zazen. Each gate increases the amount of taiji held in a being's yin and yang reserves. Those with a vin reserve also see an increase in taiji stored within. Taiji nature may also be altered with any gate unlocked

- Five Paths of Awakening

- ○ There are five stages to achieve awakening in this order: the path of self-realization, the path of preparation, the path of insight, the path of cultivation, and the path of awakening. Once all paths are unlocked, a person can enter a state where taiji is rapidly replenished from environmental sources. It allows one to heal faster, be stronger, and move faster

- Five Categories of Beings

  - ○ Every being is given a spiritual "seed" at birth that determines how strong they can become with ninjutsu. This "seed" is part of their soul. It is widely believed to be linked with Elvish heritage, where those with more Elven blood in their veins have more potential for growth. Those with a "seed" in the first category tend to be unable to use ninjutsu. These individuals tend to have mostly human blood and rounded ears. Those in the fifth category are thought to be Elves themselves and harness immense power

- Caenrya: say – near – uh

- Eirea: air – e – uh

- Taijutsu: tie – joo – tsoo

  - ○ Hand-to-hand combat

- Tonki: tohn – kee

  - ○ Physical weapons used by shinobi unrelated to ninjutsu

- Kunai: koo – nai

- ○ Double-sided dagger

- Shuriken: shoo – ree – ken

    - ○ Metal stars that can be thrown or placed between fists as a weapon

- Shuko: shoo – koh

    - ○ Metal bands that go around hands. Spikes protrude from either the palm or knuckles

- Shinobi: shee – noh – bee

    - ○ Ninja

- Caltrops: kal – trops

    - ○ Spiked metal devices

- Kusarigama: koo – sah – ree – gah – mah

    - ○ Sickle weapons with a metal chain dangling from the handle. A weight typically rests on the end of a chain

- Ronin: roh – neen

    - ○ Ninja that do not belong to a clan

- Shikei: shee – kay

    - ○ The facility where Caenrya and the other children were kept

- Duša: doo – sha

- ○ The clan that took Caenrya in

- Canecian: kuh – nee – shun

  - ○ Any person who lived on the continent of Canecia

- Daimyo: dahy – myoh (dahy rhymes with "eye" and myoh is similar to "meow" but with an "oh" ending)

  - ○ A lord with high ranking

- Shogun: show – gun

  - ○ Leader of a clan and an elite shinobi

- Oniwaban: oh – nee – wah – bahn

  - ○ Exceptionally skilled shinobi ranked above jōnin. Often in the direct employ of a shogun

- Jōnin: joh – neen

  - ○ High ranking shinobi

- Chūnin: choo – neen

  - ○ Middle ranked shinobi

- Genin: geh – neen

  - ○ Low ranked shinobi

SHIELD
OF
RUIN
THE RUINED DESTINY SERIES
BOOK ONE
S. H. BLODGETT

A Sneak Peak into Shield of Ruin

Book One in The Ruined Destiny Series

As Sayra rolled her armor-clad shoulders, she steeled herself for the coming minutes that would decide her fate. Only one victory separated her from the dream she fought tooth and nail for. A dream her brother had sacrificed his life for.

Freedom.

A short nun garbed in ivory robes stood in the marble corridor. Her hand gestured for Sayra and her opponent, Netta, to pass through the open doorway into the arena beyond. "Remember, display your prowess in battle to impress the observing Arcanists. One of them will purchase your guardianship should you graduate."

Which means I'll never see my homeland again, Sayra thought, her hand tightening around the worn pommel of her sheathed sword. *I'll no longer be forced into a life unenviable by my worst enemy.*

Sayra inclined her chin in acknowledgement, her heartbeat thudding loudly in her ears as she stepped forward. Just as her feet were about to cross the threshold into the arena, Netta's words sent an icy chill down her spine.

"Maybe if your brother asks nicely, the Goddess could trade your life for his so it won't be wasted when I cut you to shreds," she said, her dark eyes pulling at the ends. Netta tsked, her head angling down at Sayra.

Sayra knew a smirk was beneath Netta's helmet. Her nose flared, her desperation the only thing that kept the last string of her self-control intact. Grinding her teeth, she forced her dented boots to clack across the modest stone floor. Arcanists, the revered majik-wielders who protected the dwindling population of mankind, watched with burning gazes from above. They were tucked away on the second-floor viewing level, a rune-engraved column of marble at each end of the rectangular arena.

Lanterns flickered generous light across the marble walls, and a large window on the ceiling collected thick flakes of snow falling from the sky. The overseeing combat monk, Batar, gestured for Netta and Sayra to bow their heads in prayer for a safe battle. Or as safe as it could be given the last round ended with an acolyte nearly losing her entire left leg. For the prayer, Sayra mumbled some vague words, acting the part of someone who believed in the church's faith.

She breathed in, falling into an offensive stance as Batar signaled for them to be ready. A dozen feet away, Netta haughtily pulled her sword. A single brow quirked up. Exhaling, Sayra tuned out the dozens of men looking down at her and pushed back the fear of failure. Most importantly, she twisted her body so no one saw when she flipped a crude gesture at Netta.

Netta's eyes twitched, a wild grin crossing Sayra's exposed face.

Hag.

"May the final round commence!" Batar stepped back out of harm's way.

The grin slipped from her face as Netta charged. A hush sounded from the men watching as Sayra dipped low. A sword swung wide in a powerful arc, narrowly missing Sayra by a foot as she danced around Netta's slower body. Sayra attempted to sidestep, drawing her own blade across Netta's chest. Metal weakly glanced by, not even scratching the armor plate as Netta recovered with a vicious strike.

Sparks flew from Sayra's back as she half rolled, half stumbled out of Netta's reach. Relying on her strength, Netta swung her sword in wide, powerful arcs, each blow intended to cleave through Sayra.

Only a minute in Sayra's form was becoming sloppy. A grunt escaped her lips as she blocked a rough blow. She knew the only way to win was to use her nimbleness to her advantage, so she became more daring with her dodges. Her mind tracked each movement Netta made, waiting for the opportune moment.

It became a lengthy dance of Sayra navigating deadly blows. Occasionally, the edge of her blade would glance off Netta's in a minor deflection.

But then, she made a fatal mistake.

Netta feinted left, and Sayra fell for it.

Steel raced for her neck, and Sayra barely raised her sword in time to lessen the impact. A double-edged blade bit into her combat-worn breastplate, just beneath her collarbone. Netta's robust arms strained as she attempted to deliver an incapacitating blow to end the match.

Muscles quivered throughout Sayra's upper body as she held Netta's blade at bay with a lesser-skilled hand, a low grunt escaping her teeth as her hulking opponent shifted her weight forward. Sayra's right boot drug back into the snow-dusted stone, her spine bending backward.

Steel screeched further toward her shoulder, Sayra's own sword clashing on her plates from the force. Then her mind surged elsewhere. Her brother's mauled face flashed in front of her, his last words haunting her ears.

It's okay, Sayra.

It's not okay, she wanted to shout, feeling the world crumble around her as gleaming, daemonic eyes shifted to her next.

Sayra's labored breath hitched in panic, her mind struggling to repress the memory and instead focus on the match at hand. Netta pounced at the opening of weakness and drove her shoulder into Sayra's chest.

A strange sense of vertigo overcame her as she went airborne, Sayra's sense of self snapping back to reality when the ground rose to meet her. Her bare head bounced off the ground, and she tasted blood in her mouth. For the millionth time, Sayra wished her culture allowed head coverings of any sort.

Only years of extensive training had kept Sayra's grip firmly on her sword, despite the way the world teetered around her. The onlookers—sadistically intrigued—leaned over the ivory-wrapped marble railing to glean a closer look at the trial's last match between the weakest acolyte in her class and a brutal opponent.

It was Sayra's last chance as an acolyte to graduate into a Valkyrie, an esteemed guardian who protected the few remaining men in their world.

And she blew it.

"Truly a shame that our noble Arcanists have to witness such a disgraceful performance from a girl who hoped to protect them from daemons. From a girl who can't even win a fight," Netta tutted, stepping over Sayra. Narrow ebony eyes shined with victory behind her helmet. "Perhaps this performance will ensure that the likes of a Faendan remain within their failed empire. Arcanists don't need weak Valkyries guarding them."

A murmur rippled through the crowd at that, one Arcanist raising his hand to quiet the unrest. Netta sprung then, lifting her dull blade high above her. Alarm raced through Sayra at the devastating blow racing toward her stomach.

Moving her steel-clad arm to intercept the two-handed attack, Sayra knew it was a wasted effort. Too slow. The arc of her blade would never clash in time with the other, her loss imminent.

For years, she had fought harder than any other to overcome her weaknesses, and while there were few that mattered, Sayra believed she had finally amounted to more than her family thought possible.

And... for what? To fail in her last trial? Her jaw clenched, teeth protesting from the force of it.

I can't lose.

What happened next was incomparable to anything Sayra had ever felt. A rush of cool, tingling energy coursed through her body. It pressed against her skin, begging to be released.

Majik.

While Sayra could certainly feel it as it dispelled from her body and wrapped itself around Netta, it moved unseen. A force that was designed to be discovered by a new sense, unnoticed by the ones she previously relied on.

Time slowed, Netta's blow slightly slower than it should have been. Unwilling to sacrifice her impossible advantage, Sayra hastened her arm, narrowly deflecting the blade into the dirt a hair's breadth away from where her stomach had been.

Too close for comfort.

Swiveling with a dancer's grace, the flow of time resumed with fury, rippling across Netta's gaze as she beheld Sayra wringing a leg around her own. Sayra expertly maneuvered her weight, stealing her opponent's limbs from under her while gaining the high ground. Metal clanged into stone, and Netta's sword dragged on the ground beside her.

The tip of Sayra's blade drew a thin line of blood from the sliver of skin showing on Netta's neck. Their battle-flushed faces were feet apart and bearing expressions of mirrored disbelief.

Batar removed himself from a corner under the second-floor walkway, his ivory robes swishing against the dark gray of the floor. "Sayra von Lykken has—"

The young woman trembled with rage under Sayra, her voice screeching out with indignation before the overseer could declare her loss. "She used majik to win!" Netta cried.

Silence was all that remained in the declaration's wake, Sayra's still form unsure of whether to release Netta. Guilt gnawed at her gut as the truth of the statement rang in her head, though she knew it to be partially false. Majik was a force solely wielded and manipulated by men. Women never had the capability. An Arcanist had interfered on Sayra's behalf, one to whom she owed a lifetime's debt for the victory.

It was a truth she'd *never* confess to Netta.

Her eyes flicked to meet Batar's incredulous ones, his mouth firmly pressed into a severe line. Purple flushed through his tanned skin, age lines becoming more prominent at his anger at the interruption.

A deep voice lazily drifted from above, its tone reflecting someone in a position of authority—one whose word demanded unquestioned obedience. "That's ridiculous. The acolyte relied solely on her abilities to score the outcome. I, among the other Arcanists, would have seen majik should it have been summoned by a *female* no less," the figure said, his charcoal cloak rippling as he waved a hand at the display before him.

Chuckles sounded from a handful of Arcanists, the notion of Netta's claim completely inconceivable. Batar dipped his bald head in acquiescence, his features regaining their stern composure before shifting toward the sprawled acolytes before him. Folding his arms parallel, he raised his chin and glared at Netta's disbelieving face.

"As Prince Emrys confirmed, no majik resulted in your ignominious loss. This false accusation will reflect harshly on your accumulative scoring for graduation, Netta," Batar said. He practically growled the words.

Netta forcefully pushed Sayra aside, her eyes writhing with the promise of vengeance. Sheathing her sword, she took to the hallway, exiting into the depths of Saint Highburn Monastery without a final glance at the crowd eagerly lapping the unfolding drama. Sayra gathered herself and pulled back her shoulder blades. A grim line shaped her mouth at the inevitable encounter they'd later have. Replacing her own sword on her left hip, she threw her waist-length braid behind her.

Commotion caught her attention in the balcony. Several nobles quietly conversed with the Arcanist who cleared her name. The dark prince Emrys Navarre. He was notoriously known for his affinity with majik's ominous fire element, his persona embodying the aftermath of the fiery destruction he was capable of. A wink from his gray eyes widened Sayra's, the realization striking her swifter than a snake's bite. A miniscule smirk pulled on a corner of his mouth before his attention returned to the other chattering Arcanists.

For a moment, Sayra was caught off guard by the force of his attention. Her brows knitted together in response, and her mind circled the confusing realization she had gleaned from that tiny, seemingly insignificant interaction.

The dark prince ignited majik in her somehow, something Sayra had only felt when her brother had showed off his majik to her long ago. Prince Emrys had been sly about it, so the match appeared natural to spectators. Such raw talent... and he was only a fledgling Arcanist.

A chill raised bumps on her skin.

Sayra owed *him* the debt.

Batar stepped toward her, his hands rolling up parchment he annotated with the outcome of every match. Clearing his throat abruptly, the monk regained her focus before speaking. "Sayra von Lykken has emerged as victor from the final trial of strength."

Polite clapping sounded from above, lifting her chin and setting her spirits soaring. Sayra had accomplished what everyone else thought she'd grandly fail at. The fruition of her four years at Saint Highburn Monastery at long last revealed itself: her path as an Arcanist's Valkyrie. Without any doubt, she would follow in her late mother's footsteps. A woman whose name was revered within the surrounding lands and the Holy Family that ran the monastery before she died.

To Sayra, it mattered not *how* she emerged victorious, but rather solely that she *did*. Besides, it wasn't as if she had cheated.

Bowing her battered form, she took the cue for dismissal and retreated into the hallway Netta had moments before. It stung that the Arcanists barely applauded before turning to chat amongst themselves.

Two nuns closed the oak doors behind her, silencing the chatter on the other side. Within the safety of the empty hallway, Sayra rolled out her stiffened neck, removing a scratched gauntlet to free a hand. She brushed back loose strands of wheat-tinted hair across her sweat-slicked forehead, her metal-clad feet clanking against the marbled floor as she neared an interlocking section of corridors.

A heavy weight settled on her. The knowledge of her debt to the dark prince dampened the victory Sayra should have been reveling in. She only saw the prince in passing before today, only the whispered rumors shedding light on his elusive persona. She wasn't one to gather debts, so she felt strongly obligated to the Arcanist who brought her triumph. In her homeland, to owe another was an immense burden. It was better to stand by oneself than to grow weak and rely on others.

Should he not have acted, though...

Sayra would have been forced to concede her aspirations of becoming one of the best Valkyries within the surrounding countries. Forced to admit she could never one day redeem herself by saving the lives of others.

Now, though, she could make amends.

Nothing sounded more glorious than an hour-long soak in a scented tub to her aching muscles, the thought nearly making her groan at the lengthy wait ahead of her. The acolytes' trials officially concluded with her match, and the scores for each were to be tallied by the officiating monks to determine who would graduate.

Distracted, Sayra didn't notice the gauntlet until it slammed into her chest. She fell roughly to the ground, her armor clanging as Netta's creaked around the corner. A grunt escaped her mouth as Netta hoisted her breastplate, lifting Sayra's torso toward her scathing face.

"You will confess to the instructors," Netta seethed. Her disgusting breath twisted Sayra's nose. "I don't know how you used majik, and I don't give a shit where you learned it, but I felt you using it to slow me down."

Repressing the urge to headbutt the hag off of her, Sayra instead chose to do something infinitely more satisfying. After all, she knew what ticked her rival off. A laugh bubbled from Sayra's throat, a fake restraint shattering at Netta's ludicrous claim. "Everyone knows we can't use majik. It's not my fault your logs for arms weren't fast enough. Just accept your loss, and move on before you become the laughingstock outside of the monastery too."

With a noise of disgust, Netta threw Sayra's shoulders to the ground. She worked to keep the wince from her face, every aching bruise flaring at the abrupt movement. Still, the slight victory warmed her stomach more than the fear of being discovered.

Should they unearth the dark prince's machinations, Sayra could only imagine the consequences of cheating for herself. The least of which was bringing grave dishonor to her family, degrading their traitorously earned noble status and ruining any opportunity for her younger sibling to enter the esteemed Saint Highburn's Academy for Valkyries and Arcanists at the monastery. Not that she'd give a flying *dritt*—a swear word from her home tongue—about their general welfare. Only her younger sister held a place in her heart.

Ahead of her, Netta stormed into the classroom and slammed one of the thick wooden doors with every ounce of her fury. Sayra knew if Netta had stayed any longer, her thinly spread self-control would shatter and get her expelled. After all, Valkyries were supposed to be above reproach in their holy duty.

Well. That was fun.

Finding her feet, Sayra felt a pop in her spine as she followed in Netta's footsteps. Double doors opened to reveal that year's class of acolytes spread across an enormous chamber filled with chalkboards recently erased. The other young women gathered around sturdy oak tables barren of their normal study materials, many standing in collected groups with some resting in the maroon velvet chairs.

Sayra immediately spotted Netta at her usual table, tucked away in the back with her group. Several furious pairs of eyes locked on her the moment the heavy doors shut, and it took every ounce of her resolve not to stick out her tongue at the imposing image they believed they presented.

Some of them should have chosen a trade as a court jester instead.

Sayra would be an esteemed Valkyrie soon enough, and it was high time she rose above the pettiness she allowed herself to indulge in one too many times. Deciding instead to politely smile, she couldn't help but relish the snarling wrinkle of Netta's toad-like nostrils. Turning on her heel, Sayra made for her friends' table in the front, permitting one flick of her thick braid before her back flipped to the ever-troublesome group of brawny rivals. Despite her admirable effort of restraint, she knew at some point there'd be helvete to pay when they managed to find her alone.

"Netta and the hags are positively livid. You beat her, right?" asked Kimimari, drawing Sayra's attention toward the acolyte who appeared to personify the word intimidation.

Between her ebony swirl of intricate flames lacing up her arms, strong voice, obsidian hair and eyes, and severe facial lines, she was easily one of the most terrifying girls in their small cadre. A muscled arm draped over her helm, the rest of her body a picture of knightly posturing with her alert stance and ever-observing narrow eyes.

An auburn head swiveled Kimimari's way from across the table, her prim face affronted. "Of course, Sayra won Netta," Lynn rebutted, her heavily accented words lifted from her native tongue of Faenda.

Whereas Sayra had learned foreign languages from a young age, her childhood friend, Lynn, hailed from a lesser house within their home province and suffered extensive difficulties studying the common language at the academy. With the Droden Empire absorbing their homeland, its prosperity had significantly declined along with chances for females to learn the common tongue. Only due to Sayra's lineage was she afforded more luxuries, languages being one of import if she were to be married off for a suitable price. Though she had avoided an arranged marriage with a swift enrollment at Saint Highburn's Valkyrie Academy. A choice her father had no ability to control, even though he currently held an esteemed position within her conquered country. Betraying his own council to remain in power within a new empire did that to a man. He only would have gained more clout if he had succeeded with Sayra's marriage.

Throughout the last four years, Lynn had achieved a suitable degree of proficiency that allowed her to communicate what she intended to convey. However, she was still subjected to ridicule.

"Sayra beat Netta," Nes corrected Lynn, thrumming her manicured fingertips on the maple wood of their table.

Out of all the acolytes within their year, Nessika—Nes to Sayra—was easily the most attractive with her smooth darker skin, fully curved lips, high cheekbones, and stunning, heavily lashed, icy eyes. She'd been out-casted due to it. Beauty wasn't a trait coveted among Valkyries. Many presumed she'd flunk out the first year, though they were woefully wrong when she pummeled each of them with graceful ease in the sparring ring. Her hand-to-hand combat was unparalleled, her rank within the top of the class all but guaranteed upon graduation.

Lynn sniffed, but Sayra spoke first to cut off what was no doubt a terse reply with one of her own. "It was close," she grudgingly admitted, bracing her leaden arms against the polished wood. "But I was fortunate to exploit an opportunity to counter."

"Will you have graduation?" Lynn asked, the slight from Nessika all but forgotten in her concern. Her warm, earthy eyes flicked between Sayra's, tiny light freckles bunching around her nose.

Sayra chewed on her lip, considering all of her exam results thus far. In the written and field practical examinations, she succeeded in achieving top marks in her class; however, she only managed to secure one victory out of the five combat matches, all of which weighed heavily on one's score.

But she felt good. Confident. Excellent scores for two out of three were more than others received. Many didn't do well on the practical, and Sayra was more than proficient when it came to protecting her assessors from hypothetical daemon attacks.

Finally, Sayra dipped her chin. "I will. Netta's overall score in this examination was likely much higher than my own and as a result of her loss, should have increased my score quite a bit."

"I have much excitement." Lynn smiled, glancing at each of their cadre in turn. "We shall graduate all as Valkyries."

Sayra politely nodded and smiled when appropriate as the conversation continued. Her mind milled around the experience of majik and the cumbersome nuances of the matter. For one reason or another, whether mischievous or self-serving, the dark prince saw fit to interfere with her match. And she didn't like that one bit. It didn't sit right. What intention would have compelled him to do so, and why would he allow her to know of his interference?

Perhaps he thought her to become subservient, revering his holy *ræva*—yet another of her favorite swear words. Sometimes, Sayra preferred the finesse of her home tongue. While the whole incident could be rounded up to innocent boredom, she had a hunch it was anything but.

She spotted more than a handful of Arcanists spying on them during practice sessions. Many of them were likely up to no good. But until they were full-fledged Valkyries, acolytes weren't permitted to interact with anyone outside of their circle at Saint Highburn Monastery.

Several ancient doors opened opposite of the corridor in which she previously entered, the vast array of acolytes standing at attention as their superiors flooded into the chamber. Robes of ivory filled the perimeter, one prominent exception striding her way to the front center of the boards. Whereas the hundred acolytes' armor was dulled from mock battles and bore an array of damages, hers was a radiant ivory of perfection—edged with the finest runic gold lettering and adorned with the cape of the Holy Valkyrie. A stunning depiction of the warrior goddess mid-combat, flaring across the velvet, the likeness of the monastery's renowned cross carved below her left clavicle.

Out of the corner of her gaze, Sayra noted Lynn's reverence as the legendary Sanctus Catara Zefare of the Holy Family herself folded her arms behind her torso, taking in the acolytes eagerly awaiting her verdict. Despite herself, Sayra couldn't repress her own excitement at her cumulation of extensive training, and the moment she could finally feel something other than guilt with every morning she awoke to.

Not a scuffle sounded as the professors' steps halted. Nor a breath released until the words were spoken.

"Acolytes," Catara began. Her hazel sight seemingly marked each individual with a sharp astuteness akin to that of a lion with its prey. "For four years, you have striven to perfect your blade, bled to enhance your senses, and sacrificed to devote yourself to the protection of humanity's future." Closing her eyes, her platinum bun crested her head as her chin lowered. "For four years, you've endured extremes in the name of the Goddess and her blessed Arcanists, those we are sworn to protect from the ever-growing influx of daemons that threaten us with imminent extinction. Without Arcanists, every civilization's majik wards would fail, and our people would perish. With our very lives, we must ensure this never comes to fruition."

Swifter than lightning, Catara drew her blade and pointed it directly toward the center of the chamber. Above the pommel, the crest of house Zefare shone in burnished gold. Ferocious was too tame a description for her wild and determined countenance—an image painters could only hope to achieve in their most glorious of works.

"Do you still strive to uphold these values?" she roared, her passion resonating with the gathered crowd.

Sayra set her chin a hairsbreadth higher when she shouted in unison with her sisters. "We do!"

"Then, no matter what results you are given today, know that each of you has accomplished all that a solemn population could ever hope for. In your pursuit to follow our Goddess's will to become protectors of Arcanists, you have sacrificed much. You will sacrifice much more to keep Arcanists from dying. To give them that extra second to cast a spell to save their lives and that of others. In this endeavor, we have never been more successful. Let us spare a second of silence for those who have given their lives thus far in pursuit of this honor." Catara sheathed her blade and bowed her head in remembrance.

Closing her eyes, Sayra nearly shivered at the chill that raced down her back. Everyone present felt the gravity of the moment. They were all faced with the knowledge they could have rejected the Change—a majik bestowing acolytes with enhanced abilities, senses, and regeneration—upon entry into the academy. The day was scarred into their memories when the Grand Priest of the Holy Family visited to bequeath the Goddess's mark upon the nape of their necks. Only two-thirds of the acolytes survived in their class alone, the mark too great a power for some, leading to death. It was a blessing only females were chosen for the duty, else the ever-dwindling population of men would have since perished.

"May the Goddess watch over you all," Catara murmured, resuming her initial stance with her hands clasped behind her back.

"And over you," they responded, the formality ingrained from years within the monastery's Valkyrie Academy, a sister school to the Arcanist's Academy across the grounds.

Waving a hand toward Batar, an instructor of hand-to-hand combat and an Arcanist, Catara stepped aside as the monk unraveled a fresh scroll inked with brackets of names. The girls all sharpened their focus, Sayra becoming impatient from the lack of an immediate answer. The announcement was finally to be known to all, and she desperately hoped for an elite position. Her chances of making something of her life would be remarkably better if she held a greater responsibility.

There was always the chance of receiving a minor house, in which case she'd be sequestered to a single village for a lifetime. Awful. What a waste of her second chance at life. Though it wouldn't be nearly as horrible as it would be not to graduate at all.

Their combat instructor cleared his throat, every pair of eyes on his calloused hand as he wove a spell of majik. "We shall announce first those who graduate with honors, those who will receive the duty of guarding prominent Arcanists hailing from esteemed households across the kingdoms, empires, and nations alike..."

After all, Saint Highburn Monastery hosted students from every country on the continent.

Batar's voice droned on, the list of names passing by in an achingly slow manner. Sayra shifted her weight in annoyance, but when Nessika Onai's name was called, pride blazed inside of her at the accomplishment. Nes truly was one of the best candidates, and when her name was majiked onto the board, Sayra's countenance ever so slightly broke as a smile fought its way to the surface.

When the list reached thirty-eight, Batar returned his sights to the acolytes, each of them drinking in his every word. "Next are the graduates who will receive positions specially elected by the Grand Priest himself. Those who have the honor will have the holy duty of protecting the monastery, duty stations throughout the continent, and the Goddess's will," he explained as if they hadn't had the brackets drilled into them from the day they arrived.

Sayra wished he'd skip the formalities and simply copy the entirety of the list on the board. It positively killed her not knowing whether she'd graduate or if she would be assigned to an Arcanist. She only had one dream, one future she chased more than anything. While being assigned to the monastery could still lead to it, she desired nothing more than protecting her own Arcanist. After her brother died, Sayra would wreak havoc before allowing anyone else under her watch fall to a daemon's menace.

Ticking her jaw from side to side, she refrained from tapping her foot as names appeared before them. Twenty-nine were called for that bracket, none of which were her cadre.

"Two brackets remain," Batar announced in a gravelly voice. Sayra's heart pounded in response. "Those who will be assigned to lesser nobles and the unfortunates who will not be graduating with the title of Valkyrie."

Sayra gritted her teeth, ardently praying to their supposed Goddess or whatever greater power would grant her wish. Yes, it was completely awkward for her, a Faendan, to be praying at all. The very essence felt contradictory to the majority of her people. But if it worked for most of the land, perhaps there was something to it. Even if the believers looked silly doing so during their weekend congregations.

Of course, Sayra supposed she should be less critical. The slow incorporation of religion into her homeland decades ago allowed her to attend Saint Highburn's Valkyrie Academy in the first place. An individual without religion wasn't welcomed to walk within the monastery, let alone reap the wealth of knowledge and majikal benefits of the Goddess's grace.

"This year, due to the limited number of Arcanists present in your year and available positions elsewhere, seventeen acolytes will be unnecessary. Those with the lowest rankings will not be named and will be required to remain within the classroom after the next bracket is revealed," Catara said, her expression reflecting the serious nature of the next group.

Batar resumed his majik list. "And so, those in the third bracket are Zena Lekahr, Netta FeShire, Kimimari Hayashi..."

Sayra held her breath, elated to hear Kimimari's name called, though disappointed Netta's was among the chosen. Five names had been called, none of which were hers or Lynn's. Swallowing hard, Sayra's dark brows knitted together in concern.

Seven names.

Her fingers twitched, itching to know the outcome.

Eleven names.

Sweat beaded on her forehead, her vision tunneling on the ever-growing list of names.

The thirteenth name was called: Lynn von Naykarn. Her friend visibly swayed beside her as relief flung through her body, her future secured in the Valkyrie's ranks.

Fourteen names.

A slight tremor raced through her hands, her nervous energy seemingly a tangible force about her. With each passing person called, she felt her eyes grow a margin wider.

Fifteen names.

Please, please, please, she silently begged, a thing she hadn't done since she lost *him*.

"And our final graduate ranking at number eighty-four in the class, Allera Benevski."

Sayra had failed.

"No," she whispered, her voice so soft that no one beyond Lynn could hear it. Her friend's head tilted forward, a small gesture in tribute to the gravity of Sayra's loss.

Not that any of it mattered anymore. Sayra had failed, and her words carried no weight beyond her own bubble. Whether she remained collected and composed no longer affected her future. Posture was irrelevant when you held no value in their eyes. She'd be forced to return to her family in disgrace, having no purpose other than to be married off to some wealthy gentleman with a strong, noble lineage so she could contribute to humanity's growing population. The notion sickened her to no end.

Perhaps Sayra could escape and become a mercenary for hire, protecting anyone who could pay from the Horde of Daemonkind roaming the untamed land between civilizations. Any fate would be better than that of a wife, doomed only to produce heirs at all costs. She wouldn't share a husband with another for the sake of having as many sons as possible. Marriage used to be a sacred thing once, from what her mother had shared before she passed. Before the ghastly daemonic specters began hunting down men, drastically reducing the ratio of genders to a scant one male to every ten females continent-wide.

Recently, it was rumored the ratio had gotten even worse.

Only females were spared from the violent ending of a daemon's wrath. It was an anomaly when they died without provocation, only occurring when a female chose to fight back or run. Thus, they made up most of the remaining population of humankind, making them the ideal candidates for chancing their lives to protect the remaining men. Most of the monastery staff members were female as well as all the acolytes. Few monks aided in their education, those who did being masters in their trade. Sayra didn't mind. Not when the situation permitted her to become a warrior rather than a homemaker. Women weren't given many choices otherwise, only a gifted handful provided opportunities to excel in different trades.

Well, except in the southern democracy of Highlands. There everyone was equal in standing and considered apostates for forsaking the Goddess and rebelling against the faith with widespread violence.

It wasn't an appealing life to Sayra. She liked her violence in small doses. Preferably against the hags.

She had strived to be able to make a difference in the world, going as far as receiving the Goddess's mark and clumsily learning swordsmanship. As her friends glumly exited the whispering room to clean up after the day's conclusion, she couldn't bear the pitying glances or the reassuring hand Lynn placed on her shoulder before she followed the others. It was only when Netta stormed past, roughly clanging into her back, that Sayra snapped out of her downward spiral with a pissed expression.

There were options she could turn to before resorting to a return to her homeland. After all, undergoing four years at the academy earned her some prestige, even if she didn't graduate. She was only nineteen years old. She had options.

Right?

THE END OF CHAPTER ONE